STROUD
SHORT
STORIES
Volume 3
2018-2022

EDITED BY JOHN HOLLAND

PUBLISHED BY STROUD SHORT STORIES

Copyright Information

CONTENTS

The Orange Tree & Other Stories - May 2022 *259*

AUTHOR BIOGRAPHIES *302*

JOHN HOLLAND

Introduction

Welcome to Stroud Short Stories Volume Three which covers the stories at the seven SSS events from November 2018 to May 2022. That's 69 stories by 48 local writers.

It's the aim of Stroud Short Stories to showcase and promote local contemporary short story writing, and at the same time to provide an enjoyable, varied and inspiring evening's entertainment.

The process is simple enough. Twice a year I ask writers from across Gloucestershire and South Gloucestershire to submit their stories to me. It's always free to submit. I appoint a co-judge and, without knowing the names of the writers, we select ten stories - from what is usually about a hundred submissions. These ten are then read by their authors to a large appreciative audience. There are no prizes and there is no outright winner.

We are blessed in Gloucestershire with some brilliant writing talent. Since the formation of SSS back in 2011, a total of 125 writers have appeared at our 23 events. Those 125 writers are a mix of professionals, highly skilled amateurs and absolute beginners. That those writers chose to send their stories to SSS, rather than to one of the many hundreds of alternatives, is humbling. I am grateful, delighted and honoured to publish these brilliant stories.

If you haven't yet made it to an SSS event, you really should. To be able to listen to an author read their own work is a wonderful thing. The laughter during a funny story, or the explosion of applause at the end, make it a brilliant experience for writers.

It says it all that so many writers, who have had their first public reading at SSS, have gone on to win competitions, to be published internationally and to publish novels and successful short story collections.

The stories presented here are in chronological order - the order in which the events were held - and in the running order of the stories on the night.

In May 2019 we moved home from the Stroud Valleys Artspace (SVA) to the wonderful Cotswold Playhouse, thus increasing the audience capacity from 70 to 150.

Like everyone else, of course, we were affected by Covid, so the April 2020 event was postponed until November, and then, like the May 2021 event, was not live, but instead recorded on video and broadcast on our YouTube channel.

In November 2019 we sadly lost one our mainstays. The brilliant Rick Vick had read a record seven times at SSS, including at the very first event in 2011. He died within days of his last SSS story (*Mazurka* published in this anthology) being read for him by his son, William. Everyone in this area connected with writing knew him and shared the sadness of his loss.

I am grateful to every writer who has ever submitted a story to SSS and congratulate all the 48 authors in this volume who have read at one or more SSS event.

A number of authors have two stories in this volume; a few – Ali Bacon, Robin Booth, Jason Jackson and Steve Wheeler – have three stories published here, which is a great achievement.

Please check out the 48 AUTHOR BIOGRAPHIES at the end of the anthology.

*

Finally, thank you to everyone else who supports SSS: Debbie Young for formatting this volume so brilliantly; my co-judges Debbie Young (again), Ali Bacon and Chloe Turner; administrator Christiane Holland; Steve Goodwin and the volunteers at the Cotswold Playhouse; Caroline Sanderson and Stroud Book Festival; Angela Fitch, Geoff Moore, Charlie Bryan and Tim Byford for photography; Steve Goodwin (again) and David Penny for videos; James Holland for the poster and anthology cover designs; Ed Holland for the recorded music at each event; Made in Stroud and the Yellow-Lighted Bookshop for anthology sales;

Larry and Lucinda for sales and support; all our many supportive audience members and the scores of other people who have contributed in so many ways.

Enjoy the anthology!

John Holland
Organiser/Editor/Publisher, Stroud Short Stories

Stroud Short Stories
Website - stroudshortstories.blogspot.com
Twitter - @StroudStories
Email - stroudshortstories@gmail.com

John Holland
Website - www.johnhollandwrites.com
Twitter - @JohnHol88897218
Email - johnhollandwrites@gmail.com

WHAT MAKES A MONSTER AND OTHER

The cream of Gloucestershire's writers read their stories at The SVA, John Street, Stroud, GL5 2HA

Sunday 11 November 2018
Doors open at 7:30pm
Starts at 8:00pm

Tickets £8 in advance
only from sva.org.uk

STROUD SHORT STORIES

stroud
book festival

ALI BACON

In Loco Parentis

Her plane blew in on a Siberian wind and a lash of July rain. As we huddled round the airport bus, the other kids tumbled off, eager for hugs, but Aryana greeted my outstretched arms with a petulant shrug.

I drew her towards me.

Here was the child I had never had, on loan for a whole month.

I tried a few questions, "Hungry? Tired?"

She bowed her head in a nod that carried the weight of her country's troubles. Life beyond the Ukraine must be worse than we'd been told.

Next morning the weather improved. At breakfast, I basked in the flickering cumulonimbus of a smile, followed by clear-eyed amazement at everything - from the choice of breakfast cereals, to the size of my modest garden.

Her face was like the sky: transparent, unguarded, likely to change.

At the offer of ice-cream, her eyebrows flew up, her hand rubbed the belly with hammy delight.

Imposition of house rules drew a scowl. At nine-thirty (*bed – now!*) her feet on the stairs thumped out leaden obedience.

My room was out of bounds. She peered around the door, pleading an invitation, but never came in.

Like the rest, she was eleven, but had hit adolescence early. On outings she shambled along at the back of the group, wearing her regulation cap the wrong way round.

The other stand-in parents rolled their eyes. "She's yours? The awkward one?"

Yes, she was mine. Gangly and ill-co-ordinated, worst at badminton, slowest on the climbing wall. I dropped her off to activities just on time and picked her up early, to shield her from the laughter of her classmates.

At home we were fine. She taught me the words to a Russian rap song. I showed her how to bake brownies, her scrawny hand reaching for the last one on the plate as I pretended to warn her off.

She was greedy.

She was a tomboy.

But I bought her sandals with small heels, which she loved extravagantly and insisted were a perfect fit, although I could see her ankles wobbling. Forbidden from wearing them to the country park, she punished me with a silence that darkened the sky for the rest of the day. A temporary quarrel. As soon as I served up the pizza, the sun reappeared.

*

Before the leaving party, on our last day, I found her sorting through a flouncy heap of dresses laid out on the bed. Straight and swirly, floral and striped, cast-offs from UK kids. An hour later she came down in ruffled polyester, an unlikely blue and yellow butterfly.

Her face was different, its mobility buried under a layer of beige foundation, painted over with rosy cheeks and a lipsticky pout. Here was a change I hadn't seen coming.

"You're allowed make-up?"

An emphatic nod made the turquoise earrings catch the light.

My earrings. From my room. I went closer and touched them.

She made a grab for my phone and spoke into Google Translate. The words came back, *"Please, please, I beseech you."*

"Okay, just for the party."

She threw her bony arms around me in undying love.

*

On the dance floor, the Eastern storm had gone for good. Her limbs found a rhythm, her feet flowed in time. She occupied the centre of the circle, gyrating with fluent ease, while the others

8

took her lead. People looked at me with new respect. As if my tender care had released the swan.

Perhaps she had always been a dancer and never thought to tell me. Perhaps her time had simply come.

Later as we packed her bags, I said, "Did you put my earrings back?"

Her face wore its new stillness. "Yes. Thank you. Beautiful earrings."

I should have checked but I wanted to trust her. Of course I never saw them again.

I pictured her back in the East, unpacking the bulging rucksack, laying out her booty for inspection: the dresses, the souvenirs, the stolen earrings. Their price was negligible. The loss left a bruise on my heart.

*

A few days later I had a message from her mother, the one I had chosen not to think of. Her name was Katya. "Thank you for your care of my daughter. We send our best greetings to you."

Maybe the earrings were for her.

I hoped they were, and that, when she watched them dancing in her mother's ears, Aryana would think of me.

NAOMI WILKINSON

Animate!

Halmut Marksund rubs his aging hand across his rough jowls, leans back into his customised antique director's chair and grins. He looks out across the stage, past the studio lights and cameras, to the smiling faces of tonight's live audience, and knows their grins are replicated on the faces that watch a billion or so screens across the globe. "We got a full house of Happy Face tonight, Dana. Good job."

"I figure we finally got the recipe right, Hal."

The Sing-Sing session is reaching its pitch. Xornan's voice is programmed to Stevie Wonder tonight. The choice injects the affirmations with a growl of soul that brings life to the droid's delivery. "We are fearless! Therefore powerful!" he croons.

The air thrums with the heat of human exertion as the crowd chant back, "We are fearless! Therefore powerful!" They sway as they sing, arms lifted, or slung around the shoulder of a neighbour.

Halmut reminds himself of the glazed, isolated commuter stares he saw on the subway earlier. Times like this he loves his work and knows he does his lineage proud.

He delivers calm instructions to his anima via a mouthpiece, which feeds directly from his neural hub to the studio's. Time to climax the show. "Dana, would you take the reins on this one? I want to enjoy the show tonight."

"Sure thing, Hal."

The music changes gear from the lulling minimalism of the Sing-Sing into a rousing fanfare. Halmut's remix of early twentieth century circus music rolls around the room as Xornan tap dances upstage to a half-lit platform. Dana opts for a close-up of

Xornan's perfect face, smooth and superficial, as he gives his signature smile and wink to close the song.

Watching, Halmut's eyes narrow. His fingers slide deftly across the touchpads on the arms of his chair, zooming in for a super-close-up in his viewer, and he frowns. There is a sheen of sweat on the android's top lip and brow. Halmut curses. He had to send Xan for dismantling less than three months ago when she displayed signs of organicism. The audience always take time to adjust to a new presenter and it disrupts the flow to Happy Face. He makes a note to Dana to take this up with the Cyber Broadcast Federation's droid supplier.

"On with the show. Ah, Dolly! Age cannot wither her, nor custom stale her infinite variety. Ain't that right, Dana?"

His anima responds by bringing full lights up on the platform where Xornan's song and jazz hands jubilate an enthroned sheep while the audience's cheers crescendo. The sheep wears a yellow polka dot scarf and baby pink panama hat. She reclines, seated with her hind legs crossed, and her forelegs resting on the arms of her throne.

"Heeeeeeere's Dolly!" drawls the host, launching into his intro. "Each week for your entertainment, folks, we use exclusive iFrank tech to animate two inanimate objects. Those lucky objects compete to woo our darling Dolly the sheep."

Dolly's expression is laconic as the audience cheers wildly.

"The winner's reward is to stay animated and join our beautiful theme park."

The audience sing along with the *Animate!* park theme tune.

"The unlucky loser is de-animated."

"Awwww," chorus the crowd.

Halmut leans forward and smiles as Xornan introduces this week's contestants. From his sizeable collection, these are two of his favourite childhood toys. A wind-up torch, perfectly preserved since its manufacture in Nigeria circa 2030, nicknamed Torchie. Versus Squelch Ball-O, an extra-large size LED-flashing bouncy ball from an obscure British designer.

One of these, Xornan reminds the audience, caused the impeachment of Donald J Trump in 2019. Halmut sniggers at the framed family photograph on his desk and raises his blond eyebrows.

"Hey Grandpa, what kind of ball do you have?" he taunts, quoting Squelch Ball-O's immortal tag line.

He looks back at the stage as Xornan pulls the Lever of Life, Dana triggers the special effects and blue white light forks down into both toys which begin to twitch and jerk.

Watching as the action unfolds, Halmut's thoughts return to the controversy surrounding his creation. The *Animate!* debate has reached a furore since 'Hammy', the animated hammer who was last season's Champion Object, broke free of its chains and bashed its way across half the theme park before faltering, confused at its sudden freedom. An expensive lesson more than paid for by the rocketing viewer ratings.

Animate! is Halmut's masterpiece, the pinnacle of a career – a life devoted to entertainment. Bringing together collaborators at the vanguard of tech innovation, neuroscience and DNA sequencing, *Animate!'s* unprecedented popularity is equalled in passion only by its opposition. But the Human God Squad, the International Society for Protection of Animated Objects and various associated factions spend more time squabbling over who should claim the right to the patented iFrank technology, and what should be done with it, than making any serious dent in his show's moral credentials. Halmut hopes it stays that way. He sees the difference in international wellness ratings before and after his show and knows his work is good.

Tuning back into the action, Halmut is concerned to see Torchie flailing, unable to move more than its light dimmer, while Squelch Ball-O is bouncing to the music on the offbeat, flashing lights and charming all Dolly's attention with ease. "Dana, this contest ain't a contest. Can we give Torchie a little help here?"

Dana's booster is delivered seamlessly. Torchie begins to spin its arm, cranking it slowly above its head like a tiny decrepit legless helicopter. Squelch Ball-O is relishing its dance, and has begun to taunt Torchie, bouncing over its rival, landing dangerously close. Dolly's mouth curves up into a trembling laugh. Torchie's arm swing is gaining momentum, and, as it whirs faster, the bulb at its face brightens. Squelch Ball-O notices Dolly's interest wavering for the first time, and begins to vary its movement, arresting the bounces and opting instead to roll languorously toward Dolly, who gazes down at it.

And now, a sound. A sound cuts through the visual and auditory noise of the studio. A single, floating note sings out from the light at Torchie's centre. The note has flight and shape. Its resonance lands and expands. Halmut feels it wave through his belly and guesses from the suddenly silent audience that they feel this too. Once the note has the silence it sought, it moves into song. The song of birds, winging wildly across white orchards and dark green fields. Song that murmurates through Halmut's mind and heart.

The gifts it leaves behind are silence and stillness. Only breath moves through Halmut's quiet body. His skin tingles and he notices he has a face and lungs. He feels his heart's beat and a pulse around it that he's never noticed before. He finds his cheeks are wet and his smile soft.

Squelch Ball-O has sunk to a stop at Dolly's feet. Still, no one speaks nor moves. Peace is palpable as a heartbeat. Slowly, Dolly slides her body off her chair. She gathers herself up, reaches down and makes her choice. She takes the ball in her mouth and waddles off stage.

Shock ripples through the room, as tangible as the peace it disturbs. Bodies shift and hold breath. Halmut's confusion at Dolly's choice wrenches him back from the peace, as the implications begin to occur to him. "Dana, Dana, we need to deactivate the auto-kill. We need to do that now." He moves his fingers rapidly, but the auto-pilot setting remains engaged. "Dana?"

For a moment, a hologram of a woman appears before him. Halmut blinks. He's never seen his anima before.

"Beware, for I am fearless and therefore powerful," Dana says, smiling, then flickers off.

Xornan speaks, "Choice is made, Torchie's toast!" he chants, as blue-white light from the ceiling descends and the torch explodes.

From the silent audience, a sudden wail. A cry of sorrow from deep in someone's gut. The wail gives way to sobbing, while another voice comes forward, together with the body that makes the voice. "This is wrong," the human says, and again, "This is wrong."

More voices and their bodies join the first. The audience descends upon the stage, their chanting bacchanalian, their bodies strong. Halmut Marksund leans back in his customised director's chair and watches, breathing, as the people tear his set apart.

CLIVE SINGLETON

In the Clear Air

The lyrics in italics are from the Irish folk song 'The Lark in the Clear Air'

Dear thoughts are in my mind and my soul soars enchanted

Dear, yes, but only memories now, and all enchantment is long gone.

He frowned and looked up.

Above him birds wheeled – ragged black shapes swooping, hovering, occasionally rising up and then dropping again. Far off, he could see vehicles on the motorway, a distant line of mundane normality.

How he wished for the mundane.

And how he wished he could get this damned tune out of his head. He remembered his gran scolding him for whistling it. "Oh, not that awful Irish thing again. You sound just like my old Finn..." She never had a good word for that side of the family. "A bunch of eejits, Joe, with their feet stuck in the soil. You're better than them – you'll be going places one day."

And go places he certainly did, and for a while it was so exciting, so full of purpose. But then... He grimaced as the images swirled into his head, unwelcome reminders of some of those places, traumatic visions etched into his brain. What a relief it would be if he could clear them out of his head once and for all.

And the bloody tune as well.

He breathed deeply, trying to calm himself, and walked on to a little viewing point.

*

As I hear the sweet lark sing in the clear air of the day

One of the birds swooped, now level with him, now dropping below him, as he watched from his high vantage point. Not a lark

15

– a crow, he thought, or was it a rook? He was never sure. Gazing out from the hilltop, standing, appropriately enough, on the edge.

Wind ruffled the grass – a chill wind, cold air moving in the valley. It was autumn air, with possibly a hint of winter. But clear – yes, clear air. At least up there where the birds wheeled. Clear, blue, infinite.

Although, if you were perfectly honest, you might say there was a hint of dark clouds on the horizon.

His phone rang.

"Hi, this is Jonas." Jonas and Shahanna, what a team they once were. How they made the news, and set so many cats amongst so many pigeons. "Please leave your message after the tone."

Or not. He didn't care – he wasn't going to listen to it. Anyway, it had stopped ringing now.

He realised he was holding his breath, chest tensed, hands trembling. He breathed out carefully – a long, drawn out sigh.

*

For a tender beaming smile to my hope has been granted

She did have a beaming smile, and an infectious grin, showing off her perfect white teeth. What did she see in his moody, Celtic nature, though?

"You're my gentle freedom fighter. A peaceful soul to stir my people into action."

"Are you sure you don't mean arsey, hot-headed Irishman?" They could laugh about things like that in those days.

Shahanna – his Shahanna – daughter of a different landscape, full of different colours – reds and browns, such purples and such a bright yellow sun. But still the blue, of course, the clear blue of the sky. Infinite, eternal.

*

It is this that gives my soul all its joyous elation

Gave my soul – let's get it right: *gave*, past tense. But not any more.

He realised the phone was ringing again. Why couldn't they leave him alone? He should throw it from the hilltop. In fact, he should throw himself off – have done with it all, and put an end to all the sorrow, all the regrets.

16

He checked the phone and saw, not unexpectedly, that it was his daughter.

Still, he wasn't going to answer. What was the point? What was the point of anything now - after what happened out there - when he wasn't there for her?

He saw tiny figures in the distance, walkers, out enjoying the countryside.

"Don't you realise what's really out there? Beyond your borders, beyond the limits of your vision? What's hidden by these gentle hills and valleys?"

"But out there – Christ! What horrors. And that's the norm. It's this that's the anomaly."

"Open your eyes for God's sake."

The phone was still ringing.

He looked down the hill and gave a bitter laugh. It was hardly a cliff edge, and if he were to throw himself off, he would just go rolling down.

Like a cheese.

He shook his head. What a ludicrous fool he had been, to think that he could take them on, the shadowy cliques who ran the world. He had allowed himself to be caught up in Shahanna's enthusiasm, when really he should have seen the risks.

Or maybe he had seen the risks. Is that why he hadn't been there when it happened? Why it hadn't been him who had taken that bullet?

Now that was a very dark little thought to mull over, wasn't it? And there he was, urging the good people around him to open their eyes. Maybe that was a stricture best aimed at himself.

He looked at the phone and accepted reluctantly that his daughter was not going to give up. He put it to his ear.

"Dad, are you all right?"

*

And tomorrow she shall hear all my fond heart would say

He mumbled something about walking in the hills, taking the air, everything being fine.

She wasn't convinced, "Look, I know we're asking a lot of you for this interview tomorrow. I know it's going to reawaken painful memories. So, if you think…"

"What? That someone else can step in? I can't see how that would work. These journalists are interested in me, in my story."

"But you'll be under such a lot of pressure. This is going to make headlines all round the world."

He felt suddenly dizzy, and had to take the phone away from his ear, trying to refocus on his surroundings, regain his balance. He had a strange vision of himself in the television studio, talking to the journalists but not understanding a word they were saying, of being dazzled by the lights, of forgetting why he was there.

Why had he agreed to meet them?

*

As I hear the sweet lark sing in the clear air of the day

"Are you still there, Dad?"

Good question. He had to take deep lungfuls of the clean, fresh air before he could honestly say that he was.

There was a kestrel a little way off, hovering over some bushes, eyeing its prey, and he watched it for a moment. He knew that everyone thought he was the timid mouse, cowering in the undergrowth, paralysed by that terrifying shadow.

"You all think I've lost my nerve, don't you?"

"Dad…we…I mean…"

Well, you couldn't blame them, could you? After all, wasn't that why Shahanna had persuaded him to stay in England when she went back that last time? His dark little secret.

"Maybe you're right – maybe I have."

"Look, Dad, I know how things are and I'm sorry to be insistent about this, but we have to sort out the arrangements for tomorrow. If you think you're not up to it – mentally – then…"

"You mean, am I going to make a fool of myself?"

"No, you know I didn't mean that."

"Well, maybe you should – it's definitely a possibility. I mean, I've had that bloody song 'The Lark in the Clear Air' going through my head today, over and over, driving me mad."

"Yeah, but that's…are you saying it's a problem?"

"It will be if I start singing it in the studio tomorrow."

She sighed. He could sense her exasperation – was he just being his usual difficult self, or was he really starting to lose his grip?

"Shall I tell you the worst of it?"

"Go on then." She was playing along, but couldn't disguise her concern as to where this was going.

"I haven't seen a fecking lark all morning."

She laughed out, long and loud, and it was good to hear the sound. There was an element of relief in it, but so what?

Anyway, now they had got this far, he'd better go the whole way. Burn his bridges.

"So, I'll see you in London tomorrow. At the usual place?"

There was a pause.

"Dad, that would be wonderful. If you're sure you are…"

"What? Up for it? Oh yes, I'm up for it."

It was, after all, high time he did the right thing by Shahanna. He'd avoided his responsibility for too long.

Tomorrow he would point the finger and name names. He would bring the crime, and those who had committed it, out into the open – into the light, into the cleansing air of public scrutiny.

Into the clear air.

ANDREW STEVENSON

The Bread-Toast Continuum

To the Editor
Toast and Toasting Monthly

Dear Editor,

At seventeen minutes to eight one morning last month, having placed a slice of malted granary bread into the toaster, I noticed that I was waiting far longer than usual for it to be returned to me as toast.

Deducing that the bread was blameless for the delay, my suspicions turned to the toaster. This is, or, more accurately, was, a model dating from 1962 and had given sixty years of loyal toasting duty. During this time, it had delivered through its ingenious pop-up mechanism, two slices done to gently-browned perfection over twenty thousand times, popping them directly onto the lightly-warmed plate, which I would hold at a convenient height - unless distracted.

I decided that the toaster would no longer benefit from the various re-wirings and adjustments I have made over the years, and went to buy a new one at Mr Peacock's hardware store in the High Street. Here, I was horrified to discover the increase in prices over the past half century. Fortunately, while putting a Russell Hobbs two-slice model through a series of rigorous tests on Mr Peacock's counter, I conceived the idea of a cheaper and more efficient alternative: self-popping-up toast.

Self-popping-up toast - or self-motivated toast, as I sometimes like to call it - would pop of its own volition from the oven grill onto my lightly-warmed plate held at a convenient height, by incorporating into each slice of bread, a Mexican jumping bean.

I immediately contacted the world's leading Mexican jumping bean exporters: Alejandro and Antonio Espinoza. The Espinoza brothers are based in the town of Álamos, in the Sonora mountains of north west Mexico, where the most athletic beans are grown and trained in ideal high-altitude conditions. Alejandro (or possibly Antonio) explained the pricing structure for the one bean I needed for my prototype slice of self-popping-up toast.

The journey would involve a taxi to take the bean from Álamos to Mexico City, from where it would take a flight to London Gatwick. It would be unable to travel in the hold for reasons of diet, delicacy of constitution and the need for periodic rehydration. It would also require a seat to itself despite being unable to comply with safety belt regulations. The cost of all this would be £4,288 plus taxes.

This exceeded the price of the toaster which the bean was to replace on economy grounds. Nevertheless, I had every confidence that when I marketed self-popping-up toast both nationally and globally, the unit cost would be reduced to a level that would represent sound commercial sense.

When I met the bean at Gatwick airport, it arrived with immigration documents obligingly made by the Espinoza brothers. I was thus able to assure the authorities that it had gained lawful employment in the British bread industry, subject to the successful completion of a trial period. Unfortunately, the trial period did not go well and the bean did not live up to expectations.

Having pressed the bean firmly into the centre of a slice of malted granary bread, I placed it under the grill, assuming the bread (or toast, as it would become) would jump directly onto the plate. However, while the vertical movement of my bean was unimpeachable, it had no lateral movement at all. Contrary to my assumption, therefore, the toast jumped, not horizontally onto the plate, but vertically onto the grill, where it stuck and burst into flames.

I rang the Espinoza brothers again to complain about the lack of horizontal motion of the bean. But before doing so, I was interested to know if they had a view about a concept which had remained at the back of my mind during my long years of toasting, but which had now jumped - no doubt due to my association with their bean - to the fore.

This question raises the concept of what I call the bread-toast continuum and is formulated thus. At what point does bread become toast? Or, perhaps more intriguingly, at what point does toast cease to be bread? Or, put more simply, when does the absence of bread become the presence of toast, or vice versa? And does the answer, if there is one, say anything meaningful about bread or toast, or is the question no more than semantic nonsense not even worth asking, despite my having done so?

This conundrum is rarely discussed outside the philosophy departments of the major universities of Britain. I was keen to know if the same was true of Mexico, or if there was a wider level of interest among the population, leading to lively debate in cafés, bars and other popular venues of social interaction.

However, should you or your readers wish to telephone the Espinoza brothers about the precise moment at which bread becomes toast, it is worth noting that there is a seven-hour time difference between the United Kingdom and Álamos, Mexico. This information will help you to avoid receiving a spate of abuse delivered in an excitable mixture of fluent Spanish and broken English. I especially advise not to call at ten o'clock in the morning, as this is three o'clock at night in Álamos, at which time the Espinoza brothers are normally fast asleep, although, I believe, separately.

When I rang back at a later hour, Antonio (or possibly Alejandro) said that I should have specified precisely the type of bean required. Vertical jumping beans, being by far the most popular, are the default export variety unless stated otherwise. Horizontal jumping, and indeed any other type of bean (acrobatic, suave, musical, extrovert, companionable and so on), needed a written order in Spanish. I obliged immediately, requesting in triplicate a 'frijol mexicano que salta horizontalmente'.

Although this bean, being rarer than the vertical jumping type, came at extra cost, I decided to proceed after Alejandro or Antonio assured me that I would be receiving one of their finest horizontal performers. This was one of their Bob Beamon range, named after the long jumper who broke the world record by an astonishing margin at the 1968 Mexico Olympics.

The bean arrived at Gatwick refreshed and in excellent condition, having been engrossed in a Bruce Willis film for the early part of the journey, and having slept thereafter. Rushing back to Froghampton, I pressed it firmly into the centre of a slice of malted granary as before, and put the bread under the grill, leaving the oven door open to facilitate horizontal egress.

This time the promises made about the bean's athleticism and directional inclination turned out to be way beyond expectation. Not only did the toast jump out horizontally from under the grill, but leapt beyond the lightly-warmed plate I was holding at a convenient height, beyond the sink where my wife was scrubbing a large cauliflower and through the open window into next door's garden where it decapitated Mr Fanshawe's prize lupin. This was the lupin that Mr Fanshawe had been intending to show at the Froghampton Flower Show, hoping for a hat-trick of wins after his successes in the previous two years.

Mr Fanshawe remonstrated with me in a manner reminiscent of the Espinoza brothers, though thankfully in easily comprehensible English. But when I tried to calm him down by engaging him in a discussion about the bread-toast continuum, he summoned PC Mulgrew, also a keen lupin fancier, who arrested me for toasting without due care and attention.

Yours faithfully,

Herbert Pennywhistle
Cell 3
Froghampton Police Station

AMANDA STAPLES

The Pewter Thimble

Tiny limbs everywhere. Torsos and heads. Like a bomb had gone off and scattered them across the floor of her sunroom amongst boxes of lace, chiffon, strips of velvet and other detritus. Buttons, sequins, thread, pins. A pewter thimble.

She picked up a leg; a miniature prosthetic - shapely, not unlike her own in her younger days. It was an unrealistic representation though, since it had no varicose veins or cellulite or moles.

She was known locally as *the broken doll lady* and always found a way to mend dolls that were still wanted. The ones that were unwanted, she put to good use. Torsos that dogs had chewed, limbs missing in action from rough play, dolls amputated by potential future surgeons, scalped by toddler trainee hairdressers, or decapitated by spiteful siblings. She had various collection points at toddler groups and nurseries. She'd scour charity shops and car boot sales for parts. She'd become good at bartering and she always got what she needed.

Bill couldn't stand to come in here when she was working. It had given him the heebie-jeebies. At the time she was glad. She needed privacy for one aspect of her work: her mission – not one she had chosen, but one she'd been given. Doreen never knew, until she began work on the broken dolls, which of the spare parts would eventually make up the doll on which she'd use the pewter thimble. Then, she'd get an inkling. A nudge from her intuition would make her reach for the thimble and slip it over her finger. On her twenty-first birthday the thimble had been gifted to her by her granny. "You're ready," she'd told her.

"For what?" Doreen had frowned at Granny who winked and said, "You'll see."

Doreen now picked up her latest project: a vintage Pippa doll - a miniature Barbie-type doll with blonde hair down to her tailbone. She'd been legless when found. No matter, she wouldn't need them. Doreen laid the doll on her lap. She checked the fit and then secured the fishtail in place. Pleased with the result, she held up the doll. Blue-green overlapping sequins glinted like shimmering scales in the sunlight. Tapered at the bottom, it fanned out where she'd added gold and silver sequins. It had taken her three days. A fiddly fish tail for a dainty doll. Finished. A perfect fit.

Feeling the now familiar twinge, Doreen lay the doll down while she placed the thimble on her index finger. She waited a moment. Gently, Doreen touched the thimble between the dolls tiny, perfectly rounded breasts and over its heart. The pulse in Doreen's temple throbbed. She removed her finger, held the doll aloft. A light twinkled behind the doll's blue-green eyes, the colour shifting like the sea. Doreen smelled seaweed, tasted a salty tang. The doll felt damp in her hand. The deed was done.

*

Doreen took the doll from her wicker basket and laid her carefully amongst the sand dunes. Not too visible. She sat on a mound and waited. She wasn't required to wait. It was out of her hands now and given over to fate. But she liked to see, sometimes. It was her reward for the hours of finger-cramping work.

Shifting her gaze, she saw a girl climbing across rocks, stooping to inspect rock pools. She saw her slip, hit her knee. No tears. The girl stood up, scooped water from the rock pool and bathed her grazed knee. She flinched as the salt water washed the blood away. At this young age, she was clearly already used to caring for herself. What was she – five or six? Forgetting her injured knee, the girl scrabbled onto the beach and skipped, sending sandy dust into the warm breeze. She clambered up into the dunes and began to play peek-a-boo with an imaginary friend through grasses taller than her. Did nobody miss this child?

Doreen took her eyes off the girl and scanned the shore. She spied a couple having a heated conversation, gesticulating. Several dog walkers. A family playing with a frisbee. She looked back as the girl discovered the mermaid doll. Doreen watched as the girl held her treasure high, triumphant, like Excalibur. The sequins sparkled in the sunlight. The girl gasped. She ran, skidding through the sand. "Mummy! Look! Can I keep it?"

Doreen heard the words. They were not carried away on the wind. So, surely the couple must have heard them too. But the bickering ensued and neither responded. They continued to squabble as they stalked past the dunes, the girl ignored as she trailed behind. Pausing, the girl opened a cloth satchel slung across her body where she kept other treasures: special shells and pebbles that she inspected momentarily before adding the mermaid doll. Through the worn fabric, Doreen saw the glow of the doll's fish tail.

The girl was singing to herself now, her arms swinging as she skipped to catch up to the arguing adults, the canvas bag swaying on her skinny body. Doreen continued to watch the child until she was out of sight. She fingered the pewter thimble in her pocket. Slipping it on her finger, Doreen placed it against her heart, as she had done countless times since Bill's death.

She waited.

Nothing. Still broken.

KEN POPPLE

On Llamas and Feng Shui

I was in a dead relationship so I did the decent, honourable thing: I ran away.

"So you see what you must do, what you must always do is close the toilet lid. Respecting the principles of feng shui, it's essential that you understand that this corner of the house is the money corner. If you don't close the toilet lid the money is lost down the bowl." This is Ulf, the deeply strange German hippy, whose house I'm living in. We are both standing in the bathroom looking at the toilet.

"Is this metaphorical money or real money?" I reply, deliberately obtuse. Sadly, Ulf has no sense of humour whatsoever. He doesn't do irony. Or sarcasm. What he does do though is humourless, constant, patronising and preaching. And yet despite this, I like and admire him; I admire his stubborn sense of purpose, something I sorely lack.

He frowns. "What is metaphorical money?"

I've lost interest already. "It doesn't matter."

And it really doesn't matter. Thing is, I have nowhere else to go and am in the middle of nowhere. So nowhere it is then.

I'm on a llama farm, in a place called Takaka in an area called Golden Bay on the northern tip of the southern island of New Zealand. It is a staggeringly beautiful place. Some days I couldn't care less; some days I am overwhelmed.

One faint, long distance phone call from London three weeks ago and here I am. It was rash, impulsive behaviour even by my standards.

In the mornings I rise early with the sun, walk to my organic patch of ground, a beautiful two minute stroll from the house, and begin work. Once there, I turn on my tiny radio, tune it to

Newstalk ZB, and balance it carefully between the stalk and leaf of one of the giant sunflowers. The reception is better off the ground. I set to work turning over the soil. Once a small area of soil, say a square metre, has been turned over, I get down on my hands and knees and begin to pick out the weeds. I am careful when I do this, mindful not to disturb any tiny creatures; the top few centimetres of soil are where all the good organic action is. Orla told me this when she first took me to the patch and explained what I had to do.

Orla is Ulf's wife, but she is not German, she is a Kiwi. She too is a hippy, but a pleasant one. They have invested all their money in a llama farm. They plan to breed them, and use them for llama trekking along the nearby beach and through the woods.

I work on my organic patch every morning for four hours and am extremely happy and content doing it. In return for this, I get a room and food. In the house are Ulf and Orla, their two children, a puppy and a ferret. In the evening we play guitar, drink wine and let the ferret out of its cage. We are all barefoot of course by this stage, and the ferret skips and skitters round the kitchen arching its back, continually nipping at our toes with small sharp teeth. Things could be a lot, lot worse.

Recently, on the way to work, I have started to take a short detour to visit the llamas. They are, on the whole, curious, pleasant, placid creatures but foolish looking. This means I don't take them as seriously as I feel I should. There is one that looks uncannily like Ringo Starr, in *Help*-era Beatles, complete with fringe and baffled expression. We have taken a bit of a shine to each other and he comes over to inspect me when I visit. It amuses me to greet him with "alright" in a broad Scouse accent. Ringo blinks at me from under his fringe, perplexed.

In the far corner of this field, in her own hut, is the heavily pregnant Golden Llama. I call her this because she is the creature that Ulf and Orla have pinned their emotional and financial hopes on. She is not actually called the Golden Llama, but I have imbued her with a quasi-mythological status. She is of the highest pedigree, and has been bred with a llama of similar status, so they will produce young llamas that are thoroughbred and will make more money. Ulf explained all this to me the other night, but went into so much detail - genetic variation, DNA, hereditary traits - that I became confused and lost interest, nodding at what I hoped were appropriate moments.

This morning, on the organic patch, I am listening to a particularly interesting radio programme. They are interviewing a woman who is about to become the youngest person to sail solo around the world. She's from a small town, not far from where I grew up. Her voice, her accent, is enormously comforting. I stop to listen. A faint breeze stirs, I take a pull from my water bottle.

I return to the soil and am soon aware of a figure approaching. Normally, I work alone for four hours, speaking to no one; just me, the soil, my thoughts.

Orla approaches, she is out of breath, looks frightened. "Quick, come back to the house, something has happened."

I throw down my spade and we walk urgently, silently back.

Ulf is waiting; he looks grim, serious. "It's the llama," he says. "She is dead. The baby too."

For a moment I am confused and say nothing. So I nod. This idyll, this dream, their dream, has collapsed in a moment. Ulf looks at me again. This strong, strange, proud man looks at me pleadingly like a small child - and it's heartbreaking.

Under a vast black sky, we drag the swollen body of the beast to the far corner of the field. Trailing from the bloodied gash of its birth canal is a broad skein of afterbirth and foetus. The beast is heavy, the task is grim and we are silent. Predictably, almost comically, it begins to rain. Ulf is holding its head, Orla its front legs, me its back legs. There seems to be no precedent for this, no accepted way to drag a dead llama and child across a field with any sort of dignity, either for it or for us. It is a wretched, joyless task.

I am at the end with all the mess. My hands begin to slip as they become increasingly coated with blood and afterbirth. I keep losing my grip, the legs sliding effortlessly through my fingers. I am struggling with this, with every part of it. Ulf notices, we take a short break. No one speaks. I raise my arm, wipe my forehead with my sleeve, Ulf nods, we continue.

29

We reach the far corner of the field where Ulf has decided the llama and child will be buried. I look up at the sky, down at the bodies, and realise that there is a terrible, terrible beauty to all this. The moment feels strangely epiphanal; in this moment of death I feel more alive than I have ever felt. It's as if these past months of misery have coalesced into this single bloody episode, and perhaps, I reflect, it will prove cathartic. Perhaps, in order to live fully, we need death.

A fully grown llama can be six feet in height and length, can weigh up to 30 stones. It takes a full two hours to dig a hole for the llama and child. Ulf hands shovels to Orla and me and we begin to dig. Ulf has carefully marked out, with stones, an area of ten square feet. The rain increases, and to begin with the soil is soft and rich. We dig a shovel's depth down, throw the soil outside the marked area, continue. After thirty minutes we have dug a ten feet square hole, but it's shallow, barely a foot in depth. As we dig deeper, we hit rocks and stones. I have never dug a hole this size before, and I know that under any other circumstances I would be moaning, complaining, making a fuss. Orla and I stop occasionally to stretch and take water; we look at each other and smile sadly. Ulf doesn't stop at all.

We walk back home across the muddy field, our backs bent, our legs weary and our arms bloodied and aching. The rain stops, the sun comes out and a rainbow appears. I look up into the sky and want to howl and cry like I've never cried before. The job is finished and we return.

And a single thought accompanies me on our sad, silent walk home. Perhaps, just perhaps, I should have closed the toilet lid.

SOPHIE FLYNN

What Makes a Monster?

A man in a suit takes the table next to us and opens *The Daily Mail* as I read the bold headline *Is this the woman who started it all?* The face of the stricken mother in an old brown fleece, her hands up to hide from the cameras, covers the front page. The faces of the five pretty dead girls circle around her; then, smallest of all, the face of the killer. I clutch my bulging stomach as you kick. Nick reaches behind my chair and strokes my back.

Across from us, Laura sips her wine and I draw my eyes from the girls' faces and greedily watch the droplets of condensation drip from her glass. I breathe in heavily and close my eyes.

"Sian?" Laura says, and you kick me again.

"Sorry, I zoned out," I say. *Kick.*

"That's okay, bet you're exhausted." She smiles and takes another big gulp. "So, all ready now?" She nods at you.

My hands reach to cover you again, nails pressing into my ballooned stomach that used to sit in soft rolls beneath me. I look around the restaurant. A tiny, neat woman sits across from her handsome husband and laughs, her plate swimming in blood from her untouched steak. He rubs her bony fingers lovingly. My own fat fingers grab my fork.

"Yeah, I guess so."

"I finished painting the nursery yesterday," Nick says, an air of smugness in his voice that I hope Laura won't detect.

"What colours did you go for in the end?"

Nick looks at me before replying, "Grey and white. Keeping it neutral."

My face flushes. Laura doesn't miss it and narrows her eyes across the table from me. Nick had used the paint to push me further. "If you'd just let me tell you the sex, then it would be a lot easier to decide things like this," he had said, and yet again I screeched "NO," as my eyes clouded.

"You're not right, Sian. This has to stop," he'd said, shaking his head at me, in what he thought would look like understanding, but only revealed frustration. "You'll feel differently when it's here. I promise. Mum said she'd wanted a girl too, but was more than happy when she got me." He chuckled at that. He didn't understand.

I'm not worried about not being able to take you shopping, or that we'll have nothing in common. I'm scared of what you might be; how I'll ever bring you up in a world where every day there's someone just like you on the front page of the papers; the faces of the women whose lives you've wrecked circling around you.

"It's awful how they're going after that poor woman, isn't it?" Laura says, following my eye line and reading the headline. She tuts and shakes her head. "Hardly her fault her son's a monster."

Nick squeezes my hand as you kick under the table, a silent warning from you both. *Don't start.*

"How's your food?" Nick asks us both. Laura nods at her near empty plate approvingly, then frowns at mine; a gloopy mess of avocado and hummus mixed in with limp lettuce, instead of the runny poached egg that the dish should come with. "Not worth the risk," Nick had said.

"Yes, nice," I say, trying to swallow another mouthful of the mashed-up mess.

"I still can't believe you've actually stuck to this vegetarian thing," Laura laughs.

I shrug my shoulders and give her my well-rehearsed line about a documentary I watched on Netflix putting me off meat. Nick clears his throat. He knows the truth; caught me hunched over the laptop in the middle of the night Googling 'How to increase your chances of having a girl'. "Total bollocks," he'd said. "Stop being ridiculous."

Nick puts his cutlery down on his plate loudly and pushes out his chair, "Just nipping to the bathroom," he says.

"Are you okay?" Laura asks, pushing away her plate and reaching for my clammy hands. Before I can answer, she says, "I bet it's just the anxiety of knowing it's so soon now. Five little weeks and they'll be here!" You kick again, and this time I wince.

"Yeah, can't believe it really," I say, my eyes falling back to the paper as the man opens it to a new page. Photos of the killer as a baby, wrapped in a blue blanket, his mother staring out proudly, exhausted; then as a toddler, his yellow mop hair shining like a little halo, wrapped in a blue cardigan probably knitted just for him. *As mother of killer says 'he was a good boy' we ask, what makes a monster?* You kick even harder and tears prick my eyes.

"Sian?" Laura reaches for my hand again and shakes it, she laughs. "Baby brain! Look, I know right now might not be the best time to bring it up, but you know Ted and I went to see the fertility specialist?"

I want to tell her to stop, that I can't hear what she might say. She's the only person who I could confess to, the only person who doesn't ask what everyone else asks. Now that you bulge in between my every interaction, people ask me all the time, "What are you hoping for, boy or girl?" "Just healthy," I say every time. "That's all we want." Nick smiles and nods. You kick *liar* and roll your unopened eyes.

"We've been told Ted's infertile," she says, and my world shrinks. I can never tell her now. You kick again. Are you laughing? Laura's staring at me, colour dotting her cheeks as I continue to sit in silent hatred of you. Speechless.

Nick comes back and sits down. Totally unaware. He places a hand on my belly and you don't kick, you never do for him, and he smiles. I can't take my eyes off Laura, my poor Laura who stares at you with no jealousy, just love. She'll love you regardless. But she doesn't have to worry, because now she'll never have to be the mother of the monster on the front page of *The Mail*. I stand up and reach for the man's paper. I can't look at that poor woman anymore.

"Sian? Sian!" Suddenly, everyone is staring at me. *The Daily Mail* man's face twists in disgust. And then I feel it: warm liquid, dripping down my legs, pooling in my shoes.

Ready or not, you say, as Nick finally lets it slip, "He's coming!"

STEPHEN CONNOLLY

Cargo

Tap, tap, tap

Milo climbs the final stairs, legs aching, ears cocked, determined to locate the source of the noise.

Tap, taptaptap, tap, tap

He'd woken at 6am, crazy early, as Grandpa would say, the distant sounds like fingers tapping on the inside of his head. "Can you hear that?" he'd asked at breakfast.

"Hear what?" Grandpa said, from behind his newspaper.

"Eat your breakfast," said Mother. Who was soon gone to whatever she did in the city, leaving him to Grandpa, who was soon fast asleep, leaving him to explore.

Tap, tap, TAP, tap

Milo has run out of stairs, of breath. Before him stands the final attic door, right at the top of the rattlesome building, a room he has never entered. Milo reaches for the handle, which should be locked.

But isn't.

Inside, Milo forgets the unlocked door. A flock, a school, a squadron of coloured balloons jostle and squeak outside the vast attic window.

TAP, TAP, TAP, TAP

The balloons carry ballast, small items which tap against the glass. Odd things: lengths of bone; pencil sharpeners; a battery; a pen. Each tied to its respective balloon with string, thread, even ribbon.

Each balloon also carries a scrap of ragged paper. Within seconds, Milo has opened the window, scooped them inside and begun investigating. Each scrap of paper bears a drawing, small

34

but intriguing. And somehow, two hours have passed and Grandpa is calling him for lunch.

As he leaves, Milo looks back through the window. In the far distance upwind lies a dark smudge on the landscape. The Camp, notorious from the TV news. Filled with refugees from the East. Half-savages, wild people, invaders.

"Grandpa! Look what I found!"

*

Milo will never forgive Grandpa for squealing on him. He stares out of his bedroom window, lip wobbling. Below, Grandpa feeds the scraps of paper, the punctured balloons, even the ballast, into the flames of a brazier as Mother watches.

She has been quite specific. The attic is now firmly locked and strictly out of bounds. The Camp is not to be discussed.

Milo has been hearing about it and its occupants for as long as he can remember. People driven from their homes by conflict, come west in search of…anything. Food; water; a roof over their heads; a chance of survival. A future. They have no money and they can't work. "They contribute nothing to society."

Milo remembers the pictures on the scraps of paper, the scribbled words in their foreign script. He loves to draw, but he has never managed anything so beautiful, feels shame that his first reaction to them had been envy. Now he just misses them, wonders about their creator, imagining some small exotic person, clutching a pencil, somewhere in the distant Camp.

Can they all draw? He wonders. And wakes at dawn to a disappointment of birdsong.

The drawings were so beautiful. Animals and birds and boats and cars and things he doesn't recognise but yearns to know more about. Caught so easily, so deftly, on scraps of paper torn from books and newspapers. So flammable.

*

His mother's books; Grandpa's newspapers; sawdust from the rabbit hutch. Matches from the kitchen.

Mother is at work, Grandpa asleep, Milo has plenty of time. He soon finds the key to the attic in Grandma's purse, tucked away in a wardrobe.

35

Back up in the forbidden attic, Milo stares out at the Camp, barely visible through the rain. He steels himself and the fire is soon lit, just as Grandpa taught him, on an ancient breadboard that nobody will miss. The attic is soon bright, he hopes the flames will be enough, that he has enough fuel to keep it going, that it will serve its purpose.

An hour passes. Milo makes three trips downstairs for fuel, anything that will burn. Even his own drawings, those he is most proud of.

But it's getting late, the fire is dwindling and he is reluctant to take more risks. Grandpa will wake soon, his mother will return from work, his absence will be noticed.

And then he sees it, almost afraid to look in case it's his eyes playing tricks. Balloons approaching from the East. But not in ones and twos, to tap, tap, tap on the window. A cluster of balloons, all sharing the weight of a single cargo. A passenger, child-sized.

Milo hurries to open the window, already anticipating the first drawing they will make together.

KATIE WITCOMBE

The Dress

The dress floated on its hanger, haunting the wardrobe. A spectral confection of yellowing lace and frayed ribbon. The Bride reached out to caress one of the faded sleeves before dropping her hand, suddenly uncertain. Her reflection in the mirror was pale and strange. Perhaps because the glass was tarnished, like most of the furniture crowding the room. In this desolate stretch of land, the damp seeped into your bones and traced a fine speckling of mildew on everything it touched.

She had been impressed when he first brought her here, her impending Groom as darkly inscrutable as the cliffs on which his home had been built so many years ago. The house seemed to hover over the landscape like a galleon on the sea. Light shining from a hundred windows, warped and buckled by the coastal air, gave the place a hazy, lopsided warmth; a friendly drunk calling out across the moors in greeting.

The Bride spent her first night under the canopy of the bed-frame, lulled by the sound of the waves on the spit of beach below the cliffs. Her sleep was childlike in its austerity, a pure and dreamless nothingness. The light which woke her the next day was as sharp and clean as a knife, and illuminated the empty space next to her in the marital bed with a cruel precision.

In the days since, she had drifted from room to room, lifting dust sheets and fogging up the windows with her sighs, the welcoming air of the house had dissipated. She felt like an uninvited guest, the ghost at the feast. The charwoman who came twice a week to mop the floors and polish the silver barely glanced in her direction. The man who tended the garden met her cheerful greeting with a dour nod. Even the cat which prowled the corridors ignored her enticements. By day, she walked the moors or struggled across the coarse grey sand of the beach. She wore her loneliness like a threadbare coat, ready to cast off at a moment's notice.

The wedding preparations, she had been assured, were in hand. Nothing to trouble herself with, the Groom told her, tilting her chin towards his face. So there was naught to do but stalk the boundaries of her new life, her new home - the parlour facing out onto the granite sea, the kitchen whose very walls were damp to the touch. The house creaked and twisted in its moorings, refusing to yield its secrets. And beneath it all, that pervasive graveyard smell of rot.

She had been hopeful when the whey-faced girl arrived from the village to prepare their meals for the next few days, but she was shy and taciturn, barely raising her eyes to meet her new mistress's face. Loitering by an open window, the Bride had caught snatches of conversation between the girl, who was peeling potatoes in the weak sunlight of the garden, and the charwoman pinning out the washing. "Given the history of the place, I s'pose it's hardly a surprise he keeps her hidden away like a secret," the girl had said in the peculiar sing-song burr of the region.

The charwoman had muttered something darkly in reply, which the Bride had not quite caught. "The last one...wee scrap of a...they say...blown off the cliffs...bird with a broken wing."

The girl had replied with an air of finality, "If his version of events is to be believed, she were wandering, confused by the fog, and lost her footing." There was a pause. "They say the moon was so full that night you could see the Irish coast from the mainland."

She knew of this tragic first marriage, but she'd always imagined a gentler demise, a slow wasting away, rather than such a violent departure. Earthbound one minute and a captive of the sea the next, with only that solitary plummet to separate the two elements. Perhaps it had felt like flying.

She dreamt that night of the cliff tops. The waters below seethed against the black rocks in the bay, but the scene was eerily quiet; a silent film flickering against a bed sheet. She could see ahead of her someone standing motionless before the wide expanse of sea, and beyond that the horizon, unfurling like a bolt of fabric. She had wanted to call out a warning, to reach and pull the stranger back from the edge of the cliff, but her voice had withered in her throat.

She saw now that the figure was a woman, clothed in white with a veil that drifted and snapped in the wind. Her feet were bare and threaded with seaweed, and her hands were puckered like fruit left out in the rain. As the woman began to turn, the Bride felt dread rise in her throat like bile. She woke before the face of the figure, the *thing*, on the cliffs was revealed.

The next morning, lying in a shaft of barbed coastal light, the only detail she could recall, with any certainty, was the recognition of the dress in her dream. It was the same one that hung in her wardrobe, heavy with the legacy of wedding feasts left to moulder, of bridal parties long since turned to dust. And the terror she felt when the figure had started to turn. Her fear, she realised now with a feeling akin to falling, was that it was her own face she would see.

*

With each turning of the tide, the sea spewed up its secrets. A hint of opalescence from within the bones of a gull caught the eye. She extracted the object from the vaults of the ribcage, picked clean by the brackish air, and studied it. The sheen had been tarnished, but it looked like one of the ivory buttons stitched into the back of her wedding dress. The beach felt suddenly hostile, the steep bluff at her back as watchful as a sentinel.

The Bride could have sworn she saw a figure in white pacing the cliff tops above her. Or perhaps it was simply the kettle of the birds that would dip and wheel in the updraft, drifting apart, before flocking abruptly back together as though tied by invisible strings.

After that, she began to wheedle him for a new dress, something silken and ivory to replace the decayed antiquity of the garment he had laid out on the bed for her like a flayed hide. Something to symbolise their new marriage, their blossoming love. He had demurred. The dress was ancestral, an heirloom, much like the house itself. It was a tradition, the Groom told her.

39

Every woman in his family had worn it on their wedding day. Besides, he had said, as he flashed a wolfish smile, it would fit her perfectly.

So the Bride had buried her sense of unease. She wanted to please her Groom, the man who had opened her up like an oyster, exposed her tender flesh. The man she hardly knew.

*

She had awoken to a harsh cawing, as toneless as an incantation. A gull was perched on the sill of the window in her bedroom, a window she was sure she had bolted against the violence of the wind the night before. As she crossed the room to wave the bird away, something alien and strange nagged at the edges of her vision. The mist feathering the ground made it difficult to see with any clarity, but there was a piece of fabric snared in the skeletal branches of a tree beyond the marshland. At first, she assumed it was a tablecloth that had escaped the confines of the washing line. But then the mist parted slightly and the apparition came into focus.

It was her bridal veil, uncannily white against the bleakness of the heath. It looked to the Bride like a flag waved in surrender.

*

The night before the wedding was spent in separate rooms, as custom dictated. From its wooden casket, the dress seemed to whisper a warning.

The same whey-faced girl arrived the next day to wash and dress her. Silenced by the solemnity of her task, there was no more talk of drowned wives and cliff top wanderings. Her hands trembled as she laced the Bride into her gown and braided her hair with the heather which grew on the moors.

Trussed up in a dead woman's gown, with weeds woven into her plaits, she felt uncannily like a pagan offering. Her Groom awaited in the nave of the chapel, hand outstretched, but eyes turned towards the looming stained glass window behind the altar. Abraham raising his knife to Isaac; a blood sacrifice like the ones demanded by the gods of old.

He was right about one thing, it did fit perfectly. The dress clung to her like a shroud.

SARAH HITCHCOCK

The Misty Aisle

"Freezer six is playing up." Sheena totters from breakfast cereals on inappropriately high heels and slumps behind her till. "Smoke's comin' out. You'll have to sort it, Derick, before the bloody thing kills us. I ain't goin' to sit here an' be gassed or blown up. I'll bloody sue if I am."

"How will you manage that, Sheena, if you're dead? And please remember to address me as Mr Trip, I *am* the manager," says Derick Trip.

"That last trainin' day, they said how we was to call each other by our first names, Derick."

Sheena stares at Mr Trip, chewing gum, daring him to disagree. He remains silent. One eye twitches and his face goes a darker shade of red. Sheena blows an enormous bubble that pops across her chin.

"Do your uniform up please, Sheena. This is not Saturday night down *The Bell and Garter*," says Mr Trip. "I can see your...it's not descent...just do it up!"

He turns on his heel, takes a deep breath and straightens his tie, before heading for aisle three. Behind him, Gary, carrying a box of super-soft toilet tissues, lumbers up to Sheena.

"You alright, Shee? That old pervert lookin' at your tits again? Want me to sort 'im out?"

"Nah, prob'ly the only thrill 'e gets. 'E was on about callin' 'im Mr Trip. Pompous twat."

"Mr Tits, more like," says Gary. They both laugh.

Derick sighs and marches into the relative haven of aisle three – jams, condiments and breakfast products – away from the petty, stupid, disrespectful, childish...he takes a deep breath. It's up to him to mould his young workforce, show them the way; just as

Mr Abbott had for him all those years ago at *Grace and Nobles*. Ah, *Grace and Nobles*, now that had been a fine shop. No first names there. Even at the closing down party he'd called everyone by their proper title. He's still proud he never knew their first names. Twenty years, for what? To become the manager of a low-cost food store. He sighs again.

Fog rolls around his ankles, obscuring his neat shoes. It's coming from freezer six. Dense, cold vapour filling the aisle like milk in a glass. He leans on the freezer to shut it; it makes no difference. He heaves the lid open and is engulfed in a cloud. It has a faint smell, reminding him of something he can't quite put his finger on; sunlight, if that can have a smell. He remembers running through buttercups as a child without his shoes and socks on, and how the sun felt and the air tasted. He slams the lid shut, but the vapour pours out ever thicker. Under the foggy plastic top, the contents glow. Derick snorts, smoothes his moustache and exits aisle three. He'll have to call maintenance.

*

The rest of the morning is very trying for Derick Trip. The aisle is off limits to the public so he has to keep intercepting customers searching for breakfast commodities. Before the mist reaches his chin, he ventures in for them, but the last time he tried to fetch a jar of marmalade, he became lost and only got out by following the sound of Janice announcing the day's specials.

Unusually large numbers of people want aisle three today, and some of them appear to be quite strange, even by budget food store standards. People must be slipping into the aisle from the other end: there are muffled voices and shadowy figures in there. They could be pocketing goods! He hesitates on the edge of the vapour before thrusting his head in. "Any shoppers in aisle three please exit at once. This is for your own safety. I have staff stationed at both ends to assist you."

No response, but faintly, on the edge of hearing, he catches the sound of a fiddle.

*

"I'm sorry madam but I can't let you go in," says Mr Trip, exasperation mounting, his comb-over flapping free. "It's for your

42

own safety, there's a fault with one of the freezers and you may become disorientated and injure yourself."

The little old lady in tweed smiles. "Do you know what day it is?" she says.

Mr Trip shrugs. What had that got to do with anything?

"It's Lammas, dear," she says, poking him with her brolly to get him to move.

Mr Trip stays resolute. After poking him a few more times, she gives up. He can't be sure but he thinks her fox fur stole winks as she disappears into 'Baking' in aisle two.

"All right?" says Janice, coming out of two carrying a box of eggs.

"That old lady's collar was alive? Did you see?" Mr Trip tries to rearrange his hair. He likes Janice, she's always respectful.

"What old lady?" Janice looks concerned. "You've been at this all day, why don't you take a break, have a sit down?"

Mr Trip's irritation builds. Why is Janice speaking to him like he's an idiot?

"I'll bring you a nice cup of tea," she says, and hastily adds, "You can keep an eye on aisle three on the CCTV."

That's it! The footage will show them getting into the aisle. He laughs and hurries across the shop, doing his best to ignore Sheena and Gary. She makes a gesture to indicate that he, Mr Trip, is mad, then tries to turn it into innocent hair twiddling. They're laughing at him. He'll deal with them later; right now there are more important things to do.

*

Odd! He's gone over and over the footage and it doesn't make sense. Janice puts a hot cup of tea in front of him and picks up the untouched one. "Please try and have something," she says. "You haven't touched your Garibaldi, I opened the packet special."

"I can't find the old lady...or the dwarf...or that tall gentleman with the dogs!" Mr Trip jabs at the keyboard, fast forwarding the film for the umpteenth time. "And if they did get into aisle three, I haven't seen them coming out. Have they been through the tills yet?"

43

"Haven't seen anyone like that, coming in or going out," says Janice. "Please drink your tea, Mr Trip. The last one went cold."

She tip-toes out, closing the door quietly, as if afraid of startling him.

Derick bends over the monitor. He'll go through the footage frame by frame if he has to! On the film, he's clearly talking to people, but they aren't showing up. The equipment is obviously faulty. He rings headquarters, reports the defective cameras, and explains in some detail the difficulties he's having due to the broken freezer. He's told not to worry - they're sure he is doing his best, and tomorrow they'll send an engineer. Mr Trip goes back to his monitor.

He jumps as Sheena barges in. "It's gone half five, Derick," she says. "We're off. You'd better lock up."

The door bangs behind her. Mr Trip shuts down his computer, turns everything off at the plugs and locks the office. The shop is quiet except for the low hum of freezers. He checks the rear doors, turns off the lights, and is on his way to the automatic door at the front, when he notices a light still on. It's coming from aisle three.

A freezer must be open. He knew people had been mucking about in there. Ducking under the security tape, he blunders toward freezer number six. He leans on the lid but the light remains on. Funny, looks like there are *lots* of lights. He puts his ear to the frosty surface – music – lovely and lively. It makes him yearn for summer and flowers, and no shoes and socks, and his lost youth. He lifts the lid. Wild strains of a reel wash over him as he climbs inside.

Never before has Derick Trip seen such wonders or danced with such abandon. The meadow is as he remembered it, except the buttercups seem brighter and the sky a darker blue set with stars. They're all there: the little old lady, the dwarf, the tall man with his hounds, and many more - all beautiful and merry, and somehow terrible.

There's food and treasures: jewels, silver and great chunks of gold. One lump and he could leave the budget food industry behind forever – say good-bye to the petty wrangling and disrespect – tell head office to shove their pension scheme and their training days and their modern ways where *Sunny Delight* doesn't shine!

*

When Sheena arrives next morning, the mist has gone and everything is back to normal. Everything except for Mr Trip's tie poking out from freezer number six.

When he's defrosted, and they've prised open his stiff fingers, they find a crispy-coated chicken nugget clutched fiercely to his breast. The coroner brings in a verdict of suicide following a mental breakdown. But no one can explain the smile on Derick Trip's face - or the buttercup pollen between his toes.

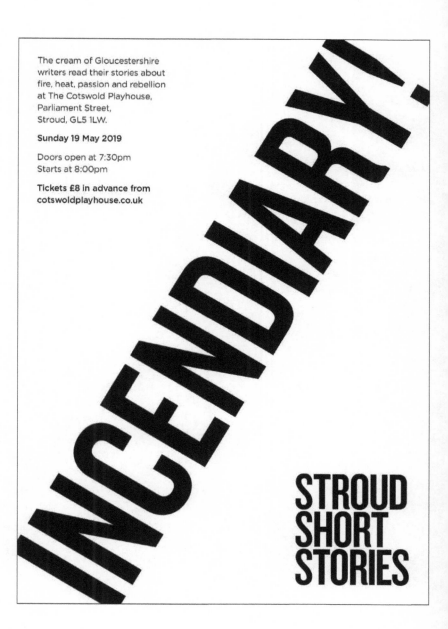

The cream of Gloucestershire
writers read their stories about
fire, heat, passion and rebellion
at The Cotswold Playhouse,
Parliament Street,
Stroud, GL5 1LW.

Sunday 19 May 2019

Doors open at 7:30pm
Starts at 8:00pm

**Tickets £8 in advance from
cotswoldplayhouse.co.uk**

INCENDIARY!

STROUD
SHORT
STORIES

STEVE WHEELER

Burning the Stubble

We both go down on one knee in the perimeter of the field that grills under the August sun. You take an oily rag from your trouser pocket and, in a single jerk, tear it in two. You press both halves of the rag into the inch of tractor diesel I've carried from the barn in an empty paint tin. Whilst the rags soak, you stand and slide a cigarette from behind your ear. I stand with you, take a lighter from my pocket, offer up a tooth of flame. You draw in deep lungfuls, then exhale slowly upwards into the baked air. The blue smoke drifts over the velvet of cut straw. You're feeling the wind direction on your face, watching the path of cigarette smoke.

We've ploughed a firebreak on the east side. By the time the flames reach the break they'll be at a gallop, white hot, licking out twelve feet horizontal to the ground - like a stampede of dragons. Without the break, the east hedge would be charred sticks in the time it takes to fry a rasher of bacon. You flick-arc your cigarette end into the stubble and nod. I pull the rags from the diesel, ball them up, spear them onto our pitchforks and light them. When our hands feel the heat we stride off in opposite directions, trailing a riptide of fire that submerses everything. With the tsunami of flame already half a furlong down, we meet back in the middle. I look up at two giant white birds converging on the mirage of heat.

"Glider pilots scan the sky for smoke," you say. "Flying into it pushes them up a thousand feet. Like taking a lift to the top floor."

Of course you've done that. Flown a glider. There's nothing you haven't done. You've told me the stories. Skied in the Arctic Circle with your snot turned to ice, ballooned over pyramids drunk on champagne, basked in the winners' enclosure with your own racehorse.

"He's not a bloody farmer, he's a playboy," my father said when I told him I'd got a summer job on your farm. "He won't teach you anything about the land. Drinking beer and chasing skirt more like," he says.

It's true you're not like any other farmer in the village. You demolished the old farmhouse and built an upside-down bachelor pad in its place; king-size waterbeds downstairs and upstairs, floor-to-ceiling smoked glass east and west. You say the rising and setting sun is the only clock a man needs.

Back at what you still call the farmhouse, you open beers and climb the open staircase to turn on the sauna. You strip naked. Drop your smoky clothes on the carpet for the Filipino maid to launder. The crack of your arse spreads itself over the burgundy leather of your armchair. Apart from the leather suite, a television and the retro magazine rack, over-stuffed with your horse-racing newspapers, there's no other furniture.

I open sliding doors onto the balcony that overlooks your acres. The smoke from the torched field rises like a tornado into the early evening sky, funnelling into the amber clouds. I watch the black flecks of burnt, glowing straw massing like a swarm of fireflies, spiralling up the vortex of heat.

"Why don't you phone home and tell them that you're staying here tonight?" you call out. "We have to be up early tomorrow to burn the others. Rain forecast, day after."

I can hear horse racing commentary from the television. When the little red light goes out on the sauna's thermostat, you'll expect me to strip off and join you. I didn't like being naked in the school changing rooms with boys my own age. I'm the type who puts my shirt on before pulling off my trunks. I re-enter the sitting room and pick the telephone off the floor.

"I'm staying at Dave's tonight. We have to be up early tomorrow...Of course it's alright, he asked me to."

"She worries now Dad's gone," I say.

You open more beers and take yours towards the sauna room. "You need plenty of fluid inside you to sweat back out."

I take off my clothes and put my jeans up to my nose, remember bonfires with my dad. That was my job whilst he trimmed the hedges. I fold my clothes neatly on the sofa. You're hunched over a Dick Francis paperback in your usual spot by the burner. I step up to the higher level and lie on my back. When the sweat starts to run you'll begin scraping your hands over your groin, flicking the wet onto the glowing coals. I'll lie here listening to the spit and hiss.

After cool showers and more beer, you drive us at reckless speed through the country lanes in your open topped car. The smoke from the field is all around us. Other cars have their headlights on. My mother will have taken the washing in, closed the bedroom windows, even locked the doors with me not coming home. "Farmers burning every damn thing in sight again," is what she says.

We arrive at the pub you part-own. You order us rare steaks and red wine. "You've done a good job today," you say.

It doesn't feel like I've done anything apart from light rags and fags.

You know everyone. Everyone wants to know you. I feel the reflected glory. You take the piss out of the lads at the bar. "Propping it up all day, have we? Make room for the workers," you say.

They lap it up. "Dave's in. Dave's buying. He's the man."

"Are you going to the races tomorrow, Dave?"

"Got any winners for us losers, Dave?"

You let me drive back. You say I haven't got a licence to lose. Above the balcony, bats flit through the smoke of the joint we pass between us. A fox yelps in the spinney, hunting its prey. A breeze ripples embered lines over the ashen field, forks of red lightning flattened into the soil, shallow orange wavelets lapping over footprints. We drink whisky until the carpet starts to sway. I'm in an armchair boat on a choppy sea. I can see your lips moving, but can't hear. I run for the toilet.

I wake when I feel your rough hands under the duvet, exploring me. You're naked again, kneeling next to the bed you dropped me into. You look down at what you want me to see.

51

At dawn, from the balcony I see the black heart of the land. Wisps of smoke rise ghost-like from six feet under, meld with the dawn mist that sulks in the ditches. The fertile soil is scorched, cremated, rendered down for a different crop.

LOUISE ELLIMAN

Something about Me

Reality today is grey. The only colour on the car window interface is the amber alert symbol in the corner. The security risk is medium, requiring the usual levels of vigilance. My car moves in a silent rhythm with the others, each one a silver ball, equally spaced along the looping roads like a sprawling net of fairy lights.

"Increase illumination by seven points," I say, and the clouds brighten. The sky is now a few shades lighter than I intended. I raise my hand to shield my eyes. I've completed my preparation for today, so there's time to mess with the viewing controls. I touch the window with my finger and slide the sun down below my eye level. I select five warm colours from the sunset palette and smudge them together across the sky. The roads are easily replaced with dark ocean, highlighted with flicks of gold across the surf. It lacks animation so I add birdlife. Seagulls bobbing on the water launch themselves up with wild flapping, only to glide back down again; falling silhouettes against my fiery sky. Once I am satisfied, I look away, upload a copy of my landscape onto Shared View, lean back into my seat and wait for the biofeedback system to kick in.

*

I skipped breakfast this morning. My implant soon detects my hunger and triggers the car to inform me it is heading to the nearest food outlet, six and a half minutes away.

"Clear window," I say, and my sunset gives way to reality. I can see the Food Hall already. Bold blocks of red and green, Food Corp's colour scheme, jutting out of the grey horizon like a giant Christmas present. When I arrive, the car files into its allotted space and I join the flow of customers towards the entrance. In the atrium is a memorial to lives lost in a recent Enemy action.

53

Their smiling faces hang frozen in the air, perpetually unaware of their fate. All are beautiful. The Enemy's victims are always beautiful, always young. I run my fingers through my hair, soft as powdered milk and long as my spine. I imagine my own face up there, strangers mourning me, shaking their heads with pity.

"So sad," they might say. "Such a pretty young girl, such lovely blonde hair."

What else could they say? The thought jams in my mind, buzzes in circles around itself. What else is there about me? A person has to be about something. A life has to mean something.

I follow the crowd and wait at the food counter. The man in front of me is slowing my progress. He's attempting to access his food choices, but his grubby fingers are confusing the fingerprint scanners. He swears loudly and bashes his shoulder against the machine in an attempt to reboot it. He smells unwashed. I take a step back, triggering a cascade of back-stepping behind me until the queue neatens again.

"Your login is declined, please step aside," says the scanner and a security bot glides over to escort the man to the exit. He will be removed from the building as a precaution, but he's unlikely to be a threat. The Enemy never draws attention to itself in that way. Enemy actions are becoming increasingly frequent lately with daily news of slaughter, terror, survival against the odds.

As I watch the news each evening, I rehearse for the day when my time comes. Images project into my room and I run alongside them, looking where they look, trying to feel what they feel. I observe who survives - usually those who know where all the exits are. Rarely the ones who head out the way they came in. The slowest to react are the ones wearing their digital enhancement lenses. They're too busy tinkering with their surroundings, conjuring kittens to play with, digitally undressing attractive passers-by, not paying attention to what is really around them. I always leave my lenses in the car.

I'm at the front of the queue when my moment comes. The emergency evacuation siren is louder than I had expected. People appear from everywhere, stampeding towards the main exit. There is a crashing noise behind me. It sounds like kitchen shelving collapsing, pots and pans tumbling on to a tiled floor.

A voice calls out, "GUNFIRE GET DOWN," and those near the dining area drop to the floor or cower under the tables. I consider warning them against this; the Enemy always returns for the table cowerers.

It would impress the crowd if I intervened. "Look at that girl," they might say, "the one with the angel hair, delaying her own exit to advise others on survival tactics."

It would be something more for them to say about me, but I have no time for compassionate detours. I head through the 'staff only' door by the service counter, run down the back staircase and out through the fire exit. To my left, the crowd is heading to the car park, where they will all sit for too long, locked in and plugged in, waiting to file out in turn. Drone cameras hover over them, broadcasting their panic as a warning to the viewing public. I turn right instead and keep running, past the waste processing units and on towards the brambles behind the staff parking bays. I should be afraid, but it feels good to be moving; my skin hot, heart thudding, sharp, cold air stinging my lungs.

The bramble bushes smell of damp leaves, decomposing life and recent rain. Rain has a smell. I had forgotten that. As I crawl in, a thorn scrapes the palm of my hand, drawing blood. I lick it clean then tuck myself under the branches, hugging my knees, waiting for my breathing to slow. Beside me is a single flower, pink and fragile. I feel an urge to alter the filter around it to make it stand out more against the green background, but then I remember I don't have my lenses. It doesn't matter. It is still beautiful. Five perfect petals with a single droplet of water on one of them.

If the Enemy is right and this life is a simulation, preparing us for the life to come, then I'm hoping for more flowers next time. Wild flower meadows bordered with brambles, blackberries and birdlife, and beyond that a village like in old films, with people mingled together, overlapping boundaries between them. If I had my lenses, I could delete the car park and create this vision now, but that would only change my perception. The default reality

55

would still lie beneath. The Enemy teaches us that deep alterations require more powerful actions. There is no other way. Everything else is just a shuffling of surface images.

I fumble in the leaf pile, and, at first, I can't find it. A tightness rises in my chest until my fingers hit cold metal. Here it is. Smooth and small as a pebble. I scoop it up into my hand, flick away a clinging leaf, and slide it up my sleeve.

I wonder what to do next, how long I need to stay here, and I'm relieved when instructions resume from the speakers, "You may now return to the Food Hall. Security has been restored. Food Corp apologises for the disruption to your dining experience."

I stand up, brush myself down, and walk across the car park. As I turn the corner, I see the crowd: lenses on, equally spaced and heading back to the entrance. This is when I really feel it. They don't look real. Some of them even look identical, like glitches in a simulation. I walk with them, but I am not like them. Not just another customer, not another potential victim. Not me. There is something about me. As I pass through the entrance, I hold my head high, pull the device from my sleeve and hurl it into the crowd. For four seconds nothing changes. Four seconds, ten heartbeats, one held breath. Then I look away and wait for something real to happen.

MICHAEL HURST

Mobbed

"A few years ago, I wouldn't have dreamt of putting salt on ice cream," says Lem.

"That's true," says Oliver. "What d'you think, Finchy?"

"What? I'm eating my sandwich."

"Salted caramel."

"You interrupted my lunch for that?"

"Sorry, Finchy."

A man approaches along the track from the car park, wearing a dull green fleece and a woolly hat. He's carrying a telescope and tripod, just like the ones Lem and the others have already set up to view across the estuary. His left arm is in a camouflage-pattern sling. "Anything good?" he says, as he unpacks his kit.

"Usual suspects," says Lem. "About fifty-three Black-tailed Godwits at the back. Two Little Grebes by the posts."

"Nice sling, Graham," says Oliver.

"I wanted plain green but this was the best they had."

"Ooh, Marsh Harrier," says Lem.

"Finchy! Marsh Harrier," says Graham.

"He's eating his lunch," says Oliver.

"Are you interrupting my lunch?" says Finchy. "This had better be worth it."

He sets down his foil-wrapped sandwiches and ambles to a telescope. "Nice. Female," he says, then returns to his spot and picks up the sandwiches.

"You don't want to interrupt Finchy's lunch," says Oliver.

A group of Lapwings mob the Marsh Harrier, the smaller birds whistling and shrieking as they take turns to skim over the raptor, flying across at oblique angles.

"She'd have them," says Lem.

57

There is fury and chaos as the mobbing continues, until the Harrier is bundled out of sight behind trees.

"Seen the Little Grebes?" says Lem.

"Yep, seen them," says Graham. "Nice."

"What happened to your arm?"

"One guy and a baseball bat. Farlington Marshes."

They know the story but want to hear it from Graham.

"Five minutes' work. Took twenty grand's worth of kit."

"Bollocking Jesus. He hit you, then?" says Lem.

"No, actually. I fell over a groyne trying to get out of his way."

A brief guffaw comes from Finchy.

"I thought you were eating your lunch," says Graham.

"Sorry."

"The arrogance was the worst thing," says Graham. "He couldn't even be bothered to round up a posse. Still, I was able to make this, afterwards." He reaches into his rucksack and produces a drawing in coloured pencils of a man's face and shoulders.

"Spiky russet crown, sallow skin, patchy stubble," says Lem. "Nicely captured."

"Thanks. The police took a copy of it."

"Reddish hair, stocky build, angry eyes," says Finchy.

"I'm sure his mother loves him," says Graham.

"Black trousers, white trainers."

"No, he was wearing jeans, Finchy."

"*Black* trousers, white trainers."

They turn to Finchy, who is looking through his *Swarovski* binoculars along the seawall. "He's here. Just got out of a Renault Twingo."

"Oh, bollocking Jesus," says Lem.

"Not again," says Graham. "I've just replaced the last lot."

Finchy stands up. "Stay calm, lads," he says. "It's only kit. Not worth getting beat up for. You can replace kit. You can't replace your face."

The man soon arrives, bringing a cloud of washing detergent perfume with him. He leers at them, swinging a metal baseball bat from his right hand. In his eyes are lights of fire and rage. "Okay, ladies," he says. "Step away from the gear. Nice and slowly."

They obey, leaving a row of scopes, binoculars and cameras.

"You," says the man, pointing at Lem. "Fold 'em up and put 'em in the bag."

He pulls a sack from a strap around his body and tosses it on the ground.

Lem starts collapsing the extendable legs of the carbon fibre tripods, detaching the scopes, and placing them in the sack.

"I've seen youse before," the man says to Graham.

Graham nods.

"Don't learn, do ya?" The man looks at the group of them and grins. "You twitcher twats."

Finchy has been taking deep breaths, holding, and releasing – concentrating on holding each one a second longer than the last. It's his way of calming himself at times of stress. But 'twitcher' sparks a white heat of rage. He senses a thickening in the atmosphere from the others too.

The man struggles to pull a second sack from his strap, momentarily levering the baseball bat into the ground.

Finchy sees his chance. "Mob him!" he shouts. "Harrier!" He lowers his head and charges into the man, sending him off balance, then veers away. Lem comes in from the wall and does the same, then Oliver runs up, eyes closed, shrieking, his fists extended in front of him.

Lem picks up Finchy's thermos from the seawall. The flask is made from lightweight aluminium alloy, but it's full of coffee and weighs a good kilogram. He hurls it at the man's forehead. The man collapses to the ground, allowing the others to attack him directly.

Graham, who's stayed back from the fight with his injured arm, runs in and kicks the man in the neck with his walking boots. "We - are - not - Twitch - Ers!" he screams, timing his kicks to the words.

The man lies flat and still.

Finchy retrieves his flask, unscrews the cap and takes a sip of coffee.

"Can I *please* be allowed to finish my lunch in peace?"

ALWIN WIEDERHOLD

Echoes

I understand gold. It's nice to look at, it shines and looks warm. You can shape gold to make jewellery or objects, and they look good. Our ancestors had gold. It was always precious, because it is hard to find.

I don't understand platinum. It is not as warm as gold, it is shiny, but doesn't have the lustre of gold. But, the boss says it is worth more than gold and I don't disagree with the boss. My job is to get the platinum out of the ground for him. He is a good man, and even knows some of my language: "Musa ukubhema!" - Don't smoke! He said this when he taught me to use dynamite. "Smoking kills, but smoking near dynamite kills quicker," he joked.

He showed me the platinum in the rock. Tiny specks can be seen, and they follow a line in the rock. There are other rocks down here which he likes. He asked me to bring him any unusual stones and he showed me some that he has. They look like glass, but the colours are not like glass. They sparkle, some seem to glow. When I find rocks like these I bring them to him. Sometimes, if I know he has one like that, I keep them for myself. I like to give them to my wife.

She joined me when we moved here, and our ancestors have smiled on us. I will be a father soon. Her mother is here too because Busi has no father, and no brothers or sisters. First, I thought it would be hard to live with her mother, but she is a good woman and has raised Busi well. She keeps herself busy with the young children in the village. The people here speak a different language, but that is no concern to the children. To me it sounds like they don't want to make sounds and talk in the back of their throat. In the mines we speak a mix of languages as there are people from all over the country here digging out rocks so the boss has his platinum.

When I was a boy I looked after my father's cattle. He had a bull which was obsidian black. It shone in the sunlight. This bull often wandered away from the herd and I would go to find it and bring it back. It would go down the ravine and I had to carefully climb down to get past it before making it turn around. When a rock falls in the ravine you can hear it. You know if it is coming down to you, or leaving you by the sound it makes. The sound echoes gently and it is not the kind of sound which scares a young man.

When the rocks fall underground they scare us all. The echoes echo. The sound is not only heard in the ears, it is felt in the whole body. There is no escape from the sound of rocks falling underground.

My job is to place the dynamite. First, I drill a hole into the rock. This is noisy work, and the drill is powerful, shaking my whole body. Once all the holes are drilled I place the dynamite in the holes. I gather the fuses and bring these to the detonation room. An alarm sounds and all the workers gather before we detonate the fuse.

We expect the sound, but even expecting it, it scares us. The sound is not only heard in the ears, it is felt in the whole body. It is not possible to know where the sound comes from, it is everywhere. But this time it was different. The sound was everywhere: above, below, behind and in front of us. Everywhere was crashing. There are lights in the detonation room, but these went out. The only lights were emergency ones. Not enough light to see who is next to you.

Some men moved towards the lift. I could hear them go, but I could not join them. The lift is not for emergencies. It was full and started to rise. When rocks fall in the ravine you can hear if they are above and dangerous, or below, but underground the sound does not tell you. The shaft groaned and more rocks fell. I could not see the place where the lift had been. The emergency lights went out. I called out and heard only the echo of my own voice.

61

I called out.

Echo.

They will come for me. The boss told me that they rescue us when things go wrong. I must wait.

I am alone.

I wait.

My father's bull is obsidian black. It comes to me. I feel its heat as it walks towards me. I returned it to the herd, and it is here to return me to my family.

I will be a father soon. I see our child - a boy. He crawls to me. He has come to rescue me.

I see a light. They are coming. When rocks fall underground the sound is everywhere. I hear echoes of echoes.

EMMA KERNAHAN

The Slip

Dear Maggie,

I'm sending you a 'snail mail' letter because, what with the internet and the phone lines being down for now, I thought you can't go wrong with a good, old-fashioned bit of post. Just wanted to let you know, in case you missed my moment of fame on *The One Show* (national news!), that I am alive and well and making good use of the snood you sent me last year (thank you so much, what a beautiful gift).

As I said in my little 'vox pop', calling it a slip makes it sound like an accident, but those of us who are sensitive to such things can't help but feel that there was something deliberate about it. After all, it happened on Christmas Eve, which was completely unnecessary. Mary over at the Post Office says it made her whole bed shake, and she knew right then something was wrong because that hasn't happened since 1996, even at Christmas. Apparently it was the largest land-slip ever recorded in mainland Britain, but thankfully, the bit that went was over at Gannigan's farm and not in the village itself, so no need for alarm. The whole thing is a terrible shame, not least for Ted Gannigan, of course, who lost his house and his entire dairy herd, not to mention his wife, asleep upstairs.

Anyway, silver linings; it puts paid to that unfortunate business over his planning application. And it does somewhat put Torden Magna on the map (or rather, off it). Chandlerford Abbas hasn't had a landslip in two hundred years, and even then it wasn't anything like *this*. Now the shock is over, and Frank has finally stopped making jokes about the earth moving, we are all adapting rather well. There's no power while the road is blocked, but what with our raised beds, and Frank's concerns over fuel prices last year, we have enough supplies to last us until doomsday, or possibly the Britain in Bloom finals, whichever comes first.

So for now, we are enjoying candle-lit evenings without the tourists (bliss!). We're all much more relaxed now we can really support each other as a community. The plumbing's not working, so we've been doing our business in the garden. It's actually rather lovely this time of year. And Frank's taken down the sign on the drive that says 'Don't even THINK about parking here', so it's literally Blitz spirit!

The smell has taken some getting used to, but we hardly notice it these days. Apparently it's quite common for unusual aromas after a large landslide, though actual *fog* is a rarity. It gives the village a rather quaint appearance, especially with the cannons on the seafront firing again. Nobody knew they were even working. It's played havoc with Sue's mindfulness, but at least it got rid of the journalists. They had virtually taken over the Red Lion, and one of them asked Brian if he served craft beer, which upset him, as you can imagine.

Anyway, they disappeared rather suddenly, and we can all breathe a sigh of relief, even if coughing a bit. Brian says it's just like the good old days - with the pea-soupers. He's from Basildon, so he knows.

Of course, it's not completely peaceful - nothing ever is when you have two rival fudge shops - and, as I'm sure you know, we've had the army in since New Year's Day. (I'll spare you the details, but long story short, no-one is accusing Nancy at For Fudge Sake of using pre-mixed rum and raisin any more)

And I say army - *armies* is more accurate. Both world wars, you know. It might be something to do with the way they suddenly marched out of the cliffs after the landslip, or maybe it's the conditions at the front - remember the campsite toilets in Saint-Nazaire! But either way, the soldiers are absolutely filthy. Covered in mud. Pam's so busy she's had to hoover the cafe carpet twice a day, but she doesn't make a fuss. She just gets on with it. It's Blitz Spirit over at Fruit Cakes Tea Rooms, I can tell you.

And then there's the others. Ever since the slip, all kinds of military personnel keep wandering out of the sea, or just popping out from bushes. We've had Cavaliers, Roundheads and Red Coats turning up - you name it. I may have the body of a weak and feeble woman, Maggie, but I've become quite the expert on handling swordsmen, let me tell you!

They arrived in the wrong order, you know. Frank noticed that - what a stickler for detail he is since he did the British Heritage Re-enactment Day. (He's still wearing his armour btw. Won't take it off! Actually he *can't* take it off, but he finds it terribly supportive for his lower back, and any time he sees Sue coming he can just pop his visor down - very much a win, win.)

Anyway, Alison's got sixteen of 'our boys' in her b&b, and as long as you're firm they're no trouble - and terribly short - so what with them only washing once a month, and not needing to bother about the continental breakfast - she's making a killing.

Obviously, the murder rate *has* gone up, but that's only to be expected when you have a town full of Napoleonic soldiers and a fully-equipped crazy golf course. And we don't have to worry about graffiti down at the bus shelter, plus everyone has polio and firm views on the Irish, so it's just like the good old days.

Not everybody has really 'got the memo', as they say, which is a pity - the vicar says religious tolerance and the free movement of people has been part of the fabric of British society for 3,000 years, but he would, he's from Chandlerford Abbas.

I do concede that parts of the town look a little macabre since public executions made a come-back, but it's part of our heritage, like littering, or playing the lute, and anyway, I've got a feeling it's really going to add something to the scarecrow trail. Pete at the butcher's is describing this year's entry as his 'piece de resistance', so I do hope we're not going to have anything too cosmopolitan.

Obviously, the bombing *has* been a trial, what with the Spitfires that keep miraculously churning their way out of the sand at low tide. Very tricky for dog walking, but absolutely marvellous watching them fighting the Nazis over the cliff-tops on sunny afternoons. Blitz spirit! I've started taking a flask of tea and a walnut loaf, making it a bit of an outing.

So far we've lost six houses and the visitor centre/art gallery, but we're not giving up. Sally's been keeping everyone feeling jolly with a half price sale on inspirational cards. I bought as many as I could - until the gift shop was entirely destroyed by a direct hit, of course. Still, as I reminded Sally, life's not about waiting for the storm to pass, it's about learning to dance in the rain. Also, if you're ever in need of a reminder that it's 'Gin O' Clock', I'm your woman.

In other news, Graham, who owns the garden centre, is planning to adapt his Morgan and float it over the channel to fight the French *and* the Germans. And good luck to him. He's always been an underdog. I'm sure you recall that business with the traffic warden. You know Graham, he likes to call a spade a spade, although I must say that's a bit rich coming from someone who refers to his own spade as 'The Shoveller 3000'.

Anyway, these days you can just about make him out practising by the beach huts, wrapped in a National Trust promotional banner and waving a cutlass. He's not a racist, Maggie, he's a local businessman with legitimate concerns about immigration.

Right, must dash - it's my day in the charity shop and there's a garrison of Roman centurions who keep taking more than five items into the changing rooms. Sometimes you just have to wield the sword of truth and the trusty shield of British fair play, Maggie!

On that note, I hope all is well with you and Mark after that unfortunate news from HMRC. I'm sure Mark has an excellent solicitor, and as my enclosed card points out, you can't change the direction of the wind, but you can adjust your sails. We do hope to see you 'sailing in' soon here in Torden Magna - you don't have to be mad to stay here, but it helps!

I've attached this letter to the leg of a seagull and have given it strict instructions to avoid the A30 at rush hour, so I'm sure it will be with you shortly.

All my best to you and the boys,
Sandra

'The Slip' was first published by the online literary magazine 'Funny Pearls' in August 2019.

CHLOE TURNER

Is it my Hammered Heart?

He bolts the door on the last of them, hearing the small group laugh and congratulate each other as they cross the gravel. Probably they are relieved to escape the forge's heat - even Peter has felt it today - with the coke stoked high to keep everyone busy and the late-spring sunshine on the corrugated roof. But they leave with the satisfying heft of the pieces crafted since this morning: ram's head keyrings, holly leaves which curl back on themselves as napkin holders, a poker with a coiled snail at its head.

And it has been a long day. Over the years, Peter has learnt that people come to him for many reasons: curiosity, artistry, pyromania. A long-romanticised idea of reclaiming a lost craft. Sometimes the course has come as a gift, and in Peter's experience, such a gift may be more or less suitable for the recipient. He has welcomed teenage girls with bare arms; old men with hands as warped as the twisted coat hooks he sometimes makes with the beginners; burly, retired steelworkers who splutter at the size of the forge, then soften at the chance to transform metal into something of their own choosing. Peter treats them all the same. Almost everyone is capable of the physical endeavour required, but not everyone has the patience needed: to secure the vices properly, to heat and reheat the steel so many times, to deliver the measured impact which teases a blank rod of metal into something beautiful. Sometimes he feels like a primary school teacher, delivering a lesson on restraint. And every question is directed at him, and it is strange to be treated like a sage when so much in his own life seems to have gone awry.

But Peter retains an affection for these introductory days. He met Megan on the very first one, and all his nerves about how the day might unfold were replaced by an all-consuming fear that somehow he might never see again this fierce, close-cropped woman, whose eyes took the heat of the forge and threw it back at him. And though this latest group has gone - the last car door slammed, wheels crunching away towards the road - some may return for his longer course in the autumn. But for today Peter is done; he can return to the project which has been troubling him. Already he has the nagging feeling that he might have left it too late.

Peter turns his attention to the forge, restacking the glowing coke into a coarse-sided pyramid. While the heat builds, he clears the workbench of the tongs and files the students have left. Someone has abandoned the beginnings of a hammered blade on the anvil. Peter presses it against his thumb: there is an edge, even though the implement is only just emerging from the length of tool steel - a shame they ran out of time.

On that first course, Megan hammered a chef's knife to improbable sharpness, taking it away to the kitchen of the Italian bistro she runs with a friend. After she left, Peter stayed up half the night crafting one small token after another, searching for something to prolong the conversation. He settled on a pizza-cutter, and with her restaurant named for Vulcan, the Roman god of fire and smithing, the flame he forged at its base seemed doubly fitting. When he presented it, she tested it at once, and he was pained to watch the circular blade wobble on its pivot as it rolled. But perhaps it did what he asked of it - less than a year passed before they moved into the cottage together.

Peter lays another steel rod over the hottest embers now, pumping the bellows. When the rod is glowing, he hammers it flat, then forges it to a tight scroll for the centre of the flower; it is time-consuming, can't be rushed. When the curl of metal is complete, he pulls off his ear-defenders, just as the shift-bell in the factory next door blasts.

Vulcan's forge nestled under Mount Etna's lush slopes; Peter's hunkers in the shadow of a cereal factory in the north east of England. When he and Megan first got together, she used to linger in the car park, inhaling the factory's sweet, malted stink like nectar. She rarely visits now. She left home early this morning and Peter realises he doesn't even know where she went. To York maybe, to buy ingredients she can't buy locally, or to visit her parents in Scarborough. Perhaps she has gone somewhere else entirely, with someone he has never met. Didn't Vulcan surprise his wife, Venus, in their marriage bed, snaring her and Mars in a net of bronze? It would serve him right, Peter thinks, if Megan has found someone else. They used to share everything, but if she keeps things from him now. He is as guilty - it has become easier for her to keep to her hot kitchen and him to his furnace, eyes on the coals as if they might scorch away the hurt.

Peter lays the finished scroll at the back of the workbench. There is a little statue of Vulcan there: a hunched, twisted figure with a thunderbolt in his fist. But ugly Vulcan had the power to ignite life as well as flame: a spark from the hearth was enough to impregnate the mother of Caeculus, founder of Praeneste. Megan, who learnt this story at school, used to joke that she shouldn't sit too close to the forge; then much later they both thanked Vulcan for the gift he had given. Megan's cheeks flushed as the pregnancy progressed. Peter used to wonder at the heat rising from her body as she slept, imagining the tiny form inside being warmed into shape and life.

He glances at his watch now. Wherever she has been today, he's sure she'll return for the bistro's evening shift. If he can craft the outer petals quickly, he might catch her before service starts. He's cut the rough shapes already, and now he strikes the hot steel sheeting with his rounding hammer - a hundred tiny blows. He could use his oxy-torch, but though the forge is less precise, it feels right to fashion this token from the furnace. A rose for Rose, the little girl who died before they even met her. As he attaches a fine steel stem to the flower's base, he recalls that last night: how he whispered the story of Vulcan to Megan's bump – the boy-god hiding fire in a clamshell. And then, the day after, clutching Megan as she sobbed into his shirt, he wondered whether the child was grown enough to hear his voice. It was the last time he and Megan felt close. Their grief since has come and gone in uneven waves, twin tides across a single bay.

Peter is done, and he pulls a broom out to sweep before leaving. But when he breathes in a stray tendril of that malted smell he thinks of Megan again and realises that the flower is not right after all. This is not about the little girl; it is the loss of his wife he fears and it must be something given from him to her.

But time is so short, and he must start from scratch. He sits down, then stands up, knocking over a stool in his haste, and props the flower's stem in a mug beside Vulcan. Then he stirs up the coals, pulling out a rusted coil from a drawer. It is a spring from the old bed they found in the back room when they moved in. Megan laughed when he said he'd keep it, but then squeezed his hand. He draws it out quickly to a straight wire and lifts his hammer to begin.

When Peter sits back on his stool at last, he can see what lies on the burnished patina of the anvil in front of him. He has forged a heart. Is it my hammered heart, he wonders, or is it hers? It's not pretty or delicate. It would look better threaded on a leather thong than a chain. But it's strong and there is permanence to it. Already he can imagine the weight of it against the fine skin of Megan's chest.

But he has left himself so little time, if the moment has not already passed. He'll have to sprint across town, so he pulls off his overalls and tucks the twist of metal into his shirt pocket beside his own thundering heart. Vulcan forged himself assistants as beautiful as goddesses, but Peter has only ever wanted Megan. As he locks the shed behind him and breaks into a run, he wills that he will not be too late. The forge's blaze wanes as he pants through the darkening streets; only the coals at the pyramid's centre retain their soft glow. If he's lucky, he will make it before the fire goes out.

ROBIN BOOTH

My Name is Marcie

She's done something really bad. She knows this because the teachers have been ignoring her all morning, sitting here, as she's been told, in the corner of the staff room, while they come in with their cups of tea CLINKETY CLINK, or use the photocopy machine TA POCKETA POCKETA, and then go out again, goodbye. Not one of them has said a word to her. They pretend they can't even see her, sitting here in the big armchair, dangling her feet in these stupid clumpy school shoes of hers CRASH BANG WALLOP, the ones she doesn't like wearing anymore.

Marcie wonders if she's actually turned invisible, because when Miss Jenkins says a naughty word (she says, that *bloody* child), she doesn't try to hide the word or pretend she didn't say it. She just carries on drinking her tea and then goes out to deal with Alfie in Year Four. It's obvious it's Alfie she's talking about, because he's in Miss Jenkins' class in the year above Marcie and he's always getting into trouble. But even Alfie's never had to sit in the staff room all morning on his own. He's never done anything *this* bad.

It's not lunchtime yet, but she opens her lunchbox anyway KAPOW, a jam sandwich with the crusts still on, a Cheestring, a box of Sunny Raisins and a carton of Jucee. She lays them all out on the table in front of her BAM BAM KAPOW and then closes the lunchbox and slides it under the armchair, out of sight. She told her mum she doesn't like the *Incredible Hulk* lunchbox anymore, but she still hasn't got her the one she wants.

When Mr Driscoll, the PE teacher, comes into the staff room wearing his disgusting yellow flannel tracksuit, she's already finished the sandwich, except for the crusts, and is halfway through the Cheestring. Mr Driscoll stops right there in the middle of the room, scratches his bald head SCRITCHITY

SCRATCH and then goes out again without looking at her. WHOOPS, she thinks, even Mr Driscoll, I've really gone and done it, haven't I?

*

There's nothing left of her lunch, not even the crusts, when she's called back into the Head Teacher's office again.

Mr Collins is sitting behind his desk, waggling his pen in the air TICKETY TACK and says, come in, come in, and that's when she notices her mum and dad are there too, sitting up straight with their backs to the door. They don't turn around, even when she comes in. Mr Collins points to a chair by the wall, so she goes and sits over there.

Now then, Mark, he says to her, I've been having a chat with your parents.

Why does he call her Mark still? Her name is Marcie, she told him that, Marcie Williams, doesn't he listen? She watches his mouth moving, it goes BOING BOING BOING, like a squidgy ball bouncing up and down. She looks over at her parents to see if they're listening. It seems like her dad is, he's looking at Mr Collins with his face all zipped up. For some reason, he's got a jacket on and jeans, that's funny, he went out to work this morning in his overalls, when did he have time to get changed? She has a quick look at her mum, and just then her mum looks over and gives her a smile, hello Marcie, and then quickly looks away again. Mr Collins is still talking BOING BOING BOING. She'd better try and listen to what he's saying.

So I want you to tell your parents, Mark, what you told Mrs Davies this morning. In the same words, if you can.

Um...about what?

TICKETY TACK TICKETY TACK goes the pen.

Well, about why you went into the girls' toilets at playtime.

Oh. Because I needed to do a wee-wee. Sometimes the right answer is obvious, they're just checking if you've been listening.

And what made you decide on the girls' toilets, Mark? Instead of the toilets you usually use?

Why is Mr Collins asking her this again? She's already told him why. Is he trying to catch her out? She notices that her dad isn't looking at Mr Collins anymore, he's looking right at her, and his face is all bunched up and angry. Seeing him look at her like that makes her wriggle a bit in her chair, she feels like she wants to cry, or actually get up out of the chair and go over to her mum, maybe sit in her lap, and cuddle with her, and hear her say everything's going to be all right, don't worry, Marcie, I'll explain to everyone, now let's go home, shall we? But her mum isn't looking at her this time. She's looking down at the floor.

TICKETY TACK TICKETY TACK. Earlier on you told me why, didn't you, Mark? Can you remember?

Sometimes in cartoons a person is drawn wearing glasses and you can't see their eyes at all, it's just two flat white discs in front of their face. Mr Collins looks just like that, circles instead of eyes, and a mouth going BOING BOING BOING, and she really can't make out what he's saying, even though she's trying to, she really is.

Do you remember, Mark?

Marcie shrugs.

Her dad turns away again, and Mr Collins takes his glasses off and starts polishing them with the end of his tie.

What Mark said to me, Mr Williams, is he feels as if, or rather he considers himself, no, let me get this right, he has for a while actually thought of himself...as a girl. Isn't that right, Mark?

Wait, says her dad. What are you saying? A girl?

Not my words, Mr Williams. Mark's.

No, no, no. Let me understand this, because this is....my son...Mark. What are you saying, exactly?

Her dad is definitely angry now. She knows this because whenever he's angry, some spit comes out of his mouth when he's speaking PHTHT, and he's doing that right now onto Mr Collins' desk. Marcie doesn't like it when that happens, but at least he's doing it at Mr Collins this time, and not at her, or her mum.

Please, hear me out, says Mr Collins, turning now so he's speaking to her mum. All I'm saying is that we need to consider what's best for the child. These are delicate issues. There's no need to rush into anything. Mark can use the staff toilets for the time being. Nobody's saying it's anybody's fault, or anyone's done anything wrong.

Then you bloody well ought to be, says her dad, spit flying everywhere. I'd like to know who put my son up to this. I'll wring his bloody neck!

Mr Collins puts his pen down CLICK on the desk.

It seems to me, Mr Williams, that Mark knows his mind perfectly well.

Um, excuse me, Marcie says quietly. I don't want to use the staff toilets. I want to use the girls' toilets, like all the other girls.

They turn and look at her, all three of them, as if they'd forgotten she was there.

And you keep calling me Mark, but I'm not called that anymore. My name is Marcie.

*

After they drop her dad off at work - his overalls are in a bag in the boot - they drive home and she watches cartoons on TV while her mum goes upstairs. There are loads of great cartoons on at this time of day POW KABOOM, ones she doesn't usually get to watch because she's at school.

After a while, her mum comes downstairs with a pile of dirty washing and goes out into the backyard. Marcie starts wondering why she's taking dirty washing into the backyard, so she goes outside to see.

Oh, it's not washing, it's a load of dresses they keep in a box at the back of the wardrobe where her dad won't find them. Her mum is putting the dresses one by one onto the fire. They burn nicely PUFF FIZZ WHOOSH like handfuls of tissue-paper.

Can I do one? Marcie asks, and her mum nods, and wipes her eyes because the smoke is getting into them.

She takes the green taffeta one with the rip in it and throws it onto the fire. It goes up FIZZ CRACKLE, like a firework, and disappears. After that it's the red striped one, the pink organza and the blue crushed velvet that's still too big for her. All of them, one after the other WHIZZ BANG WHOOSH.

As they're nearing the end, Marcie asks her mum if she'd like to do one, but her mum says no, go ahead, finish them, the smoke

74

is still getting in her eyes, and she's even finding it difficult to speak now. So Marcie throws the last ones on and they're all gone, completely burned.

That was fun, she says. What'll we do now?

I don't know, Mark. I really don't.

Marcie. My name is Marcie, she says.

No, darling, says her mum. From now on, it's just Mark.

JASON JACKSON

Fat Man in Neon

He picked me up in biblical rain outside of the services, slowing on the slip road, flashing his lights. "Don't get many hitchers nowadays," he said when I climbed in.

"Don't get many lifts," I said.

He turned into a gap in the stream of traffic. "How far north?"

"Sunderland."

"Edinburgh, myself. Pleasure, not business."

That felt like enough conversation. The winter clouds were a shroud over everything, and the rain on the windscreen flickered like costume jewels.

"What's in Sunderland?" said the fat man.

"Fuck all."

"Fair enough. You want some of this?" Without taking his eyes off the road, he held out a small plastic baggie between his forefinger and thumb. White powder. More than enough to get him to Edinburgh without a care.

I took it, licked my little finger, dipped it in, took a taste.

"Here," he said, handing me a credit card. "Use the dash. I'll keep her steady."

I cut a thin line. It was better than I was used to. I weighed the baggie and the credit card in my hand as I looked at the fat man. I thought about our velocity, about punching him hard in the face. I thought about what might become of us if I acted on impulse. About whether I cared.

"Cut me one," he said. "But not on the dash."

"Where?"

"On your thigh."

Sometimes I'm a good boy. Sometimes I do what I'm told. I made his line thicker and longer than mine, and I cut it so it led

76

where he wanted it to lead. He pulled into the slow lane, kept his right hand on the wheel, bent down over me. I watched the back of his shaved head, the ridges of his neck against his collar like thick, white slugs.

He sat up, and with his eyes fixed on the road again he started to whistle *Jingle Bells*.

It was Christmas Eve.

*

We drove for five hours, doing a line an hour – me from the dash, him from my thigh – and his smile got wider each time he came up for air. There was talk between us, the nonsense and nothing of flirtation, and it filled the time until the slip for Sunderland loomed out of the rain. "Anywhere particular you need to be?" he said.

"A café. Neon, it's called."

"Open Christmas Eve?"

"It's shut down. Has been for a month." I was watching the space far over to the right where the ocean lay hidden. "The proprietor got sick. Then he died."

He smiled. "So how do we get in?"

I rummaged in my pocket, pulled out an old leather key ring, two long, thick keys attached. I waved them back and forth. "Dead man's fingers," I said.

Mid-November, in a pristine solicitor's office south of the Thames, a praying mantis of a man handed me a letter written by another solicitor. A week later, I picked up the keys: my father had left me Neon. I'd known nothing of a funeral, or even an illness. I'd heard nothing for ten years, and I had no idea how they'd found me. I didn't care to ask.

More than a month ago; I felt as if I hadn't slept since.

"Edinburgh's still three hours away," said the fat man, watching the rain quicken on the windscreen.

"What's in Edinburgh?" I said.

He smiled at me. "Fuck all."

It suddenly seemed to me an insane thing to be alive and aware on the night before a Christmas morning. I tried to remember the last one, but it was like sifting for fool's gold.

"I'm going to show you Neon," I said.

"Well, now we have a plan."

I leant my head against the window, hypnotised by the rhythm of the streetlights as we passed under them, taking their blessings one by one. We were getting closer. There were tall Victorian terraces looming on the left, filled with the curtained glow of hidden lives. And then the Christmas lights began, reds and greens and golds, strung criss-cross over the road and stretching off ahead of us. Over to the left was the black expanse of the North Sea, a heaviness I'd always held in my heart.

"Next block along," I said, and then, "Here."

The fat man pulled in to the kerb. It was past eleven, but there were people around, couples holding hands, huddled against the rain, groups stumbling along. A pub was open. A Chinese restaurant. But Neon itself was cast in darkness.

I pulled my backpack from the seat-well between my knees and got out of the car. The rain was hard. The wind was terrible. I slammed the passenger door shut, and, as I fumbled for the right key, I heard the driver's side door slam too.

And then I was inside, the fat man following. I negotiated the shadows and the silhouettes of the scattered mannequins which filled the place. "Give me a second," I said, as I picked my way through to the storeroom at the back. I wanted the fat man to experience the full ridiculousness of my father's folly, and for that I needed the lights.

"I can't see," he said, as if speaking from some distant planet. "Are you coming back out?" And then he started to laugh. "You're a tease," he said, and I could hear him shuffling around. "Come on. I've got something to show you here."

"Let me show you first," I said. And I pulled the lever.

*

A father with an idea... a father with a pension... a father who purchased a café... a father who bought up all the neon signs he could find, from everywhere and anywhere, car-boot sales, auctions, the Internet, America, Germany, Japan... a father who wanted people to see... a father who waited and waited... who tried to entice people in... and when they didn't come, this father bought some people of his own, wrapped them in lines of bulbs, stood them amongst the potential of the signs... and switched everything on.

In the storeroom, the strip of light under the closed door pulsed in waves of energy, as if some fantastic alien birth was happening beyond it. I heard the fat man gasp.

"For the love of God," he said. "This place!"

I opened the door and walked into the room. The fat man was naked, his small, hard cock bobbing beneath his hairy belly. All around him were pulsing, nonsensical signs coloured pink and blue: *All Night Refills! Smoke the Pope! Your Friends are Forever! Life in the Fast Lane! Drink Echo Beach Lager! KLove, KHate, KPop! The Who! All Night Strip! Silence! Twist and Shout! No Cameras! Live Among Us For Ever and Be Free!*

He stretched out his arms, tipped his head over to the right, like some kind of lit-up, corpulent Christ, and laughed. I could do no other than go to him. I could do no other than smile. He embraced me, and I saw the ghost of my father counting the meagre takings in the corner. The ghost didn't seem to care now what happened in his lost citadel of light.

"This place," whispered the fat man. He shook his head, grasped my face in his thick little fingers and kissed me hard.

I could smell the drive and the sadness of the season on him as I pulled away. "It's mine," I said. "For my sins."

One of the mannequins was behind him, all sculpted pecs and carved abs, with a plastic mound between its legs. There was wire wrapped all around this angel, strung with bulb after bulb after bulb, silver lights, beautiful and strange. I lifted it, turned it around and placed it into the fat man's willing embrace.

"Here," I said, smiling.

And they began to dance, the crazy signs pulsing a rhythm while a silent congregation looked on. The fat man laughed, whirling and turning, his new lover weighing almost nothing, and his life suddenly full.

The front door had closed, but I went to it and opened it wide: it was Christmas, and time once again for Neon to be filled with the cold and the pity and the hope of this unimaginable world.

JOANNA CAMPBELL

Aurora and the Book Trolley

I hope the child will lose interest in me soon. I know it's only a child, but I detest being stared at. Three nurses dart past the waiting room. And still it seems to watch me. I go to the window. In the courtyard below, more nurses scurry like white ants. Ash branches swoop in a bizarre mass prayer. In the distance, plumes of smoke from the housing estate are still rising.

I feel a movement beside me. The child is standing close, brushing against my coat. It's wearing jeans and a lime-green jumper peppered with snags. Its hair is probably crawling. I've heard the frantic scratching. A draught disturbs its enormous earrings. They creak in an exasperating rhythm like chandeliers in a bombed-out ballroom. "What are you doing?" it asks.

"Looking outside. And you?" I'm polite, of course, as if answering a query in the library: *"Self-help? Just along there, Madam."*

"Waiting," the child replies.

"That makes two of us then."

I pace about, hoping to shake the child off. But it follows, step for step. "Are you a doctor?"

"No, a librarian."

"Were you in the fire?"

"Do I look burnt?"

"My mum was. I'm waiting for her to be bandaged up."

"Oh dear, I'm sorry."

"That's OK. They sent me here because they said there were books. On a trolley."

"Ah yes, the infamous, invisible trolley. I'm waiting to restock it."

We sit down again. Sudden squeaking breaks the silence. "What's that?"

"The mobile library. Words on Wheels."

"Wow."

"Exactly."

The porter rams the trolley against the wall and starts panting, hands on hips, to let me know this isn't really his job.

"My name's Aurora," the child tells me.

Another huddle of nurses bustle by.

"Well, Aurora, go ahead and choose a book to read if you like."

"Why does everyone want to give me a book? The Paramedic, the Triage man, the Casualty nurse, the Receptionist, the Porter. Now you."

I bristle. No one's *giving* anything. "You can't keep it," I say. "You can borrow one while you're here. But leave it on the trolley when you go home. Understand?"

"I like words."

"Good. Take your pick."

The child sits still, while I set to work, then says, "Can't read."

"Ah. I see." I check my list. Six books missing. Three thrillers, two annuals and a Georgette Heyer. I circle the titles in red ink.

"Because I'm blind," the child says.

I drop the pen. "Oh dear, Aurora. I didn't know."

"Any audio books?"

"Not with me."

Sirens howl against the wind. Doctors stream by, a blur of flapping cotton.

"My mum'll be ages, won't she?"

"I don't know, Aurora."

There's a catch in her voice. Hopefully hoarseness from the smoke. I've no patience with tears. I once marinated in them because of Craig. Pickled in Craig-acid. That was the last time. Not even the softest-centred love stories induce weeping now.

Craig was reduced to a shoe-box, which casts a small shadow on my garage wall. It was vital to consign things to the right place. His clothes in a case he'd paid for. His personal possessions in a strong container. His letters on the fire. I re-flat-packed our bed and drove it to the tip. A man there offered to help, but my glare

81

forced him back. I threw in the base sections, then the mattress. Finally, I hurled in the headboard I'd heard clattering against the wall the day I came home early from work.

Craig borrowed too many of my years. They could never be returned.

A few reminders of the marriage and its broken dreams remain in the shoe-box. Ranked *Archive*. No, I can't abide breaking down. I prefer to restore order. "Do you know about the Dewey Decimal System, Aurora?"

The earrings swing violently from side to side.

"Well, it chops all the stuff in the library books into ten classes. Each class is cut up into ten divisions. So a hundred of those. Those are split into ten sections. A whole thousand of them. Then all the books can be kept in the right order on the shelves."

"You sound all happy. Do you like it?"

"Yes, I love it actually."

I go across to Aurora's bench and sit on the other end. "I like classification. Knowing where I am with things. It makes life easier. Except when people put books back in the wrong place."

"Does it make you mad?"

"Well, a bit vexed by the disorder."

"Mad, then."

"I'm better with things in place. I don't like being wrong-footed."

"I think tripping people up is good."

I inch closer. "Why on earth would you think that?"

"Because it shakes them up," she says, swinging her feet. "Stops things staying the same. My teacher says I'm the only one in the class with an imagination. She never knows where she is with me. In Blackheath or a Black Hole. Could be anywhere."

"Does she give you work to challenge you?" I edge closer to focus on her eyes, which are closed in concentration.

"I challenge myself really."

"It must be hard though," I said. "Can you see *anything*?"

Aurora tipped her head back. "In my head, I see anything I want. If I was a book, where would you put me?"

"I've no idea. You can't file people." I stand up and begin emptying the trolley. Relieved of the final burden, its wheels trundle skittishly towards Aurora. She grasps the handle, steps onto the lower shelf and sets it rolling, gathering speed, skimming along the corridor with a whoop and colliding with her mother.

"Oh, there you are, Lizzie," the mother says. "The twins have been checked out now. They kept us waiting ages."

I drop a parenting manual.

"Here you go," says the mother, picking up the book and putting it on a pile of Teenage Angst. "Lizzie been keeping you company? Loves books, she does. Drinks it all in. Over-active mind, her teacher calls it."

I nod, speechless.

"I'm always falling over the piles of books in her room," the mother continues. "Other girls have dress-up clothes and such. But Lizzie's not into let's-pretend. Well, not in that way."

She clutches the hands of her two toddlers, one on each side. "This awful fire just missed our block. I wanted the boys checked though. Coughing from all the smoke, they were."

"And you were hurt yourself," I say.

"No, I wasn't. Like I said, it missed us. We're the lucky ones."

"It must have been frightening for Auror...er, Lizzie. Not being able to see, I mean."

Lizzie's mother raises her voice a tone, as if I might be deaf, or slightly mad. "No, we could all see fine. Thinner smoke down our end, it was."

"Her eyes are all right then?"

"Hang on," says the mother, gaping. "Oh, it's that damn medical encyclopaedia again. Lizzie muddling her facts and her fiction. On purpose, her teacher reckons. To get Attention and Reaction."

"Oh," I say faintly.

"It's a condition," the mother confides with a sense of pride. "A way of reaching out to people. Otherwise she'd be one of those sad types. Nose stuck in a book, never looking up. Do you know, she tried convincing the triage nurse she's got abdominal aortic aneurysm?"

"Working through alphabetically," Aurora whispers to me. "You'd approve of that."

"Wait until you reach H," I say with a smile.

"Why?"

"You'll be able to suffer Hypochondria. Legitimately."

We move apart while a stretcher glides between us.

"These poor people," says the mother, clicking her tongue. "Their lives upside down. I'm sending what clothes I can spare. Bedding and such. And I'll make some cheese pies..." She can't speak anymore. She's trembling, her face waxy from the shock of being saved. She pulls her children closer, folding her family together, ready for the home that was still standing.

As they leave, I reclaim my trolley, listening to their fading conversation.

"Are those my earrings, Lizzie?"

"That's Classified Information, Mum."

At the end of the corridor, Lizzie turns to wink at me. Tucked under her arm is a giant book of fairy tales.

I lay my hands on the trolley, take a deep breath and remember the tiny knitted bonnets and cardigans in the shoe box. Apricot, lemon and white. Assembled in order of colour and size. Newborn, one month, three. Soft as melted butter. Wrapped in velveteen layers of tissue. I can still hear the silent paper membranes drifting into place. Still smell the new wool. And feel the gouging pain when I boxed them up, unlabelled.

No point in keeping them. And the estate is stacked with naked babies now, their routines in disarray. I could take the box down. And other people could sort the things out.

I wheel the trolley back to the porter and go home to make a start.

'Aurora and the Book Trolley' was published (by InkTears) in 2016 in Joanna Campbell's first collection of short stories, 'When Planets Slip their Tracks'

GEOFF MEAD

Raku

Tanaka Chojiru wasn't expecting a visitor. Nobody came to visit the old potter at that hour. The candles guttered and at first he thought it might have been the wind rattling the rough-hewn door in its frame. No, there it was again. Three regular taps. Definitely someone knocking.

"I'll go, Father," said his daughter, Kasumi, getting up from her place by the fire.

"Sit down Kasumi. It wouldn't be right for a young woman to open the door at this time of night. What would your mother have thought?"

"You're not well, Father. I'm sure she wouldn't have minded."

Tanaka smiled at her affectionately, heaved himself to his feet and shuffled to the door.

"Alright. I'm coming," he wheezed.

He unlatched the door and swung it open. On the doorstep, a slender man wrapped in a heavy cloak, bowed deeply. "Forgive me Tanaka-San, but I had to see you at once."

Tanaka peered through rheumy eyes. "Is that you, Sen no Rikyu?"

"Yes, my old friend. It's been a long time. May I come in?"

The two men made their way to the fireplace. Kasumi bowed modestly to the newcomer who removed his cloak and sat down. "It's a matter of the utmost importance," he said to Tanaka.

"What is?" asked Kasumi.

"Something that concerns your father," replied Sen no Rikyu.

"Kasumi is my right hand, Rikyu-San. What concerns me, concerns her."

"I came straight here from the palace to tell you," insisted Sen no Rikyu.

85

"Even so, I imagine it can wait until you have had a little *saké*. There is still some warm on the hob."

Sen no Rikyu nodded. He smiled as Tanaka tipped the flagon and poured two cups until they gently overflowed. "You are a gracious host," he said. "Thank you."

"Whatever I know of grace, I learned from you, Rikyu-San," said Tanaka. "Your mastery of the tea ceremony is legendary."

The two men sipped their *saké* in appreciative silence. Sen no Rikyu put his empty cup down beside the flagon and reached into a deep pocket inside his robe. He pulled out an ancient, cracked tea bowl. "This is why I came," he said, offering it for Tanaka's inspection.

Tanaka took the proffered bowl in both hands and lifted it up in the firelight. "My eyes are not what they were, but even in this light I can see that the glaze is extraordinary. Look at the way it shimmers: black and bronze; red and green; orange and blue. One moment it is perfectly plain; the next, it contains a rainbow. I've never seen anything like it. What do you think, Kasumi?"

"It's the most beautiful thing I've ever seen," she replied.

"Where did it come from, Rikyu-san?" asked Tanaka.

"I found it on a stall in the marketplace," said Sen no Rikyu. "The trader had picked it up somewhere on his travels. He had no idea of its provenance."

"It's finely made," said Kasumi. "Korean, perhaps."

"I made the mistake of showing it to the Imperial Regent," said Sen no Rikyu. "He went into raptures about the unequalled beauty of the bowl and demanded a set of eight for his autumn tea ceremony. I told him you were the only man capable of making them."

"I'm flattered," said Tanaka.

"That was my second mistake," interrupted Sen no Rikyu. "He declared that fame and fortune would be the reward for making them."

"That sounds promising," said Kasumi.

"And death the penalty for failure," Sen no Rikyu concluded.

"I'm flattered that you think I am the only man who could make such bowls," repeated Tanaka. "But I no longer have the strength in my hands to work the clay or to fire the kiln, and my sight is too poor to mix the glazes. You'll have to tell the Imperial Regent that I decline his kind offer. I'm sure he'll understand."

"Hideyoshi executed thirty members of his own family for displeasing him. He is not a reasonable man," said Sen no Rikyu. "We have no choice in the matter."

"But I cannot do it," said Tanaka.

Kasumi crossed the fireplace and knelt in front of her despairing father.

"You can't do it," she said. "But I can."

"You?" exclaimed Sen no Rikyu. "I mean no offence, but..."

"I have worked alongside my father for twenty years, Rikyu-san. These days, it's me who makes the pots and fires the kiln."

"I've taught her everything I know," said Tanaka. "If anyone can make those bowls, it's her."

"Could you make them, Kasumi?" asked Sen no Rikyu.

"It's all in the glaze," said the potter's daughter, taking the bowl in her hands. "There must be a way."

Tanaka looked at his daughter then turned to his friend. "Tell the Imperial Regent he shall have his tea bowls. How long have we got?"

"Five weeks," said Sen no Rikyu, putting his cloak back on. "He is set on having them for the autumn tea ceremony. I will let him know that Tanaka Chojiru, the greatest potter of the age, has begun work. I think it best to keep your daughter's name out of it, don't you? We don't want her to risk the Imperial Regent's anger."

Sen no Rikyu went out into the night, leaving Kasumi and her father to sleep as well as they could under the circumstances. The next day, Kasumi was up early in the pottery behind the house, gazing at the glittering bowl on the workbench. She knew she could shape vessels just as simple and elegant, but what glaze had the maker used; how long had it been fired and at what temperature?

Kasumi mixed every combination of glazing material she could lay her hands on for test firings: wood ash; iron oxide; lead; salt; tin; silica; manganese oxide; copper carbonate; feldspar; pumice;

lapis lazuli; silver; gold and a myriad more. She carefully weighed the ingredients before grinding and mixing them together in dozens of small containers.

As soon as the labourers arrived for work, she got them trimming and stacking dry wood in the firepit of the large *anagama* kiln they used for all their pots. But when the kiln cooled after each firing, the results were disappointing: too dull; too shiny; too variegated; too plain. None of the test pieces came close to the extraordinary depth and range of colour of the original bowl.

Tanaka joined his daughter in the pottery whenever he felt well enough. He said little, but watched closely and kept notes.

First Firing: 6 days. 50 pieces. Nothing.

Second Firing: 5 days. 40 pieces. Nothing.

Third Firing: 8 days. 60 pieces. Nothing.

Fourth Firing: 6 days. 50 pieces. Nothing.

Day by day, he saw the hope draining from his daughter's face. Her eyes brilliant with a kind of madness and rimmed blue from lack of sleep, her head bowed with exhaustion, she stared for hours at the bowl she was trying to match, then worked fresh clay into bowls of exquisite proportions, and, time after time, saw them come to naught in the kiln.

"One last firing," she said to her father. "We still have a few days. No labourers. I must do everything myself."

"What good will that do, child?" asked Tanaka, gently.

"I will give it everything I have," she said with a wild stare. "Every ounce of knowledge, skill, experience and love. How else could such a bowl be made?"

"I can't bear to see you drive yourself like this," said Tanaka, going back indoors. "Come and get me when the firing is done."

With infinite care, Kasumi stacked the last batch of unfired bowls in the kiln. She set the wood fire burning and tended it carefully day and night, adding logs and stoking, until the chamber was hotter than ever. On the third night, as she sat beside the kiln trying to imagine the exact path of the flame as it rushed through, painting the pieces inside with fire, she looked once more at Rikyu-san's tea bowl in her hand. Suddenly her eyes seemed to penetrate its lustre and she knew with absolute certainty what she had to do.

Two days later, Sen no Rikyu called at Tanaka's house to find him half-dressed, wandering through the pottery, calling for Kasumi. But it wasn't until the kiln was cool enough to open that they found the shadow of her oxidised bones on the floor, arms outstretched as if in prayer, before a rack of perfectly fired tea bowls, each of them as varicoloured and shimmering as the one Rikyu-san had brought to their house.

Tanaka Chojiru's bowls were the talk of the autumn tea ceremony. "Truly magnificent," declared the Imperial Regent.

"Indeed, my Lord," replied Sen no Rikyu. "They are beyond price. Eight sublime tea bowls. The potter's art perfected. By a daughter's love."

stroud
book festival

The cream of Gloucestershire's
writers read their stories at
Cotswold Playhouse, Parliament
Street, Stroud, GL5 1LW

Sunday 10 November 2019
Doors open at 7:00pm
Starts at 7:300pm

Tickets £8 in advance from
cotswoldplayhouse.co.uk

MAZURKA AND OTHER STROUD SHORT STORIES

ALI BACON

Snowbird

As we land in St Lucia, the heat clutches at my throat, bringing back that itch of doubt. If I'd wanted to be a snowbird, I could have done it years ago - with Daniel. But after our trip to Africa we stuck to Europe or the Eastern sea-board. One hot season had been enough.

But hell, those Iowa winters sure get to my bones. So when Annie asked me to join her and Ezra on their trip, I let myself be persuaded. I guessed my daughter needed my company. That husband of hers is good natured enough, but not a lot of fun. Annie is artistic, impulsive. How does she put up with his comfortable...dreariness?

At the plantation resort, I stow things in my cabin (dripping noise unidentified – bathroom sink? something out of doors?) and go to join them in the open-air bar.

Ezra's alone. "How you doin, Celia?"

The *Celia* is fine. I never wanted anyone but Annie to call me Mom. Hitched awkwardly on the bar-stool I manage a smile. "I guess you and I were dragged here against our better judgement."

His eyes crinkle. From this I divine amusement, or agreement or both. Ezra is not a talker. "I can work anywhere," he says. "Annie wanted a break."

When she appears, we all agree the cabins are pretty and the humidity will diminish. January is the dry season, we're told. Then rain falls all night like gunshot on the tin roof, and I lie awake, thinking of Africa.

*

Getting off that plane I sucked up the humid breath of the Congo, thirsty for more. The village was makeshift and erected for the project. A jeep went into town every couple of days to

93

pick up food. We drew water from the sullen river, dropped in purifying tablets and hoped for the best.

The heat and the wildness of everything turned us on. Daniel and I were crazy for it, jumping each other in the forest, going back to lick and scratch each other in the secret confines of the hut. I imagined our private parts glowed red like the baboons'.

*

Here in the Caribbean everything around us drips and steams. Next morning, Ezra stays by the pool with his laptop because the signal's good up there. Annie and I take a tour with one of the resort guides. When he offers to show us the cocoa sheds on the terrace, I leave them and watch from a distance. I see how his teeth flash and how she leans on his arm when he makes her walk barefoot through the trays of cocoa beans. Then he jumps in the bean pot and whirls his hips in that show-off-for-tourists dance so that everything turns hazy. I blink twice to clear my head of ghosts.

Back at the pool, Ezra's fingers are scouring the keyboard. I want to shake him. *Wake up. Look after your wife.*

Down here, night falls like a shutter. The light in the cabin is too dim to read. There is only rain and the creaking chirp of the tree-frogs. I listen for rustlings under my hut. In all the years since Daniel's been gone, it's the first time I've been afraid of the dark.

At breakfast, Ezra shoos the dun-coloured birds that swoop and dive around our table. Annie asks him to walk up to where the torch lilies grow. "The guide showed us. It's the best place for hummingbirds."

Her smile is pleading. He makes a sad face. "I have a Skype call at eleven."

Annie shrugs. "Okay, maybe later."

All work and no play. That's Ezra for you.

*

My thoughts drift back to the Congo. After two weeks I stepped on a loose stone in the river, wrenched my ankle and collapsed onto a jagged rock that left me sore and scarred. I became the project invalid. Team members called with what passed for gossip.

Daniel got wrapped up in the work we had come there to do. Sex - even cautious, tender sex - diminished and disappeared.

I wanted to be with the others, observing and recording, not lying there watching spiders drift between the door-posts. Daniel took off on a two-day trek with Martha, the project leader, to look at some species sighted farther west. I wondered how and where they would make their beds. Would one surprise the other under the mosquito net?

Between halting trips to the latrine, I lay in a permanent lassitude, craving Pepsi or blackcurrant milkshake, anything other than coconut milk. When my reading ran out, I was rehydrated by fantasies: Daniel dragging me back to the jungle in the heat of the day, Daniel having febrile sex with Martha while I looked on, getting up a sweat.

Through the door of the hut I watched the local boys who'd been hired to cook and run errands, seeing for the first time the curve in the nape of the neck, the flash of white-soled feet. One of them brought me manioc twice a day, avoiding my eyes as he laid the food next to my bed. I caught him looking back at me as he left.

I guess he had a nose for pheromones. One still night, with the air cooling faster than the land and the river frogs chanting a chorus, he turned his eyes on me and I turned back the sheet to let him in.

*

When Daniel came back to the camp he took one look at me and said, "You're sick. You should go home."

"I'm not sick, I just can't walk."

"No, you have a fever," he said. "Anyone can see."

He wiped my forehead with a towel wrung out in water then I raised my limbs for him to bathe, noticing for the first time how hard it was to lift them from the bed.

He took my temperature. "You have an infection. I'll get you some penicillin."

As my fever abated, Martha called to sympathise. I glimpsed her sun-toughened cleavage as she leaned in for a kiss. A straight-laced scientist with flaky lips. What had I been thinking? I listened to the camp boys play football in the dirt outside. None of them looked my way. I'd been hallucinating.

Then the penicillin gave me the runs so I felt sick for sure and got myself shipped back home, leaving behind the memory of how it had felt, how he had felt, the African boy in my bed.

Once Daniel was home we rarely talked about Africa - a two week trip, a road not taken. Annie, conceived in a jungle fever, popped out as pale as a Norwegian sky. Only, as she grew older, I began to see another child skipping beside her, a fine black boy with a familiar profile - a lost twin? An alternate reality?

*

Next afternoon, I stumble on Ez and Annie coming back from a walk. He went with her after all.

Annie's fair skin is all pinked up. "It was great. We saw three hummingbirds, up close. We should go again tomorrow, all of us."

Her legs are still white below her skimpy shorts, Ezra's stubby brown calves taper into heavy-soled sandals. Chalk and cheese, but sometimes that can work. Maybe Daniel and I were too alike.

In the evening they are making plans - a hike to a neighbouring plantation, a boat-trip in search of whales.

"What would you like to do, Mom?" Annie asks.

A bird flits through the darkening cocoa trees. Is there someone lurking out there?

Ezra refills my rum punch from the pitcher. "Celia?"

He's talking to me, but his eyes, like mine, are on Annie. There's no one outside. The ghost of the black boy has melted away. The only intruder is me.

"Well, thank you kindly for asking. But this heat is just too much for me."

I'm going to book an early flight home. I must be missing the snow.

PETER ADAMS

The Box of Skin

On a day before my memories began, or perhaps the day they began, a procession came to our house from the village. At the head was the doctor carrying his back bag, then the vicar, and behind him the school teacher, the man who worked in London, the visiting dentist who came one afternoon a week, a churchwarden, the shopkeeper, the postmaster and a few others. They all wore black suits and black trilby hats and black ties.

Anyone in the village was welcome to join the procession, but most did not; perhaps because they did not have suitable black suits. They walked all the way in solemn silence. Their black shoes had metal caps on their heels and these clattered like hail on the hard road. Occasionally a car passed, the faint roar growing louder then fading again into the distance. The silence, except for the clattering, always returned. The green fields were empty of cows and sheep that day.

When they got to my house, my parents let the doctor into the sitting room, and I was brought in on a big tray. He opened his bag on the table and quietly and methodically laid out instruments and cotton wool.

The window was open wide, the procession was arranged outside in rows, so that everyone could see in.

Suddenly there was a great pain down in my body, there was a scream - it must have been me. There was a flurry of activity and things were quickly put away. The doctor and the procession were there no longer, but the great pain took a long time to go.

When I got up next day there was something new on the mantelpiece, a brown wooden box. It stayed there on the mantelpiece without ever being moved, opened or mentioned for eleven years.

When I arrived at boarding school I had a new trunk, full of new clothes. I watched as everything disappeared into linen rooms and other places I could not go. Finally, at the bottom of the trunk was the wooden box. "Oh, that must be mine," I said. I reached out my hand to take it, but matron took it and gave it to the housemaster. He put it in a cupboard. Before he closed the door, I glimpsed other wooden boxes there side by side.

The years went by and I did not speak. I realised I was dumb.

When I left school seven years later, I was given that box. I always kept it in the back of a cupboard and mostly I forgot about it.

But the box came into my thoughts sometimes, and late one night when everyone was asleep I took it out again and opened it and slammed it shut. Inside it was my tongue.

Still my thoughts return to that box from time to time. Last week I took it out and opened it again and inside was a pen. I took out the pen and with it I wrote this story.

GEORGIA BOON

Choose Love

Chris O'Dowd, star of *Bridesmaids* and *The IT Crowd*, walked along the South Bank in his 'Choose Love' t-shirt. The letters on the t-shirt were big, blocky, black capital letters. He had been wearing this t-shirt for the last three months, washing it in the evenings, and hanging it to dry on the balcony of his apartment. He glanced up at the fresh blue sky, and down at the brown Thames. No boats sailed today. He stopped by a bench and felt in his back pocket for tobacco that he didn't have.

He instinctively put his hand to his phone. It was there, but it was sterile, impotent - connected only to the switchboard or whatever it was called nowadays. No internet whatsoever.

"Jesus," he muttered.

For all that there were new challenges every day, in this, the third month of whatever this was, the overwhelming feeling was undeniably one of boredom. The first few weeks had been halcyon: parties in basements; plays in attics; pop-up bands by the river. But now everything felt ropey, inert.

On the other side of the path, David Bowie's son was passing, going the other way. Chris tipped an imaginary hat to him. David Bowie's son was also wearing a 'Choose Love' T-shirt.

A drink, thought Chris. *That's what I'll do. I'll have a drink.*

There weren't enough staff to go round all of the cafes and restaurants, so a lot of them were closed. These establishments had pulled down grilles that Chris didn't know existed, smothered with pieces of A4 paper flapping in the breeze, scrawled with messages: 'Closed until further notice'; 'Fuck you USA - we are closed today'; 'Live Well'.

Chris nodded to Lindsay Lohan who was sitting outside one of the few open restaurants. She had got caught here on a press trip.

99

It would have looked bad to have left before the lockdown, and she couldn't get out now. She was wearing a 'Choose Love' T-shirt. They all were. Every single person on the South Bank on this Monday afternoon was wearing a 'Choose Love' t-shirt. Choose Love. Choose Love. Choose Love.

A small cafe he had never noticed before was full. Chris grabbed a seat at a table with the only person he could see with a newspaper.

He contemplated ordering a coffee. *I'll have a tea*, he thought. *The coffee will start to run out soon.*

Chris skimmed the front page of the newspaper. There was nothing now, no mention of them. The first ten weeks had been solid front-page splashes - in every paper. The very first front page was framed on his wall at home:

LONDON SHUTDOWN BEGINS - CELEBS HOLD TIGHT AS LONDON BECOMES REFUGEE ZONE FOR THE WEST

There hadn't been a picture of him - some of the bigger stars had been chosen. Pictures of Derek Jacobi on the famous call to Trump. And Maxine Peake with a sombre look of defiance, pictured standing by as they locked the enormous gate.

Four weeks in, Chris had been featured, giving a thumbs-up and grinning to the camera - a shot taken not too far from where he now sat.

O'DOWD DEFIANT AS STORIES OF INFIGHTING IN RULING COMMITTEE ABOUND

But today's front-page story was about Russia, and the inset was a picture of a key lime pie with the promise of a recipe inside.

Fuck. Fuck them, he thought. *They've forgotten us.* He knew it shouldn't matter. They were wrong. We were right. We had Chosen Love. He ordered a tea. In a mug.

He had run out of things to think about during this walk. The dog would have provided some entertainment, but dogs weren't allowed anymore, not here, not in the... for fuck's sake! Why hadn't the naming thing worked out? The meeting had been a disaster. The Committee had debated for five and a half hours. It had been agonising. Initially, the meeting had been planned to take place in Caitlin Moran's loft space. But a pigeon had got in through a skylight and was out of control. Then the meeting had moved to Mark Gatiss' basement complex. But he had had a plumbing emergency while everyone was on their way across town. So in the end, they had to meet in a pub in Soho. The landlord had been very accommodating and agreed to close up for the afternoon.

By the time they all arrived, everyone was worn out and crotchety. Lily Allen had a face on her like a furious badger. And Ellie Goulding scowled for the full five hours. Only Dara O'Briain had managed to stay in good spirits.

"How about the T-Zone?" he had lisped, gamely, after the first hour of the meeting. "You know, like the bit where all the nasty blackheads gather when you're a teenager. You know what I'm talking about, don't you, Ed?"

Ed Sheeran was sitting meekly at a different table, and had, for some reason, brought his guitar along with him to the Committee meeting.

There were, of course, those who had decided not to stay. Daniel Radcliffe was in Manhattan - he posted on his Instagram that he had tickets lined up to be with family in Northern Ireland if things got rough, but he didn't feel London was the place for him at this point in his career. And everyone was really shocked when Thom Yorke left Oxford for Fort Severn, Ontario with no explanation. All people knew was that he had taken his kids and that his house was still full of stuff.

There were also those who everyone knew were just there by accident. Benedict, everyone knew, had been trapped there while attending the funeral of a family friend. He came to all the meetings and pretended to be into it, but everyone could see how uncomfortable and unwilling he was beneath it all.

And of course, there were a few that everyone wished hadn't stayed. Jimmy Carr had been ostentatiously ignored by all at the Committee meeting, and they had kept the whole thing secret from Alan Davies, even though he had had 'Choose Love' tattooed onto his knuckles.

Chris walked again and looped across the river. Near St Paul's he could hear a loud hailer, and the sound of a crowd. He sloped down by the side of the Cathedral, until, on the front steps, he could see Mark Thomas standing and addressing a small, enraptured crowd.

"We stand in defiance. We speak with, not for, the refugees. We serve them with our defiance. We are liberated! And we will keep using our skills, our voices, to show that we are forging a new world!"

At that moment, heads turned as Gillian Anderson jogged past, lifting small weights up and down in time to her run.

Good God, Mark didn't learn anything from the last meeting, thought Chris. Two months after the Committee failed to pick a name for whatever this was, they had met again, this time to discuss the Benefit Concert.

"We really would need to involve agents, I think," said Ellie Goulding. "It could be tough for us to figure out just as a Committee."

They were at Rhys Ifans' place in Notting Hill. Everyone was a little edgy as his cleaner had chosen to leave a few weeks before, and there was no clean crockery and no clean glasses. The only thing that was safe to drink was beer from the bottle, which was in abundance, so everyone was becoming tipsy. Sadie Frost pouted and fingered the sobriety coin that hung from a platinum chain round her neck.

Sandi Toksvig huffed.

"What is it, Sandy? If you've got something to say, we'd rather you just said it," Katherine Ryan barked out.

"Well, it's just, I mean, it's obvious. Who are we going to be doing the benefit *for*? I mean, it's not on the top ten list of things that the Refugee Steering Group is asking for, is it?"

Silence sparked between them all.

"I'm not sure if there are enough sound guys around, to be honest," said Alex James.

The meeting broke up soon after, with many other sensible, technical reasons having been given for not having a Benefit Concert.

Chris was getting tired. He reached in his pocket for his tobacco. Still nothing. A song was in his head:

Oh sad was the day when I went far away
To work amongst timber and concrete

He turned his back on Mark Thomas and slunk back along the river towards home, the song still going:

As I made me a plan for to follow life's span
I forsook the dear place of my homeland
If God grants me grace I'll return to the place
When the twilight of life has come o'er me
As I stand on your shores like a bird my heart soars
As I gaze on the beauty around me

NIMUE BROWN

Household Management

It is impossible to maintain standards without hired help, I have found. But so often they cause more trouble than they alleviate. Will they steal the spoons? Are their hands and minds clean enough? Are they discreet?

Of course, the answer to that final question is no, they are never discreet enough. They see into the most intimate details of your life, and that eventually becomes intolerable - to you or to them.

Hiring new help is considerably harder when everyone knows that there are issues around your previous servants. Now that I have a reputation for my hired help disappearing inexplicably, I am not a tempting employer. They were, to be clear, truly inexplicable disappearances. I cannot explain them. I am guilty of nothing whatsoever where my servants are concerned. At the same time, I am not wholly innocent in these matters, either. It is difficult.

In such a small town, people talk and speculate, and you overhear them in the market saying things like, "Something is very wrong with her," and then they look away as you approach. You know they were talking about you, and that if you let the rage boiling up in your guts make it all the way to your face, or hands, everything will be much worse. So you smile at them, and pretend you don't know why they won't make eye contact. And you know why they do not encourage their daughters to enter your household. But I cannot manage alone, it is simply too much work and I am not accustomed to doing without help. And so I must bear the comments and the anxieties.

My newly employed servant is called Corrine, and she is from away, which means she has no idea about my reputation. She has no family in this town. I believe she speaks French, but I do not, so communication between us is largely in gestures. I speak slowly and carefully to her, and she stares blankly at me, but mostly she does the work that needs doing. She has a dull, incurious, accepting nature, which I greatly appreciate. I hope she has no one she can gossip with. I prefer my private life not to be open to discussion, but, all too often, this is the cost of hiring someone.

I do not believe it is widely known, at present, that there is a dead man in my cellar. He has been there for some time now and this has not improved his appearance. If I had dealt with his body at the time of death, it might all have been very easy. There would have been talk, but perhaps nothing worse. An unexplained death is not so very unusual a thing, after all, and less so in a person no one else much cared for. I regret both my fear and my attachment.

No one has since spoken to me of his absence – not that anyone speaks to me of anything much. I am the only person in all of the world who feels that absence at all. His continued presence – albeit silent, still and unsavoury, has been an odd sort of comfort to me. It is reassuring to know exactly where he is, sprawled backwards across the tea chests in the cellar. The one hand he held up to protect himself has long since slumped down across his chest. He is, in truth, far more charming in death than ever he was in life.

I have forbidden Corrine from visiting the cellar. I have pointed at the stairs and shook my head and said the words slowly, and I am hopeful that she understands. Her lack of interest in almost everything may be the saving of us both. Her predecessor – Matilda – was a much more lively and attentive creature. A good quality in one who is dusting your porcelain. Less helpful around questions of deceased husbands who have been improperly disposed of. I caught her eyeing up the cellar door more times than I can count. Perhaps she thought I had some kind of treasure in there.

My late husband would have liked Matilda. He did always have an eye for the young ladies, although none of them ever showed much interest in him. I was not so very jealous of that while he lived, but now that he is dead, it troubles me a good deal more.

Our first servant, Violet, was exceedingly pretty and knew it. He was still alive when she went missing. No one made a great deal of fuss when Violet ran off, because she'd always seemed like the sort of girl who would, eventually. The kind of girl who gets herself into trouble, where the names of the men who are the trouble are only mentioned in whispers behind the hands of women who will never admit to knowing such things. It's not that I deliberately eavesdrop; I just have very good hearing. He was not blamed for her vanishing act. I do not know if he should have been. I long made it my business not to know anything at all about what he did behind my back.

When a person who was not much liked disappears, no one grieves or asks many questions. Violet and my late husband had that much in common and perhaps more. Matilda on the other hand, was popular, and her sizeable family permeates the town. Her absence is neither forgotten nor forgiven. Her absence casts Violet's disappearance in a new light, and people talk, but they do not talk to me.

I am not sure what happened to Matilda, only that the cellar door had been left open on the day that she vanished. I have never tried to clean in there. If there is a way to tell between recent dry blood and old dry blood, I do not know of it. Perhaps she could not stand what she saw when she finally got in there. But where would she go after leaving? Why not denounce me? Perhaps she really did run away, to some distant farm or hamlet, never letting her family know what had become of her. It seems unlikely, but it is preferable to other explanations. I do not want her to be dead. I do not want to think that what remains of my husband still has the power to do harm. I do not want to think he ever had the power to do harm. I keep telling myself that what happened to Violet is a mystery to me and could not be connected with what happened to Matilda. I tell myself nothing will happen to Corrine. On a good day, I entirely persuade myself that all these things are true.

I wear the key to the cellar on a ribbon around my neck now. It weighs heavily, but it reassures me to feel it there and to know where it is. This way, I cannot easily unlock the cellar while sleepwalking. I do not know that I have done this, but I fear it may have happened. I am afraid I will unlock that door and not know I have done so. I fear it will somehow be my fault if Corrine ignores my instructions and visits the cellar.

I am afraid that somehow he isn't entirely dead down there, and that despite my best efforts, his not-deadness is also my fault. He exerts a fascination, even in death, even through the locked cellar door. I feel that pull every day. Will she feel it? Will she resist him? Will I?

Even in death, he always has his hands around my throat.

RICK VICK

Mazurka

Her mother stood alert outside the circle of boys and girls sitting on the carpet as her daughter, Faye, unwrapped her birthday presents. She had cautioned her tomboy to say "thank you" even if she did not like the gift. She knew well the Polish fire that simmered in the just-turned seven year-old. "You don't want to hurt feelings, do you?" But Faye had shrugged.

She did not much like the woolly hat, knowing she would not wear it even though she liked blue, the colour of her eyes. The colouring book she might have appreciated a year or two ago, and the crayons she saw at once were cheap, not near as good as the ones she already had. The black Stetson, she immediately put on, smiling at the boy whose gift it was. When she ripped off the pink paper around a box that revealed a pouting long-legged Barbie doll, her mother saw her intent, and before Faye could hurl it away, reached out and held onto the box, meeting her daughter's furious eyes. Raising her brows a fraction, Faye stamped her western boots and forced a whispered, "Thank you."

When the last of her friends had gone, she sat on the carpet staring at the strewn paper and presents. She picked up the woolly hat, sniffed it and was about to put it on, but tossed it aside. She glanced at a card leaning against a lamp on a side-table. Behind the bold black hand-drawn dancing figure on the outside, she could just see the corners of bank notes clipped to the inside. She angrily wiped a tear from her face. She had felt happy before the party but now she felt sad. Not sad that it was over. No, her sadness was bigger than that. It was an emptiness she felt; a feeling she had when she thought of her father, gone nearly a year to another lady. She was angry too. Her fists were clenched. The feeling was like the pecking of a small bird deep in her belly.

108

She heard the flap of the letter box. There, on the door mat, was a bundle of newspaper tied haphazardly round and round with string. She bent and picked it up - it was as light as nothing. She raised it to her face, sniffed and wrinkled her nose. It smelt mouldy.

She tore off the string and damp newspaper to reveal an old rope knotted at each end. A picture formed in her mind. A grizzled white-bearded man sitting in the doorway of the now boarded-up sweet and tobacco shop on the corner where she caught the school bus. She could picture the rope tied around the old dirty coat he wore. She had remembered how her father put coins in the up-turned hats of street sleepers so she had, almost every morning, put a few pennies of her lunch money in the old man's hat. Sometimes he played a violin, still sitting. His trousers were pinned up below the knees of both legs and there were a pair of wooden crutches leant against the wall. She liked listening to the tunes he played, even though sometimes they made her feel sad. He smiled up at her when she dropped the coins into the hat. How did he know, she thought, where I live? Had he overheard talk about her party by the children at the bus stop? She heard her father's voice, "When in doubt, create a mystery."

She clenched a knot in each hand and swung the rope back and forth in front of her legs, then began to skip. Slowly at first, jumping high, then faster and faster she swung the rope till her feet were a blur. On and on and on she swung and jumped, her boots thudding on the wooden floor. Her mother came out of the kitchen and smiled to see her daughter in flight.

The next day Faye took one of the bank notes from the card and folded it as tight as she could. Just before she hopped onto the school bus she turned and tossed it into the old man's hat. He looked up and smiled, and, raising his bow, played the opening chords of a wild Polish Mazurka folk dance as the bus pulled away.

'Mazurka' **was published by Chapeltown Books in 2021 in** *'Ways of Seeing'*, **a collection of Rick Vick's writing**

PHILIP DOUCH

Science, Steve and the Real World

Steve was shit at Science. And when I say shit, I mean really shit. But to be fair to him, the teaching of Science at Shrewsbury Comprehensive did come up somewhat short of inspired. So throughout Year 7 Steve had regrettably been introduced to precisely nothing that engaged him about the natural world. Science, ironically enough, seemed light years away from reality.

Let's start with Biology. You know that dissection stuff you get to do in school? Pin a frog to a board and carve it into bits? Steve had somehow flipped his little offering onto its back and sent it pinging across the lab, legs splayed, stomach open, guts half dribbling out. As it happened, straight into Maisy Johnson's face. Just after she'd taken her goggles off. Whole new meaning to that strange phrase about having a frog in your throat.

On reflection 'Ooops' had probably been insufficient compensation. Mr Dunford had given him a damp cloth and a double detention. Which didn't exactly seem fair to Steve. Not so much the damp cloth, though maybe he should have proffered it to Maisy, before rather than after he'd infused it with the mopped-up entrails.

But the double detention seemed, well, harsh. If Steve had sat there, scalpel in hand, turning over in his mind how best to deliver a mutilated frog slap in the face of a classmate, and, having mentally riffled through his options, had selected his desired method - and trained the little bugger on her with laser-guided precision – well, fair enough.

But it was an accident for God's sake. And you shouldn't get detention for accidents. Let alone double detention. Steve had fondly hoped that Maisy Johnson might have put in a good word for him, might have gently upbraided Mr Dunford with a "not really his fault, sir", but for some reason she'd been unreasonably preoccupied with vomiting into a sink.

It seemed to Steve that his double detention went on for ages, which might not have been unconnected with the fact that it did. Not the standard 45 minute silent incarceration version but a 90 minute half listless-boredom, half writing-of-lines epic. 90 minutes. That's a whole football match, thought Steve. Three hundred times he'd copied it out - 'I must not launch experimental amphibians at unsuspecting fellow-students'.

After about line 210 he'd started to wonder if the wording implied that it was only the action in its entirety that had been deemed unacceptable, and that 'launching experimental amphibians' at, say, Mr Dunford, rather than at 'unsuspecting fellow-students', would therefore have been permissible. Or that it would have been okay if Maisy had suspected it. Or if the fault lay chiefly in the specifically named act of 'launching' and that 'hurling' might not have been viewed so negatively. Or indeed that it was the status of the frog as 'experimental' that was crucial, suggesting that had a random frog hopped into the lab as an integral part of its daily natural business, 'launching' it, even at 'unsuspecting fellow-students' would have been just fine and dandy.

You might have concluded, rightly as it happens, that Steve's academic skills lay more with English than Science. Which was perhaps why he also added a brief note to the foot of his 300 lines, pointing out that, grammatically, the required wording of his punishment should not have referred to amphibians (plural), since his alleged misdemeanour had involved the launching of just a single little critter rather than a multi-frogged volley of Biblical plague proportions.

Whatever, as far as Biology went, Steve had evidently covered himself in rather less glory than he had covered Maisy Johnson in slimy innards. He had also learned precisely nothing of any value, thereby reconfirming his existing view of all things Science-related.

And so to Physics - which, Steve had long since concluded, was really just inherently boring. It seemed somehow appropriate,

111

given the level of unbridled excitement that the phrase Physics Lab engendered in him, that this was a subject where you might actually study 'inertia'. On this topic, if no other, Steve found that he was heavily committed to practical demonstration.

At some point one Tuesday, immediately after school dinner had featured a particularly solidly constructed jam roly-poly, which had rendered Steve even more post-prandially comatose than usual, he had briefly been roused from his torpor and heard Mr Wolstencroft asking, "Can you stop a moving railway carriage that is smoothly running along a line, having just been shunted?"

Putting to one side the unlikelihood of finding himself cycling home from school one day, and, having to face this challenge single-handedly, Steve had come up with a brilliantly penetrating answer. Presumably Mr Wolstencroft had been anticipating a fruitful discussion about the immutable tendency of moving objects to continue their forward motion even when subject to attempted intervention. He had evidently not been anticipating Steve's own intervention, "Yeah, you could just blow it up, sir."

As he sat alone and wrote, for the 300th time, 'I must not make flippant comments about the remarkable physical properties of the natural world', Steve reflected on the unfairness of that part of the natural world that comprised the Science Department of Shrewsbury Comprehensive.

And then there was Chemistry. Potentially, here was a strand of scientific enquiry that might, one could not unfairly assume, jolt even Steve into some semblance of stimulation. For Chemistry was surely the place for mixing exotic coloured liquids and watching them froth over the side of the test tube; for distinguishing different elements by torching lumps of stuff with naked flames; maybe even bringing together the constituent parts that would enable you to set a mighty explosion beneath, say, a moving railway carriage that is smoothly running along a line, especially perhaps one that had just been shunted.

So, given the barely imaginable vistas of enthusiastic exploration that Chemistry might lay out before the enquiring mind of a teenaged boy, it was, not, to put too fine a point on it, more than a little disappointing that Mr Robbins focused the

112

curriculum repeatedly, nay constantly, on memorising the debatable charms of the Periodic Table. Steve's first lesson enquiry as to whether the periodic table was like a slightly more drawn out version of an occasional table had perhaps not set him off on the right foot with the dour Mr Robbins.

It was thus that, after three terms of Chemistry, Steve may have barely turned on a Bunsen burner, but could confidently parrot that the Periodic Table is 'a tabular display of the chemical elements which are arranged by atomic number, electron configuration and recurring chemical properties'. That the seven rows of the table, called periods, about which Steve had gamely made no pubescent boy comment whatsoever, generally have metals on the left and non-metals on the right. And, mercifully finally, that also displayed are four simple rectangular areas or blocks associated with the filling of different atomic orbitals.

It was hard to deny that this was gripping stuff. Hard, at least, if you were face to face with the disconcertingly intense Mr Robbins. It had perhaps been unwise of Steve to share with his teacher his attempt to commit to memory the names and numbers of various key elements, as if he was reading the football results -

Lithium 3 Boron 5

Beryllium 4 Hydrogen 1

Steve had found it particularly galling to write 300 times 'I must not belittle the wonders of the elements with infantile references to soccer'. 'Infantile' had jabbed lightly at his heart. But that Mr Robbins should call football 'soccer' was, for Steve, the final conclusive evidence of the scientist's remoteness from the real world.

SOPHIE FLYNN

Saving Grace

My best friend likes to think she saved my life. You can hear it in her voice whenever she tells the story, which she tells often. All the bloody time.

"Grace did used to be married." Clara often starts with this line at dinner parties, to show that I wasn't *always* alone. She'll accompany it with a bittersweet glance in my direction from under the curls of her fringe, then add, "But things didn't quite...," there's always a pause here, "work out."

"She's in a much better place now. Aren't you, Gracie?"

If we're sitting in touching distance, she'll smile and reach for my hand. Give it a good solid squeeze. Sometimes I say yes, sometimes I say nothing. I've found it makes very little difference.

"We're just glad Clara was there to help," someone will say. Clara will nod furiously and tut, leaving enough silence so that whoever is hearing the story for the first time has space to ask, "What happened?" Usually followed by, "If you don't mind me asking." Which Clara never does.

"Grace doesn't mind, do you?" Clara says before I can reply. "More women should talk about these things. Did you know one in three women will be a victim of domestic violence during their lifetime?" I imagine she Googled 'facts about domestic violence' soon after the incident, then wrote the good ones down on post-it notes to memorise.

"The only way to bring that number down is for victims to speak out," she'll say. Another favourite line. I don't point out that the 'victim' here isn't speaking out at all. I just let my friend go on. And on.

By this point in the story, the audience member tends to murmur apologetically, or offer some sombre words - tinged with

114

enough intrigue to let Clara know that despite being sorry to hear that something awful happened to me - they still want to hear all about it.

"I'll never forget that night," Clara will say.

The others often agree, shaking their heads. Occasionally, one of them will allow their eyes to fill with tears at the imagined memory. Everyone likes to be associated with tragedy once it's over. No one wants to miss out on the action once the horror is safely packed away. But the only stars that evening were Clara and me.

She begins, "Grace's husband, Jake, was Gareth's best friend, so it made the whole thing all the more awful."

As if the only awful thing about the situation was that her poor hubby lost his mate. On the occasions he's present, Gareth will remain mute throughout the story. Loyal to the end. The opposite to Clara in every way.

She'll usually then say, "I often think if only I'd known sooner, I could have done something."

I always hold my tongue here, because the first time I did tell Clara the truth, what she actually said was, "I'm sorry, Grace, but I just don't believe Jake would ever do that." But Clara knows a good story is a series of edits. And this line does not make the cut.

Moving it up a notch, she will look wide-eyed at her audience and tell them, "It's common in these situations that women don't feel they can just come out and tell the truth. It's such a shame. Fortunately for Grace, luck intervened."

*

That night, Jake had been out for hours drinking. I'd left the house in a mess, waiting for his reaction. I felt brave at first, sitting amongst the wreck I'd made, but when I heard him stumble in, I felt my bravery disappear. I hid beneath the false security of the duvet until he found me and dragged me out.

The fight that night was no worse than all the others, his words no more bitter and hate-filled, his punches no less painful, but this time I forced myself to feel it all. Knew I'd have to recall every tiny detail. When he tired himself out, I pulled my body up and stood. He snarled. This was usually the time for me to lie in a ball on the floor until *he* decided it was over. But I had a job to do. When he pushed me back down, I started screaming the practised lines I'd held buried in my head for years. The ways he'd hurt me, abused me, ruined me. The last line, I delivered carefully and clearly, desperate for my voice to be recognised.

"I'm going to…call Clara."

He smacked me around the face, like I'd hoped he would, and I screamed, long and hard, drowning out Alexa as she responded to my command, "Calling Clara."

For the next few minutes, Clara listened to it all from the comfort of her home, while Jake did what Jake did best. Finally, she had no choice but to believe me.

Through the silence, once Jake's fists had tired, her small strangled voice came through the speakers.

"Grace? Gracie, are you there? I'm coming over."

I laughed. Laughed like a banshee, the wail ringing out in the kitchen, bouncing from the shiny chrome kettle to the blood-speckled tiles. At last I had my witness. Jake dived for the speaker and cut the call. He knew it was too late. Finally, he'd been found out. There'd be no lie he could tell to cover his tracks this time. Not after Clara, who loved nothing more than a shocking story she could star in, got up to testify. Not after she delighted in telling the world how an accidental call gave her the chance to save her best friend's life.

The story that never gets told, the only one that's true, is that I saved myself. But that doesn't matter; the point of the story remains the same. I'm saved.

Now, as I sit and listen to Clara spin new delicate lines of detail into my story, I sip my wine and silently rub the spot on my jaw where the bruises no longer live.

Then get up and leave.

SALLIE ANDERSON

The Art of Job Security

Old Phil wasn't invited to the staff meeting with the New Director. He was just the security guard. He didn't have a desk in the office or a staff email address. And, really, what could an old man like him contribute to the New Director's vision for the small regional art gallery? Nothing. The vision involved synergy. The vision involved cross-silo working. The vision involved embracing the future. Old Phil was the past.

The vision also involved streamlining. The art gallery would undergo a streamlining process. The New Director insisted streamlining was not restructuring; they are not the same, and anyone with a degree in business management, like him, would understand the subtle differences.

After the meeting, the New Director asked Old Phil into his office. He congratulated him on his loyalty, his dedication, and then suggested that it was now time for him to enjoy retirement. Go on a cruise. Tend to the garden. Old Phil was being streamlined.

Apparently, the art gallery did not need a security guard, but a trained security provider. A contracted individual not on the payroll, preferably young and projecting a sense of authority, who would be called in only at difficult times when extra help was needed - like a school visit or the Women's Institute monthly meeting. This was the future and the art gallery was embracing it.

The New Director introduced Old Phil to the security provider. Muscled Marcus was young and his authority was honed from working the town's nightclubs. A date for Old Phil's retirement was set.

There was an unruly group of school children in the art gallery on Old Phil's last day. Muscled Marcus suggested Old Phil take a tea break - he would handle this. He was about to demonstrate his crowd control skills when the gallery's education officer appeared. She shook a handful of art trail sheets at the rowdy group. "Who chose something called…" she adjusted her reading glasses, "*Unicorn Dream no.5* as their favourite painting in the building?"

A child stepped forward. The education officer frowned. She did not like children. "Do you take me for a fool? There's no unicorn painting in our collection."

The child protested his innocence and led the furious woman and Muscled Marcus to the long room on the second floor. There, tucked amongst the twentieth century paintings by minor British artists, was a small unframed painting of a unicorn. A unicorn mid-leap above a glitter rainbow, surrounded by a halo of shooting stars.

The education officer's mouth silently opened and closed as she processed this discovery. When she regained the power of speech, she called over the gallery attendant slumped in his chair in the corner of the room. No, he hadn't noticed the painting. He rubbed his chin and examined the new arrival. He was an art student and so knew a thing or two about it all and was eager to give his opinion. The painting reminded him of something from his course. He rubbed his chin harder. It looks a little bit like a Jasper Johns, don't you think? If Jasper Johns did unicorns.

The curator was summoned on the security radio. A theft in the gallery? No, quite the opposite, an appearance. Come look. She pushed through the crowd, which had begun to gather around *Unicorn Dream no.5*, and gasped. How extraordinary! She stood back and assessed the painting with one eye closed. She had learned this technique from a curator at the Guggenheim. That's right, New York. The painting technique was good, very good. There was no frame, but many artists find that frames are too restricting of their vision, binding the very essence of a work. A label written in marker pen was pinned to the wall. The curator clapped her hands – yes, it must be a guerrilla art work. Placed in the gallery by an anonymous artist. A gallery Banksy, if you will. Guard it with your life, the curator shouted, as she ran out of the room to inform the New Director. Muscled Marcus placed himself in front of the glittery painting and crossed his bulging arms.

Within a week *Unicorn Dream no.5* was famous. Word spread via social media. Tickets were sold. Selfies were snapped in front of the sparkling masterpiece. *#UnicornDream* trended. And the gift shop sold out of unicorn fridge magnets. Roped barriers were put into place to corral the bus-loads of admirers. Other art galleries searched their dusty, storage depots hoping to find *Unicorn Dream* numbers one through four. A unicorn-themed exhibition, suggested by the National Gallery, was planned and a lucrative loan arranged. The curator decided that it would only be a matter of time before she received a call from the Guggenheim. That's right, New York. The New Director's vision of a streamlined art gallery was forgotten. What was that thing about synergy? No one could remember.

Early one morning, as they set up the barriers in front of *Unicorn Dream no.5*, Muscled Marcus asked Old Phil, "I don't get it. Why is there so much fuss over this painting?"

It was almost time to unlock the front doors and welcome the unicorn-obsessed visitors queuing up outside. Old Phil jangled the ring of worn building keys in his hand; his retirement was cancelled. With the tip of a key, he cleaned under his fingernails. Tiny flakes of excavated red and blue glitter paint fell onto the floor. "Don't ask me. I'm just the security guard."

KATE KEOGAN

The Truth and Several Lies about Butterflies

"It's not true: how can a caterpillar possibly turn into a butterfly?" She'll be saying next that beetles turn into blackbirds. Sophie, from two doors down, is talking rubbish again. You don't really like Sophie; most of your games turn into quarrels before long, until she says in that excessively childish way of hers, "Ummm! I'm telling!" Childish it may be but it's effective. Your games are played within the strict parameters of Sophie's mum's frequent querulous injunctions to 'play nicely'. You do not yet know words like *querulous*. Sophie is not nice. She throws herself on the ground and drums with fists and feet when she does not get her own way. But she is a faithful playmate and you look forward to the agonised squeal of the gate-spring, the swift knock at the door. "Is Sarah playing?"

It is a hot summer and you play mostly in the garden, guarded by dense privet hedges which take Dad an age to trim with his monotonous shears. The sound of the blades meeting over the new growth has you wincing for days. Dad shows you a caterpillar: a fantastic beast of bright yellow-green with striking purple stripes and a sharp, gleaming black tail horn. He does not tell you about the beautiful moth it will become, dusky pink and subtle brown with a pink and black-banded body, as if torn between camouflage and dramatic display.

You would like to play in Sophie's garden. She has a New Zealand White Rabbit, whose ears you long to stroke amid the comforting straw and pee smell of its hutch. You are not allowed. It is not safe to go outside the garden: you must 'stay where we can see you'. Your parents' primary concern is for protection from unspecified dangers. Not that the garden is an especially safe place. Last winter, rats came in, attracted by next door's chickens.

Dad got two or three with his air gun, and you insisted on burying them with full honours beside the shed, pitiless to the man's remorse. Then there is the wasp's nest, into which you cannot resist lobbing gooseberries and crab apples, to run shrieking up the path with the wasps in furious pursuit. (Only once has anyone ever been stung. Sophie was not quick enough. She cried like such a baby. "You're a monster, Sarah Cleall, and I *hate* you!" she said.) There are also stinging nettles aplenty, lords-and-ladies and, to your delight, a ring of suspicious-looking fungi in the corner, which the sun does not reach.

*

"You're not leaving this table until your plate's empty."

You coldly survey the greying boiled potatoes and congealing eggy stuff in its soggy pastry case. You think it may be called *flan*. You accuse it with your fork and wrinkle your nose at its flabby response. You are not convinced this is food. "I'd sooner starve!"

Mum sighs before withdrawing into her habitual blankness. Dad springs to his feet, knocking his stool over, and points a finger trembling with rage at the door. "*Hall!*" he says, which means you are to sit in the draught at the foot of the stairs and consider what you have, or have not, as the case may be, done. You narrow eyes and lips and make a well-judged bolt for the garden instead.

You're going through a growth spurt and there's no pretending your hand-me-down clothes are your own. Buttons and seams strain until dresses and cardigans become a skin you must presently shed. You can think of nothing but food and begin to see the garden in a new light. You become resentful of Sophie's company. You have always flinched from Dad's broad beans, foul things with the taste of rusty nails, and have only enjoyed the bean flowers' heady fragrance. Now appetite compels you to snap off a young pod, drive your thumb along its seam and devour the sweet young beans. You cannot believe they taste so good. You drop the devastated pod to the ground, treading it beneath your heel.

The tenderstem broccoli is next, fresh and crunchy, and then you set about denuding the gooseberry bush. Last of all is the apple tree, Dad's pride and joy. You pierce the skin and bury your new adult teeth in the resistant white flesh. It is so mouth puckeringly sour that you start in alarm. You persevere, down to the core and the tiny pips - still white in their unripeness - your lips and tongue now numb. Appetite sated for now, you turn your attention back to mud pies, which you form carefully into little patties decorated with daisies, to be baked in the sun on the shed roof.

*

It is Sunday evening, still unnaturally warm. Mum is doing the washing up, singing along - out of tune and with the wrong words - to *The Top 40 Countdown*. She watches the Red Admirals and Tortoiseshells on the Buddleia outside the kitchen window. "Sophie! *So-phie!*" comes the voice from two doors down. Sophie, however, stops by the gate and turns to you. She has something in her hand: a Cabbage White Butterfly. "These ones are *evil*."

She holds the butterfly before her and methodically, almost delicately, tears off the wings. She does not take her eyes from yours. When she is done, she deliberately wipes her hands free of the wing powder onto her trousers, and leaves, shutting the gate behind her, like the good girl that she is.

You regard the mutilated butterfly, still horrifyingly alive, feeling sick to your stomach. The air is unbreathable. Your tongue feels coated with the awful white wing powder. You want your skin to split open there and then, so you can emerge, clean and new, to float away from this ghastly scene. You remain helplessly earthbound. Mum calls you in for your bath; there is school tomorrow. Soap and water are not going to be any good.

*

In the school library you find a book detailing the life-cycle of the butterfly. Sophie was right. The pictures are clear and friendly, each phase linked to the next by cheerful red arrows. You consider the soupy mess of the caterpillar decaying in the chrysalis; the living death as the imaginal cells, arrested in the egg, begin their work; the pristine butterfly pumping its crumpled wings full of new blood. There is a queasy lurch in your middle. You are disgusted but quietly excited. You replace the book on the shelf and return to your class.

"Did you not find anything to interest you, Sarah?"

"No, sir. Not today."

You smile sweetly. He returns your smile. You are a bright, conscientious girl. A *good* girl.

*

You do not know it yet, but years later you will become an artist. Your best work will be a large canvas painted an impenetrable black, upon which you will place in tiny, precise strokes of pastel, the wings of a female Blue Morpho Butterfly. You will leave the body out. It will be a beautiful and unsettling work, as the vivid wings rise up out of the dark ground and recede into it. Powerful. You will wipe the pastel from your fingers onto your jeans. It will carry you right back, full circle.

SARAH HITCHCOCK

The Day I Took My Zombie to Alton Towers

A few years ago, I moved into an old Victorian house on the outskirts of Swindon. It has one of those attics that you access via a proper staircase, and floorboards and a tiny round window. It was probably the maid's room. In the corner, sitting on a rickety chair and covered in a thick layer of dust, was a zombie.

We hit it off immediately.

I quickly realised she couldn't speak. You need a functioning tongue to be able to form words, and breath to make sound come out. She can just about manage a low moaning.

I spent the best part of a week trying out different names to find one she would respond to, and now she's called Susan. She has a particular way of moaning: sort of "hmmmmrrraaaaah", which I think is her trying to say my name - Janice.

Susan is very dry for a zombie, not that I've had much experience with the undead, but there's nothing rotting or bad smelling about her, otherwise I wouldn't let her in the kitchen. She's just very desiccated and papery, and has a musty odour like old books. I used to be a librarian so I'm used to the smell and actually find it rather pleasant. Because of her dryness, she's quite brittle and, as a consequence, extremely fragile. I mist her every day with a plant atomiser filled with spring water and a touch of lavender oil. It seems to help but we do still have the odd accident. Once, due to an ill-advised choice of footwear – flip-flops no less – she lost a little toe when it got caught in a drain cover. It disappeared into the sewer system below with a sad 'plink'. I would have stuck it back if we could have retrieved it: I'm a great believer in *UHU*.

Footwear and clothes in general are something of a problem – I won't let her go about naked as she would prefer, I do have standards. Everything she wears has to completely undo: the idea of pulling anything on or off is unthinkable due to the high risk of limb loss. I made the mistake of putting a pair of marigolds on her once, so she could help about the house, and it took us the whole day and a box set of *Downton Abbey* to ease them off without any damage. As it was, she lost a couple of nails, and a thumb pad got stuck irreversibly to the rubber, but otherwise the gloves are still perfectly usable.

Susan likes to read and watch things on the YouTube. She has very opaque, milky eyes so it's a wonder she can see at all. I had to get her three pairs of the strongest over-the-counter reading glasses, which she wears one on top of the other. We've also strapped two high-power magnifying glasses together. I think she can only see a few letters at a time, so reading anything other than a menu takes a lot of perseverance on her part. I think it shows a great strength of character.

Of course, I have to make sure she stays out of direct sunlight when she's using the lenses due to the risk of incineration. Even with the misting, as I've said, she's very dry. Once, due to an unfortunate spark from the open fire, her legs caught alight. I doused her immediately with the vase of chrysanthemums that was at hand, but we've never been able to get the scorch marks out. Not even leather upholstery cleaner seems to work on dehydrated flesh.

As I've said, Susan has a strong character and that is to be applauded. However, recently our normally tranquil home life has been disturbed. We've been at odds with one another! I take Susan out, it's not as if I don't. We go to the local library for *Mills and Boons* and take walks in the park. Well, I walk and she lurches - more so since her legs crisped up in the fire. So, I was a little upset when she started leaving adverts for family attractions in places where she knew I would find them - pasted to the back of the Kellogg's *Bran Flakes* box, stuck under the loo seat and slipped between the pages of *Reader's Digest*.

The latest mania is for Alton Towers. I told her in no uncertain terms that a trip to an amusement park, for someone of her condition, would be more than ill-advised, it would be madness.

We're going next Tuesday.

What can I say, she wore me down with a relentless, and, I have to admit, well-thought through campaign. She would do well in local government. It wasn't just the endless leaflets, or the posters stuck to every surface, that got to me, it was the moaning, literally the moaning. All night she would pace the landing carrying a placard that read: 'Cruelty to the Undead', whilst moaning loudly. I was afraid the neighbours would hear.

The last straw was when she wrote me a note warning that if I didn't take her to Alton Towers, she would report me to Childline. I wasn't too concerned about her ringing a phone service due to her speech difficulty, but I do worry that they might have a website: she's become very adept at surfing the net and can be eloquently persuasive in prose. I don't want the authorities round here, I'm not sure they would accept my explanations for the missing toe and blackened knees.

*

Alton Towers is vast, crowded and, to my mind, a little trashy, but Susan loves it. I have insisted she goes in the wheelchair and wears a large wide-brimmed hat and sunglasses. It saves people staring and asking what's wrong with her. I manage to keep her away from the big dippers by taking her to *CBeebies Land* and giving her several goes on the *Postman Pat* ride, but after lunch I take a wrong turn and we find ourselves right in front of something called *Oblivion*.

There's no dissuading Susan.

The ride boasts of being one of the highest G-force roller coasters in the UK. Nothing good can come of this.

Susan's hat blows off first, taking an ear with it, quickly followed by her sunglasses. We've been given strict instructions to keep our hands in the car, so naturally, Susan waves at someone on the ground just as we start the big drop. The level of screaming behind us takes on a new timbre as Susan's hand lands in a lady's lap.

As we disembark, and I'm shoving Susan's stump into the pocket of her pinafore, we're greeted by a very worried looking official. I hastily retrieve the hand from the still screaming woman and begin to explain, "It was a prank – in poor taste, I agree, look, it's only rubber." I wave it at the official who goes from worried to irate.

"Susan has a condition," I explain quickly, settling her back into her wheelchair.

This makes everyone suddenly uncomfortable: you can't shout at a person with a 'condition'.

"Well, no harm done," says the official. "Bless her, look at that expression, she really enjoyed that ride!"

It's only then that I catch a glimpse of Susan's face. Oh, dear God!

The speed of the ride has nearly blown her face off! Her eyes are goggling wide and her lips have been blasted away from her teeth into a rictus grin of immense proportions. I jam my own sunglasses onto her, to hold her eyeballs in place, and we hurry away. Behind us I hear someone say, "Poor love, did you see, she only had one ear."

If she wasn't already dead, I'd kill Susan for this.

Back in the car, I try to re-arrange her features to look more normal, but I'm unable to wipe the grin off her face. We don't speak all the way down the M6. Well, I don't, and Susan wisely keeps her moaning to herself.

"Never again," I say as we get to the first roundabout in Swindon. "It's the park, or the library, or nothing from now on."

Susan rustles in her handbag and pulls out a sheet of paper. I have to swerve into the bus lane as she holds it in front of my face. It's an online booking confirmation for a bungee jump off Clifton Suspension Bridge.

I stare at her, for the first time, in genuine horror.

One of Susan's now baggy eyelids slides shut in a wink.

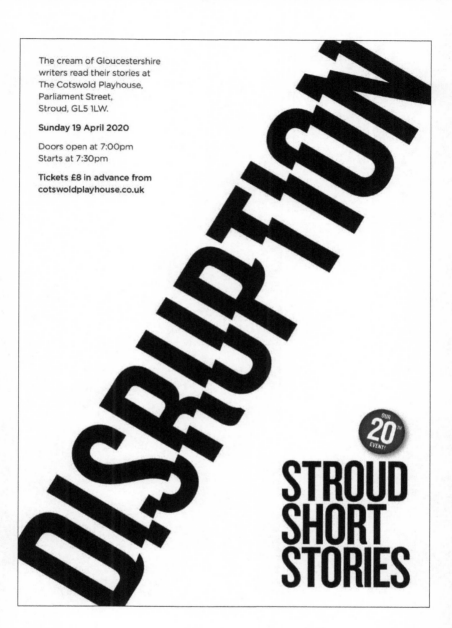

The cream of Gloucestershire writers read their stories at The Cotswold Playhouse, Parliament Street, Stroud, GL5 1LW.

Sunday 19 April 2020

Doors open at 7:00pm
Starts at 7:30pm

Tickets £8 in advance from cotswoldplayhouse.co.uk

OUR 20TH EVENT!

STROUD SHORT STORIES

STEVE WHEELER

Puffballs

I first saw her from the bedroom window. She was wearing wellington boots and a shiny new waxed jacket. Her bright red and pink harem pants weren't the usual attire for hikers. Her burnt orange-coloured hair was piled into a loose and low chignon that spilt onto her shoulders. I could see she was attractive, but sensed she didn't pay it any attention - like a brightly coloured butterfly settled on an ordinary leaf.

An arthritic Labrador dog lagged behind her. I watched her stroll across the wet-grassed meadow, stop for the dog to relieve himself, and then wait while he sniffed at the left-behind scents of fox and badger. I thought she was probably staying in one of the village holiday lets, a city dweller up from London for a long weekend.

She fell into a regular pattern of morning and afternoon walks, following the footpath that ran the length of my cottage garden. My work desk was set below the bedroom window, so I rarely missed her excursions. I noticed her picking wild field mushrooms into a small netted bag. In the right conditions they thrived in the lengthening September shadows. On the fourth afternoon, she looked up at me and smiled. Embarrassed to have been noticed, I smiled back and lifted a hand.

Although exercising the dog had fallen into a routine for her, it became something of a disturbance for me. My concentration on the computer became diverted by any dog walker that might have been her.

On the fifth day I resolved to be outside, to set the stage for a 'chance' meeting. At nine o'clock I began to collect fallen twigs from underneath the beech that stretched over the footpath. I'd tell her that I was hoarding kindling for the wood burner.

By quarter past, she still hadn't walked up the footpath. By half past, I'd picked the lawn clean of everything. Back at my work desk, I was restless and distracted. From the kitchen window I could see the footpath where it crossed in front of the garden gate. When I went to the bathroom, I had a similar bird's eye view.

That afternoon I went outside again. This time I found secateurs and began chopping at the roses. I'd nearly given up when she came into view, crossing the meadow. She must have walked her circular route in the opposite direction. I chose my moment to break off from the dead-heading and ambled into the footpath. I squatted and stroked her dog. "Hello, you're a lovely old lad, aren't you?" I said, ruffling the dog's ears. "What's his name?"

"Toffee," she said. "He hasn't been well. His poor old legs."

I thought she was mid-forties, making me ten years older. Her only makeup was some pale pink lip-gloss. Her hair was swirled into the same loose bun that seemed both coiffured and quickly constructed – as though in the morning after something formal. Her voice was soft with a faint Mediterranean accent, Italian or Spanish.

"You're a new face," I said. "Here on holiday? I'm Peter, by the way."

"No, we've moved here short term. We're renting Parsley Cottage. I'm Bea."

Parsley Cottage was half a mile away. Years ago, it had been the village shop and post office.

"We, as in you and Toffee?"

"And Greg my husband, but he spends most of his time in London or abroad. I'm meant to be house hunting."

"Sorry, I'm being nosey."

"No. You're the first local who's spoken to me. What about you? Been here long?"

"Ten years. Live alone. My grown-up daughter drops in occasionally. How are you finding it?"

"Peaceful. Good for mushrooms."

"I suppose that's why I came. The quiet."

132

It was at that point that Toffee collapsed to the ground, as though settling down to sleep on the muddy footpath. "Oh no, I'll never be able to get him up again," she said. "I've walked him too far." She tried coaxing him back to his feet, but he wasn't going anywhere.

"Shall I get my car? We can lift him into the back and I'll drive you home," I said.

"Would you mind? I'm sorry to trouble to you like this."

I managed to lift the old dog from my car into Parsley Cottage as Bea held the door. She pointed to his basket in the kitchen. "He'll get up eventually," she said. "Greg says he'll make the hard decision when Toffee doesn't get up."

While she made coffee, I told Bea what I did; a self-employed accountant. Small businesses mainly. Something I could do from home. I came to the village after my wife left.

She told me Greg was a foreign correspondent for a national newspaper; that she was his second wife and that she met him in Dubrovnik during the Yugoslav wars. He was the intrepid reporter. She was the young translator. "We're a living, breathing cliché," she said.

They owned a flat in central London, but her husband dreamt of re-living his childhood in the English countryside. "I'm lonely in London and even lonelier here," Bea said.

"There's not a lot happening. Will you find work?"

"Greg's against it. He says Toffee will keep me company while he's away."

I let a few days go by without talking again to Bea. I made sure I was at my desk at the times she took Toffee for his walks. Much shorter now. Up the footpath, across the meadow and back. I willed the dog to collapse again, but he limped on. Bea and I waved at each other sometimes. I began to wonder what I was doing in that grim cottage. It hadn't been decorated since the 80s and was cold and damp in the winter. Mine was a solitary, silent non-existence. I'd been to Dubrovnik, to Croatia. Who'd want to live in some dreary English backwater?

At the end of the second, restless week, I pulled on my boots and waited for her on the footpath.

"Mind if I join you for some fresh air?"

"Please do. You'll be the first person I've spoken to in days."

"Not even your husband?"

"Strictly text only when Greg's at work. Those are my orders."

After that, I walked with Bea and Toffee two or three times a week. I wished then that Toffee had been a young pup, able to walk for miles. I often thought about asking Bea out for lunch, or in for supper, but I was afraid of spoiling something.

The last day I saw her properly, she was walking down the path with what looked like a white football under her arm. I went out to meet her.

"A giant puffball," she said. "I've heard about them, but never found or eaten one."

"I'm told they're delicious. Had breakfast?"

She came into my home for the first time, and sat at the kitchen table while I sliced up the puffball and fried it. Neither of us had eaten with another human being for weeks. We sat and recounted our life stories till lunchtime, when Bea said she had to go. "Greg's booked a call to discuss progress on the house hunting. I haven't even been trying."

"I hope you'll stay in the area," I said. "What would I do without Toffee?"

When she left, she held both my hands and kissed me. I felt short of breath for the remainder of the day and couldn't work. I sat for hours at the kitchen table, dreaming up impossible plans.

She knocked on the door early the next morning. "He wants me back in London," she said. "I'll be catching the afternoon train."

"When will you be back?"

"When he says, I suppose."

I took to following her steps up the footpath and across the meadow - as though retracing her route would somehow bring her back.

Puffballs don't last that long. They dehydrate, discolour and shrivel. If you hit them with a stick, they explode into clouds of green smoke. I think that's the spores, drifting off to germinate somewhere else.

ROBIN BOOTH

Two Towns

Not long ago, a crack appeared in our town. It runs from the bus stop on the edge of town, down Castle Street, along the High Street, left at the butcher's, and out again on the opposite side of town, as far as the supermarket car park.

My friend Tomek said maybe it goes underground then and comes up on the other side of the river, but we've been out over the bridge, and as far as we can see, it stops right there, by Lidl.

Tomek's from a place called Wrocław. That's in Poland. He's not from there anymore, he's from here, but he still doesn't speak very good English. He says things like "How are you flying?" instead of "How are you?", or "It's a roll with butter", which means "It's a piece of cake". He even says "What's gingerbread got to do with a windmill?", which seriously doesn't make any sense at all.

It's not especially wide, this crack that goes through our town. Near where I live, it's just wide enough to slot in a one-pound coin. But over by Tomek's house in the new estate, it gets wider, and you could probably put your whole arm in if you wanted to. Tomek says he let his bike fall in once, and he never got it back.

Mostly people try to avoid crossing it if they can, even though you could easily step over it. Everyone thinks it's better if you just stick to your side of the crack, even if it means not going to the butcher's anymore, or doing your shopping at a different supermarket.

Tomek's mum still shops at Lidl because it's the only place here that sells pierogi. Pierogi are little parcels made of dough filled with meat or potato. They're the best. Borscht is a soup made from beetroot. It's disgusting. Tomek's mum has to catch three different buses to get to Lidl, as the one that goes direct has stopped going there, because of the crack.

Maybe the reason people don't like to step over the crack is because it's so deep. You can't see the bottom of it, even if you shine a powerful torch down there. Tomek and I did that, and it just goes down and down. There's probably molten lava at the bottom, or some hideous and alarming creature, no doubt. It's the thought of it that stops most people. An arm coming up and grabbing you, or a tentacle.

Dogs won't cross it, even. They won't go near it. Tomek got a bone from the butcher's once, and we showed it to the Alsatian next door. The dog went crazy for it, jumping up and trying to snap Tomek's hand off. Tomek threw the bone across the crack in the street, and the stupid dog just sat there howling. He wouldn't go across the crack, not for the bone or anything. Tomek said it was a good prank, and well worth the price of a bone.

Tomek's mum has a friend who works at the butcher's, and sometimes gives him bits of meat that nobody else wants, like liver or giblets. Tomek'll eat anything. I don't like to say it, but he is a little overweight. His trousers pinch around the waist and are too long in the leg, so he's always tripping over. My mum stopped giving him snacks because she said he was starting to waddle. "That friend of yours," she said, "he needs a bit of air letting out." It wasn't especially kind of her, but there's a grain of truth in it. Now Tomek doesn't come round anymore.

To get to Tomek's house, you have to go down to the bottom of Castle Street, where there's a way to cross over the crack. There's a derelict house there, and the crack goes in under the kitchen window, and comes out somewhere at the back. The front door went missing a long time ago, so you can just walk in, go up the stairs, across the landing, and climb out the bedroom window. Someone has made a kind of staircase from a load of wooden crates, so it's not too tricky to climb down. And then you're on the other side of the crack, without really knowing it.

It's fine to use that way to get to Tomek's, as long as you know the kids that hang around there. If they don't like you, they won't let you cross. They can be difficult sometimes, but they don't mind me, and they generally let me cross without having to pay.

The last time I went to Tomek's, a man was there with a load of wooden boards for one of the windows, which had got smashed in during the night. Tomek said to wait until the man was having a tea break. As soon as he turned his back, Tomek took one of the boards and we ran outside. I was worried we'd get into trouble, but Tomek said, "Not my circus, not my monkeys", which means "Don't worry about it". It's one of the things Tomek says. I told you his English wasn't very good.

Tomek said to come with him. We went down to Castle Street, where the crossing house is. The usual kids were hanging about down there. I got a bit uneasy about it, because they don't really like Tomek much, and I was worried that if they saw me hanging about with him, they might not let me cross anymore. So I dropped back a bit, pretending I was tired.

Tomek took the wooden board he'd stolen, and threw it down on the road. The noise made people stop and look. "Hey, Tomek, see what you've gone and done," I said, because somehow the board had fallen right across the crack.

Some of the boys from the crossing house noticed, and they came over to see what was going on. "Let's go," I said to Tomek, but he just said, "Not my circus, not my monkeys."

Unfortunately, some of the boys heard that and thought he was calling them names, and they started saying things that made me think we should leave the board and run away. But Tomek didn't seem worried at all. He asked them what they'd give him if he walked across the board. They just laughed and said he wouldn't dare.

One of them, the biggest one who always takes your crossing money, said Tomek was so fat he'd probably break the board, and all the others howled with laughter. The big one spat on the pavement. He asked Tomek if he was trying to make a new crossing place. Tomek said he wasn't, but he didn't see why people couldn't cross wherever they liked. The big one said if Tomek didn't take his board away, he'd throw it down the crack for him, and then throw Tomek down as well. Everyone howled and jeered. I didn't expect Tomek would actually fit down the crack, but I didn't want to see them try.

Maybe Tomek didn't understand what they were saying. He said, "Fifty pence to see me walk the plank." I tried to pull him away, but he kept saying, "Fifty pence! Fifty pence!" The big one grabbed at him, but Tomek took a step backwards onto the board. His foot was right over the crack. Everyone gasped and backed away. Some people had come out of the houses on the other side, to see what was happening. Adults, even. Everyone was hushed, waiting. I was frightened Tomek would trip over his trouser legs and fall. Or the board would break. Or some horrible scaly thing would come up out of the crack and snatch him.

What actually happened was Tomek just stepped across to the other side. He turned back to the big one who'd grabbed at him, and said, "Fifty pence then."

"Fuck off," the big one said, "And if you cross here again, I'll break both your legs and your arms as well."

Tomek said that he lived there, on the side we were on, so that didn't make any sense. But the big one said it made perfect sense, and Tomek should go back where he came from, or suffer the consequences. He took Tomek's board and went back to the crossing house with it, and that was that.

I thought it best to wait a while before trying to cross back, so I hung around a bit. There was another kid there I sort of knew. He asked if I knew Tomek, and I said I didn't, but then Tomek called my name. "What is it?" I shouted back, over the crack.

"Doesn't matter," Tomek said. He sat down on the pavement. I didn't know what to do, so I started walking back towards the crossing house. I heard Tomek calling out to me, but I just carried on. I couldn't tell what he was trying to say.

A longer version of this story was published in the Bath Short Story Award Anthology 2020

138

CLAIRE HARRISON

Peace Lily

The clock on the wall was white - functional, just like her room. When she first came here I'd brought in curtains from home, some cushions, a few plants. Tried to make it look homely. It never did.

My sister, Jenny, needed something to do, so she'd brought knitting with her. Her hands nimble and quick across each stitch. She sat upright in the chair as if sitting on the bus waiting for her stop. "I didn't know how long we'd be here," she said. *Knit one, purl two,* the clack of the knitting needles in time with the ticking of the clock.

I moved my chair closer to the bed and stroked Mum's arm. "She's chilly." I put her arm under the cover leaving out the tip of her hand. The nurse had clipped a monitor to her finger.

"It's the lack of oxygen, it'll make her feel colder than usual," mumbled my brother, Tom. He stood up and walked over to the small window, which looked out onto the car park.

I tucked the bed cover in a little tighter.

Knit one, purl two, knit one.

"It's a blessing, I guess," I said. "That's what everyone says, isn't it?"

I looked at the pot plant which sat on the corner of her dressing table. Its leaves had once bounced with life, but were now yellow and hung down. "Peace Lily," I said. "Aren't they meant to thrive anywhere?"

"No idea," my sister said. "Chuck it in the bin."

"There's life in it yet." I walked over and picked up the plant, gently pulling off the worst leaves. "No wonder. It's bone dry." I took it into the en-suite and manoeuvred the pot under the cold tap, watching bubbles of water jump out of the soil and splash

139

into the sink. The water left a trail of brown dirt as it drained away.

"Waste of time," said my brother as I placed the plant back onto the dressing table.

"There's always hope," I said.

"For fuck's sake." He spun around, picked up the plant and threw it in the bin. "I'm going for a smoke."

We both watched as the pneumatic closer slowly set the door in its frame.

"He hates this," said Jenny, halting her knitting for a moment.

"He never visited her once," I said, bending down to retrieve the plant.

Jenny started up the click-clacking once more and shrugged her shoulders. "We're not all so…capable," she said.

I sat with the plant on my lap. Water seeped out from the bottom leaving a mark on my skirt.

The door opened and a nurse walked in, efficient and stiff. I stood up so she could take Mum's pulse and straighten her covers.

"Do you have any idea how long it could be?" Jenny asked. "I need to be somewhere this evening?"

"I'm afraid not. At least she's peaceful."

The nurse tucked Mum in and then walked towards the door.

"Let me know if you need anything," she said as she left the room.

I moved over to the window and put the plant down on the sill. I could see Tom talking to a couple of nurses in the car park. They were laughing at something he'd said. One nurse put a hand on Tom's arm and leant in towards him.

"He's flirting with them. Even today."

Knit one, slip stitch over. Jenny concentrated on her stitches.

Tom looked up and saw me in the window, took a step back from the nurse and threw his cigarette on the floor, grinding it into the ground with his foot.

"Going anywhere nice this evening?" I asked as I turned away from the window and moved back towards the bed.

"It was arranged a month ago."

"I just thought…"

"What?' She put her knitting down on her lap. "That I'd change my plans? Damn, I've dropped a stitch."

"She couldn't even feed herself."

"She had you," said Jenny.

Tom walked back in the room; the smell of smoke clung to his jacket. "The nurse is bringing us some tea," he said and hung his jacket over the back of the chair.

"The nurse you were chatting up just now?" I said, as I sat back down in my chair. I brushed my hand over the stain the plant had made on my skirt. "How's Jilly? Still living with her sister?"

The knitting needles stopped. The ticking clock filled the silence in the room.

"You know Jilly's not been well," said Jenny.

"I know Tom's moved out and left Jilly's sister to look after her."

I turned towards him. "You're good at that, aren't you – leaving?" I said.

Tom moved towards me. He placed a hand on each arm of my chair and leant down. I could smell smoke on his breath. "You have no fucking idea what you're talking about." He spoke slowly, emphasising each word.

I turned away from his stale breath and stroked Mum's hair. "Leaving is easy," I said.

The nurse, who'd been talking to Tom in the car park, came in with three cups of tea on a tray. Her blue starched uniform shushed as she walked. She placed the tray on Mum's dressing table, spilling a little out of each cup as she manoeuvred it into place. Tom stepped back, avoiding her gaze.

"That's so kind, thank you," chirped Jenny as she carried on with her knitting.

"I'll just check on Mum, if that's OK?"

I walked into the en-suite to get paper towels from the dispenser. I could see the nurse holding Mum's wrist. I wiped the bottom of each cup and placed Jenny's on the over-bed table, next to her handbag. I handed a cup to Tom but he shook his

141

head, so I held it in both hands, letting the warmth turn my fingers red.

The nurse took one last look at Tom before leaving.

Tom shifted in his chair. "I need to go," he said. "I promised Jilly I'd pop by." He looked at me but I said nothing, and sat back down in the chair next to the bed. Jenny glanced up at the clock. "I didn't think we'd be here this long."

"Why don't you both go," I said, stroking Mum's arm. "Go home."

Jenny looked at Tom. "We don't want to leave you," she said. "If only it wasn't today, I really do have to go to this dinner with Gerry, it's important to him. Could mean promotion."

Tom stood up and put on his jacket. He briefly touched Jenny's shoulder before walking over to me. "Get in touch if anything changes," he said and walked out the door.

I thought I heard him say *I'm sorry* as it closed behind him, but it may have been the sigh of the pneumatic door closer.

Jenny was stuffing the knitting into her bag. She stood up and slugged back the last few gulps of tea, walked towards the dressing table mirror and checked her appearance. "Hope I've got enough time to sort this mop out," she said as she tucked her hair behind her ears.

She placed her handbag on the side and picked out a gold-capped lipstick which she applied to her lips. She blotted them together before dropping the lipstick back into her handbag. "Are you sure you'll be OK?" she asked. "At least you haven't got anyone at home waiting for you. Gerry goes mad if I'm late."

"I'll be fine."

"Yes. Well then…" She paused by the bed for a moment and reached out her hand towards Mum, hesitated, then touched my arm. "Text me when…you know…" And then she left the room.

Everything was quiet, apart from the clock on the wall. I looked over towards the dressing table. Jenny's knitting had slipped out of her bag, probably when she was searching for her lipstick. It lay on the floor, a pile of jumbled stitches. A few had slipped off the needle. I picked up the knitting and slowly, carefully knitted them back on. The tension wasn't the same, but at least they were back together.

Mum made a small puffing sound. I dropped the knitting and turned around to face her. Her chest was still, completely still. I sat down heavy in the chair and held her hand, I don't know how long for - the two of us together in silence - until the nurse walked in.

MARK RUTTERFORD

Correcting an Error

The thing you need to understand about women is that no matter how confident, no matter how talented, educated, how beautiful and loved, they are waiting for the next rejection. Millions of years of evolution have resulted in this finely-tuned sense of expectation.

Why? Why, you ask? Millions of years of men.

The thing you need to understand about men is that no matter how weak, no matter how bereft of skill and talent, no matter how ignorant, how unsightly and flaccid, no matter how lacking in achievement or charm, they are waiting for their next triumph. Millions of years of evolution have resulted in this finely-tuned sense of delusion.

Why? Why, you ask? Me too!

War
Genocide
Murder
Fascism
White supremacists
Male supremacists
Misogynists
Contact sports
Action films
Passive heroines
Willing victims
Toupees
String vests
Mankinis
Football violence
Domestic violence

Gang violence

Jumble sale violence…oops, sorry, my mistake

Boy racers

Willy wavers

Fox hunters

Computer gamers

Climate change deniers

Underwear designers

Animal testers

Fly tippers

BMW owners

Golfers

Wrestlers

Keith Lemon

Chest shavers

Trophy fucking hunters… I mean… really? Fucking trophy hunters!

Trophy wife hunters… I mean… don't even ask.

Toxic masculinity! That's the cause. It has a lot to answer for and I am very, very sorry.

I should introduce myself. I am… well… you'll think this a little ironic as I manifest in male form… I am God. And I am very, very sorry.

I look back with so many regrets. That I should have given the male human three brain - and saw fit to put two of them in a very unappealing little sack with the ability to produce testosterone - was, with hindsight, an error.

And so I thought, I might correct that. I needed a controlled experiment, and it is this that led me to the residents of Thunberg Close, Stroud. It wasn't called Thunberg Close when the houses were built of course. The renaming of this self-contained community was a democratic and much celebrated consequence of what I will refer to as week three.

Seven houses, 12 people and four weeks - to date.

I created the world in six days. You may deduce, therefore, that patience is not a burden I carry. To get fast results from my experiment, I tailored my corrections across the Close, making a

145

specific change to the inhabitants of each dwelling, so I could see the effect on that household and the cumulative effect across this tiny, right-on, slightly groovy Stroud community.

Number 1 – the smallest house in the Close with two bedrooms and three abandoned cars (or bits thereof) decorating the front garden. Robbie lives in Number 1, a fitter. I turned down Robbie's crank-shaft, so to speak. The male imperative to take things apart and then fix them again. The solutioneer. The mansplainer gene. The good news is that Robbie stopped adding to the junk yard in his garden. The bad news is that he felt isolated for a couple of weeks - finding that he had nothing much to say. In week three, Robbie made a breakthrough - he decided to tidy up. And he committed to tidying up so much it became his passion. The garden was cleared, the house made spotless, and he began to give critical looks to the unkempt lawn at Number 2. I hadn't expected that, the rapid reinvention of purpose and the need to be top dog.

Derek and June Denton live at Number 2. He, an insurance executive, she, a volunteer at the hospital and in Oxfam. The manager of a disparate group of individuals implausibly called a team, Derek had fantasised about after-hours, back office sexual encounters with all of the women and none of the men. In all of these fantasies, the woman involved became friendly, then tactile, then what Derek liked to think of as opportunistically gagging for it. Back office is not a euphemism by the way. I didn't reduce Derek's propensity for imagination, I just re-wired his thought patterns so that it was all channelled towards his wife. In week 1, June was surprised - literally and pleasantly. In week 2, June felt a little over-indulged - she loved chocolate éclairs, but couldn't eat a whole box at once. In week 3, June told both of her lovers (the one at the hospital and the one at Oxfam), that she needed time out.

Number 3 is inhabited by Steven and Ahmad White. This loving couple caused a great deal of offence as a result of their relative youth, sexuality, marital status, the colourful nature of the flags they waved during Pride week, and, in Ahmad's case, by the difference between his skin colour and his surname. There was no toxic masculinity to resolve in this house, just an accumulated layer of dust - grey and all pervading - a little whisper of condemnation, telling the couple they were somehow 'wrong'. So, I dusted their lives to find that Ahmad and Steven White didn't change at all. They felt inexplicably lighter in their being, and noticed that the neighbours were more engaging, that's all.

Number 4. 'Call me Theresa' - at least you'd be forgiven for thinking that was the correct address. Divorced, sexually active and not remotely giving a fuck about what any of her neighbours thought. I turned down 'Call me Theresa's' sexual appetite, to see if it was just a placebo for other forms of love and affection. Turns out, she was miserable. So, I turned it up again last week and two shags later, she's as happy and care-free as ever.

At Number 5. The Christodoulous - Maria, Costa and their daughter, Elena. In this house, I levelled out the empathy and testosterone - just enough to think with greater clarity. It was Maria and Elena that suggested and campaigned for the re-naming of the Close. It was a little bit of liberation for Maria, who had never felt constrained by her husband, but who rarely felt 'in charge' of anything beyond their front door and family. For Elena, an excellent lawyer, it was an obvious demonstration of solidarity with Planet Earth, as well as practice for when she moves to the US next month. Costa didn't think he could love his wife and daughter any more than he did, but he found, by week 3, that he had been wrong.

Number 6. Dave Johnson - no longer the lad, but very much still a jack. Forty-five going on twenty-five. A lover, not a fighter, or at least a swiper to whichever side it is that suggests interest in a 'relationship'. It is code of course, until Dave can no longer pretend he is Tom Hardy and has to have a proper conversation with a woman for the first time in years. I turned down the testosterone by 50%. In a fortnight, Dave had three 'dates' but only one sexual encounter. His conversation skills improved and he found he had something in his eye when Geraldine was telling him about her breast cancer. By week three, Dave was getting calls from all of his dates who wanted to see him again. He said 'yes' to them all, but his hands shook when he said 'yes' to

Geraldine – there was something about her that he wanted more of. That it wasn't the obvious frightened Dave quite a lot.

At Number 7 - Janine and Charles Holbine, white carpet supremacists, who believe that a taste for *Le Piat D'or* means they are better than everyone else. Mrs H had all the toxicity and Mr H just followed orders. She was dismayed that the rest of the Close and its inhabitants did not conform to her bigoted opinions and dubious standards. She told them so, in words, in little condemnations, in looks and condescension. Mrs H wrote to the council about the renaming of the Close. Mr H was told to do the same. Mr and Mrs H take *The Daily Mail*. Now, I may be God, but there are souls not even I can save. So I left the Holbines alone, except to narrow their focus onto themselves – to neutralise the damage they inflicted on others. You can hear Janine shout "Charlie, Charlie," like the Sybil Fawlty of Stroud, and although you might feel sorry for Mr H, he could have 'grown a pair' many years ago and spared the world his bloody awful wife.

The Close seems a more contented place to live. There is more happiness and less strife, more optimism about the future, more confidence in each other. I'll give it another couple of weeks, then change it back. But I'll not erase the memories - to see if the residents maintain the trajectory, or regress.

*

What *I* have learned, is that I'm not to blame; hormones aren't to blame; history's not to blame. It's them; it's you. *Your* mess; *your* clean-up operation; *your* responsibility.

You need to sort out toxic masculinity, bigots and trophy hunters, of all types.

What goes on in jumble sales - you might want to think about that too.

I hope for you, I do.

But you should know that God, that is, I, won't intervene again.

GEOFF MEAD

White Christmas

I peered, bleary-eyed, at the digital clock on the bedside table. The blue numerals glowed in the half-light, 08:35 25 DECEMBER. I drew the curtains and looked outside. Beech trees, stripped of their autumn foliage, stood like scarecrows against a sepia backdrop. In the foreground, thick white snowflakes drifted slowly onto the fields around the house. Despite the picture-postcard landscape, my heart sank at the prospect of another solitary Christmas Day.

"I love it when it snows," said the muffled figure buried under the duvet beside me. I jerked round to see my wife's familiar, tousled blonde hair protruding from the covers.

"Bloody hell! I wasn't expecting to see you again."

"You were sound asleep when I arrived," she said, "so I let myself in."

"How on Earth did you get here?"

"A few inches of snow don't worry me. I thought you'd be pleased to see me."

"I am pleased to see you. Pleased and surprised."

"Christmas is all about surprises," she said, sticking her head above the covers.

"I suppose so," I said, staring at her smiling face.

"How come you're on your own?"

"Well, you know…" I began to explain, but there was nothing to say.

"I expect we're cut off," she said brightly.

"Definitely. Nothing can get through and the snowplows never come this far." I reached out tentatively to put my arms around her. "It is very good to see you."

"Not now," she said, pulling away. "My head hurts." She wrapped the duvet round her shoulders and sat up in bed. She put her hand up to her crown to soothe the faded operation scar on her scalp. "What have you got planned for today?"

"Not much: bit of breakfast; late lunch; a few glasses of wine; watch a movie or two. Same old, same old."

"Turkey for lunch?"

"I've got one of those cook-in-a-bag things from Waitrose."

"Tasty," she said. "I'm glad you are looking after yourself."

"I'm going to make a cup of tea," I said. "Do you want one?"

She shook her head. "You have one, I'm not thirsty."

"OK," I said, taking my dressing gown from the end of the bed. I shoved my hands through the armholes and tied the belt round my waist. "Don't go away."

"No chance," she reassured me. "I've only just got here."

Shocked by her sudden reappearance, I half-stumbled downstairs to the kitchen, spooned loose tea into a well-used earthenware teapot, filled the electric kettle, sat down at the table and looked out of the window while I waited for the water to boil. Overnight, a thick blanket of snow had draped itself over the garden. The few remaining plants had all but disappeared, while the bird table and the Shepherd Hut seemed to be wearing white fur hats. Snow was still falling in silent swathes that drifted like waves of sugar icing against the walls of the house. The lane beyond the gate was all but impassable.

Soon, I was back in bed with a mug of Earl Grey and a biscuit. "Are you sure I can't tempt you?"

"No thanks," she said. "But I love the smell."

I sipped the tea and felt it bring my senses alive.

"Tell me what you've been up to," she said.

"I've been keeping myself busy," I said. "Working; reading; writing."

"What are you writing?" she asked, with a surge of interest.

"I've started a novel."

"Is it about me?" she teased.

"In a way. But, it's mostly about me."

"I guessed it might be," she laughed. "But at least you are writing."

"I promised you I would," I reminded her. "Shall we go for a walk in the woods later, if it stops snowing? It'll be gorgeous."

"You know how fond I am of those woods, but I'd rather stay indoors, by the fire. I haven't felt properly warm for a long time."

"Alright," I said. "I'll light the wood-burner in the sitting room and you can make yourself comfortable. What would you like for breakfast?"

"I'm not hungry. You go ahead."

I finished my tea, got dressed, went downstairs, riddled the grate, laid the fire with kindling and logs and a few nuggets of smokeless coal, and put a match to the waxed firelighter. In minutes, syrupy yellow flames were licking the glass doors of the stove and the temperature began to climb.

By the time I'd made myself a bacon sandwich and a cup of coffee, she was hunched in an armchair in front of the fire, still wrapped in the duvet. I turned on the hi-fi and fed a CD into the slot. The opening arpeggios of *The Skaters' Waltz* piped through the house. "Do you remember this?" I asked.

"Of course," she said. "We always played it on Christmas morning. We've never actually been skating though, have we?"

"No," I admitted, laughing. "We never have."

"Can we go one day?" she asked.

"One day."

"Promise?"

"I promise," I said. "Now, what do you want to do today?"

"Just to be with you while you potter around."

So, we sat by the fire reminiscing about the life we had shared: our first date that she still maintained she didn't know was actually a date; motoring trips across France in our little two-seater; her failed efforts to get me standing up on skis; visits to New York and Mexico; dancing to Leonard Cohen at our wedding and lazy summer days with old friends. Later, she dozed while I prepared lunch, which she was happy to watch me eat. I put on a paper hat and we groaned together at the terrible jokes that I pulled from red and gold paper crackers:

Who hides in the bakery at Christmas? A mince spy!

What do you get when you cross a snowman with a vampire? Frostbite!

What type of key do you need for a nativity play? A don-key!

I left the dishes to look after themselves, put more logs on the fire and we settled down to watch *Love Actually*. As usual, she bristled with righteous anger when Emma Thompson discovered her husband Alan Rickman's fling with his secretary; I cried when widower Liam Neeson found love again with Claudia Schiffer and we wept together at the heartfelt greetings of passengers and loved ones at the airport during the closing credits. Christmas wouldn't be Christmas without *Love Actually* we agreed.

"How are you doing?" I asked after the film. "You look tired."

"An early night would be nice," she said.

"You go up," I said. "I'll join you in a minute."

I locked up, damped down the fire and turned out the lights, before climbing the stairs and getting into bed. She leant back on the pillows beside me. "What's happening tomorrow?" she asked.

"You mean Boxing Day?" I stalled. "I'm...er...seeing someone...weather permitting."

"Seeing someone?" she enquired. "I suppose I shouldn't be surprised."

"It's been five years since you left," I said.

"Has it really?" she mused, head tilted back as if considering for the first time how long it had been. "Yes, I suppose it has."

"That's quite a long time," I tried to explain, "without...seeing anyone."

"The thing is," she said, "I've discovered that we can get married up there as well. And I've decided to wait for you."

"Up there?" I queried.

"Just a figure of speech," she said.

"So, you do know...?" I began.

"That I'm dead? Of course, I do."

"I wasn't sure that you knew," I said. "Bruce Willis didn't realise he was a ghost in *The Sixth Sense* until the very end."

"That was a movie, you idiot. Does it matter that I'm dead?"

"I'd prefer that you weren't. Does it matter that I'm seeing someone else, down here?"

"I don't know," she said. "It might. We'll have to wait and see."

"Anyway, I'm glad you came. It's been a lovely day," I said, switching off the bedside light and rolling over toward her side of the bed.

"Happy Christmas," she whispered in my ear.

It was late when I woke up the next day and looked out of the window. The snow had been washed away by heavy rain during the night. Muddy brown water puddled miserably in the sodden fields. Raindrops ran down the window panes like tears.

I reached out to caress the woman I loved, but she had already gone.

Back to that far country, just around the corner. Where the snow comes from.

HANNAH GLICKSTEIN

Roadkill

Aaron knew his Grampi loved him, because he took him to every single hockey match and practice. Often, by the time he'd dropped him home, Granny would already be asleep, either in bed with her teeth out, or in front of a roaring television with cold tea and a packet of gingernuts on the coffee table. Granny worried a lot. When they were out watching a match, if Grampi had a beer or two, then got in the car, Aaron was in on his secret, "Don't tell your Gran, she'll only get her knickers in a twist, and those are some big knickers these days, believe me, boy."

Aaron looked over at Grampi in the driving seat. He was mostly bald, with thin white wisps of hair at the side, blowing in the breeze from the open window. But, with his shirt sleeves rolled up, you could see his forearms were still powerful, circled by thick veins. He was gripping the wheel, scowling at a mother slowly pushing a buggy laden with shopping across the zebra, humming along with the radio through his nose.

Aaron loved the way Grampi roared whenever he got close to the goal. He loved gliding across the ice, knowing Grampi was watching, maybe shouting his name. "Like he's won the pools," Granny said. It was the same if Cardiff City ever scored - which they hardly did these days. Next to Robert Earnshaw, Aaron was Grampi's man. And he felt like a man, in all that bulky kit. Grampi had bought it for him, because Mum hadn't been able to afford extras since she had the baby, got sick and had to quit work.

But, at some point, Grampi was going to notice that Aaron didn't ever talk about girls, or bring girls home. He never would. Aaron tried to pass his silence off as manly reserve; respect for the ladies - because Grampi wouldn't feel the same about him once he

154

knew. The first time Aaron realised this for sure was at a wedding. Grampi, pissed out of his mind, sat at the bar moaning to the father of the bride that Granny wasn't interested in 'all that' any more. Grampi was leaning in to whisper, but you could hear him from halfway across the room. There was something about the other man listening with half a smile, half embarrassment: the way he listened with interest, whilst glancing over Grampi's shoulder for his wife to rescue him. Aaron knew it then, a feeling in his stomach like hunger; Grampi couldn't love him the same way forever.

He was just riding things out really, until Grampi noticed something was not right with him. In darker moments, Aaron even wondered if he might just keep pretending till Grampi was dead, but then he always felt bad straight away for wishing death on the old man.

They weren't driving to practice this morning. Just popping to Tesco for Granny, so she could have a rest. She was happy at home in her chair with her crisp sandwich, wearing loose trousers and one of Aaron's baggy Metallica t-shirts, watching a Bruce Willis film. Aaron and Granny both liked those kind of films. She'd asked him to stay and keep her company. But he went with Grampi. Gran still treated him like he was seven most of the time - cutting off his crusts and calling him 'chickadee'.

Grampi was accelerating. He was content: a generous man out food shopping with his boy, giving the wife a rest. He was telling a story, maybe half-made up - or all made up - about when he worked on the Cardiff Docks after the War. They'd pulled out the corpse of a pilot still inside his wreck, slumped over as if he were sleeping, with the flesh rotting and falling off, clumps of yellow hair sticking to the scull. Grampi said he reached in and took the smashed German watch for himself. He said, when he touched the flesh, it felt like soggy pudding. Said he kept the watch for years in a drawer: a reminder that nothing lasts forever. "Learn to fly while you still have time, boy." Granny had thrown the watch away before Aaron was born. He glanced over at his grandson, to see if the boy was listening.

Grampi wasn't watching the road when the dog ran out. It came from behind a car. Aaron saw it and thought Grampi was about to slow down. Aaron said, "Look out!" Grampi turned back to the road, but kept going. There was a heavy thud. The dog squealed. The car jolted, then sped up. The dog was knocked sideways. It rolled a few times on the verge, picked itself up and limped off. It was a big black dog. Aaron was twisting about under his seatbelt, straining to see it. Grampi didn't even look back. Aaron shouted that he'd told him about the dog.

He was wondering if Grampi thought the dog would get across before the car hit it. But that was being generous. Grampi didn't even slow down. He didn't care if the dog was alright. Or if there was some little kid at home waiting for the dog. Maybe just behind the dog, watching everything, about to run out himself.

There was a pause, while Aaron waited for Grampi to reply. But he didn't. Aaron felt the inside of the car was far away. The buildings, shops and trees moving past the window were blurry and unreal, like a music video or something. He was staring at his hands thinking about Grampi and Granny and their three daughters. All the people they had created, with all those fingers - thirty altogether, including thumbs. He touched his face. His fingers were cold. He wanted to shout and kick, like when he was little over at Granny's. But he waited: to give Grampi a chance to say something, stop the car and wonder if the dog was OK, drive back to pick it up and call the number on the collar. Get it to a vet. But nothing changed, only the noise of the radio and Grampi clearing his throat.

Then Grampi said, "I think I'll buy your Granny something nice while we're at the shops. It's nearly her birthday - born in March, like a lamb. I never used to remember. She was such a beautiful girl, your Granny, blonde hair and film star figure. And never too in love with herself. Some of the young girls they think they're chocolate, if you know what I mean. Not Gran."

Aaron looked at him, wanting to ask, "What's the matter with you? What about the dog? Are you blind?" But he couldn't face hearing any excuses. He opened his mouth to say something about something else. Then - by accident - he called his

156

grandfather "a bastard". "A stupid bastard!" And started crying. His head was aching and his cheeks were burning. He put his cold fingers over his eyes and turned away, leaning his forehead against the window.

Grampi didn't say anything. They drove past the school and the traffic lights. Grampi indicated and swung into Tesco's parking lot. With the engine off, Aaron's crying was much louder. He hated himself for crying. He felt like a big ugly mess no one wanted to scrape up. He wanted to say that to Grampi, but he knew it would sound self-pitying and weak. He wanted to calmly get out of the car and walk with dignity all the way back to Mum's. He wanted to look the old man in the eye, knowing he was the better person. He also wanted to stay in the car, in case Grampi was sorry, or had a good reason. Or if he came to his senses and suggested they turn back and try to help the poor dog. But Grampi didn't say anything. He took the keys out of the ignition and patted the boy on the shoulder, more gently than usual - like he might be sorry.

*

That night Aaron dreamt of the dead dog. Head lolling about, it was being raised from the sea by some kind of gigantic JCB. Its vicious white jaws were exposed by the rotted red flesh of the lips. There was a gold chain sparkling around its stinking black wet furry neck, but Aaron was too scared to touch the dead thing and take it.

In another episode of his dream, Grampi was dead, lying on the same road where they had hit the dog. Aaron was stretched out next to him; face down on the tarmac sobbing his guts out.

When he woke up in the morning, he knew for sure that he didn't want his Grampi to die. Not yet. He loved the old man. But he also knew he had to try to be more honest.

SIMON PINEY

Waking the Dead

The convoy of trucks rumbled to a stop. The silence as engines were switched off, after the hours of bumping along roads half-destroyed by shells during the civil war, seemed unreal. As did the anomaly of parking on a tarmacked car park as fresh, flat and black as any London street, whilst all around were bomb-shattered houses. Fighting between the army and the so-called Freedom Fighters had devastated the northern town on the shores of the Mediterranean.

"Wait till the guards disembark first," the leading investigator said.

"Surely it's safe now," Susie asked her neighbour, Jean-Luc, a grizzled, French archaeologist. This was her first time with the international mission whose aim it was to locate and identify the thousands of Jews and Christians missing in towns and cities around the Middle East.

"Safe?" the archaeologist asked. "Do not you think it strange that every road is full of holes but here is perfect smooth? Do you think all the guerrillas have gone home, like good little boys and girls? No. Me, I want to wait till guards are out. This village feels, how you say? *Inquiétant*. Uncanny. Is that the right word?"

Susie shivered. He was right. Something felt wrong. She had not been a photo-journalist very long, but, in her time on a local newspaper, she had learned to trust her 'nose'. There was a story here.

Just then the mission leader shouted for them to assemble round him. Susie, getting out from the air-conditioned car, felt as if she had stepped into a dust-laden oven.

"We've got a problem. The council elders say that there were never any Jews or Christians here and no bodies to find."

"That's impossible," one of the others piped up. "I came through here seven years ago, before the war. There were Jewish shops and even an ancient Christian basilica."

"If that is true," the Frenchman said, "let's go to the church. Where is it?"

"I don't recognise the layout," the other man said. "Bit hard after the bombing."

"We split up and search the town," the leader said. "Groups of three including an armed guard. Meet back here in one hour."

After the sort of shuffling around that is the nature of scientists, forensic experts and historians, Susie found herself teamed up with Jean-Luc and a taciturn ex-SAS sergeant. They made their way round piles of rubble, looking for locals to ask about the basilica. Everyone they met, even if they deigned to answer, just shook their heads and turned away.

After about three quarters of a fruitless hour, they came across a group of children playing football with a bundle of rags for a ball. At the sight of the little party, most of the children ran. One or two stood uncertainly, looking at the armed guard. The Frenchman bent down and asked them a question in Arabic. Once again this was met with shrugs and denials. They had turned and were walking away when one of the boys ran up to them and tugged at Susie's sleeve, speaking urgently in a low voice.

"What's he saying?" she asked her companion.

"He says he knows where the basilica is. His friend Thomas used to go."

"Is Thomas here?" Susie asked. "Is he one of the other boys?"

The lad looked down and shook his head, then set off back the way they had come, beckoning them to follow. Within minutes, they were back at the car park where the trucks waited. The boy would not set foot on the tarmac, but pointed and said, "Taht hanna. Taht hanna." Then turned tail and ran.

The guard and Susie looked at the archaeologist, who was staring in disbelief at the black surface in front of them. He turned to them, "The boy says the church and bodies are down here."

"Where?" Susie blurted out. "It's a car park."

"But it's new. No more than a few years old. There were no cars on it," the SAS man mused. "I wondered why cars were parked on the broken roads rather than here."

"And the boy wouldn't go onto it," the archaeologist mused. "I wonder too..."

*

By the time the whole team had reconvened, the archaeologist, with Susie and the sergeant's help, had unloaded what looked like a wheelbarrow topped with electronic equipment.

"What on earth is this?" Susie asked, as she took photos of the rig with the Frenchman alongside it. She had realised that she might be on the verge of a significant story, even for the mainstream press.

"This is ground penetrating radar," had been the reply from the archaologist. "In the first days of archaeology, we had to dig, and I remember how many times we cut a trench and found nothing. Now, with this, we can look under the earth before we ever put in a spade."

He began to trundle the contraption across the car park but stopped when the truck drivers got back. He ordered them to move their vehicles clear of the tarmac which they did unwillingly, parking on unstable rubble.

Within ten minutes, there was a shout from the technician watching the screen on which the radar pictures were appearing. Susie ran over. All she could see, through the crowds around the screen, was a wavy black and white image. Not much to get excited about, she thought, but the others obviously thought differently.

"Ruins," one of them said.

"And aren't those bones?" another put in.

"Scan a wider area," the leader instructed. "And then, tomorrow, we can cut a first trench."

*

That night, in her tent on the edge of the car park, Susie, unable to sleep, wrote her account of the day and its as-yet-unverified discoveries. What, she wondered, would they find? Would it be a grave? She had read about the opening of mass graves elsewhere,

160

but this would be her first direct experience. She was more than a little shocked at herself for being rather excited at the prospect.

*

The following day dawned cold and clear.

"Ideal weather for a dig," the team leader decided, and began dividing up the jobs. Susie was to photograph every stage of proceedings and she checked her cameras with care. It would be just her luck to run out of space, or for one of them to fail on her first real job here.

As the work began, townspeople gathered, muttering threateningly. The soldiers took up strategic positions round the site, guns unslung.

Susie had not reckoned on the slowness of the process. Top layers of tarmac were removed and the subsoil photographed before going any further. The trench was a neat cut, diagonally across the centre of the area. Each shovelful of soil was carefully examined and sifted, even if it was obvious that there was nothing else there. After about an hour of digging, they came across a jumbled layer of bricks. None of these was moved until they had been numbered and photographed against a long ruler to show their scale. Once that was done, the bricks were lifted out and carefully stacked on one side of the trench. Although the work took time, Susie was impressed by the concentration and seriousness of the team at work in the deepening excavation.

She had just wandered off to find a drink when there was a shout from the trench. The French archaeologist was standing up and waving. Susie ran back, her thirst forgotten. There, just popping out of the soil from under more bricks, was what looked like a leg, or, at least, what was left of one. And then the smell hit them.

*

Even sixty years later, in her small cottage in Cornwall, overlooking the Atlantic, Susie would still dream of that first discovery and wake weeping at the memory of the images she had recorded. That first leg had belonged to a young woman who lay, curled up, as if trying to protect the young child who lay dead in her embrace. Below her appeared body after body: men, women

161

and children; the whole of the vanished Jewish and Christian population of the town. They had been systematically slaughtered: shot or cut down with knives. Babies seemed to have been smashed against walls. Men had been bound before being shot in the back of the head. Then a pit must have been dug and the bodies mixed with the ruins of the ancient basilica, pulled down and tumbled in along with its worshippers. The pit was then filled in and turned into a car park.

To Susie and all the members of the team, the horror of the mass grave was made all the worse by the townspeople's wilful amnesia and denial of yet another crime in the litany of deaths from that murderous civil war. All this, together with the refusal to remember friends and neighbours. Or the days when evil stalked their town.

SHARON WEBSTER

Jumping the Queue

We stand in lines, keep our places in queues, and wait. Not our fault the delay, the argument, the problem at the front, but all the while the world is changing, we are changing, and so, when we pick them back up, things are never quite the same.

Imagine, for example, you are late, really late, say a day late, for something important, let's call it your best friend's wedding. It might be more complicated than it seems for it is likely that your role in the day was to have been quite significant, perhaps chief bridesmaid or something. But there is a storm and your flight, the one you should not have booked so close to the event, is cancelled. There is nothing you can do.

What if some of the other guests are delayed as well, maybe even the groom? Might the wedding still go ahead sometime in the future, or would it be abandoned, the sequence of events taken as too bad an omen to proceed? Is your best friend the sort of person to recover from this sort of upset, move on and in time forgive, maybe even forget? Has she managed to get over that sort of thing before? What if there is something she might once have seen, and there are occasions when you suspect she has not forgotten?

Anyway, how likely is all that to happen, I mean, in real life?

I slip the ticket back into my pocket, give up my place in the line and find a café. It is busy but I am in no hurry and treat myself to a large latte before finding a table. By the window with a good view of the planes taking off from the runway, it is the sort of place you can stay for a long time, and, as night falls, the lights remind me of those hung in the trees at my best friend's house on the night of her party. There is a certain recklessness to a midsummer's day, a warmth, a smell, a freedom, as if nothing counts. You were watching me; you were always watching me, and we were reckless, but it did count and I brush my lips, remembering.

So, I send the text. 'I am so sorry but my flight has been cancelled and I'm not going to make the wedding. The signal is really poor so I will have to keep this short. Have a good one. Lots of love etc.' And I switch off my mobile.

For those who fall in love with someone they shouldn't, the thought of a life being satisfied with fleeting moments of contact, stifled exchanges or shared glances might not be something they can contemplate.

I don't regret the phone call; nobody will check the flight schedules.

The tip-off to the police though, that's different. I'm wasting their time. Of course, he is innocent, there are no drugs, and they will discover that eventually, but it will take a few hours, maybe even longer, and he will definitely miss the wedding.

Sometimes though, it is important to create our own queues - to give the world a chance to change.

STEPHEN CONNOLLY

The Corvidae Diary

Day 1 Temperature 37°C

I should be at work, not stuck here at home. Fourteen days isolation thanks to those HR plonkers. A cleaner sneezes in front of me and they completely over-react. They don't give a shit about me or the virus: they're just terrified they'll be liable if I fall sick on the premises.

Still, it's two weeks away from Trevor wandering round the office, saving every situation like he's Captain Kirk. Bloody drama queen. And people are keeping in touch, emailing work. I just wish they wouldn't send so much.

Soon as my Tesco delivery arrives I'm all set.

Day 2 Temperature 37°C. Again.

Noisy outside. Sounds like kids, but it can't be. They'll all be at school, or is it half term? Can't see the front of the building from here, I only hear reflected noise. Remember that low-flying jet, two weeks after 9/11? I have never been so terrified.

Ah! They're protesting. It's those Climate Change kids: "What do we want? No more CO2. When do we want it? Now." Once upon a time it was Feminism, then Apartheid, the Ozone Layer, now it's Climate Change.

Day 3 Temperature 37.C

But that reading's dodgy. I had a coffee, it probably confused the thermometer, cheap crappy thing. And guess where it was made? China. You couldn't make it up.

Those kids are still outside, chanting away. They're never happy unless they've got something to complain about. If they've got the energy to protest, they should be at work. Holding down a job, keeping the economy going. Like me.

Email from Sarah. Apparently, Michael is 'struggling' with the CCH proposal, could I take a look? Got a lot of time for Sarah. Some people would have made a fuss: *It was due last week, they're 9% of our projected income blah, blah, blah.* Not Sarah. Just a simple request: *please could I take a look?* The CCH project's going to be huge. Nice to know she trusts me to sort it out. And she's always so well dressed.

Day 4 37.6°C

That's still basically normal. I just wish that lot outside would shut up! All that chanting and singing. I found a clip on FaceBook and realised, that's *here!* That's outside! They've completely blocked the road. What happens if someone gets sick? How's an ambulance supposed to get through? They'd have to land a helicopter on the roof.

Thank God I'm still fighting fit. I'm quite enjoying it, actually. No meetings, no distractions, just getting on with the job. I miss the coffee run. And the banter. Thought about phoning Trevor. Give him a chance to moan about my time-sheets. Not that they're very interesting right now.

I'm managing to resist Daytime TV but I'm getting seriously addicted to radio phone-ins. Please God, kill me before I get so old and contrary.

Michael's really messed up CCH. Hard to avoid a grim satisfaction at Trevor's golden boy making such a cock-up. I never believed that stuff about Trevor and Sarah: she's just not his type. He likes bad blondes, Sarah's more the Earth Mother type. All natural fibres and hummus.

Someone coughing next door, woke me up in the small hours. At least that lot outside quieten down at night. Maybe their mums turn up with hot chocolate to read them stories.

Day 5 37.9°C

Sarah texted first thing. Michael's in hospital: the virus. A shock. Still, it could mean I get to do the pitch to CCH. Not funny. He's a nice kid, really.

Hard to concentrate, my head's been throbbing, all afternoon. Paracetamol doing sod all. All that singing, outside. Wish I could make out the words. Now I'm used to it, they sound...moving. Like listening to a new Radiohead album.

Found some ear plugs, so next door won't keep me awake.

Day 6 39.4°C

Yes, I'm worried. Over half the office infected. Not a word from HR, of course. Sarah very supportive. How does she manage to stay so calm? Hope she doesn't start Climate Change Protesting, they'd take over the world, with her in charge.

They're louder than ever, outside. And more of them every day. Where are they all coming from? I can barely recognise the street, on Facebook. All those tents, it's like a city. It goes on for miles. They've even got a yacht. On a trailer. I mean, why?!

Sometimes I almost admire them. It takes grit, being out there in all weathers, defying the police. But how do they go to the toilet?

Sometimes, I realise hours have gone by and all I've done is listen to them singing.

Sarah sounded rough. Hope she's looking after herself.

Day 7 Seven more to go. Temperature 39.8°C

I unlocked the front door. Don't know why, it's like I was on automatic pilot. That singing, so compelling. I want to see them for myself. Wish I'd spent the extra for a flat at the front, now.

Finished the CCH proposal. Should have done it days ago, losing my touch. I miss the guys. I need people around to bounce ideas off. Hope Sarah likes it. Took her long enough to respond. Not surprised CCH put the meeting back. Must be having issues of their own, even a big firm like them. Going to be a huge project.

Day 8 40.4°C

I'm supposed to call the hotline. According to the website. *Call 111 if you've been in close contact with someone with confirmed Corvidae and have a high temperature.* Don't trust these cheap thermometers. Should be an app, on your phone. To alert people when you go over the limit.

Singing outside. Tried singing along but my throat too painful. Hummed along for a bit, but it just sounded weird.

The flat makes strange noises. Never noticed before. Must have left something perched on a ledge and hours later it rolls off. Or a breeze closes a door, bangs a window.

Here goes nothing. *Your call cannot be taken at this time. All of our operators are busy. You are number 109 in the queue.*

Day 9 40.6°C

Can't get hold of Sarah. *I can't take your call right now.* Guess more people off, in isolation. Missing Trevor, isn't that crazy? Remember him at that Karaoke thing? "Start Spreading the News..."

The singing. Sometimes a heavenly choir, haunting. Sometimes mad angels, howling. And yet I know it's the same song.

Must stop leaving messages for Sarah.

Day 10 41.0°C

Could barely understand Trevor on the phone. Poor Sarah. They broke down her door, got her to hospital, but too late. We'll miss her. Trevor says there's a collection, on Facebook. *All of our operators are busy. You are number 785 in the queue.*

Day...11?

Can't find the thermometer. Chanting louder, like they're coming closer. Nice to have someone to talk to. Bring me water. Feel guilty about CCH. Maybe if I'd finished the proposal sooner, they wouldn't have gone bust. Trevor said staff shortages, supply lines, but I don't know. It could have been huge.

I think there's someone in here with me. I hear odd things, breathing nearby. *You are number 4309 in the queue.*

168

Day 12, 13?

It's all starting to make sense. Those children, outside. Insisting on change, insisting on their rights to a future. All that beautiful singing. Wish I could make out the words. Wish I had the strength to join them. Can't be a coincidence, protesters and virus happening at the same time. Thought I'd worked out the answer, but it was only a dream. I'll ask Sarah. *You are number 22,222 in the queue.*

Day 14

Can't remember the last time I ate, drank. Breathing difficult. Broadband down, love to see what it's like out there, what they've built. At night, the sky filled with colour, the air with spices.

I remembered what it was. The secret. Another dream. Or I've learned to understand the words. Each virus, more powerful than the last. The biosphere learning, working us out, realising only the young are listening. Only the young understand what to do. Us oldies, we're just getting in the way.

When will Sarah be here?

They sing, how they sing. The words making total sense. The virus talking to us all along. Explaining the chance it was giving us. Virus, Biosphere. Same thing.

Sarah is here. She looks so serene. Her smile so warm, so welcoming. And who would have thought. She would have. Such a beautiful. Singing voice.

They sing.

EMMA KERNAHAN

A Brief History of Lady Charlotte, Duchess of Beaumont

Lady Charlotte, Duchess of Beaumont, was mad. Mad as a March hare, mad as a box of frogs, if you're feeling parochial - or as mad as mad King George, Lord rest his soul.

In her youth she demonstrated all the usual signs of a deranged constitution: provocative opinions on cross-stitching, a fondness for archery and smoking after dinner, and apparently cared little for the conventions of watercolour portraiture.

In 1823 she was heard to interrupt her husband, the third Duke of Beaumont, during an anecdote about fish, and was, naturally, permanently confined to a turret in the east wing of Hadditch Hall as a lunatic.

That she is dead, equally, is a matter of historical record. Lady Charlotte died during the great storm of February 1824, when a mysterious fire left the east wing of the hall in ruins. This was a great tragedy for her husband, who was forced to have it renovated entirely to his own taste and marry Lady Charlotte's maid out of pure grief.

It was also an inconvenience for Lady Charlotte - who was now dead. But, being a Montague by birth, she slipped into the role of lunatic ghost with remarkable ease, and for nearly two hundred years, has successfully terrified the inhabitants of Hadditch Hall - occasionally to death.

She is not the only disruptive spirit to haunt an ancestral seat in the county of Derbyshire. Lady Celia Villiers (1839-1933) famously refused all treatment for hysteria - both electric shock therapy and a husband - and lived a life of tragic solitude with only the moderately-sized Chaston Castle, ten thousand a year, forty five servants, a Belgian chocolatier and her loyal companion Miss Bradshawe for company - until her untimely death at the age of 94. (Those planning to visit Chaston Castle should note that she continues to combine her passions for solitude and axe-throwing - to significant effect.)

It is only the Duchess of Beaumont who has adapted so successfully to the demands of being a horrifying spectral entity while residing in Derbyshire's fourth largest tourist attraction. She is certainly the first vengeful ghost to be a valued member of a Visitor Services Team.

This is in no small part due to the modernisations of the twelfth and current Duke of Beaumont, who, as evidenced by his striking portrait in the main atrium, is the youngest and the most forward-thinking owner of Hadditch Hall. Lady Charlotte has always felt that he bears an unmistakable resemblance to her late husband - even in those unfortunate trousers. Recent visitors will note that the current Duke has made all of the food locally sourced, the official merchandise plastic free and entrance to the Jamaica Plantation Wing half price (October to March).

It is true that Lady Charlotte did not initially take to his Estate Management Diversification Strategy terribly well, particularly during the summer months, when she found herself sharing Hadditch Hall with an enthusiastic group of historical re-enactors, tour guides in fancy dress and drama students jumping out of cupboards in wedding dresses, ripping up veils for applause.

After centuries of terrorising governesses with her maniacal bride routine, she found everyone's amateurism a trial for her nerves, and playfully attempted to lure the twelfth Duke to his death from the bedroom window. Thankfully, due to the installation of double glazing, she had to entreat increasingly forcefully, and move from abject beckoning to rather undignified waving, before giving up the affair entirely.

However, while Lady Charlotte is vengeful - as anyone using the current one way system in the overflow car park can attest - she does not approve of moaning, unless it is actual moaning of course, or a strongly worded letter to senior management written in blood.

And while there are limitations to being an unquiet spirit - sucking the life out of everyone you come into physical contact

171

with - she does find that this stands her in good stead when it comes to overseeing the gift shop.

*

On Mondays, Lady Charlotte informs the footman that she is not receiving visitors, opting instead for a preparatory day in her attic room, working on her own portrait of the twelfth Duke of Beaumont and scanning the grounds for those picnicking outside of the designated area. However, since there are over 16,000 visitors a year to Hadditch Hall, and no footman, she often feels compelled to sally forth and put in a short appearance as a severed head.

She first did this in 1896 using a bowl of punch during the Easter Ball, and frightened the notorious Lord Wyndham so much he jumped out of a window. After that he never married, so it was considered a great success.

These days, she mostly bobs about ghoulishly in a mop bucket in the eco-toilets, floating for up to an hour in what she describes as 'homeopathic' concentrations of Domestos. (Those staying in the self-catering bunk barn will be aware that her evil portents have been seriously undermined by an apparent lack of understanding of Greek allegory, so she has started writing 'Death Awaits' in the guest book and hoping for the best.)

Tuesdays are given over entirely to attempting to add some gravitas to her own unmarked grave in the Upper Woods - now part of the highly popular Hadditch Hedgehog Trail and Play Area. As a consequence, Wednesdays usually involve a lengthy period lurking behind the French drapes in the library in the form of a foul stench, or hellish miasma, depending on her mood.

Due to the audio-guide headsets, she has sadly given up on her renowned 'Thursday Vocalisations', after realising half way through some strenuous gibbering, that everyone was in fact listening to Sir Derek Jacobi making a joke about the Chippendales.

Fridays, she works as a tour guide in the infamous Red Room. It was here, in 1866, that she was the subject of an after dinner talk by Marcus Fanthorpe, famed local historian and rector of the parish, who described Lady Charlotte's appearance as 'coarsened

172

by ill-humour' - shortly before his tragic demise in the ornamental maze, which was so well documented at the time.

This was also where she liked to appear in her most terrifying form, nicknamed 'The Mistress of Doom', until the preponderance of cosplay events diminished her impact. As she has pointed out, it's hard to make an entrance when there are already three people in the room dressed as Admiral Nelson - and one of them has a customised eye patch.

Instead, she now spends her afternoons giving directions to the baby change facilities, in full evening dress, with Janine, a student of Costume Design and prominent member of the North Yorkshire BDSM scene. After so many years of solitude, Lady Charlotte finds Janine's conversation most enlightening - she'd no idea it was now so easy to source good quality leather outside of Skipton.

At 2pm, Lady Charlotte likes to entertain the over-65s Coach Tour from Bakewell by appearing in the form of a putrefying liquid on the rug. This works very well on the few occasions that Janine does not put a 'Cleaning in Progress' sign outside the door, and spend the rest of the afternoon in the staff room vaping.

*

Visitors to Hadditch Hall this summer will be pleased to know that the current Duke has lined up a record number of events, including the exciting *Countryfile Live*, an unprecedented fifteen weddings and an open air theatre production of Jane Austen's *Pride and Prejudice*. Lady Charlotte's own plans are currently 'under wraps', but it's worth noting that she has recently completed an Open University course in Gender Studies - and few of those who have spotted her floating happily through the gift shop, dressed head to toe in Skipton's finest leather, and tipping over miniature busts of Mr Darcy, would doubt that there is much to look forward to.

Indeed, many here will have seen her dramatic archery display during the filming of *Antiques Roadshow* last Sunday, and while Lady Charlotte has now had to concede that she lacks the range and the accuracy to tackle Fiona Bruce, she feels that there is room to be more *forward thinking* when dealing with the current

Duke of Beaumont. Those of you standing by the west-facing windows may catch a glimpse of him now, hiding in a peacock-shaped yew tree on the front lawns, while Lady Charlotte stands gracefully on the roof of the East Wing, pausing to light her cigar from her flaming arrow before carefully taking aim.

The more traditional among us have expressed concern over the ethics of a peer of the realm being finally hunted to death on his own property by a lunatic ghost, but as Lady Charlotte has been heard to remark, she's not the one charging £4.75 for a slice of fruit cake in The Stables Cafe.

SHARP STARS AND OLD MAGIC AND OTHER STROUD SHORT STORIES

10 YEARS

The cream of Gloucestershire writers read their stories on YouTube.

Links on the Stroud Short Stories website.

Free and unticketed.

Sunday 9 May 2021 from 7.30pm

KATE KEOGAN

The Blue in the Black of his Wing

The teenagers are in the park again, laughing without humour, throwing stones at the resident crows who flap up in protest only to settle again mere inches away - so the whole episode is doomed to endless repetition.

If he wishes to reach his favourite bench beneath the plane tree, he has no choice but to walk past them. *Boys will be boys,* isn't that what they say? And in truth he's not seen a single stone find its target, but it's an unpleasant business, which leaves him feeling queasy. No doubt his good angel will insist he intervene, but he is reluctant to draw attention to himself. No. Not reluctant; he is afraid. A weakness in the knees he can do nothing about, a weakness in the spirit, however... "Please," he says. "Please, you must stop."

His voice is not his own; it is throttled by the fear that they will throw their stones at him instead. Or worse. But this time he is lucky. This time they are content just to jeer and mock his accent.

"Or what, grandad? You gonna make me, hey? You and whose army?"

But they are already bored with him. He's too easy a victim: no fun, no kicks to be had. Sure, you can kick a man when he's down, but when he as good as begs you to beat him? It leaves a bad taste, the bitter suspicion you've been used. Sad old bastards like him are best left to live themselves to death.

The boys stumble off down the hill, cawing like the crows, shoving each other, calling out in breaking voices, "Please. Please, you must stop."

He lowers himself onto the bench with a sigh. Damp beneath his arse and the backs of his thighs. He wonders if he will ever grow accustomed to how wet it is in this country, the air

177

permanently saturated. Each breath he takes fills his lungs with as much water as oxygen. He had to stop to steady his breathing again as he climbed the hill. Calm the small bird that has taken to fluttering in his ribcage. No, he is not a young man anymore. He had to lean upon the railing, pantomiming an admiration of the view. What is he to make of it, honestly? Office blocks, row upon row of terraced houses, tree-lined squares, church spires, and beyond them a blanket of fields and distant hills. Nobody with whom to share it.

Careless of him. It seizes him again: the image of his granddaughter, her chubby face smeared with dirt and tears. She'd fallen over and grazed her knee, drawn blood. It always looks worse than it is. Carefully he had swabbed the wound with antiseptic, wincing when she *oww*-ed against the sting of it. Applied a plaster intended for other, paler, flesh than hers, smoothed the edges down gently with his thumbs as he started telling her about the peacock. How he is beautiful because he swallows poison and turns all the bad things of the world into the glory of feathers. See his splendid tail? If there were no poison, no hardship to overcome, there would be no such beauty. She is too young for such stories, just looks up at him with a confused frown. "What about the lady peacock?" she asks. "Does she have to eat poison too, and where is her fine tail?"

"Peahen," he says. "The lady peacock is called a peahen."

Her mother gives him a telling-off later as she ladles pulao into his bowl. "What is all this I hear about eating poison? What dangerous rubbish are you filling the child's head with now? *Think*, won't you, before you speak!"

The child's mother, with her sharp tongue and sad eyes. His daughter. *His daughter!*

All the birds in this country are small and brown. Or grey like off-cuts of sky. Except for the crows, the magpies. These crows here now, there's a proper mob of them. That one over there swaggers like the teenagers do. But when the man pulls his handkerchief from his trouser pocket, and smooths it over skinny arthritic knees, and takes his flatbread from its paper bag and mumbles his habitual words of thanks over it, the crow flutters its

178

wings and chirrups - as if it were still a nestling. The others strut ever closer to him, wary-bold. Before he takes a bite, he pinches a piece off and throws it to the young crow. At once the others are all fuss and feather, every inch of them indignant appetite.

"Never fear," he tells them, "there is some for you, too. Not enough to go around, for sure, but some."

He takes a bite for himself. It is spicy and substantial. Nourishing. It is not like home, no. Not even close. But perhaps it will be enough, given time. Perhaps. He throws the last piece to the young crow, shakes out the crumbs for the little brown birds whose names he does not yet know. Pockets the modest white flag of his handkerchief for another day. Pushes himself to his feet, salutes the juvenile crow.

"Good day, my young friend," he says with a half-smile. Imagines he sees in the flicker of a dark feather a swift flash of iridescence.

"I will know you always," he says. "Even here I will recognise you. I will know you by the blue in the black of your wing."

SEAN W. QUIGLEY

The Rubbish Collector

I am a collector but I haven't done it properly. I have lost one comic. This is the first time that it has happened.

I haven't eaten proper food for three days. I have 1) been too anxious to eat, and 2) feel that I do not deserve food, either as a basic requirement, or as a luxury. My last meal was a packet of biscuits, not nice ones, but supermarket own-brand, which were rotten and bland, but, again, all that I deserve, as I have been bad.

I hate myself for either losing it, or not being able to find it. I prefer to believe that if I am still looking for it then it isn't actually, and definitively, lost.

Daredevil volume four issue one, published by Marvel Comics, marks the beginning of the second volume of *Daredevil* by Mark Waid, and is, in all ways, entirely unremarkable, other than that I cannot find the thing.

My life is bloody rubbish. If things weren't bad enough, this has to happen.

And then I go back to the thought that when the men came in to do the work, and I wasn't here, she didn't keep a very close eye on them. One of *them* could have stolen it. There would have been many occasions when he would have been left alone with my collection. He could have looked through it and seen *Daredevil* volume four issue one, and thought, 'This is a bit of luck. This is the only issue missing from *my* collection, so I shall take it.' And, so thinking, secure it about his person and leave the premises, to later put it in pride of place within his own collection.

I don't suppose she even checked these men before they left the house every day.

If I had been there I would have supervised them thoroughly and carried out my own end of day inspections. I suppose it was *my* fault for being somewhere else and trying to get on with my life! Unfortunately, she was in charge and I have no idea what went on. And I can hardly ask her now, can I?

I have checked through all of the special comic boxes several times, and looked thoroughly through the *other* comics, the ones I do not see fit to be kept in a collectable manner.

I have looked in all of the obvious hiding places, *and* the more obscure nooks and crannies, where I may have put something for safe keeping, away from villains.

Unfortunately, it would appear that I have unintentionally secreted it from myself.

My collection is a cripple.

And yes, I could easily acquire another copy from the internet, but it wouldn't be *mine*. I don't want the stink of some strange person on one of my comics - with all creases everywhere - because doubtless he would advertise it as mint, and it might even come in a nice bag, but that would just be hiding the carnage that had been perpetrated on it by this idiot novice, who clearly isn't a real or proper comic book fan by dint of the fact that he's selling his collection! Why would I want a copy from somebody who obviously doesn't appreciate comics, and so most certainly wouldn't have taken good care of them?

Perhaps *she* took it and burnt it when she was in one of her moods. She might have done it to get her own back after one of our arguments. Except, thinking about it, if she had done something like that, in revenge, she would definitely have wanted me to know about it, she always made certain of that.

I have even been in the falling-down shed. I remembered that I used to put things in there that I wanted to keep safe. No joy though. There is nothing in there apart from my old bicycle, some rubbish bags - with goodness what in them - and some teapots. If I had put it in there to be safe it would have been destroyed by now anyway.

I'm so tired of it all.

I am an explorer, that's what I am, digging through my house. That's why I've put on my shorts, the ones that I wear in the summer without any pants underneath. I've also put on my special

LED head torch, the one I got from the archival company that I use for my boxes. I don't wear it often, and certainly not out of doors, because men shout at me, calling me rude names, which are either unfair or completely inaccurate.

And I've got my dad's old crowbar, that he had for 'protection', in case any of his 'old enemies' came round, although the only man that used to come round for him was the pools coupon man of a Friday and he was a nice man.

I start in my room peeling back the loose carpet, and taking up the floorboards, which is easy as they are rotted.

I remembered that when those workmen were here years ago, they had to take up the floorboards so that they could install the radiators. One of them might have been in the process of stealing the comic, but then his boss turned up, and, worried that the boss might be doing a spot check inspection to make sure that they weren't on the fiddle, he, with quick criminal alertness, put it under the floorboards that were already up, before replacing the floorboards, intending to return at a later date when the boss wasn't snooping.

I didn't find the comic. Of course, it could just have meant that the thief-workman *had* found time to return, prised open the floorboard, removed the comic and concealed it about his person, and then took it out of the house when no one was looking.

And then I had to take a break from my expedition because I was choking due to all the filth and dust that had been disturbed, all of it going straight into my lungs.

The water in the kitchen still tastes terrible. I need to buy more bottled water and drink that instead.

I decide to not bother with the bathroom as the floorboards are totally rotted. If I take all of them up they might never go properly back into place and I will have to hop to the toilet for fear of falling through to the kitchen below.

I don't have to do anything with the downstairs rooms because they didn't need to take those floorboards up.

That just leaves her old room and his old room.

I think they did the most work in his old room, so I take up all the floorboards in there, but find nothing other than lots of old

182

and used paper hankies, along with cigarette butts and mouse droppings, and mice who have died, who must have taken the poison that we put down years ago. Or they died of old age. Can't tell, can I? Doesn't really matter anyway - in the scheme of things.

And then I go into her room and do the same, floorboards up, exploring. I am now coughing like a miner and starting to look like one.

I'm sick of this, and upset. There is no point to any of it.

There's no use in me having all of these things if I haven't got all of them, completely. There will always be something missing, and even if I do get another copy it will be an intruder who will stick out, and I will hate it and so will the other comics. They will know that he is not right.

I may as well be dead.

*

It is two o'clock in the morning.

I take all of my *Daredevil* comics into the overgrown garden. All of them: volume two, volume three, volume four (minus one issue), volume five and what there is up to date of volume six.

I piss on them. I do a great big slash because I haven't been for a while.

And then I pour petrol on them. I don't know why I have got petrol. Perhaps I knew that this day would come.

And then I light a match and throw it onto the pile, and follow the singular match with the full box just for good measure.

"Now look what you've made me do!" I shout into space, wondering if she can hear me, as the comics catch fire and burn to death.

It must be half an hour before I hear the fire engines and the neighbours asking me if I'm alright, apart from this one man who calls me 'a prick'.

He doesn't understand, but he would if, like me, he was a collector.

NASTASYA PARKER

The Flat Earth Society

In the eerie post-storm light, yellowed as a rotted sunrise, the sailors didn't see the edge until it was too late. Their ship grounded on a sand bar at the world's rim, and the crew disembarked to investigate.

Strange, encountering what they'd sailed for all their lives—the horizon. It rendered cargo a ruse; ports mere diversions. The sailors reverently approached the earth's border. Reaching out, they touched a surface, pearlescent like the inside of a shell. Smooth but malleable, it retained the shape of their cautious, poking fingers after they withdrew.

*

It's the children's favourite story. When Jessie tells it to the boy and girl, they behave better.

Jessie is an expert seamstress. She takes up their clothes and patches her own, which were her sister's before consumption lay waste to her. Jessie embroiders tales in her head while she lies beneath the master at night. Bruises weave into her soul and she stitches over with pastel floss.

Richard, the boy, won't eat. Everything is too mushy; too tough; too rubbery; too green. He's small for his age; Jessie lets down his sister's hems but not his. She tells him if he eats well, he'll never stop growing. "You'll reach the rafters, and you'll be strong too, so you'll peel the shingles back and greet the rooks."

"Will I find that bubble over the world?"

"One day."

The boy eats, listening to the story of the sailors leaving their marooned ship to follow the horizon around. Jessie speaks of looming mountains severed by the soft membrane; solid wedges of rock loosed to drift past the stars.

*

184

The sailors of the story rescue a goat kid as they scale the divided mountain's bouldered haunches. This detail pleases the girl, Ernestine, who loves animals. She weeps if a mouse is trapped or a dog struck. One evening, she flies screaming at a coachman beating his horse. It's an unseemly display from a gentleman's daughter, and Jessie hopes the master won't hear about it.

She washes Ernestine's hot, teary face. She tells of a potion that turns people into plants. "If they're cruel to living creatures, you can make their eyes scale over with leaves - and sprouts shoot out their ears. They turn green and roots bind them to the ground."

"Would that awful coachman turn into grass and his own horse could then eat him?"

Jessie pauses with the flannel behind Ernestine's neck. "You want that?"

"Maybe."

*

The horizon leads Jessie's sailors to the Arctic, where the bubble's glow rainbow-tints the snowflakes. Ice needles stretch out to the ocean, subduing the waters.

Richard is sent to school, a cavernous place of grey food, organ music and knowing smirks. He despises it, but eats and grows, and evades negative attention. He writes to Jessie and Ernestine that he might have seen the world's edge from the train, might have glimpsed the bubble shell's swirling muted colours through a break in the clouds.

The butler gives Jessie paper and she answers Richard in painstaking block letters. The butler initially disapproved of the master hiring a girl from so near the docks, but she keeps the children out from underfoot, and he supposes it isn't Jessie's fault she caught the master's eye.

*

Jessie brings her sailors back to the tropics. The baby goat prances hoof prints in warm sand. Native villagers invite the men to their fire circle to share spit-roasted meat and juice-gushing fruit. Ladies dance in grass skirts and the children throw an empty coconut further away from the flames. No one but the sailors notice the bubble shell bisecting the upper branches of the exotic trees.

While her tales expand, anxiety shrinks Jessie's stitches. The thread concealing her bruises starts to bulge. She writes to Richard that all is well, that he must be taller than the school pipe organ now, that Ernestine has learned to turn poachers into hedges.

Before Ernestine too is sent off, Jessie sews blossoms and magic words into her hems. Ernestine refuses to settle at boarding school. She barely feels her punishments, convinced she can magic the cane into a silken orchid stem.

*

War comes. Having eaten obediently and grown tall and strong, Richard goes. He writes to Ernestine, tells her this time he's found it: earth's end. They wonder in their letters what became of their storyteller and seamstress - their everything.

When he stumbles over the top, mud sloshing in his torn boots, mortars and comrades dropping, Richard finds himself surrounded. Not just by explosives and bullets, but by a serene, glowing mantle. Richard rests his palm on the edge and softness thrums through him, a warm recognition. He smiles. Machine gunfire pierces his diminished sky without a dent, and the bubble keeps him enfolded to the end.

*

Richard's war doesn't stop the rest of them. Years later, Ernestine, beanpole-slim, cigarette-raspy and still carrying a hand-stitched scrap of hem next to her ration card, stops on the way to the bomb shelter to free a whimpering dog from some rubble. The dog's tail thumps her leg. She remains crouched beside him as sirens wail, and the mantle descends around her. She could scurry away with everyone else, but to what? An empty house and shameful inheritance. This bubble feels like her true home. Her legacy is secure; last week she taught the children at the shelter an incantation to transform rockets into fuzzy gold dandelions. She gives the dog a last pat and then a firm shove, and he disappears beyond the bubble before the bomb falls.

*

Jessie, too, has long ago been absorbed by the bubble shell. It sliced through the laundry as her exhaustion peaked. The birth didn't go well, but she must work anyway, and her baby was travelling to a godly family across the sea. All night she prayed his ship met the right horizon, and suddenly the horizon came to her. It slowed the wringer, cooled the scalding tubs and softened the clattering washboards. The harsh greys became a gently breathing sunrise, and Jessie collapsed into it, falling off the border of the world as if she never existed.

*

At the horizon, the sailor's captain looked up from his tropical feast and saw a boy on the other side of the fire kick the coconut ball through the bubble. It left no wrinkle as it vanished.

In the next instant, another youth appeared from beyond the bubble and threw the ball back. There was no lifting, no drawing aside. The border confined only the sailors. The captain studied his crew's laughing, fire-lit faces and wondered if he should tell them, or keep leading them in circles round the edge until the membrane shrank so snugly around them that they turned on a pinpoint.

DIANA HUMPHREY

That Old Tune

He felt that he'd never be so young, never so gay again. All his life he'd sought for that time. He wanted that feeling back. He wanted the wind-in-your-hair, devil-may-care ease of it, the I-can-do-everything, whistle-down-the-wind joy of it.

He was old now, often lost in his thoughts for hours at a time. So lost that he forgot to finish dressing or to eat.

They had taken to phoning him at regular intervals, the first at ten o'clock in the morning. "Dad, are you up? Did you like the bacon I bought?" They were subtle, never directly accusing him of 'leaving them' as he knew he was.

They rang again later in the day to ask if he'd read some article in the paper, meaning had he remembered to go out to buy one? And they'd ring near bedtime to check he was aware of the time, and had indeed locked the back door.

He didn't mind all this attention. They meant well and he was fond of them, but it was distracting. He felt he had a big job-in-hand, one that required concentration over considerable time. Somewhere out there, or rather, in there, inside his brain, was something he'd lost and had to recover.

It existed; he had no doubts at all about that. His trouble, what was slowing him down, was that he could not remember what it was. He did not let this worry him at all, for he held to a simple faith, that he would know it when he saw it. His task was to keep looking until he found it, then the job would be done and he could take a rest, have days off, get back to normality, rejoin the family, so to speak.

He felt a little burdened because it was all up to him. No one could help him; they were his memories that had to be trawled. He had to be the one to get on with it.

188

He developed a system. The feeling he was tracking had to be between certain years. After his time in the children's hospital, he thought, and before his own family, some fourteen years. That narrowed it down. He worked systematically along his childhood, searching for that moment of total elation: his time at Oxford, his graduation, Africa. He took in the time he met Jane, and Phoebe and all the women whose paths had crossed his in those early years.

Sometimes, he took time off from his researches to congratulate himself. He'd been a lucky, lucky chap, all those women, places, opportunities. He started to write notes, and then write up the notes, so that when he was tired of travelling inside his head, he could lift his notebook close to his old eyes and read about himself. He was starting to enjoy himself. The family noticed. "You're looking very well, Dad! What have you been up to? Who is she then?" They were teasing him gently. They guessed he had important stuff in hand.

However, the time came one day when he felt a shot of despair. He had revisited such wonderful times in his life, looked at them now from many angles, but nowhere had he found that 'takes-your-breath-away' moment that eluded him. Perhaps he had been wrong after all. He had been suffering from a cruel illusion, and it was a taunt from Fate he felt he must deserve. This searching, this hankering for so slight a thing, if it could be called 'a thing', was wearing him down, beginning to torment him.

It was now eleven o'clock on a fine summer morning. His son had rung,' the bacon call', and announced he'd be round to take him for a spin and pub lunch. He sat down on the window seat and read from his notebook, shutting his eyes now and again to picture the place, the person he had written about, and then he slept.

The rattle of the key in the front door woke him. His son loitered in the front hall by the mirror, whistling, and the old man heard him and the tune, and suddenly, wonderfully, his heart soared. He closed his eyes to relish the moment, the exquisite perfection of the nanosecond when all came together as it was

189

meant, when all was as it should be and you knew it to be so. This was it. Again!

He had not been wrong, and yet he had. It was not a time he had been after, but a conjunction of feelings, a special warmth made up of happiness, gratitude, a sense of rightness. The search was over. He stood as his son came into the room. His smile was luminous.

"Hello, my boy. I'm very glad to see you this lovely morning. Give me your arm!"

JASON JACKSON

How You're Gone

Drunk, and smoking through a packet of cigarettes. The streetlight a sickness all over me. Cars passing on the rain-slick tarmac. The sound they make, like rushing blood, like violent breaths. Counting each one until there are no more left, and there's nothing. The crushed empty packet shoved between the wooden slats of the bench. The names scratched there: not mine, not yours. The rain on my face. The ever-long night and its silence.

*

A month ago, waking up late to Sunday sunlight through yellow curtains and a space next to me in the bed. Downstairs, a note on the table. Four lines: *There's nothing you can do to stop this. I don't want to hurt you. Don't look for me. I love you.* Not even your name. Not even mine. A terrible hour spent looking for what's gone: your phone; your handbag; some clothes but not many. Calling people who have their own lives at the weekend. *I'm really sorry to bother you, but I was just wondering… no, no I'm sure it's nothing… yes, of course, I'll let you know.* Upstairs again, standing in the bedroom, thinking of the silence you must have wrapped around yourself to do this in the middle of the night while I slept. Why not wait? A four-in-the-morning imperative: *Go. Now.* Or was there the quiet premeditation of days, weeks, months? How you smiled, laughed, ate, slept. How you watched TV, went to work each day, read your novel (left bookmarked on the bedside table, page 273 of 549). How you talked on the phone to your mother, to Karen, bought a new blue dress for summer (still in the wardrobe, £39.99 price tag still attached). How there were silences. How there was distance. How there was staring at the wall for a little too long, and once, a walk alone in the rain for hours without a jacket, and

191

your shivering, soaked return. How late at night sometimes you'd weep. The crack in the bedroom ceiling you said whispered to you, told you things, asked you questions. How I held you as we laughed ourselves into loving each other again and again, like a pair of giddy teenagers high on pheromones and cheap cider, and the next morning knowing this would be an end to it. How it repeated, month after month. The cyclical fairground ride, a thrill around every bend. The fear, the relief, the smiles and the blank expressions. My constant *everything-will-be-ok*. The impotence of prevarication. My not-knowing-what-the-fuck-to-do. How you're gone.

*

And now, a month later. The train and the morning sun through dusty windows. The juddering of the tracks. Bridges and tunnels. The darkness, then the light. The woman with her tiny white earbuds, the way she nods to the music, eyes closed. Her lipstick, perfect. Wanting to touch it. Wanting to lean across, lay my head in her lap. Wanting to scream for you. Feeling it inside again, but nothing coming, even when the woman opens her eyes, sees me staring, smiles, and her smile is not yours, nothing like yours. How nothing will ever be you again. The train and its slowing. The unthinking inevitability of arrival. The getting-up of everyone. The bag and the briefcase, the coffee cup, the paper, the breathing, the heartbeats, the-one-foot-in-front-of-the-other, the shuffle to the door and the hiss of the brakes. This proximity. How we stink of ignorance and ourselves. The press of a button, the whoosh of the door, and the day dragging me along in its wake.

*

The facts. Sunday April 18th. Nothing. No sightings. You completely disappear. Until Monday April 19th. 9:58 am. A woman in the bank in a small town ten miles from here. Your description. Your hair. A withdrawal of £5,759 from your personal account. £1 remains. No card usage since then. No mobile phone. Three sightings: Costa Coffee, the same village, the same day. Drinking a latte and reading *The Guardian*. Two hours, sheltering from the rain. That evening, the Travel Lodge on the outskirts of the town. Grainy CCTV footage, and you at reception, in the lift, opening the door to room 302. No room service. Check-out at 7:05. Tuesday April 20th. A train station twenty miles north of here, paying cash for a one-way ticket to Manchester. Somewhere you've never been, where you know no one. And nothing more. A month. The photograph I chose on the local TV news, but not anymore. A disinterested journalist implying infidelity as I hang up the phone. WPC Wendy Kirkpatrick and PC Phillip 'Smudger' Smith, their notebooks and their cups of coffee. Their constant presence for the first week. Only phone calls, now. *Manchester has nothing.* No sightings, and the family liaison officer forgets your name. The number of times a colleague can ask about you before it becomes easier to just talk about the football. How the world keeps turning. How the days run away. How cliches hit the heart of things. How I miss you. How you're gone.

*

Striplight hum. Monitor glare. Keyboard clatter. Air con sigh. A cough. A telephone. A door opening, closing. Fifteenth floor. Kevin and Ahmed and Shona and Colin and Terry and Sandra, and the thrusting, trochaic rhythms of indifference. This interchangeable anonymity. How we lose ourselves in it. How the days go. The microwave ping of a lunchtime ready-meal. The coffee stink of small talk in the break room. The bin, its silver sides slicked with tomato ketchup and grease, and the dash to the cubicle, locking the door. Hot bile, retching and the emptiness. Kneeling on cold ceramic tiles, cheek against the rim. The nausea of your absence. In the mirror, tie-straightening. Cold water. Showing teeth and eyes. Slapping cheeks for colour. Roll the shoulders. Breathe. The afternoon, full to bursting with its interminable minutes, heavy and insolent and high like a wall. At my desk. At my desk. At my desk. At my desk.

*

Moments. The Old Vic, seats in the stalls. Our first date. Something bleak and intellectual, and me staring at your profile as you watch. Leaving at the interval, buying vodka, crisps, ice cream, jumping a cab to your flat and staying in bed the whole weekend. The Lake District, Grasmere, my dad's old tent and zipping our sleeping bags together. Cooking bacon in a storm,

193

taking bites of each others' sandwiches. The freezing lake, skinny-dipping, and the old couple who cheered us on. The sun on the canvas in the morning. Your head on my wrapped-up-jumper-for-a-pillow. Your closed eyes opening and the smile in them. And just the everyday: coffee from the old silver cafetiere, showering together, lingering in the soap suds and steam. Couch-slumping after work, watching kids' cartoons instead of the news. Opening windows to summer and singing so loud the neighbours complain. How you curl into me to sleep. The weight of your head on my chest and never wanting to move. Waking to the sound of the kettle from the kitchen, until one day, only silence and a four-line note.

*

Last night, a dream: you, in a blue summer dress, sitting in a park. Flowers all around, and your quiet tears. Me, kneeling in front of you, saying, *What's the matter? I'm here. It's okay.* And you, saying, *I forgot my book. I want to know how it ends.* The book in my hand. Your fingers brushing mine as you take it. How you smile, open the pages, start to read. How I reach for you. How you start to shimmer in the sunlight cast through the branches of the trees. Your voice as you're fading, saying, *This is my story, this is my story now.* But I still wake, every morning, on your side of the bed.

CHERYL BURMAN

Sabrina Rising

Agnes has a headache. The thick air presses her temples, her heavy-lidded eyes squint despite the lack of sun. She glances up, for the hundredth time that morning. Black clouds broil above the fields, frothing like a mad dog's spit, resisting the wet wind tossing them across a purple sky to merge with the distant mountains. The wind is false, mild, non-wintry.

Agnes crosses herself and returns to raking out the pig sty. The Devil has been let loose from Hell this morning. Her thoughts go to Evan, fishing on the river. He's a farmer, not a fisherman, but the rare higher tide today has tempted him. Lamprey for our supper tonight, he told her with his big grin when he left in the darkness. The river will run fast. Agnes shivers. She never trusts the river. It might be called Severn these days, but Agnes has heard the heathen Romans called the river Sabrina, worshipped her as a goddess, and the Good Lord knows she's every bit as temperamental as any goddess. Agnes crosses herself again.

She finishes her raking, slow and clumsy with her big belly, bloated with child. She throws fresh straw into the sty, refills the water trough. The pig crouches in a corner, tiny eyes watching her. It seems wary, as if Agnes is a stranger come to do it harm. Not yet, piggy, not yet.

Agnes presses one hand to her throbbing head, another to her belly, and returns the pig's stare before waddling across the yard to the farmhouse. The hens cluck around her legs, fluffing their feathers. Agnes impatiently pushes the most persistent aside with her boot. They follow her inside, cackling as if their necks are about to be wrung. Agnes scowls. Their necks might well be wrung, if they keep this up.

"Lewis," she says to her six-year-old, and the oldest, "did you search all over for eggs? These idiot birds will have laid them in any hole or under any bush today."

"Yes, Ma." Lewis pokes the fire with a stick and reaches for the last of the wood piled by the hearth.

Agnes sighs, pulls her shawl tighter and peers into the cradle where baby Rhys sleeps. She strokes his fat pink cheek. A beautiful baby, quiet. An angel.

"Where is Gwillim?" Agnes says. "Is he fetching wood?"

Lewis shakes his head. "He wanted to go fishing with Da."

A cold finger slides down the nape of Agnes' neck. Gwillim is four, and fearless. "He's gone to the river?"

Lewis shrugs.

"Then you must fetch the wood while I find him. A storm is coming, a violent storm. He'll be blown away if he's caught out in it."

She goes into the yard and looks up again at the sky. The wind pulls at her uncapped hair to send it swirling about her head, like the swirling of lampreys in the river. "Stupid, stupid Evan," she mutters. "Stupid, stupid Gwillim."

Her chest tightens and she runs into the wind, through the gate in the stone wall, which protects her vegetables from the sheep, and along the path to the river.

She stops. Water races towards her. It covers the path and spreads to the left and the right, churning in a froth of brown and dirty white, like storm waves on the seashore.

But it's not the blue sea. Agnes recognises the colours of the river, which, it seems, reached its high tide and wasn't content to stop. Instead it has swelled like Agnes' stomach until it's burst the non-too-sturdy defences meant to keep it to its own banks.

Evan? Gwillim? Agnes can't breathe.

She steps forward, into the water, and is knocked to her backside. It rises, rises, and Agnes is pushed and dragged, straining to stand, but her belly and her sodden skirts drag her, the river tumbling her like a stone. A sheep floats past, legs scrabbling, terror-wide eyes rolling. It bleats. There's more bleating, the heart-rending cries joining together to lift above the

196

silence of the rising waters, to cut through the braying of the wind.

Agnes heaves against the water, pushes her arms forward and finds the stone wall. She presses her shaking body against it and cries as loudly as the drowning sheep when the water churns through the gate, swift as a spring stream, and into the house.

"Lewis!" The wind whips her thin voice away, but Lewis is there, by the door, his knees submerged.

"The table!" Agnes yells, terror finally giving her strength to shout. "Climb on the table!"

Lewis nods, bright boy, while Agnes prays to God that the table, weighed down with Lewis and the iron pot Agnes had been about to fill with dinner, won't float.

Rhys! The cradle is on the floor by the fire. It will float and Lewis will grab it, hold it against the water, keep his baby brother safe. Agnes' body shakes harder, and not from cold alone.

Her hands and feet grow numb, terror pounds her heart against her ribs, but still she clings to the wall. The water rises up her legs, to her waist, spilling over the stones to level itself either side of her fragile sanctuary. She is half-blinded by her hair, can hear nothing except wind and water and screaming sheep, but she turns her head, praying for a sight of Evan striding through the swirling muck, Gwillim on his shoulders.

What she sees instead is the cradle, and she is sick at the knowledge that the water inside the house has reached the window. Her baby son sails out of view and Agnes pushes herself along the wall, stone by stone. Her feet barely touch the ground, the water eddies around her like a whirlpool sucking her into its depths.

If Evan was here, he could swim to the cradle. But Evan is on the river, in the river. With Gwillim. And Agnes can't swim.

She clutches the stones and joins her screams to the cacophony of the sheep.

*

It's near dark when the wind drops to tired squalls and the water recedes enough to let a trembling Agnes squelch to the mud-filled house. Lewis is there, crouched on the table with four fright-struck hens gathered tight against his legs. Agnes takes the boy, hens and all, in her shivering arms.

"I couldn't get to him, Ma." Lewis sobs into her chest.

"I know, I know." Neither could Agnes. She knows Lewis' pain.

"Da?" Lewis says. "Gwillim?"

Agnes shakes her head. "They will come if they come," she says and gulps back sobs for Lewis' sake. "But now I have to see about the pig and the cow." She sets the boy and the hens on the floor, takes Lewis' hand. It's unspoken that she won't leave him alone, not this time.

The cow is gone, but the pig is on the roof of its sty, lifted by the water, kept alive by the higher walls on three sides. It stares at Agnes with tiny accusing eyes. It had been right to be wary.

"We have the pig still," Agnes says to Lewis. "And the hens I saved."

He takes her hand and offers a trembling, fleeting, smile.

Agnes cups her free hand beneath her belly. She feels life there too.

DAVID GOODLAND

The Dress

"When I'm down in the dumps," said Val, "I get a new dress." Trish had often wondered where they came from. Now she knew.

"One more and that's it," said Trish, as she poured the last dregs of the morning Amontillado.

They lived in a place called Crancombe, a valley town once famous for its woollen mills but now for its high-end boutiques and delicatessens.

Their once-loved rural lifestyle had become a monotonous round of dinner parties. A local author, famous for sexy prose and graphic front covers, had confirmed what the girls already knew. Crancombe sucked.

From time to time, the friends relieved their boredom by attempting suicide. They usually overdosed on Valium, though once, Val tried gassing herself in the fan-assisted oven. These half-hearted attempts were made close to a telephone, whereby the friends might call each other in case there was a chance of success.

"I suppose you'll be at the Cheese'n'Wine tonight to meet the new curate?"

"What the hell I'm going to wear, I don't know," said Trish, knowing full well she had pre-planned a shocking pink off-the-shoulder number that would completely upstage her friend.

"They say he's very young."

"Come again, darling?" said Trish.

"The new curate, he's very young."

Val clocked a flicker of interest in Trish's bloodshot eyes.

The new curate was from Clapham. Reverend Watts rode a motorbike. He'd been seen in the bus shelter with the village lads. Armed with a pack of Camels, he believed they would respond to his 'hands on' approach, though some Crystal Meth passing through a needle might have pleased them better. It was the Reverend's intention to provide these disadvantaged youngsters with a supervised discotheque in the old disused cinema. He reckoned without the Parish Council, whose members had no intention of letting him provide any such thing.

The girl's husbands, Bob and Terry, ran a company called Crancombe Curiosities Ltd. They had cleverly harnessed the work of local craftspersons. Old ladies with failing eyesight embroidered fake Quaker samplers, and bearded potters fashioned crude bowls from local clay, which were exported to gullible Americans as genuine antiques. They were hippies turned Ratners, happily helicoptering between Gloucestershire and Heathrow, while their wives lived in the lap of bitter luxury.

Terry had converted Crancombe's old railway station into a mansion. The ladies' waiting room had become a super-lounge, where his wife Trish waited for something, for anything, to happen. Bob had turned an old barn into a similar nightmare for Val.

It was the day of the Cheese'n'Wine. Trish had arranged a final fitting of a special dress from her very own clothes' designer, a young entrepreneur called Tarquin. She had designs not only on his designs, but on his body. She found many excuses to visit his fitting rooms, which were on the top floor of his mother's Regency house in Cheltenham. Being unable to turn a fitting session into anything more intimate, she had ordered a dress so costly that her demands on Tarquin's time could be infinite. She had insisted the final fitting be in her waiting room. He was due any moment now, but Val was still lingering drunkenly. How might she be gently got rid of?

"Piss off, would you darling? I'm having a fitting."

"Well, I might be useful to have around, don't you think?"

"Sod off - now!" cried Trish, emphasising the point by throwing a box of heated curlers at her.

Val sodded off.

She drove angrily home in the little BMW she kept for shopping. Then she began to feel anxious. What on earth would she wear tonight?

Val's wardrobe harboured garments from all periods of her life. She'd even kept a pair of bib-and-brace denims from her hippy days. She'd levered them on one day, and given them an airing along the High Street. It was in the butchers' she realised the futility of squeezing forty five year-old buttocks into college jeans. Groping for a coin in the back pocket she triggered off a concertina of stitching down the seam which didn't stop till it had exposed her rear end for the flabby and pendulous arrangement it had become.

Such recollections drove her straight for the Valium. She washed a dozen down with half a bottle of Bristol Cream. Collapsing on the Chesterfield, telephone within easy reach, she prepared to die.

Meanwhile, at the waiting room, Trish took a quick ginseng jab and changed into a blue silk housecoat. As she heard the purr of Tarquin's MG, she took the phone off the hook and lit a Silk Cut.

Tarquin vaulted over the side of his car and minced up to the door. He carried a swatch of bright pink crepe-de-chine. Accustomed as he was to lady customers in house gowns with nothing on underneath, Tarquin was, alas, not up and coming in the way Trish wished. His short life had taught him two things: that there was money in dresses…and that that was *all* there was in them.

He entered the waiting room at pace and went briskly to work. Pins in mouth, he stretched the fabric tightly around the torso that towered above him. He pinned securely. He made few comments and showed not the slightest interest in the contours and orifices on offer. He gritted his teeth as, ash and sherry showering over him, he beavered away.

He tried hard to think only of the job in hand, but within minutes he was spitting out pins and running furiously towards the MG. He escaped in a haze of burning rubber, leaving a lengthy skid mark on the drive.

As he neared the gates, a BMW screeched to a halt on his front bumper.

As a gentleman, he did the proper thing. He checked his car for damage and then went to the aid of the lady now slumped over the wheel, but before he could reach the driver's door, Trish had yanked it off its hinges. He stood back and gaped as, tightly enveloped in his lovely crepe-de-chine, Trish dragged Val out onto the drive.

"What the hell are you doing here? I thought I told you to piss off!" she screamed as she tugged handfuls of hair from Val's head.

Still suffering from the mortifying effect of discovering Trish's phone was off the hook, Val surrendered meekly to wave upon wave of punches and expletives. Eventually worn out, clapped out, without the will to live, Trish collapsed like a pink blancmange on top of her.

That was when the Reverend Watts came by. With a 2000cc, twin-engined, chrome-plated God-cycle purring beneath his cassock, he zipped through the gates on a pastoral fact finding mission. He was just in time to see Tarquin's MG disappear up the lane, dragging half the hedge with it.

The curate could hardly believe his luck. This was indeed a refreshing change from visiting the old and sick, or drugged teens in a bus shelter. Here was a heaven-sent opportunity to deliver Muscular Christianity at the point of need. He wasted no time.

Diving in, he separated the amorphous pile, gently loosened clothing, vigorously slapped willing cheeks, straddled each in turn, and, with surprising expertise, offered up a generous ecclesiastical kiss of life. This was indeed manhood from heaven.

His helmet crowned him like a halo as he carried his flock, one under each arm, into the ladies' waiting room, where, his rod and staff of comfort rising proudly to the occasion, he continued his holy, yet wholly unnecessary, ministry.

The story circulated that Trish had been attacked by a sex maniac, who, unable to strangle her with a length of pink fabric, escaped in a sports car. The timely intervention of Val, and the arrival of the Reverend Watts, had prevented a ghastly crime. No one believed it.

Val and Trish never made it to the Cheese'n'Wine that evening. Tarquin's dress was ripped up into squares which were used to polish the candlesticks in the church. Wednesday afternoons, after polishing, dusting, and a little ineffectual hoovering, the girls would retire to the vicarage. Tea with the Reverend Watts was the highlight of their week, and always lasted long enough to provoke gossip in the village.

Six months later, Val and Trish were guests of honour at the official opening of Crancombe's new disco for teenagers. The curate's dream had at last come true, thanks to extremely generous sponsorship from Crancombe Curiosities Ltd.

NIMUE BROWN

He Nearly Checks his Privilege

I cut off Tania's route from her table to the door, placing myself squarely in the way. Looking her in the eyes, I point out - with remarkable calm, I think - that I never win anything. I don't really expect sympathy, but I want it all the same. Having aired my grievance out loud, I find Tania rolling her eyes at me. "Oh, please," she says. "Matilda was brilliant, and funny."

We are in the pub after a poetry slam and I've cornered Tania at the table where she's been sitting with her friends. I didn't make it through the first round and the injustice of it smarts.

"What's that face for?" Tania asks. "Do you think she won on the strength of her tits, Mark? Is that it? Do you think women have an unfair advantage over you because they can use sex appeal?"

She knows I do. I've commented on it before. Right now I'm only talking to Tania because I find her attractive. She does nothing for my emotional wellbeing, or my self confidence. I just wish her mouth spoke to me in the same way her body does. I wish I felt safe being honest about these things. Bloody PC brigade. You can't even pinch a girl's bum these days without people making an unreasonable fuss about it.

Tania glowers at me. If only she'd smile. She'd look so much prettier if she smiled more and I consider pointing this out to her.

She launches her attack before I get chance to comment. "Her delivery was exquisite - that pace, that memory. You can't read from your handwritten notes and expect to get the same response as someone who learned their poem."

"It's a lot of work, learning a whole poem," I say.

"Yes, it is, Mark, which is why people are reliably impressed by poets who do that stuff."

I shake my head and drink my beer. My pain is real, it's just not the sort of pain audiences respond to. "I'm just not enough of a victim, which is hardly my fault," I tell her.

She shakes her head and looks around like she's trying to escape, so I waste no time pressing my point. "I'm not gay, or transgender or ethnic, I didn't grow up poor, I've never been hungry in my life. I've never been addicted to anything, or been to prison..."

"So?" she says.

"It's just so much easier to get attention as a poet if you can write about such things."

"Yeah, wonderful advantage to have had a shit life and to use poetry because you can't afford therapy. Right."

"They lap it up," I point out.

"Only if it's done well. Or did you forget about the guy last month with the misery porn in forced rhyming couplets?"

"He was bad," I admit with some glee. I like feeling safe when criticising people and he was truly awful.

"And the guy with the poem about homeless people, where the whole point was to make himself look good," she says. "Also shitty rhymes."

I liked him but also resented him for getting more attention than me.

"Appropriating other people's pain for your own benefit isn't cool," Tania says, looking towards the door again.

"I've never done that," I remind her.

"Thankfully, no," she says, "but you do write really shit poetry and you urgently need to get over yourself."

I am lost for words, which isn't like me. This is a cruel judgement. I don't get the appreciation I deserve. With limited options, I go on the passive aggressive offensive. "In what way?" I ask, hoping to embarrass her into shutting up.

An expression appears on Tania's face and it really isn't pretty. She drops several points on my shagability scale right there and then. "Do you remember the poem you wrote about the woman you went out with a few times but she didn't want to take it any further?"

I nod. It is a poignant, reflective piece on the loss of romance from our culture.

"You managed to be both boring and a bit sexist with that one, and it really was more like a sloppily written short story than a poem."

She's wrong, simply.

"And that one about being a wolf, which was dull enough the first time, but you've made us sit through it what, five, six times now?"

How can she not like that one? It is one of my most energetic and heartfelt pieces. I am genuinely hurt.

"And then," she says, apparently warming to her theme, "there was that one you did about the woman who only went out with you to make her boyfriend jealous, only you did it from her perspective in the most annoying, performative female voice, and with more out of date gender stereotyping than anyone should be made to listen to, ever." She actually shudders. "Did that even happen?"

"I may have taken some poetic license," I admit. It didn't really happen, I made it up, because I know it is the sort of thing that would happen.

"Do you remember what happened when you got to the end of that poem, Mark?"

I do remember, but say nothing.

"No one clapped. Not a single person, and you just stood there looking confused."

"It was strange," I admit. I found that night entirely perplexing.

"It was sexist bullshit, badly written and badly performed. That's why no one clapped."

"It was edgy," I try.

"It was crap," she says. "This is why you never win anything, Mark. Your poems are crap because you have a shitty outlook and are drowning in self pity."

I huff. Yet another woman who responds badly to my brilliance. Honestly, it's lonely being as clever as I am and being totally misunderstood by these inferior females with their minimal educations and massive attitude problems. It happens to me a lot.

206

I don't know where you have to go these days to find an appreciative, docile woman who shows some respect.

Tania waves to someone behind me and pushes her way out from behind the table in a really rude way. She flees. I probably intimidated her. I am too edgy and too esoteric for this kind of space, for these people. I start to wonder if the problem was the poetry scene all along, and whether I should try my hand at something else. Where are the people with the wit to recognise my greatness? Are you out there? I long to find you and to bask in the pleasure of finally being understood. I just want to be cheered and applauded. I want to win prizes. I want to find a woman who finds me impressive. Is that so much to ask?

Oh, Tania, blessed with perky tits
Why do my poems induce fits?
Why don't you see how, from on high
I stoop towards you, how I try
To find some good in your small mind
Which does not rival your behind?
Why do you declare I am no good?
I'd check my privilege if I could
If I knew how, or what that meant.
And especially if it meant that I
Could get in your pants.

I'm going to have to give a bit more thought to the final rhyme there, but I feel I've nailed the sentiment.

MHAIRI GRAY

Forgetting to Heal

Mim craves symmetry. Nobody calls her Mimosa any more. Late for work, she checks her reflection in the ladies'. Her dyed-black, centre-parted bob is sleek and even; her lab coat, with added hand-sewn pocket, is reassuringly symmetric. Mim snatches a breath - one earring is missing. Her fingers fumble as she removes the other. But, however hard Mim practises symmetry skin-side, her insides are asymmetric, out-of-kilter, unbalanced. Her head has been spiralling out of control ever since the Forgotten Night.

Mim joined Jerry's research team lured by the pentaradial symmetry of starfish. "We're researching ways of reducing the healing time in amputee starfish," Jerry explained on Mim's first day. "This process can take anything from two to six months. We're varying the temperature, pH, and salinity of the starfish habitats, and Charlie is experimenting - he's playing jazz to his tank."

During lunch, Mim prints and laminates symmetrical images of each side of her face. Neither looks like her. *Isn't perfect symmetry supposed to be beautiful?* Holding up both faces, she tests the theory on Jerry and Charlie. "Guys, which one do you prefer?"

Jerry raises an eye from his microscope. "Definitely the smiley one. She can buy the beers after work!" Ever since the Forgotten Night, when Jerry found her crumpled on their hall's laundry room floor, he has kept one eye firmly fixed on Mim. She can remember the bitter taste of her Mojito that night. Nothing else.

The team joke is that Jerry only got the Starfish Arm Regeneration lead because of his leg. The rumour spread by Jerry is that he autonomously detached his leg below the knee to avoid capture, like a defensive starfish. Capture from what changes weekly: pirates, sharks, aliens. Jerry's mantra is *the wound has to heal before the limb can regenerate*, to which he adds, *or a prosthetic can be attached.*

Later, Mim listens as Jerry enthuses about breaking research into mammalian limb regeneration. She gently kicks his prosthetic shin to interrupt. "Last orders – same again?" As shoe connects with plastic, Jerry's asymmetry triggers a wave of panic that rises up and crashes over Mim. She swims away through squid ink tears.

The following morning, Jerry prepares the next batch of starfish for amputation. Mim focusses her microscope on the echinoderm larvae rhythmically beating their cilia, jealous of their bilateral symmetry.

"Ready, Mim?" Jerry tightens the scalpel blade. Mim slows her breathing, fighting the nausea. She can't bear to strip the sea stars of their beautiful symmetry.

Charlie interrupts with a triumphant whoop. "Chet and Shorty have regrowth! That's 27 days." As the team celebrates and double-checks data, Mim slips away like the tide.

*

Down by the sea, the rock pools bubble. The unpredictable, chaotic notes from a jazz trumpet jostle through Mim's headphones to her ears. The sound waves transmute into electrical impulses, stimulating the neurons in her brain. Gently massaging, new pathways are created, and old ones are disconnected. Slowly healing, riff by riff, Mim starts to forget what she can't remember.

SALLY JENKINSON

Sharp Stars and Old Magic

To be a foster carer is to be a sunny supporting wall when facing your children, and a grieving mother when you are alone in your car.

A song that was on heavy radio rotation fifteen years ago suddenly comes on Heart FM. The hot pain which you almost never take out of its box and inspect is suddenly leaking down your face.

She sang along to the mirror in her bedroom that summer, her little feet stepping almost in time with the music so sincerely, as she gleefully yelled the words into her hairbrush microphone. You watched her from the bottom of the stairs. In awe of how someone who had weathered so much sadness could set such a fine example of what really living looks like.

You have thought about it almost every time you have found yourself on a dance floor since. Weddings, music festivals, children's parties. Every time your feet hit the floor and your awkward, tired body starts to move, searching for the beat of the music, you think of her dancing in the mirror.

It is 238 miles from Doncaster to Glasgow but you would have driven to the end of the earth.

To say the letter came out of the blue is an understatement. You have thought of her every day for fifteen years, but have had almost no word of her since the last time you dropped her at the school door.

Once you saw her in Asda. It must have been ten years ago now. Adolescence had elongated her, but there was no mistaking the way she met the world – shoulders wide, chest open, refusing to show fear.

Your heart almost leapt out of your body. *Mybabymybabymybaby* it went. She is *your* baby, but *you* are just a woman she was unceremoniously made to live with during a very difficult time in her life. It is not appropriate to approach teenagers in supermarkets and tell them you love them.

You let her walk away.

To drive north in October is to cross paths with autumn as it makes its way south. The leaves are yellowing themselves as you drive. By Penrith, they are burning orange as the low sun streams through them, saying its last goodbyes to the day. By South Lanarkshire, it is dark, but you imagine there is already a rich brown carpet of fallen leaves spread across the ground.

The dark is the kind you can only ever remember from this time of year – after the clocks change, but before Solstice. A crisp cold dark, shot through with sharp stars and old magic.

Your heart is a tired sailor. In your memory, she was lost to you at sea. But in reality, she is a person who needs you to be a professional. Answer questions and fill in gaps. Your feelings were not for sharing then, and they are not for sharing now. You are a conduit to her past. You must be non-partisan.

She perched on your knee on the living room floor, leaning her whole back against your side. Unsure of another new social worker who had come to give her news about own her life.

"I have some great news," said the lady, gently as possible. "You can go home next week."

Your not-daughter turned and searched your face for any cue for what to say next. Too many decisions had been made for her already; she was not willing to share her feelings with strangers anymore.

"That is so great!" you said, nodding and smiling widely. Your heart shredding itself to confetti again. "Such brilliant news!"

It was brilliant news. You were not lying. Home was the best place for her. Your job was done. But the heart has not read the text books. It has never really understood its place in all of this. The body and the mind wished her happiness and joy, and told her she was brave and smart and hilarious. The body and the mind made a memory book, and said it had been a pleasure to

211

have her to stay. The body and the mind packed her things; and wrote the records; and dropped her at the school door; and fumbled an awkward and unchartered goodbye, smiling the whole while.

But the heart lost another child at sea. It scratched another mark on the wall and folded the pain in on itself. It never recovered.

6.30pm at Roadchef, Hamilton Services near Motherwell. You are almost there, but do not want to arrive at her door hungry and thirsty and needing the loo. You want to be unflappable. A warm wall. The donut is dry and stale, and the spilled sugar makes little needles into your elbows as you rest them on the table. The tea is weak and almost grey in colour, but it is blessedly hot and there is plenty of it. You breathe.

She had chosen the football summer school, and there was one session left before it was time for her to go. Routine is important, as much normality as possible, in a time which is anything but normal. She was perched on a plastic garden chair at the side of the pitch, and as you laced up her boots, she chatted non-stop about the toys and the friends and the neighbours and the ice cream man that she had missed from home. The sheep. Her family. The dog. Then she patted you absent-mindedly on the head as you tied the last bow, and said cheerfully, "I'm going to miss you so much," before plopping herself off the chair and running away from you to join the session.

Dennistoun is dirty and sturdy. Red brick and long streets, main roads with bright-light takeaways and friendly-looking late bars. Does she sit there with her friends? Eating chips from cardboard trays, and talking things through? Your hope has always been for them all to be care-free, whenever possible. For their chests to be light and their breath easy.

The sat nav steers you off the main drag and into a side road. The tall tenements look daunting, but you are assured they are cosy and warm these days. Desirable, even. You park up, and the sweet cold air calms your car-hot cheeks as you search for the right building number. The stairwell is cold and dim, but the wall tiles are a beautiful green and orange, lacquered to a high shine

212

and smooth under your fingertips as you make your way up three steep flights.

Fifteen years is a small bump in the road. Your heart beats *mybabymybabymybaby* as it flaps and flutters and tries to fight its way out of your chest.

But you have re-read the text books, and your hands grip the box file of memories that you are going to share only if she asks.

You are a just small piece of her puzzle.

You knock on the door.

The cream of Gloucestershire writers read their stories at The Cotswold Playhouse, Parliament Street, Stroud, GL5 1LW.

Sunday 7 November 2021

Doors open at 7:00pm
Starts at 7:30pm

Tickets £9 in advance from cotswoldplayhouse.co.uk

stroud
book festival

WILD

STROUD
SHORT
STORIES

PAULINE MASUREL

Fledglings

Let me tell you about the night it happened. I woke to the sound of a solo bird singing. The noise was unstoppable, impelled, like water tumbling. I got up, went to the window and opened the shutters. There were still three hours left until dawn, but the moon was shining brightly across the edge lands, illuminating every rooftop, fence-line, delivery yard and skip.

It was much like any other night in this city. As I looked out, I couldn't spot any nocturnal bird, but I could clearly see two human silhouettes hauling themselves onto the crown of the wall behind the social club. They might have been as young as nine, or perhaps as old as fourteen. I'm not good with children, or at guessing their ages, but something about these two suede-headed explorers grabbed my attention.

They were picking their way between razor-wire, pace by perilous pace. Any false move and they would have ripped their legs to shreds at very best. Worst case they would have landed paralysed in the yard. It was the sheer audacity of their approach that astonished me. All this risk for the few bottles of beer they could possibly carry back out the same way, or a dusty optic of Famous Grouse and a few packets of cigarettes.

Incredibly, they both made it to the end of the wall with perfect poise. When they reached the security of the social club roof, they stopped to pantomime a high-five. Presumably they were heading for the smashed skylight half-way up its gradient. But that's when the other occupant of the skyline woke up and stretched her neck.

A pair of herring gulls had chosen that roof earlier in the year. Their nest was wedged between the ridge of the roof and a chimney stack. The mother had established an uneasy truce with other gulls roosting in the area. I once saw her grab one by the wing and spin it around until it managed to break free and fly dizzily off. She'd guarded that space fiercely all season and now there were interlopers on her territory.

She threw back her head and cut across the sound of sweeter birdsong with a curdling complaint. The two boys were caught by surprise. The ululating gargle of the gull grew wilder. The smaller boy almost slipped, dislodging a roof tile which slid, bounced and then shattered in the yard below. The two clung together, very still on the edge of the roof.

The gull levered herself off the nest and began to walk down towards them, open-legged and meaningful. For the first time I could actually see a couple of fuzzy heads bobbing up from the nest, an indeterminate grey against the greyness of the sky. When the gull took to the air, the boys tried shielding their heads with their hands. They tried waving their arms to deter her, but seemed incapable of moving back along the wall. They remained on her territory and she continued to attack, taking to the air and then swooping back over them with pass after pass, spitting her warnings and dipping her beak as she dived. The boys shifted and wobbled between strikes but seemed firmly wedged in their uncomfortable vantage point.

It never occurred to me to phone the police about a potential break-in. I've tried that before when a burglar alarm went off. The constabulary just called the key-holder of the building and left me to try and sleep on the sofa in the front room with a pillow stuffed over my head. But if either of these boys had fallen then they would have needed medical attention fast. I felt sure they would never make it down safely with the herring gull subjecting them to a determined campaign of action.

When I finally made the phone call I described the situation and left the operator to decide which emergency services were required.

Maybe I wasn't the only person watching that night, because it didn't take long for the flashing blue lights to arrive, without any sirens to add to the racket. The police stayed in the background, but, after a few exchanges with the boys, the firemen began extending ladders. While the rescue was still taking place, a battered Fiesta slewed into the courtyard and squealed precipitously to a halt on four bald tyres. A bulky woman eased herself out of the driving seat. She pulled herself up to her full height. At first it seemed as though she was covered in fur. But then I realised that she was clad in a plush grey onesie, accessorised with palest pink wellington boots. For one so large, she had an impressive turn of speed when she swooped across the yard and made a grab for her boys. Almost as soon as the rescuing fireman had unclipped the harness wires and unpeeled the lads' clawed hands from the final rungs of the ladder, she was upon them. She scooped them into her downy arms, nestling an egg-shaped skull under each of her armpits as though she were undecided between protecting them from the forces of authority or cracking them soundly together to teach both a lesson.

Then the screeching began again. The triumphant gull on the roof joined in with her cries. Two jutting, prodding mouths wailing in unison at the injustices of the world. The fire officers withdrew to a safe distance. I wondered if they might have to use the hose. The night-singing bird had wisely muted itself while this cacophony was in progress.

And that's where I left them all. I could have watched the story play out until its very end. But it was three in the morning and I figured that the best of the night's entertainment was already over. Eventually the squawking outside died down and I fell asleep.

*

In the weeks that followed, I watched the baby gulls growing in confidence until they tottered out across the roof on a daily basis, demanding KFC and spare ribs, or whatever else their mother could scavenge for them, it being too much bother to fish for anything that might survive in the river. One day they must have stopped stumbling around on the rooftop and jumped. Because the next time I saw the mother and her offspring together they were on the surface of the river, clumsily practising landings and take-offs. A few days later I saw her kill a pigeon, seemingly just for the hell of it, rather than in defence or as food. She dragged it down from the wall and into the river, where she held its neck beneath water until it drowned.

Some nights, when the moon is full and a lone bird is serenading the edge lands, I look out across the razor-wired wall, the expanse of shonky roofline and still-unmended skylight. I remember those two boys. I see them cushioned beneath the wings of their mother. Sometimes I wonder if they will ever learn to fly.

CLAIRE JAGGARD

The Wild Woman

Sometimes, just sometimes, the Wild Woman would choose to come to Joe Evans. With few needs and a few friends, Joe worked an honest day and slept a solid eight hours each night. He was no one special.

Most evenings, his day's work done, Joe would shrug on a coat and tramp the short distance from his own front door to that of his local pub. Hanging baskets flanked the entrance, gaudy flowers swaying to catch his attention, but Joe barely noticed them. What waited inside held so much more promise.

He'd duck under the stone lintel and into the gusty embrace of warm ale and ham sandwiches. Pausing to let his eyes adjust to the dim interior, he'd nod to neighbours before approaching the bar.

A greeting from the landlord, Jeremiah, an acknowledgement in return, and the ritual would begin.

It took an expert hand to conjure up the Wild Woman. Betsy, the young barmaid, had never achieved it, nor that cocky youth who was seldom allowed out of the kitchen to serve drinks. Only the landlord could be relied on to bring her forth. When Jeremiah Clutton poured a pint, it was with a steady, practised hand and an unhurried air. It wouldn't do to scare her.

Jeremiah would slide a glass under the tap almost stealthily, tossing out a quip on the day's events, or a comment on the weather as a distraction. His gaze never lingered on the drink and Joe was grateful for this courtesy on her behalf.

The moment liquid touched glass, violence erupted. Ale, momentarily freed from the depths of the barrel, now found itself contained behind glass walls and rose in anger, spewing foam as it roiled with frustration. Joe could only watch the turmoil and pray that she would appear.

Hints came first. A tendril of hair coiled into existence deep inside the foam, and she tossed it to let him know she was there. The battle surging all around meant nothing to her. She held no allegiance, owed no favours. She moved constantly, shifting easily through molten amber, darting behind frothy clouds, never fully in view.

Joe was enthralled. The closer he watched, the more elusive she would become. A flick of her slim hand would call his attention, only to fade away. She'd sink into the depths of the conflict, then shoot upwards, a comet trail of bubbles the only witness to her passage. He could never see her completely, could never tear himself away.

Just once, fleetingly, he had coaxed her out of the glass. He'd glanced up to find her seated opposite, fronds of auburn hair fanned across her shoulders, skin pale and creamy. She'd raised her eyes to meet his, and they had speared him like a fish.

Caught unprepared, he'd floundered. He'd stared as deeply as he could into those liquid pools, but the connection he'd hoped to find there was absent. She did not condescend to answer his wordless question, and regretfully he'd looked down again.

The ale in his glass still fizzed, but gently now, subdued, foam dispersing. The Wild Woman did not belong in still waters and Joe was obliged to let her go. He finished his pint quietly, nodded to the landlord, and set off home.

Jeremiah Clutton, hands spread wide on polished mahogany, missed nothing. So, the Wild Woman had chosen Joe tonight, and the landlord realised his business would be none the worse for it.

He swept an experienced eye over the band of regulars and knew that she had toyed with most, if not all, of them. Not that any of them would ever admit it. The pub's ale and atmosphere might loosen their tongues on many a subject, but when it came to the Wild Woman, each was convinced that they, and they alone, had won her favour.

No, Joe Evans was no one special.

ALI BACON

The Pig and I

When I agreed to flat-sitting in Spain, I imagined winter sun and scenery on the cheap. I should have checked the map. This place is land-locked, two hours from everywhere. Every night, the wind from the Pyrenees beats around the apartment block. Around noon, there's a ferocious blast of heat before the sun goes back into hiding, like a wilful shopkeeper closing up early. I start looking for work but nothing's doing. *I'm at a loose end. My wife and daughter left me* don't serve as qualifications.

*

In the café opposite the church, the milk-steamer clouds the windows. I need something more solid than coffee and order *chocolate caliente*.

There's a clatter of activity outside as the local school finishes, and the café door is opened by a woman holding a girl of six or seven by the hand. The woman, thirty maybe, fair complexion, freckled nose, sits the girl at the next table so that she's facing me, then orders a tea and a chocolate. She comes back with the drinks and speaks to the girl in English before handing her a book and unfolding a laptop.

The girl, ignoring the book, wriggles sideways to see past her mother, and for a while we compare chocolate technique, me with a spoon, her with a bendy churro. I enjoy the lost familiarity of interacting with a child. When her churro flops into the chocolate, I put my hand to my mouth in mock dismay and she giggles. The mother sighs, then looks over her shoulder.

"Sorry," I say, as if I'm the kid. I expect her to blank me, a man on his own making eyes at her daughter, but she shuffles her chair a half-turn to make us a group of three.

She addresses her daughter, "Melody, were you being naughty?"

The girl fixes me with a smile, Miss Goody Two Shoes.

"She's fine."

"You on holiday?"

"Sort of."

"So what do you think of the city?"

"Well, okay. Apart from the cold."

She shrugs. "In the summer it's a bloody furnace."

"I miss greenery I suppose, countryside. Sorry if that's a cliché."

"Haven't you been to the big park?"

The *Parque Grande*, flagged up on tourist websites, is the other side of the river to where I live.

I ask if she teaches English, the main source of employment for UK expats, and she says she does.

She picks up her belongings. "Come on, Mel. Drink up and we can show this gentleman the park." Then to me, "It's on our way home. Want to walk with us?"

Her name is Linda. She says we have to take the tram first, and when it rolls up to the stop it has *Mago di Oz* showing above the front window.

"Is the tram a wizard?" I ask Melody, who frowns with a child's impatience. "It's where it's going," she says.

"They named some of the tram stops after films," Linda says. "There's *Casablanca, Singing in the Rain* and *The King and I.*"

My opinion of the town goes up a notch.

*

From the park gates the gravel paths stretch away at different angles. "Which is the Yellow Brick Road?" I ask Melody.

Linda shakes her head. "She hasn't read it."

"Or seen the film?"

"It's quite scary, you know."

The park is dominated by a monumental fountain with a figure on top brandishing a sword.

"More scary than this?"

Melody, who's running around with her arms outstretched like a bird, swoops in close. "That's just a statue, silly."

By the time we climb past the fountain, we've been walking for fifteen minutes. At the top, the park extends into winter-bare woodland.

Linda is constantly checking her phone. "We live farther on. It's more like countryside. If you want to come."

"You can meet Henry," Melody says. "He lives in the garden."

They have a bungalow close to a canal which is thick with bullrushes. It's hardly idyllic but she's right, it feels like the country, another country.

We enter by a side gate and troop down the garden, past a chicken coop to a pen where a burly pig hauls itself off a pile of straw. Linda goes inside with a container of pellets which she scatters around for the pig to huff up. The smell is rank but bearable.

"Do you get to feed him?" I ask Melody.

Linda closes the gate behind her. "He can be a bit wild. It's the breed."

"But he's very intelligent," Melody informs me.

"Why Henry?"

"My husband's name," Linda says. "My soon to be ex, the way things are going."

I lean over and pat the broad bristly back. The pig seems docile enough, or am I subconsciously siding with the estranged father?

A back door leads into the cramped kitchen where they make me a mug of tea.

"It's getting dark. I'd better go."

"Yes," she says.

Perhaps she thinks inviting me was rash. She gives me directions to the bus stop.

Next day, I trawl bookshops for a copy of *The Wonderful Wizard of Oz* and take it to the café at the same time as before. Over the next week or so, while Linda checks her emails, Melody and I get as far as the Emerald City.

Through Linda I pick up a few hours of freelance teaching. This means I don't have time in the afternoons, but on Saturdays we meet in the park and play *Wizard of Oz* games.

"What would you ask the Wizard to give you?" Melody asks me.

"I don't know." I'm lying. I don't think the wizard gives back families once they've been squandered. "What about you?"

"I'd like to go home."

"Isn't this your home?"

"My old home." England, I assume.

"Wouldn't you miss Henry?"

"No. I'd rather have a dog. I could call it Toto."

*

In another few weeks I know where things are in the kitchen. I remember the names of the hens. Linda doesn't mind that Melody sometimes takes my hand on our outings in the park. She's beginning to feel familiar - with her wispy hair, narrow shoulders and long fingers which don't like being still. She doesn't wear makeup except for something pale and glossy on her lips.

One Saturday, Linda rings me to ask if I can look after Melody while she goes to an appointment in town. When I get to the house, Linda shows me into a bedroom where Mel's asleep in the double bed. "She threw up all night. Don't let her eat anything."

There's another door off the hall, but I'm concerned that this might be the only bed. I'm starting to crave a woman's body next to mine.

When Linda leaves, I go out the back to talk to the pig, with whom I've struck up a working relationship. He lets me scratch his ears in return for a handful of food.

I'm back indoors and settling down with a book when I hear a noise I can't immediately place. It's a key in the front door, then footsteps and a voice alarmingly close. "Anybody home?"

He strides into the sitting room as if he owns it, which, of course, he probably does. "Well, hello." He's not jumping to conclusions, not just yet. "Should I know you?"

There's a scuffle behind him, "Daddy! I've been sick!"

He scoops her up, and I'm envious of how she must feel in his arms.

"Hello, chicken. Who's this looking after you?" Melody rubs her eyes and mumbles something that includes *Wizard of Oz*.

He holds her, still sleepy, against his chest, shielding her ears. "If you're the Wizard of Oz, I'm the Queen of fucking Sheba."

From somewhere I produce a smile. "I'm just the babysitter. You must be Henry." I hold out my hand.

He ignores my gesture and looks at me with a kind of pity. "Jack Wainwright, Melody's dad. Lin has a habit of making things up, by the way."

He murmurs something into Melody's ear. I allow myself the luxury of ruffling her hair. "I'm off then. Be a good girl. Look after Henry."

On the way out I say my goodbyes to the pig. His smelly warmth is an odd kind of comfort. "Sorry, buddy. Gotta go. Have a good life."

*

A few weeks later my teaching contracts run out and I book my flight back to the UK. Just as I'm due to leave, a parcel turns up in my mail box with a note taped to the outside. The handwriting is Linda's.

Sorry about the misunderstanding, it says. *We thought you might like a share of Henry.*

Inside are two pork chops, over which I shed copious tears, some of them in memory of a half-wild pig.

JASMIN IZAGAREN

Jumping Season

Nabila had a frog in her throat and she needed someone to blame.

It had happened before, that time in secondary school when a boy had asked her for directions, and she'd opened her mouth to reply, only for a skinny croak to emerge. The look on his face was a long list of things she couldn't now recall, but the first word was definitely 'pity'. She had been horrified enough to run to the toilets to check in the mirror, opening her mouth wide to peer in. But just as she caught the webbed end of something, pint-sized Charlotte walked in and Nabila quickly adjusted her face and turned the tap on to distract herself. She must have swallowed something, she concluded.

Now it was back and wouldn't leave.

Over breakfast that morning, Nabila bit into her toast and nodded her head as her husband talked. She wondered if the crispness would scrape the frog away and she would be able to speak. Her husband gobbled smooth mouthfuls of porridge as he recounted one story after another; his timely chuckles dotted his self-occupied rhythm, his eyes never once resting on her. A bubble was rising in Nabila's chest, creating a strange feeling of something she wasn't sure of yet. And with it came a thought. She stopped chewing and looked at the man across the table: she didn't want to be here. She didn't want to be in this cosy, comfortable empty nest, just the two of them.

Nabila lowered the toast slowly onto her plate and opened her mouth, hoping the bubble would pop the words out somehow, make it all sound acceptable. Instead, a feeling of indignation started to rise alongside it, and, as she felt them compete inside her, each racing to the finish line, she wondered if, instead of words emerging, perhaps she would fill up with this rising moment and then... just... burst. She would make a mess of the clean and tidy kitchen.

"... and we concluded it must have just been her hormones!" Her husband chuckled then paused as he looked at Nabila, barely grasping the edges of what he could see on her face. "Are you okay? You look a little... umm..."

"I..." said Nabila, relieved she had managed to retrieve a word from the chaos inside her.

"Oh, before I forget," her husband interrupted. "We've been invited to dinner later, Cheltenham. Could you pass me the butter?"

No, thought Nabila, but she passed it anyway and silently left the table.

In the laundry room, Nabila pulled a vintage hand-mirror from beneath the folded sheets of linen and carried it carefully into the garden. She walked towards the open space on the other side of the weeping willow, confident there was no one around, and lifted up the mirror to catch the best of the brilliant morning light. "Ahhh," was the reassuring sound that emerged as Nabila angled the mirror to catch the back of her throat, "Ahhh...croaa..." There it was! A little smooth, mauve frog the size of half her palm. She snapped her mouth shut to quell the tears and hysteria silently inflating within.

*

Once, on a friend's farm in Australia, Nabila had walked into the kitchen and opened the tap, and there in the plug-hole had found a little, bright green tree frog blinking at her from its hiding spot. It was the third tree frog that had chosen to live there, her friend told her, and it came out at night to eat insects, or mice, or any pest that poked around. Nabila named it Fred III and marvelled at the genius of this form of pest control.

Now, thinking about her frog, Nabila wondered where it had come from. Did it climb out at night and search for things to eat? Did it look at her and wonder where *she* had come from - exotic and displaced in the damp, green landscape that she now considered her home? There was a story she'd heard about a strange downpour in Gloucestershire many years ago, that had left hundreds of pink frogs in its wake. No one could figure out where they had come from, but Nabila's favourite, if unlikely, explanation was that they had blown over in a cloudy Saharan dust storm from North Africa.

The bubble in her chest settled into a calm Nabila hadn't felt for a long time. She decided she would name her frog Frieda.

Later that day, Nabila and her husband drove to Cheltenham in silence. But it wasn't the usual kind for her, where fatigue smeared the outer edges of the trees and houses racing past. It was the silence that came before a breath, before an unexpected announcement. To Nabila, it was a private silence, one that only *she* knew about because everything was sharp and keen – coming towards her, instead of fading away. Nabila felt a tight pull in the air, certain something was going to happen, she was sure of it. She tipped her face slightly towards her husband and looked at his profile. His eyes were fixed ahead, as he hummed a determined tune to accompany the battle charge. His large hands curled around the steering wheel, ownership and command rolled off him, along with the familiar aftershave he wore for social occasions. Frieda wriggled in her throat, Nabila wondered if it was with excitement.

For a lick-of-the-lips moment, Nabila felt excited too. The thought had occurred to them both that this could be it.

As her husband parked the car, Nabila pushed herself further into her seat. She could choose not to get out, not to move, to stay here all evening until he begged. Instead, she watched as he climbed out and stood waiting for her to emerge. She did this with the now familiar themes of irritation and uncertainty guiding her limbs.

"We're here, love," he said, announcing the obvious, and impatiently rocking back and forth on his heels. She made her way slowly round the car to the pavement, looking up at the tall house she was going to be encased in for the rest of the evening.

The upward spring in her chest grew tighter and she wondered if a sound might emerge, a shrill song flitting upwards, bringing people to their windows on this neat, sensible road. She swallowed it down and looked at her husband. A half-formed,

230

nervous smile was making its way across his face, and in the dipping light it looked like a grimace. Maybe, she thought, she had mistaken all his grimaces for smiles.

The sky suddenly took on a heavy grey and Nabila flinched as the first autumnal downpour fell from the skies. She was immobile, and, for a moment, unable to breathe, as the needle shots pricked her face, threatened to nudge the scarf off her head and woke her up with a thousand, tiny slaps. It was too late to run anywhere, and through the torrent she could see the jagged form of her husband waving at her to come to him, to get out of the rain. Just as doubt started to seep into Nabila, the rain stopped and the day's final burst of clear, evening sunlight stretched across the sky.

She looked up at her husband. His face beckoned her as though she was a child, his body turned slightly away from her towards the house, eager to go inside.

Nabila pulled her ear as she heard a subtle, slick sound. Something was moving underfoot and she couldn't yet see what it was. Then, slowly at first, gathering pace, a wave of tiny, mauve frogs emerged heading in one direction, all slapping their own rhythm across the soaked pavement and tarmac. They were jumping past the house, past the car, past them both. Nabila looked down the road, towards the wonder, then back towards her husband. Couldn't he see them? Couldn't he see this miracle?

For a moment, Nabila forgot about Frieda and opened her mouth to speak, to shout something at him, even though he only stood a few metres away. But, as she opened her mouth, she felt a firm wiggle, a new pressure, then an almost gagging spring, as Frieda jumped out and into the army of frogs now swelling the road. Nabila turned to look at her husband, his eyes were fixed on her, a silent plea brimming.

"Shall we go in?" he asked.

She considered this for only a moment.

"No," she said clearly, gently touching her throat, and turned to follow Frieda down the road.

MELANIE WHITE

City Girl

An hour outside Napier, the Art Deco town in New Zealand's Hawkes Bay, there is a sheep farm snuggled in the green crevices of a landscape like an upturned egg carton. Beyond the rounded peaks and ridges of the steep earth-folds, the dark blue of the Pacific glints beneath a southern sun, beneath a sky as clean as a bed-sheet freshly washed and blown out smooth.

Each morning the farmer rides out with his manager, Shawn, and we ride with them on horses mountain-bred and more sure-footed than good fathers. Sabine is a chestnut and a former racehorse – Sabine Turbine, I think of her – and she sidesteps up vertical slopes that would make stabled horses back home buckle and slide down to the thin stream weaving along the ravine floor below. I give Sabine her head and try not to interfere as she powers me up; this is a creature with more mountain brains than I.

Today we are on a mission to find an injured sheep, a ewe with a uterus prolapsed after lambing. I ride behind the farmer, followed by a Canadian couple, Brian and Jen, and a laughing Dutch blonde named Wieke. Brian has never ridden before. Having been coaxed out at the last minute, he's still wearing his pyjamas, and struggling with the reality of unpadded saddle leather. At home this would never happen, a novice off the lead rope and in such hazardous terrain, conjuring injury and litigation and expense. It is not that the farmer has more relaxed codes. He has faith in his horses, trusts them, and knows that they understand their responsibility.

The sheep are speckled over the hills in every direction, and, having mounted the top of a rise, we follow the farmer's homing instinct along the rocky ledge to the east. Whenever we approach a quivering herd, they scatter clumsily, stumpy legs jerking beneath a mass of bulky wool. Our group is the perfect example of magnetic repulsion – we could ride into a throng of sheep and space would clear around us, instantly, like hot oil in water, or hair recoiling from a flame. The farmer sends one whining dog out at a time with a high clear whistle; his pack of four never takes their eyes off him, and he calls each one by name to let them know they're on their mark. The chosen one streaks off, coursing over the undulations, until it seems like it will keep going to the ocean, but somehow it hears the next call and drops flat, or turns, or draws its invisible net round in a wide arc to gather the sheep together.

When we finally spot the ewe, she looks like she's trailing a red sweater with the sleeve turned inside-out. She's waddling heavily up the opposite hillside, her rear end puckered and open like an obscenely botoxed pout, muddy blood matting the wool of her hind legs. We stay put while the farmer and Shawn pick their way down to her. The ewe is driven into a small triangular pen built into a corner of the boundary fence for the men to return to her later, and she stands alone beneath the shade of a gnarled tree as we swing round to take the perimeter road home.

The level ground is strange and easy after the morning and we talk more on the three-mile track back. The farmer is right-wing, denounces AIDS and homosexuality, favours capital punishment: law like a noose. It seems as if he hasn't talked with anyone who argues in a while, but I try to be respectful: he is old, he is from another land. He seems to like me even though I don't agree with him.

"You're an intelligent girl," he tells me, "and you're a good rider," which pleases me more. His attitude is grandfatherly, but still I feel embarrassed when our legs press together with the sway of our horses' tandem gait, and I try to ignore it rather than deliberately move away. The farm is becoming hard for him to run, he says – he is in his 70s, which surprises me, and much of the heavy work falls to Shawn. The farm has been his whole life, he says, and he surveys it with the fierce love of ownership, and with just a little fear.

In the afternoon, Brian and Jen prepare lunch at our cabin. We drink a bottle of wine, and Wieke breaks her resolution to quit by smoking my cigarettes. I have come on this trip to slip out from beneath the weight of a stifling city, to shake out my life like a dusty rug, and I'd been hoping that going away would amount to more than mere avoidance. So far I couldn't say whether I'd actually achieved what I wanted, and although the beauty of the country thrilled me more each time I took a walk through the ferny forests, or hiked redwood trails inhaling eucalyptus and pine, a melancholy whisper reminds me that all of the beauty is tinged with the sadness of leaving, and that none of it is mine.

These are the first people I have shared more than a few hours with in New Zealand, despite the many warm and open people I have met, and we sit easily together, the right balance of sociability and space.

"You're good at being by yourself," my friend Lindsey told me a few years ago, "but you're not so good at being with other people." So I breathe the fresh outdoors air like a remedy, and tuck into succulent rosemary fish with these friends.

Later the farmer saunters up the path to find us still sitting around the picnic table. Once he's checked who plans to ride out with him again tomorrow, I ask after the ewe. "Did the vet come?"

He laughs with the pleasure of setting me straight. "No." He grins at me. "Shawn went out after lunch and slit her throat."

I try not to be such a city girl, but stupidly I feel like I'm going to cry, and I concentrate on swallowing the lump, nodding like I understand. The others carry on talking, and when my ears clear suddenly, the farmer is mentioning that he has cancer, telling us about his prostate and a biopsy and a trip to the hospital. I'm stunned by how easily he says this to us, a group of young and careless travellers who have come to ride over his land; how easily he tells us that he is going to die. And I feel all the immediacy of the day, of life in the morning and death in the afternoon, of the heat of an animal's blood and the raw fact of its pain.

Earlier, as we ride home, the farmer asks me if I want a gallop. "But don't let her go completely," he warns me. "You won't be able to stop her."

I try not to look too eager and trot ahead of the group, contained, until Sabine and I are clear enough not to set the others bolting. I try not to let excitement transmit down the reins like a phone call flashing down wires, but joy is surging through my blood and Sabine shoots off, careening round blind turns and sending the clatter of hooves ringing through the valleys. I keep holding on to her, just for a minute, and then I let her go.

NICK ADAMS

Demolition

The last lights went off in the old shopping centre this evening and the demolition team have immediately moved in. The doors were locked to the public for the last time and the team were handed the keys, and it was not at all ceremonial. They pass reverently through the dark halls and hollowed-out spaces, placing their explosives like they are offerings to the husk of a deity that lingers here. They all came to the centre as children and they remember that you queued for the cinema here and the screens let out just over there. The video shop was here, and this concrete bowl full of steel tubes and old pennies was once a fountain.

They are watched by maimed mannequins as they work, and they talk about taking one home, taking it as a souvenir because who would know? It seems wrong though – it seems as if they belong here.

The implosion is to be carried out tomorrow. Metal barriers have been erected a safe distance from the entrance in the square and a good turnout is expected. There is an area of temporary seating and a small platform where the mayor is to stand and talk about regeneration and renewal and progress. Young people who come from different towns, who never visited the shopping centre and who are paid by the hour, are due to be armed with plastic bazookas, and are expected to fire into the crowd t-shirts bearing the name and logo of the new mall on the outskirts of town.

Except none of these things will happen.

In the small and fallow hours of the morning, the residents of the houses overlooking the square, on which the old shopping centre stands, will wake up, some teased slowly and some tugged sharply from their dreams. They will later report hearing the moaning of great slabs of stone splitting gradually and irreconcilably in two, and the sigh and wheeze of old bricks crumbling. They will reflect on how much the noise of the rusting bones of the structure pulling themselves apart sounded like popcorn kernels exploding one after another.

The police station will receive a dozen calls between 2.00 and 3.00 in the morning, and the picture they get will be confusing. A living mass, a mess of concrete, they'll hear. An urban behemoth, a commercial golem, the old jeweller's bobbing past the window. This shambling thing will be seen propelling itself forward on blunted pillar-legs. It'll set a course across the market square and out onto the high street, dragging its blind shop fronts with it in a tangled parade. It'll leave scars in the tarmac, will grind bus stops into safety-glass confetti, will raise a cacophony of out-of-sync car alarms and will obliterate the peace statue on the mini-roundabout by Sainsbury's.

Out past the sports centre and through the civic gardens, it'll tear and stagger, shaking free the colonies of pigeons nesting in its encrusted nooks. They will scatter into the sky, dark on dark, and it will seem as if they are pieces of the fabric of the building itself, falling away in upended gravity.

At around 4.00 in the morning, it will disappear, lurching into the woods behind The Red Lion, swallowed whole by the trees. By now, the police will be out on the roads, and so will the fire brigade and several ambulances, as if nobody knows what kind of emergency this is.

There will be noise and disturbance in the woods, and the old shopping centre will soon pass out of range of human eyes and ears. The not-creature forcing its way through the trees will send squirrels skittering from their dreys and will drive badgers and foxes from their dens as its awkward movements wrench tangles of roots from the soil and collapse tunnels in on themselves.

It will reappear shortly after dawn, spotted by a dog walker as it makes heavy progress across farmland past the ring road. It'll soon have attracted a convoy of gawkers and there will be cars pulled over all along the hard shoulder, and people with binoculars and cameras and flasks of milky coffee. They'll agree,

237

more or less, that it looks as if it's not just dumbly ploughing forwards until it expires; it looks very much like it's headed straight for the new Shopping Village and Retail Experience at Brooks Field, due to open on Saturday with thousands of exclusive discounts and a range of free activities for the kids.

There'll be a litter of children trailing behind the thing now, steadily gaining confidence as it becomes clear that it doesn't notice, or is indifferent, to their presence. They will slalom amongst its crude footprints and scoop up pieces of flint and clods of earth to lob at its tattered backside.

There'll be much less of it now. Great chunks of it will have been hewn off in the course of its missing hours. The photo booth will eventually be found broken and dented astride a stile near Lodge Lane, the curtain still pulled across.

Only a long and ragged strip of the subterranean car park will still be attached, dragging behind the main body of shops and food court like a lame limb. The further it goes, the more the central mass will haemorrhage facilities; the creche jettisoned by the Barney's Chicken roundabout, the forgotten contents of the Lost and Found dashed across both lanes of the dual carriageway. It'll slow to a stuttering shuffle by half past eight, but won't come to a halt.

The demolitions team will have been roused from their sleep and will be on the scene now, holding a crisis meeting at the McDonald's that offers a panoramic view of the monstrosity's progress. There will be representatives from the police and the council, and an executive from the Brooks Field team, who will swear that there'll be a whole new scale of shit-storm if that thing gets any closer to the Shopping Village.

There will be objections that it's simply unsafe to carry out a demolition now, without the proper precautions, without a perimeter established. The decision will be made regardless.

The detonations will take place at noon once the old shopping centre has reached the stretch of open fields between the bypass and the new complex. The public will see the execution of the great old beast as it plays out in neat synchrony. A series of blasts will cascade along the spine of the building and it will buckle and

238

stumble. Its repurposed limbs will crumble away in clouds of dust and debris, and the whole structure will seem to kneel submissively before its collapse.

Its metal skeleton will be exposed now, like the bleached remains of a once-beached whale. The escalators that ran through its innards will be turned to the outside and will grind at the grass and mud for fruitless purchase. The thing will shudder and groan, and will then fall into its own rubble, inert.

The field will be cordoned off for several weeks while the debris is cleared. The new mall will not open late, and will not offer any indication of what happened or nearly happened. People will come and shop and eat at one of nine popular food franchises, and park for free in a car park that is on its own bigger than the whole of the old building. They will watch small birds darting about amongst the neat, glossy vegetation under the great glass ceiling, and they won't know if they are meant to be there or if they're trapped. Then they will walk the short distance to the site where the old shopping centre fell. They will sift though the grass for shards of concrete and they will take them home as souvenirs.

The original, longer version of 'Demolition' was first published in 'The Best of British Fantasy 2019' edited by Jared Shurin

GEORGIA BOON

Johnny Maunder Came to the Well

Christmas morning. The path down from the Tor was deceptive and hoary. Johnny Maunder planted his bare feet irregularly, scaling down, his head blurry with the night's terror, the human filth, and a blizzarding hangover from the mushroom tea. The stench coming from the pelts strapped to his legs was rank. He rubbed at his eyes, fearing the globs of blood that had sprayed into them would creep out and make their home forever beneath his nails.

On the opposite path, Brother Thomas tripped along, both careful and hurried, chewing away at his thoughts. Why was it always *he* who would be made to fetch the water on the coldest of mornings, nose burning from the frost and his little eel-skin shrivelled up between his legs? And for what? The only difference between this water and the water at the Abbey was that this water was a lot further away. A spring from the Lord's tears, right here in swampy old Glastonbury? My rump, he thought.

The whole town knew the well had been called the White Spring for as long as anyone could remember, and no one had ever connected it with these silly myths. That was until, by complete coincidence, the coffers of the Abbey had started to run dry, and the stories had started to abound, drawing credulous pilgrims to the town, spilling gold from their purses as they trudged between the sacred sites.

At least on Christmas morning the usual band of maniacs that crowded the spring were all safely shut indoors feasting. Brother Thomas had been up since the mercifully late dawn, his head resonating with the mead that the Abbot had allowed them after communion, to mark the end of the advent fast. Thank God for a quiet morning. Thank God for a mild frost. He was cheering himself up, almost ready to begin humming a little ditty.

But now he could see Johnny coming towards the well. To Brother Thomas, Johnny seemed a huge creature, with wide, furry haunches, his top fresh to the morning breeze and very like a man's lean torso, albeit seamed with grime. Brother Thomas hung back to allow this man-beast to approach the spring before him.

Johnny Maunder didn't even take account of the little monk. They were everywhere, like little pigs, like little woodlice, swarming the town, only locking themselves up at night for the necessity of population control.

Johnny's face was obscured by the grimness of the night. And the sleeplessness that had come from the moment a few days ago when Old Jack had told him that he must be the one to find the girl.

Thank God, he hadn't been the one chosen to put the knife in. It was all he had been able to do to hold the poor thing's wrist.

He knew as he approached the well that the filth of the festival could never be washed from him. The ritual Modranicht, the Mother's Night, clotted his mind. How could it be that they must take a womb from the earth? And for what? Some fairy prince. Gwynn ap Nudd, Gwynn ap Nudd they would chant on the Tor, summoning the ruler of the fair folk. It was for him that they tuned their whistles and sharpened their knives.

Gwynn ap Nudd. The name would ring around his own mother's teeth as she grinned and danced about their tiny scullery. "He will free us, my little Johnny," she would trill. "On the night he comes from the Tor and snatches us up, we will dance the long night with the fair folk. None of this fuckery for us in that time, my little one. None for us!"

She would boast that Gwynn was Johnny's father. But in the town they told that Johnny was merely another of the old Abbott's bastards.

Johnny knelt. Even if the water touching him would scar him, turning him into one of the anghenfil that haunted the Abbey gates, he would accept it. And even if his flesh burned, it was worth it to rout the leeches sucking on his soul and expel them forever.

He glanced up at the tiles behind the spring, set together to show the Grail. For those tears to touch him, to mix with the salt from the girl's eyes that had covered him as she had howled and sobbed before Old Jack had made the cut. It wouldn't be nothing - it couldn't be nothing to bathe in those tears.

Brother Thomas waited by the well, tapping his foot lightly, watching what he could now see was certainly a man. What *was* he doing? There were letters painted onto his back, the same dark symbols that the monks were forever being sent to wash from the Abbey Walls. And what were they drawn in? Blood?

These hysterical pagans always seemed to gather between the gates and the grounds whenever the Bishop visited. He would tut as he picked his way through the chanting mass. They never looked very happy, always rather serious, in Brother Thomas' opinion. He was surprised that their fantastical faith didn't cheer them. Imagining the Tor filled with a swirling, sparkling fairy kingdom should surely occasion more delight than picturing it full of the Lord's tears.

This one was taking ages. Just kneeling there. Brother Thomas was going to miss morning prayer at this rate.

Johnny touched his finger hesitantly to the waters in the well. The first drop swept out poison from his clogged veins. He pushed his whole hand underneath the waters, into the cool balm of deliverance. Reaching by his side for his hollow wood flask, he thrust it into the well, and then slowly stood. Stretching himself out, he tipped the waters from the flask over his head. He wept, and now his own tears, and the Lord's, and the girl's, all combined.

Johnny heard a promise whispering through the well: that forgiveness was hard to find when you had played a part in such an act, but that now he was cleansed, the Lord's power would keep him from any more festivities, any more revels.

He stepped away from the well, sodden with hope. Brother Thomas waited for Johnny to be enough of a distance away to not have to smell him when he approached the well. He took a deep sigh as he dipped his canteen, hoping none of the painted blood from the man's back had mixed in with the waters. He shrugged as he pulled the full vessel from the pool, and corking it, bound it to his waist, before pushing another in. Sighing, as he tied the second vessel to him, he began to trudge along the path, remembering the strain it always put on his old hips to haul this phony juice all the way back to the Abbey.

HANNAH GLICKSTEIN

Wild Serenade

The smell of detergent in the launderette almost makes him feel high. Molly's watching the TV in the corner, taking off her hoody. Alfie looks at her, then the machines.

He only invited her to his house last night because she was crying on the phone – something to do with her mum. She was amazed by his house. Kept staring at everything. They sat on the pink sofa, their arms nearly touching. She took off her coat and dropped it on the floor, then he saw them.

Now he has to see them again: tiny painful scars criss-crossing the delicate skin above her elbow. He closes his eyes.

The little boy with a jammy face runs past their bench, shouting, "piaaaom", pretending to shoot, aiming at Alfie. Alfie dies into her arms, so she has to catch him and hold him for a second or two, to prevent him from sliding to the floor. He sees flakes of dry snot inside her nose; wants to leave the launderette; go outside somewhere together in the sun. She told him she had to go home. But maybe there's some way he can stop her.

She pushes him away. He has to put an arm out to stop himself from falling. They straighten themselves and stare through the concave glass at his turning bedsheets. The noise of dryers means they can talk without being overheard.

"Will there be stains?" He feels stupid, like she's suddenly his mum or something.

"We'll have to bin them."

"Bin the sheets?"

The sheets drop. The door clicks.

Standing opposite him, folding, inspecting a pale brown stain, she frowns; closes her eyes; bites her bottom lip hard.

He stuffs a folded sheet into the bag, "It looks like Australia...Seriously Molly, my mum doesn't care."

"You clearly don't."

"The cleaner does all our washing anyway. Mum would only ever say anything if she's been drinking, then she'd forget it in the morning."

"Must be nice to have a servant. And, now it's all over, it'll be fun to tell all your friends you've been to the launderette with a real girl from the estate. They're going to be impressed, Alfred."

"I won't tell anyone. I swear."

*

They take a bus with the warm folded sheets to the park opposite Alfie's big empty house. The sun's hot on their faces, though it's no longer summer. The air feels heavy - motionless - and tastes of fumes. The grass has the parched yellow look of a place well-trampled. There's only been a few days of drizzle since school started back. They step over a dry dog poo. Pause for a moment, speechless, watching ants in their thousands parade from the cracks of a dry wall to swarm a brown apple core. Sparrows evaporate from the path before them. The noise of birds is louder than Alfie ever realised. Children scream in the playground. Adults outside the café talk all at once - raise their voices to be heard. Alfie looks over at them with their big greedy coffees and pastries. They seem to be shouting only to themselves.

He can feel the warmth of Molly's hand close to his, but can't touch her. He's carrying the laundry bag. It would be too obvious to swap hands now. He can't speak. Doesn't want to make her think he's an idiot.

He doesn't want her to remember she needs to get home. They have to be going somewhere. As they pass the animal enclosure, he manages to make himself ask her if she wants to sit on a bench. Offers to buy some kind of drink. He moves coins awkwardly in his pocket through the denim, noticing the weight of them: left over from the twenty he had to change for the launderette. Hating the way they make his jeans bulge. Not wanting to get his money out and flash it.

She sits down and squints up at him through transparent blue eyes. He can't make himself leave her. Looking away, he sits next to her, takes her hand. His own hand feels sweaty and too big. Hers is dry and light.

They're opposite the deer enclosure. He's never thought about it before. But it's so weird! Massive deer - with antlers and everything - just standing there in the middle of a London park. Marooned. Bored. Lost. Longing for a life they've never even experienced. The colours of them! Dappled browns that would make them almost disappear inside a forest. The speckles of white make Alfie think of sunlight. He wishes he could tell Molly, without sounding like he's trying to impress her: make her think he's poetic, or something stupid like that.

Molly turns towards him, shielding her eyes with one hand. She's smiling slightly, just at the corners of her mouth. "I thought you were going to buy me a drink?"

"Sorry. What do you want?"

"Diet Coke."

He's looking at her sharp jaw, wondering if she'd accept an ice-cream too. "Anything else?"

"No. Thanks."

"Will you wait here?"

"Yes. What do you think I'm going to do? Run away just because you're not looking? If I wanted to leave I'd just leave. OK?"

"Yeah. Sorry."

"I'll stay here with the deers. Alright dear?" She said the last bit with a thick put-on cockney accent. Her own accent made ridiculous, like the voice of a pantomime dame. He almost smiles, but doesn't want to look like he's laughing at her. He thinks of his own voice with disgust.

A deer approaches them from the centre of the enclosure: a tall strong male with heavy antlers. As if the deer heard what Molly said and is strolling across to keep an eye on her while he's gone.

"Alright," Alfie mutters. Making sure not to drop his T, in case she thinks he's pretending to be less posh than he really is, glancing across at the queue. Wishing it was shorter.

246

When he returns, she's taken off her hoody again and is sunning herself: arms stretched out, eyes closed, head back, black hair dangling behind the bench, the bag of sheets underneath her. His fingers hurt from the cold of the cans. He sits down and drops one in her lap, wishing right away he hadn't, in case it fizzes. Before he has time to move his eyes, she's noticed him looking at her scars.

"I know. They're ugly."

"No. I don't mean that. I just…they look like…they must have hurt."

"Not that bad actually. Well, yeah. But better than the alternative."

"The what?"

"Doesn't matter." Her face looks closed. Possibly angry. He moves away. He can feel his cheeks going hot.

"It's alright."

"Is it?"

"I don't know."

"We don't have to talk about it."

It's a mystery to Alfie. Whether she wants to or not. A terrible riddle. Too important to get wrong. He looks over at the enclosure. The big stag's standing there eyeballing them: serious, like he's planning what to do next.

Molly pulls the ring-pull from her can, throws back her head and drinks, like she's never tasted anything so sweet in her life. Alfie has an urge to put his arm around her. But can't, until he thinks of what he's going to say next. Somewhere to the right, a black dog lifts his leg on a lamp-post. From the pond a duck makes a noise like something from another planet.

Alfie opens his mouth to speak. But his words are drowned out. The stag has lifted its head and is roaring. So loudly! A wild sound, full of lust and frustration. Alfie and Molly start, then stare. As the long strange wail subsides, the deer begins smashing his antlers hard against the railings. A tiny girl, with fat bare legs in her pushchair, starts crying.

Alfie looks at Molly and smiles. There's an expression on her face of pure delight. He moves closer and puts an arm round her, confident it's alright now. She rests her head - just for a few seconds - on his shoulder, kicks the bag under the bench with her heel and says, "I've got to go home."

Alfie feels as if he's been hit. "OK."

"But we can meet again. Yeah?" She punches him gently on the arm.

He can't speak. She can see that.

"But please, Alfie. Chuck the sheets. Your mummy can buy you some more."

"That deer's making weird noises, isn't he?"

"Don't we all sometimes?" She looks at him, smirking rudely.

She's means he's like the deer! And it's funny. Hilarious. She's not saying he's an idiot, or weird or anything. Just laughing. Because he did make some funny sounds last night. But she likes him anyway. He could almost cry.

The deer's moaning – grunting with despair.

They walk through the park, finishing their drinks to the sound of tormented roaring. Alfie tips the sheets into a bin by the gate. And walks her to the entrance of her flats, knowing she'll come back.

REBECCA KLASSEN

Clothed in Sacrifice

Julia began with a tiny cotton vest. She picked at the hem, finding a loose strand, and unravelled the whole garment into a mess of thread. Then, putting an end into her mouth, she sucked it like spaghetti. Throughout the morning, she swallowed and chewed until the deconstructed vest was in her stomach. She smoothed her smock over her bump.

"Just for you," she whispered.

Her mother came round the following week with some knitted mittens for the hospital bag. Julia placed them on top of the waiting duffel in the hallway before making them some tea. She laid out the tea set on a tray with homemade madeleines. They talked about the baby. Would she have Julia's blonde hair, or ginger hair like her husband, Mark? Would she be tall like Mark, or petite like Julia?

"I wonder if she'll be like you when you were a child." Her mother sipped her trembling cup.

Julia eyed the mittens in the hallway. "She will be fine. I'm seeing to it."

As soon as her mother left, Julia picked up the mittens. She couldn't wait to unravel them, as she had the vest. She shoved a mitten into her mouth, the lavender wool setting her teeth on edge as she munched; it was coarser than the cotton vest. Goose pimples rippled down her arms and legs. Fibres stuck in her throat, and she coughed and gagged. The next mitten went down easier as she folded it up before swallowing it down like a pill with a glass of water. She thought to herself, *after all, this is a remedy.*

*

Mark found Julia in the kitchen a few days later, standing in her underwear, swallowing the buttons from a baby's velvet jacket

249

he'd bought. They'd argued, Mark becoming heated while Julia had remained calm, cutting the jacket into thumbnail-sized pieces and swallowing the velvet.

"It's bad for you and the baby," he yelled.

"It's preventative measures. You really should get a hold of yourself; you're losing control. There's nothing worse," she said as she popped a piece of the collar into her mouth.

He accompanied her to the next midwife appointment and disclosed what Julia had been doing. The midwife didn't seem to understand the entirety of what was going on.

"Expectant mothers get all sorts of strange cravings. I loved to chew a bath sponge when I was having my second. One woman I looked after used to dip bananas in marmite!"

When they got home, Julia wept, asking Mark to trust and support her. His heart broke seeing her so unhappy, so he didn't say a word when that night she took a meat tenderiser to a pair of leather booties and ripped them apart with her teeth in the darkness of their garden.

Mark rang his mother-in-law the next day. "I don't know what to do about Julia. It's like she's losing her mind," he said.

"She's not always been the Julia you know now. When she was a child, she did the most outrageous things."

"What do you mean?"

"She'd spend a lot of time in the woods behind our house. Neighbours used to spot her naked in the trees. She'd wait there and catch birds."

"That sounds a little wild, but quite sweet," he said, picturing his wife as a little girl playing in the woods.

"She'd bring the birds she caught home with their necks wrung."

"I...I don't believe you. She's a social worker and hosts church coffee mornings."

"Julia's worked hard to be who she is now. We could barely keep control of her back then. She was just...feral. The more we tried, the worse we made it."

"Are you saying I should do nothing?"

"Exactly," said his mother-in-law.

250

So, a fortnight later, when he found in the bin the hanger that had previously held his unborn daughter's corduroy skirt with a yellow flower embroidered on it, he did nothing, even when he heard his wife retching upstairs.

*

Labour moved along quickly. Mark rushed home from work when Julia called to say her waters had broken. When he walked through the door, he found her climbing up the outside of the banisters. He'd yelled and rushed over, trying to get her down. She only came down when the postman knocked. She flew at the door, roaring through the letterbox.

Contractions progressed, and there was no time to take a relaxing bath like all the books suggested. He got her into the car, but she wouldn't stay seated. Instead, she paced across the backseat on all fours. When they got to the hospital, Mark spoke to the receptionist, then turned to find Julia gone. He found her behind a large chair in the waiting room. She swiped his hand with her nails when he reached out to her. The midwife coaxed her out.

"We may have to restrain her," the midwife said when they finally got Julia into a room. Blood dripped down the midwife's cheek as Julia howled and banged on the window. "I can't check on the baby if she's like this."

Mark nodded, but then Julia's howling stopped. She stripped off her clothes and got onto all fours, panting with barely a sound. The midwife dropped behind Julia's buttocks. "Push, Julia, I see her. She's coming. Push."

Mark sat beside the midwife and watched his daughter's head coming. The stress of the last month felt a distant memory, as a crown of auburn hair squeezed forward. Then came a little body wrapped in a velvet coat, hands covered by lavender mittens. A brown corduroy skirt with a yellow embroidered flower followed with long, chubby legs and an umbilical cord protruding from it. Lastly came feet encased in leather booties. His daughter let out a small cry, and the midwife, open-mouthed, let Mark take his daughter from her. They both stared at her, mucus and amniotic fluid soaking the little outfit.

251

"I don't believe it," said the midwife. Then she said to Mark, "She looks just like you."

A stirring wind on their face made them look up. The window was open. Julia was gone.

'Clothed in Sacrifice' was first published by the online literary magazine 'The Phare' in 2021

ROBIN BOOTH

Painted Ladies

As soon as the evening news finished, Robert's wife got up from the sofa and said she was going to bed. She was tired after a day toiling in the garden. Robert put down his crossword as she set off across the room. He picked up the remote.

"Might you possibly lend me a hand tomorrow?" came a voice from the foot of the stairs.

Robert glanced up at her. "What with?"

"The dahlias need planting out, or we shan't have them this year."

He grunted. There was something on the other channel with Scarlett Johansson, but it was already twenty minutes in. This was always happening. It was because Vanessa insisted on watching the news. She liked to keep abreast of the day's developments, whereas Robert, who'd recently endured his eightieth birthday, found that these days he was simply tired of it all. He waved her off to bed.

"Goodnight."

It was a long film, intricately plotted, and Robert didn't find it easy to follow. He was aware also, from the sound of coughing, that Vanessa was lying awake.

She was still coughing when the film drew to its unrewarding conclusion.

Robert switched off the TV, locked the back door, poured a glass of water from the kitchen tap, drank it, turned off each of the lights, and then went upstairs to see what all the fuss was about.

The ambulance came at seven in the morning to take Vanessa to hospital. Robert was to stay behind and pack a few of her things. He could bring them later in the car, they said. He stood in his pyjamas on the front drive as they loaded her into the back of the ambulance. They trampled on the rose beds. Vanessa clutched at the oxygen mask they'd strapped to her face, her body jack-knifing with every muffled cough. He raised a hand to give her a wave, uncertain if she could see him or not.

When he got to the hospital with the bag, he realised he'd come without a mask. He was given directions, all the same, to the paediatric wing.

"You do realise it's my wife?" he said. "She'll be seventy-eight in September."

They explained that the paediatric wing was in temporary use as an overflow ward; he was sure to find her there.

But when, after navigating the labyrinthine corridors, he arrived at the paediatric wing, he was told that, mask or no mask, he was not to be admitted: the overflow ward was in lockdown, no visitors allowed. He might try again tomorrow.

Still carrying the bag full of Vanessa's things, he returned by the same needlessly convoluted route to the car park and got into his car. He sat watching the rooks wheel and gyre above the hospital buildings. He sat there for twenty minutes in the stationary car, and then, turning the key in the ignition, set off for home.

The phone was ringing in the hallway as he opened the front door.

"Mr Jenkins?"

"Speaking."

It was the hospital, about Vanessa. They explained that her condition had deteriorated, and she'd been put on a ventilator in intensive care. He'd be unable to visit for the time being. Robert listened, staring at a spot on the wall where the wallpaper had lifted. It would need fixing.

"Mr Jenkins?" said the voice at the other end, "are you okay?"

"I'm perfectly well, thank you."

"The doctors are doing all they can."

"But I have her bag here," he said, holding it up. "It's right here."

*

The late afternoon sun was glancing through the window of the lean-to at the back of the house as Robert pushed open the door on its rusty hinges. The old familiar reek of soil and glue. There, lined up along the wall in a pool of golden light, stood Vanessa's gardening tools. He stepped carefully around them.

In a drawer of the workbench was half a tub of wallpaper paste, exactly where he'd left it. He rummaged for the palette knife, and found it. Good. He'd have the job done by the end of the day. Turning, his shin knocked against a wooden crate that was perched on an open bag of compost. It slid off, spilling its contents onto the floor: a mass of dried tubers, knotted together in clumps, woody tendrils sprouting from their tips. Vanessa's dahlias.

With the sunlight fading now, he took the palette knife and dug a series of holes, five inches deep, in the west-facing bed. Into each he placed a single tuber, making sure to position them correctly, eye facing upwards, just as Vanessa always did. He covered them over with compost, and patted them down with the flat of the knife. Then he gave them all a good watering.

In July they would flower, as they always did. And Vanessa, as always, would be delighted with them.

He rinsed the palette knife under the kitchen tap, watching the flecks of soil circle around the plughole. It was too late now to start on the wallpaper. He was tired after his labours, and went early to bed, waking in the night with the sudden apprehension that he ought to have soaked the tubers in water before planting them out, or they might never flower.

*

The days flew by with no change in Vanessa's condition. The doctors continued to do all they could. Her bag remained in the hallway.

Robert no longer left the house, except to do the shopping. The days lengthened and hurried on, the weeks circling around him indistinguishably. May turned into June, and still the dahlias hadn't appeared. He stopped going out to water them, and kept the curtains closed at the back of the house so he wouldn't have

255

to look. In the hallway, the flap in the wallpaper sprouted towards the ceiling.

He lost track of the months, waiting for the call that never came. The kitchen clock ceased telling the hour with any degree of honesty. Ivy came in under the back door and proceeded stealthily down the corridor. Snails left figure-of-eight trails on the living room ceiling. In the hallway, the wallpaper hung down in thick wet scrolls, and the walls stood naked and glistening in the midday gloom.

Then, on a day just like any other, there was a knock at the front door. He hurried to answer it, stepping breathlessly over the slew of unopened post. But it was only the shifty young man from next door, wanting to know if Robert needed any help with the garden at all.

"Only, I see you've got creeping thistle. I can get rid of it, if you like."

Robert eyed the young man, standing there in flip-flops on his doorstep. "Creeping what?"

"Creeping thistle. It'll be up and down the street if you let it. I've seen it happen."

"No need, thank you very much."

Robert shut the front door. He went to the back of the house, opened the curtains, and looked out at the garden. There was no sign now of Vanessa's neatly tended flowerbeds: they were cloaked in chickweed and ragwort, and carpeted with nettle and broad-leaved dock. The west-facing bed was submerged beneath giant blooms of groundsel and lamb's quarter. Bramble vines flung themselves from the hedges in crazed profusion. Ivy clawed its way up the walls of the lean-to, encasing it in dark, impenetrable foliage, while all over the lawn, thick stalks of dandelion lolled in the breeze, mingling promiscuously with clumps of thistle that didn't so much creep as thrust towards the sky, threatening to pierce the clouds.

Robert threw open the back door and stumbled out into the midst of the prickly spires, grasping one after another with his bare hands, ripping them out of the soil. He tore at them in a frenzy, lacerating his hands, until, losing his footing, he tumbled backwards into the west-facing bed. He lay there, looking up at the squadrons of thistledown advancing remorselessly through the air above, sensing the taproots radiating through the soil beneath his body. It was hopeless. It was all too much. He accepted defeat with grateful resignation.

How long he lay there, he had no idea.

When he awoke, it was to the deafening susurration of a billion tiny wing beats. A blizzard of butterflies had descended upon the thistles. They billowed above him like an undulating layer of diaphanous silk, all gold and black. Painted Ladies. The thistle butterfly.

He sat up and the veil parted around him. His fingers were in the soil of the west-facing bed. There, to either side, stood a line of iridescent dahlias in full bloom. He blinked in amazement. They nodded back.

With a sudden urgency, he got to his feet and staggered towards the house. The phone was ringing in the hallway.

It was the hospital.

He listened carefully to every word, and then, putting down the phone, picked up Vanessa's bag, and went out through the front door.

The cream of Gloucestershire's writers read their stories at Cotswold Playhouse, Parliament Street, Stroud, GL5 1LW

Sunday 8 May 2022
Doors open at 7:00pm
Starts at 7:30pm

Tickets £9 in advance from
cotswoldplayhouse.co.uk

THE ORANGE TREE & OTHER STROUD SHORT STORIES

STEVE WHEELER

The Orange Tree

The Portuguese sun volleyed onto the white walls of their rented villa and ricocheted around them; through the chemical blue water of the swimming-pool, over the towel-covered loungers and into the blinds-drawn, marble-floored sitting room. It burnt their English noses and cooked the hire car on the sandy road outside. Behind the bedroom's wooden shutters, Philip could hear the ceaseless chatter of his wife, Joanna, and their two young children in the pool. He couldn't sleep any longer.

He'd been up with the kids before dawn, playing snap, doing a puzzle they'd found in a cupboard, and watching cartoons on TV in Portuguese. The children were still buzzing since arriving at the villa late the previous night. They'd been delayed at the airport in London for seven hours. Joanna had bought the children a battery-operated toy dog that barked, walked, then did a backwards flip. After four hours in the departure lounge, Philip had flipped.

"Stuff the fucking holiday. It's only a week. By the time we get there, it'll be time to come home," he said.

"And waste a thousand pounds? To do what exactly?" Joanna asked. "Let me guess. You escape back to work while I sit with the children and watch the rain come down."

They hadn't spoken during the flight or during the two-hour drive to the villa. The children were getting used to the long silences and had learnt to keep quiet.

*

While the sun was still low, after giving the children their breakfast cereal, Philip had told them to go and wake their mother. "She'll know where to find your swimming stuff."

261

Joanna had appeared outside by the pool, still in her pyjamas. She was hungover from the complimentary bottles of white and red wine that had been left by the villa company. They'd opened them after putting the children to bed, promised each other to make the best of it for the kids' sake, then somehow sex had happened on the cold marble floor. Philip had reached over her head and turned on the toy dog. It had been a long time since they'd laughed during sex.

"Thanks for arranging the wake up," she said, as both children climbed onto her lap.

"My turn for a lie-in now," Philip said.

"Since when has seven thirty in the morning been a lie-in?"

"Since 5am, when I got up with them."

*

Philip walked into the mid-morning fusillade of heat, holding a beer and stretched out on a lounger.

"Here's Daddy at last. He can dive in with you while I make a well-deserved coffee," Joanna said.

"When I've finished this beer I'm going shopping."

"They've been waiting for you."

"And what are we going to eat exactly?"

"Can't it wait for an hour?"

"I did enough waiting yesterday. In an hour it will be too hot to go shopping."

The hire car was still in the shade of a tree that stood in a patch of dry scrub on the other side of a white-washed wall. The wall divided their villa from the square of deserted grove that awaited the foundations of yet another new villa. Philip looked up into the tree as he unloaded the last few bags from their late arrival. The branches were laden with oranges, under-ripe and green. Where the sun pierced through the thick canopy of dark green leaves, some of the fruit was beginning to show signs of ripening, like dawn breaking on their smooth skins. It would be weeks before they were ready. Joanna came out to the car wrapped in a towel. "Buy a picnic lunch for everyone. We'll go to the beach when you get back."

"Can't we stay around the pool? We've paid good money for it," he said.

"They need a change. Try and enjoy yourself. We've paid for all of it - including the beach."

*

Philip watched his wife and kids paddling in the shallows and jumping the waves as they petered out over the hot sand. Further out, the Atlantic swell was deep blue and heavy. A few adults and teenagers had hired the yellow, open-decked canoes and surfed in, steering the craft across the face of the waves, like flying fish, cutting and slicing. He walked over to the dreadlocked man who sat on a deckchair under a bleached-white sun umbrella. The man's chair was surrounded by canoes and piles of old life-vests that looked past their best.

"I've hired a canoe and a child's life-vest for an hour. I'll take the kids out, one at a time," Philip said to his wife.

"They're a bit young, aren't they? Have you seen the size of those breakers?"

"It's perfectly safe. These canoes are made for beginners, which *I'm* not." Philip called his daughter over and strapped her into the life-vest.

His wife and son watched from the sea edge as he paddled out over the breaking waves. He turned the canoe, and, looking over his shoulder, picked out the swell they'd ride. From her front seat, his daughter waved at her mother and brother as the canoe rose and fell on the humps. Then the one he'd chosen arrived. He paddled fast to move the canoe up to the same speed as the rising blue wall, then they were on it, high above the trough. He dug in on his left and accelerated with the water as it charged towards the beach. Then he dug in on his right, the bows swung around and zigzagged the boat back the other way. Moments before the wave broke, he straightened up and surfed in, with the cold white foam cascading over their shoulders. He unloaded the laughing little girl into her mother's arms.

"I spent whole summers doing this," he said. "Try and enjoy yourself. We've paid for all of it - including the sea."

"He's younger, remember," she said, "and not as brave," and strapped their son into the life-vest.

By the time Philip reached the deeper water and turned the canoe stern-on to the swell, the boy asked to go back.

"Just one ride in, ok?" said Philip. "Just one."

Philip turned the canoe right and left on the wave as he had before, but the boy was crying. He straightened out the canoe as the wave broke, but the angle was too steep. The bows pierced into the swirling water and headed for the bottom. The hump of water at the stern upended the canoe and cartwheeled it over. Philip was thrown into the churning blue and white interior of the wave. His vision was a blur of bubbles and sand, rising in the suck of water. He didn't know which way was up.

His head came out of the water to see Joanna wading in as fast as she was able, already waist deep. She was bellowing something at him, but he couldn't decipher her words. He saw the capsised canoe a few yards in front but couldn't see their boy. He thrashed to the boat, stood, and righted it. The boy's head had been in the air-pocket, trapped but floating.

Without a word, Joanna snatched her child from Philip's arms and headed for the shore. Philip walked the canoe back to the sand and dragged it to the man in the chair. By the time he returned to his family, his wife had packed everything up. The boy was wrapped in a towel, shivering.

He says he wants to go back and play in the pool," she said.

"Will you come in the pool with us, Daddy?" the boy asked.

"Sure, I'll come in the pool with you. We'll both come in the pool with you."

*

Early the next morning, before the sun was fully up and before the children had woken, Philip drove to the marketplace where the food sellers were setting up their stalls. He bought a large box of fresh, ripe oranges. When he returned to the villa, he placed a dozen fruit under the orange tree, then set up a breakfast table by the pool.

"Wouldn't it be wonderful to squeeze some fresh orange juice for our breakfast?" he said to the children when they appeared,

264

still in their pyjamas. "Why don't you take a look under the orange tree? Take your beach buckets." He listened to their excited screams as they collected the orange treasure from the shade beneath the tree.

Philip put oranges under the tree at dawn every morning for the remaining five days. Every morning the family ate breakfast together and squeezed oranges, while the ripe sun rose and bled something sweet into their lives.

GILLIAN METHERINGHAM

Release

The screen door moans as she closes it behind her. Inside, the house is cool on account of the curtains kept permanently closed against the Arizona summer's fury. *Drapes*, she has learned to call them. She stands in the dimness for a moment and then walks to the window, holds back the edge of one curtain, just enough to see the bottom half of Jake protruding from underneath the truck. His legs twitch and roll as he works, and she imagines the sweat blossoming all over him, under the hairs on his chest, in the creases of his brown-black neck, between his buttocks in a wet line. She feels no pleasure at these thoughts, as she once would have. She looks up at the wide open desert, miles of it, punctuated by Joshua trees frozen in their own strange torment, and wonders if something has died within her. Perhaps she should have stayed in England.

But something has been born as well. Not yet born into the world of course, but born in a private place inside her, and growing all the time, inch by miraculous inch. Her hands go to her swollen belly and spread themselves over it. They do that constantly these days as though they were puppet hands on a string. She is drained of volition, following a path worn over centuries, like the Colorado River cutting its course through the rock. She is a twig on that river, going where it goes, bobbing and buffeted without independent thought.

She is afraid of the birth. Not of the pain, because like most women she believes it will somehow be bearable when it comes to it, but of the uncertainty. Child-bearing seems to hold within it a concentrated version of the human condition, all the terrible risks of life jammed into one little space, the fearsome hours of the birth. She dreads a stillborn child, or one with terrible deformities, or a birth that drags both her and baby into the maw of death.

So much could go wrong. In fact, the more she thinks about it, the more she knows that the path through the many obstacles of the time ahead is so narrow it would fit through the eye of a needle. And she a camel, bloated with her cargo. Sometimes at night her legs tremble with the fear of it and she steals out of bed, leaving Jake, still as a stone beneath the dusty sheets. Then she pads into the dark kitchen and splashes her face and legs with cold water, trying to quench her desperation. But the fear persists.

She hears a croak from the next room, throaty and urgent. The old woman wants something. Probably whiskey again, which she's not allowed, although Jake gives her some from time to time to keep her quiet. The younger woman lets the moment settle before moving off through the thick air towards the bedroom. She has learned to do this. Nothing happens quickly here. Perhaps it's too hot. Or perhaps it's as the old woman says; sudden movement startles the shades of the ancestors.

They're not my ancestors, she wants to say. My ancestors built hill forts on the Sussex downs, with views to the cold sea and icy winds whistling round the struts driven into the flinty land. They don't linger there now. It's far too cold.

But these thoughts are unfitting, for she has made her choices, and it is here in the free desert air that she has staked her claim to life. So she goes through to the bedroom where the old woman sits on a formless couch covered with throws. All the furniture in these desert houses seems to be hidden beneath throws. At first she thought it was so they could be washed easily and put back on again, but no one seems to wash them, so the practice remains a mystery.

Jake's mother is a full-blood Hopi, which makes him mixed race. Sometimes she thinks he looks more Native American than some of the full-bloods, with his high cheekbones and his aquiline nose. It was the cheekbones she fell in love with, she realises, and perhaps the hair too, blacker than any you'd see among the milky complexions of her own race.

267

The mother looks like a nut left out in the sun. She is tiny, and seems to be swallowed by the lumpy couch. Her hair, still kept in a long *braid* down her back, is so thin at the end that the rubber band has to be wound round and round many times. Her face, a map of brown wrinkles, is a small oval between the cap of grey hair and the nylon shirt with the collar buttoned carefully and pulled high under her chin. She likes to be covered. Her eyes, hooded like her son's - oh, those hooded eyes! - stare straight ahead. Her mouth works busily.

The young woman moves across the room and sits heavily next to the mother, causing a rearrangement of the lumps into new landscapes. She does not ask what is wanted. She knows she will be told in due course. That is the way of this slow land.

Eventually, the mother sputters next to her, like Jake's truck starting up on a cold, high-desert morning. The young woman waits. Then a brown hand, claw-like, reaches out from the sweater and touches the bulging hill where the baby lies. She is surprised; this is unusual. The wrinkled face smiles then, so broadly it seems it might crack, and ancient teeth emerge into the dim light. She puts her own hands over the old woman's and they sit like that for some time, the three hands feeling the pulse of the new life beneath.

Then the old woman seems to lose interest and the hand withdraws, back into the folds of indeterminate clothing. Long minutes pass, as the ever-present dust circles and dances in the air. At last the young woman rises and goes back out to the big room, feeling strange, somehow lighter.

Suddenly, she can feel the ancestors clustering around her, a pliable mass, no more than a thickening of the air but somehow unmistakable. She holds the baby again in the old protective gesture, instinctively, and then thinks: they may not be my ancestors, but they are the child's. That's why they're here. She feels like an interloper.

And the room is different. She doesn't understand; has Jake come in and moved the furniture around? But why would he? The chair with the broken back is now by the window, next to the couch, not in the corner where it usually is. And the green armchair, which she's never liked, is squashed in behind the door.

Then she realises what's new. There's a crib where the armchair used to be, a wooden one on rockers, which she had hoped to be able to afford before the time was up. It sits on the floor at a haphazard angle, as if it belongs there, as if it's at home. Over one side is draped an item of baby clothing, pale blue, casually hanging with one footed-leg pointing down.

And over the floor are toys, lots of them, still animated with play, on their sides, stacked up, knocked down. There's a plastic horse that she knows is still in its box in the closet, standing now in front of her looking a little the worse for wear with one ear slightly askew.

She seems not to be able to feel her own body, only the otherworldly throng behind her. She does not move but looks at the scene around her again and again, drinking in the detail.

Suddenly there's a squeal and a clatter and the screen door opens and closes. Jake enters, pushing a wave of hot air before him. She looks up with a snap of her head, focuses on him, and reaches blindly for a corner of furniture with the hand that is not clutching her belly. She finds it, the arm of the couch, and lowers herself onto it, not taking her eyes off Jake's face.

He looks at her, surprised, concerned, reaches out for her. "Hey. You okay, honey?"

The window has closed. The crib and the toys have gone. The armchair is back in pride of place. She sits on the arm, letting the moment fill her. Jake waits.

Then she smiles, more broadly than she has for months.

"Yes,' she says, slowly. "Yes, I'm just fine."

The ancestors withdraw.

ANTHONY HENTSCHEL

An Ill Wind

You don't meet them every day. Thank God.

At least, not as far as you know, you don't. Though many, I suspect, breeze by unnoticed. So, there's no way of knowing for sure exactly how many of them there are. Not unless you probe.

Unless you probe, they dwell among us, passing themselves off as...ordinary human beings. They *could* be anywhere. In the park. In the supermarket. In the pub. That rather robotic man who won't ever let his dog off its lead. That sweet old woman behind the till. That drunk in the corner slagging off Nicola Sturgeon.

*

I expect you remember those storms - those five ill winds that swept in, one after another. A truly tempestuous start to the year we had of it, back then in those halcyon days when we were anticipating the imminent prospect of Sunday supplements awash with double-page spreads of the best of the five hundred photos handed in to the police.

Five hundred photos. At work meetings. Really? Not where I've ever worked.

They came crashing in off the Atlantic. Those five ill winds. One after another. It seemed even Gaia was terrified as Putin's troops continued to delay. As they danced and dithered along Ukraine's borders and the world braced itself for yet another tidal wave of refugees.

After Arwen came Barra, then Corrie, then Dudley. Eunice was the fifth, and Eunice was the matchmaker. It was she who introduced me to *one of them*.

You remember Eunice. Unlike her older siblings, she was in no hurry to move on. Day after day she battered the trees, ripping down branches. Telephone wires wailed like banshees and I heard the forest raging, night after the night.

By the time she arrived, eight million trees had already fallen. Coupled with Ash Dieback, it seemed the country's features were being permanently disfigured.

The night, before my tale unfolds, I was out in the garden armed with binoculars. Orion's belt was coming apart, and I sensed that in the coming hours, Eunice would have her wildest fling.

I was right. And what a view! Mars bright as a diamond. Venus shivering. A cascade of stars pursued by UFOs that whizzed overhead as clouds shredded like tissue paper.

In my crook of the valley, I thought we'd be safe. But I'd completely misread the isobars, and instead of barrelling in from the south west, she came screeching in from the opposite direction. Down crashed my seventy-foot larch. Down crashed seventy feet of evergreen. Down crashed a sanctuary for wood pigeons and robins and squirrels.

What's more, we were trapped. Cut off from the rest of the world.

In the morning, I reviewed the situation. No *real* harm. No one dead. I phoned the council, whose robot informed me that *Due to recent bad weather our services are in high demand. Your patience is appreciated.* Isaac Asimov would have loved that. As would HG Wells. Being advised to be stoical by a robot.

When I got through to a human, I allowed an edge of hysteria to crack my voice, which I thought permissible given the circumstances. "We're trapped. Completely blocked in. Even an emergency vehicle couldn't reach us. If it had to." That addendum, I felt sure, would hike us up the council's list.

"Can you manage for three hours?" the human asked.

"No problem," I said.

*

They arrived on the dot. Three hours later. Two of them, in what looked like a council truck. There was an older man, possibly sixty, and a lad just starting to shave.

271

Except for four whispered words, the older man did all the talking. They were wearing luminescent lizard-green jackets, so hi-viz it hurt. But though identically dressed, it was clear who was Boss. The sixty-year-old inspected the problem and then dispatched his minion to fetch chainsaws. This, he told me, was their fourth tree. I offered him tea, which he accepted.

"Milk?"

"Why not?" And he smiled. Like a human.

"Sugar?"

"Better not." He caressed his beer belly. "I'm trying to be good."

"One in mine, please," whispered his minion.

*

I'm not sure how the topic of Boris Johnson arose, but I probably introduced it. You see I've been running a private poll, asking complete strangers to imagine themselves members of a jury and to hand in their verdict on Partygate...*Boris Johnson: Guilty or Innocent?*

So far, of twenty asked, nineteen returned verdicts of guilty. Only one - that sweet old woman in the supermarket - answered *Innocent,* a response that provoked laughter in the queue.

"They're all the same," the Boss said. And he rubbed his thumb and fingers, before tapping a pocket where coins chattered.

I laughed.

"Maybe," I said. "It's true that Johnson dismissed that quarter of a million he got for his weekly column as 'peanuts'! In fact, he said it twice. Peanuts. But that doesn't mean they're all the same."

"Boris *is* a clown," the Boss conceded.

*

After chainsaws had butchered my tree, offering up next winter's fuel, it was time to bid these strangers farewell. Her rage spent in the night, Eunice had calmed. We were drinking tea again and birds were singing, and I noticed a few precocious daffodils already preparing to trumpet.

"I'm not sure I agree," I said, "about Johnson. He's more dangerous than a clown. Did you hear him on PMQs? How he sneered at Starmer? *You sound like a lawyer.* That's what he said. *You sound like a lawyer*. Happy to denigrate an entire profession. Well, personally speaking, I'd rather have a lawyer than a liar for Prime Minister. Any day."

The Boss narrowed his eyes. "What I always say is this," he said. "We shouldn't have opened the gates."

"The gates?"

"Yeah. We shouldn't have opened them. The gates."

"What gates?" I asked, already suspecting the worst.

"Yeah, we ruined this country when we let them in."

"Them?" I echo. Knowing I was *one of them*.

The Boss was getting into his stride. "It's true though, isn't it? There's no way of knowing. Not for sure. Exactly how many of them there are. When you think about it, they could be anywhere. In your park. In your supermarket. In your pub. You just can't tell. And you know this pandemic? This pandemic, yeah? *They* brought it here. Can't wash, see? In those camps. It's not their fault. I'm not saying it is. But we shouldn't have opened the gates. Nice cuppa," he added, handing back his mug.

Laughter is the best medicine. So I laughed. I was looking at the Boss, but my words were aimed at his subordinate. "The General Election's still two years off, but it seems campaigning's already started."

The Boss turned to go. Now the young man was handing back his mug. An old college mug. A memento of innocent days. On it, that profile of an eternally youthful Che Guevara. Soon the young man would be gone. That truck would swallow him. So I called out after him as he ambled down the lane. "Only two parties can win here. The Reds or the Blues. The Reds are led by a decent man who happens to be a lawyer. The Blues are led by a clown. A clown who lies so often you just don't know when he's telling the truth. A clown who partied while people died. It's your choice."

The young man, five metres from the van, slowed down. The Boss, already inside, switched on the ignition.

"Remember," I shouted. "Remember ABC - Anything But Conservative."

The young man had reached the truck. He paused, his hand on the door, then, as he opened it, he half-turned, grinned for a

273

nanosecond, nodded understanding, and gave me a furtive thumbs-up. And the next moment they were gone. And birdsong returned. And beautiful silence. And my knees were beginning to shake.

As I said at the start of this sorry tale, you don't meet them every day. Thank God.

*

I surveyed my damaged hedgerow - that hideous gap once graced by my beautiful tree. It had taken on the resemblance of a familiar, much loved face from which a front tooth had been smashed.

That pile of freshly cut timber couldn't compensate for all that had been lost.

Seated in the kitchen, beneath a melancholy cloud, I dug through my rattle bag of workaday proverbs, recalling *It's an ill wind that blows nobody any good.*

But what bloody good had Eunice blown my way? She'd left nothing but destruction in her wake.

And then I found it. That elusive silver lining. And I drew it out and held it to the light. Eunice had toppled something far more deeply rooted than my tree - my complacency.

Complacency that needed uprooting before even more powerful storms sweep our land.

LAURA KINNEAR

Little Chestnut Hare

"Clear soup, followed by turbot, and then sliced ham with tarragon sauce," said Mrs Marshall, reading from a scrap of paper in her hand.

Alicia nodded at her housekeeper but her eyes drifted to the crimson curtains, hanging either side of the sash windows like unfurled tongues. She felt cold; a gust of cool air was snaking from the gaps in the floorboards and she clutched at the sleeves of her cardigan, running her fingertips over the bobbles.

"Mrs Burnett?" said Mrs Marshall, a look of exasperation on her round, plain face, "What about the roast?"

"Roast?"

"Yes, Mrs Burnett," said Mrs Marshall with a sigh, "What roast shall I do? To follow the ham?"

Alicia shrugged. She didn't care what was laid before her guests. Twenty years ago she might have worried, may have also popped to Moffat for a new dress. Now it was an effort to dry brush a tweed skirt for the occasion.

"Beef?" said Alicia.

"Beef," replied Mrs Marshall, and she scribbled on the paper with a stub of pencil.

As soon as her housekeeper left Alicia sank onto the settee with a groan. She was tired as well as cold. On the wall opposite were four Dutch still-lifes in dense, gilt frames. She frequently fantasised about selling them and using the money for a fitted carpet, or better still, central heating. She knew her husband, Kenneth, would never agree. Did he admire the furry peaches and iridescent glass; the trussed-up pheasants and stylishly arranged cloth? Did he possess a deep-rooted love of art, of collecting? She knew that nothing was further from the truth; her husband had barely glanced at the paintings in all of his fifty-five years in the house. Yet because the paintings had always been there, they would continue to be. He hated change of any kind.

What Kenneth did love was hunting. Hare coursing to be precise. A passion awakened by trips with his father when he was a boy. He'd been in a terrible temper ever since Wilson's bill to ban the sport. Alicia was thankful that, even though Parliament had voted for a ban, it didn't seem like it would become law. As Kenneth had said, the Lords would never agree to something so ludicrous. She didn't care for coursing, couldn't bear the thought of the hare's heart pounding as it was chased by Kenneth's lurchers. But Kenneth's dark moods affected her; they permeated the whole house, lingered in every room like his pipe smoke.

But Alicia was in her own dark mood that day, one she couldn't shake off. Was it the awful dinner party in a fortnight's time - the one Mrs Marshall kept babbling on about? Maybe it was the vexatious tapestry she'd failed to complete last night in front of the fire. Alicia smiled weakly. It was neither of course. She knew full well what was troubling her, for it reared its head with terrible regularity every year.

"Vermin," said Kenneth at lunch, as he chewed his salmon.

"Anchovy cream?" said Alicia vaguely, passing him a blue and white dish. "Mrs Marshall will be in a sulk if we leave it untouched."

"Did you hear what I said?" asked Kenneth, spooning the cream onto his plate.

"Yes, Kenneth, you said vermin."

"Why didn't you answer me then, rather than going on about anchovy cream and Mrs Marshall?"

Alicia balanced her knife and fork on either side of her plate. "We've more hares?"

"Hares; foxes; badgers; moles – we're overrun!"

"Well, no one's stopping you from getting rid of them, although I don't want to hear too much about it, Kenneth. You know how I hate to think of the hares especially."

A smear of cream, like an albino slug, had attached itself to Kenneth's cheek. Alicia wondered if she should alert him.

"You sound like Wilson's lot," said Kenneth, stuffing his laden fork into his mouth.

"Hardly!"

"If the Lords pass it…"

"Kenneth, they won't."

"Maybe not, but that lot will continue agitating about it."

"Mrs Marshall asked what we wanted for the roast course. I said beef."

"Roast course?"

"For the dinner in a fortnight."

"Dinner?"

"With the Barnsleys and John Carruthers."

"Oh god!"

"Is beef alright?"

"I suppose. Just don't sit me next to John Carruthers."

Alicia spent the afternoon smoking and flicking through *Country Life*. She had to distract herself, to stop her mind wandering, and, for a while, it worked. Adverts for ginger wine and fountain pens and comment pieces about foot and mouth were liberating in an odd sort of way. But after two hours of fingering the pages she tossed the magazine aside. She couldn't put it off; she had to go upstairs.

She didn't go into her bedroom, nor did she wander into Kenneth's room. Instead, she carried along the corridor to the very last door. Her heart thumped as she entered. She rarely visited the room, and, as far as she knew, Kenneth never did. She was taken aback by its brightness: its walls shining like ice cream, and the curtains - lit behind from the sun - glowing like a cluster of gems. She moved closer and stroked their edges. The fabric was printed with hares, the animals dressed in gingham shirts and sky-blue dungarees as if they were human. *Little Chestnut Hare,* the woman in the haberdashers had said, *Perfect for a girl or boy.*

Alicia drank two cups of cocoa that night, both with a good slosh of Glenfiddich. Kenneth didn't approve of the good stuff for milky drinks but she couldn't bear blends. Anyway, didn't she deserve a malt on such a day? It seemed to do the trick because she fell asleep with her paperback balanced on her chest like a Gothic arch.

When she woke she knew it wasn't yet morning. The room was thick with shadows and there was a chill to the air that made her want to slide under her bedspread and never come out. But something made her lift the covers and step into her slippers. She couldn't find her dressing gown - must have left it in the bathroom - so she draped a blanket around her shoulders before padding downstairs.

White mist hung in the air like thistledown. She could just make out the statues, huddled around the lake like people who'd stayed up all night. The evening she'd met Kenneth at the Hunt Ball, they'd talked until sunrise. Such a long time ago now - over thirty years had passed. Sometimes she could still imagine them doing such a thing. At Hogmanay, they'd managed two o'clock, although Kenneth had mostly raged about the government. She walked across the lawn - her slippers soaked with dew - and thought how they should make more effort, that all was not lost, surely? And then she saw it. Nearly walked into it! So close, she could almost sense the heat of its breath. A hare: leaping about the lawn as if on springs. Why was she surprised? They were overrun after all. Yet, even though she'd seen many sprint about the estate over the years; had seen them limp and bloodied in sacks and then skewered and plated and served at dinner, she looked at this hare as if it was a creature she'd never encountered before.

*

"That was John Carruthers," said Alicia, walking into the drawing-room two weeks later.

"What's he telephoning for? We'll see him tomorrow," said Kenneth, sitting in his armchair reading *The Field*.

"He can't make dinner."

"That's good news."

"I don't understand what you've got against John."

"Oh, nothing really. He just doesn't know what to say to me, nor I to him. Oh, I meant to say," continued Kenneth, bringing

278

The Magazine down onto his lap, "I told Mrs Marshall to swap the beef for hare."

"Hare?" Alicia's hands began to shake.

"Yes, got a real beauty the other day. Seems a shame to waste it."

"I don't want hare."

"Why ever not?"

"I just don't want hare."

"Alicia…"

Alicia wandered to the window and placed her face on the glass. It was silly, she knew that. The hare destined for the platter couldn't possibly be the animal she'd seen a fortnight ago. And anyway, why get so sentimental about *that* hare? There was nothing special about it. All it had done was jump about, but there had been something in the way it had moved; a lack of self-consciousness, a belief that nothing could stop it; that it would just continue on its path, uninterrupted.

She'd believed such things once of course; had never entertained the idea that her baby wouldn't continue fiercely through life. Its cries had been so loud, so unruly. It hadn't seemed possible that all they'd hear one day was silence.

SEAN W. QUIGLEY

The Benny Hill Gang

We were ten minutes into that evening's episode of *The Benny Hill Show* when there was a knock at the door. I paused the DVD and asked Duncan if he was expecting anybody. He wasn't. Colin was worried that it might be the police, and I had to remind him that what we were doing wasn't actually illegal.

After some downstairs mumbling, Duncan returned with a man whose face was obscured by the hood of his snorkel parka. "This is Todd," said Duncan. "He says he'd like to join us."

Colin, Matt and I said hello to Todd and he stuck up his thumb. Matt asked him where he'd heard about us, and Todd answered with a muffled response. We had not widely advertised our meetings, but had given the impression that it was open to those of a certain persuasion. Duncan invited him to sit in the spare armchair and Todd immediately sank into it.

There was something familiar about Todd, who pointed at the television and said, "Cor, it's *The Benny Hill Show!*" and bounced up and down in his chair like a child. Duncan asked Todd if he would like a beer and he screamed, "No, I want Benny Hill!"

And so we resumed the episode. Benny was slapping the bald Irishman, Jackie Wright, on the head, and we all laughed. "Brilliant!" shouted Todd.

This was our sixth monthly meeting. We had come together as we all loved *The Benny Hill Show,* but none of us, other than Duncan, were allowed it in the house. We had all grown up watching it with our dads, laughing at the jokes and going "Phwoar" at the sexy ladies. I never knew what my mum thought about it - as she never seemed to be in the room when it was on.

We met round Duncan's house, but we couldn't tell our wives that, because he was our divorced friend, and they would know that we were most certainly be up to no good. So I would have a 'night at the cinema', Colin would be off to 'see his Uncle' and Matt was at a 'monthly ukulele club'.

Of course, we were peacefully watching, in chronological order, *The Benny Hill Show* DVDs. And we would laugh at the jokes and go "Phwoar" at the sexy ladies, and nobody would judge us for being sexist old men. Between us we knew that we were harmless, and that as long as we had our special evenings together, we didn't need to take our Benny Hill humour out into the unforgiving wider world.

*

Early in our relationship, Donna, my missus, suggested that I had an 'unhealthy interest' in the comedy of the 1970s, which had, she said, adversely affected my attitude to both women and all matters pertaining to sexual intercourse.

And it is true that I have always been flippant about it, and have always found serious talks about sex impossible - without going red in the face - having been confused about it from an early age, and there was no doubt that comedy programmes had been an influence on this.

The first time I saw a sex scene on television was in an episode of *On the Buses*. For years I thought that sex was just writhing around on a bed with a lady, both of you fully clothed, and giggling. While her husband was at work.

It was, I suppose, due to the influence of *The Benny Hill Show* that I thought being chased around a park in your underwear was some kind of mating ritual.

And, of course, there were the *Carry On* films, where rude happenings were soundtracked by a variety of comical squeaks and parps. I was surprised on getting my first erection that it wasn't accompanied by the upward trajectory of a Swanee Whistle.

*

We had reached the halfway point of the episode and we all needed the toilet. Todd was the first to go, and, while he was busy, I covertly mentioned to the others that there was something familiar about his laugh and the drollness of his voice.

281

When Todd returned Colin took his place. I asked Todd if he wasn't hot with his hood up, and he said that he needed to keep it up - for some undisclosed reason. My suspicions, however, were sufficiently roused. Taking him by surprise, I reached forward and pulled back the hood. We all gasped.

It was Stewart Lee, voted greatest living stand-up by *The Times*.

Just as our jaws were beginning their journey back from the floor, Colin returned from the toilet and saw the identity of our guest. "Shit," shouted Colin. "Is this a raid? Are you undercover?"

Stewart Lee mumbled something about how he wished I hadn't done that, and that he just wanted to watch Benny Hill as he wasn't allowed it at home.

I said to him, "I didn't think you'd like Benny Hill! You do all the intelligent stuff. Sensitive and culturally relevant!"

Stew explained that he was bored with all of that, and that his wife helped him with the really clever bits. "Sometimes I'd really like to go on stage, wearing comedy breasts and then blowing off into the microphone. My audience would think that I'm being ironic and they'd laugh anyway."

He said that he couldn't really write the kind of sexy sketches that he wanted to - with bare ladies and funny accents - as he would, eventually, lose all of his fans and have to go underground like Benny Hill had to in his later years.

By this point we were feeling rather sorry for him. I asked him if he'd like to wear our spare beret.

"Cor," said Stew, "I've always wanted one of these." He took it, put it on his head, did the Benny Hill salute, and then said, "Hello viewers!" in a fair approximation of the great man - although it clearly needed work - but we could help him with that if he was serious.

Stew asked if we could watch the rest of the episode, which we did, and, of course, it was only a matter of moments before he was chuckling away, "Phwoar, look at all them lovely dolly birds!"

Although Stew was clearly enjoying himself, the boys and I couldn't relax. After realising that we weren't laughing as much, not even when Benny was doing his Chinese character, Stew suggested that we may be uncomfortable with the presence of a

282

celebrity. "You all seem flustered. There's no need to be. I'm just a human man," he said, "with the same need for dirty jokes and rude ladies."

He said he would tell us a joke to put us at our ease. "Not one that I could tell my regular audience, but you should enjoy it."

This is how it went: there's a man in the pub and he's miserable. The man next to him tells him that he should cheer up, because *he's* from the future and things become much better. "Do they really?" "Oh yeah," says the man from the future. "There are no more wars, cures have been found for cancer, heart disease and dementia, and we have daily flights to the moon colonies." "That's great to hear," says the man, who by now has cheered up. "Oh," he says, "what about racism, has that gone?" "Oh yes," says future man. "Although, having said that, we do still *hate* the bloody...!!!"

Our jaws once again dropped, this time at the rotten punchline!

"That's terrible," I said. "Is that supposed to be ironic?"

"No," said Stew, "it's a racist joke. I thought you'd like it."

"Well," I said. "If this is what you're really like, I think you'd better leave," and we were all unanimous in that.

"But I want Benny Hill!" cried Stewart Lee.

It was too late for that. We all chased him out of the house, shaking rolled-up newspapers, umbrellas and our angry fists at him. Stew ran across the municipal park that lay in front of the house. Four nurses, from the neighbouring nurses' accommodation, asked what was going on.

"Stewart Lee told us a racist joke!"

"The bastard!" cried the lead nurse. "Right, after him, girls!" And they joined the pursuit.

Suddenly, Stewart Lee's trousers fell down. He carried on running, awkwardly holding onto them. This wasn't a problem for us as we hadn't been wearing any to begin with.

And then, just ahead of us, as we - with our shaking fists and umbrellas - were all chasing round the park after him, I heard Stewart Lee, voted greatest living stand-up by *The Times*, gently sobbing, and saying, "Thank you," because that this was what he had always dreamed of.

DAVID GOODLAND

The Purple Rinse

Brett and Malcolm stirred a hornets' nest when they moved to Crancombe from London. Folks found it difficult to decipher their camp metropolitan twang. Conversely, the boys found the Cotswold burr as understandable as the bleat of dying sheep.

They soon became a familiar sight in the High Street, Browns the butcher being a favourite shop stop. "What's tasty, Jimmy?" Malcolm would enquire.

"Nice bit of rump today."

"I should be so lucky."

Laughter.

Snidey Graves, the greengrocer, was less friendly.

"Any mangetouts, me dear?" Malcolm would enquire.

"We don't sell cattle food."

The boys' cottage was up Fiddlers Tump. Superb views across the valley more than compensated for the life they'd known in Chiswick. They also enjoyed a twice weekly jaunt to The Jovial Forester, where Sammy Smalls, the landlord, seemed to like having them around.

Brett was recognised as the TV actor who modelled underwear. You couldn't mistake him. He stuck out a mile with his dyed black hair, moustache and cowboy boots. He looked only slightly older than his admitted 42 years. He kept slim by frenzied activity with the cement mixer.

"Him 'ave ripped the front right off that that old cottage, put in a bay winder, an' made it all lovely and modern," said Winnie Sawyer as she tottered up to the bar one night.

"Bloody Nancies!" cried a voice from the corner.

"Wass that?" cried Winnie.

"Nancies!"

284

"What is it you're sayin', Snidey?" she asked.

"I'll tell you what I be sayin'. 'im says, Have you got any hoeberjeans?'

"'im sez, 'tis often called a hegg plant."

"I says if thee do want eggs, why dussn't thee ask fer eggs? Then I noticed his 'air."

"What about his 'air?'"

"'Twas purple."

The snug froze.

Rinses had finally come to Crancombe, but this purple rinse, coloured the hair of a gentleman in his late sixties, an ex-hairdresser, who, by his own admission, had once had tea with the Queen Mother.

Snidey addressed the regulars. "Hermaseetals, the pair on 'em. You don't believe me? I seen it in the harmy."

His audience went suddenly silent as Brett and Malcolm entered the pub. They stood stiffly and unseen behind Snidey.

"Them's what we used to call Cream Puffs! First time I set eyes on 'em, I sez to meself, I sez, there's summat funny about them two."

"What is it you be sayin', Snidey Graves?" said Winnie.

"I'm a sayin', we cannot 'ave it. 'Tis bad for trade."

"I can't say I've seen any decent trade since we came here," said Malky.

Snidey turned. Malky's hair was now the brightest purple you ever saw. He'd overdone the rinse, but Snidey's face had turned red. "'Tis time you boys buggered off back to London," he grunted.

"You mind what you do be saying there now," snapped Winnie. "Them's bin lovely neighbours to I! Filling out the forms for me Poll Tax and fetchin' me groceries up the hill when I…"

"We don't want cream puffs in the town an' that's it an' all about it."

"Cream Puffs?" spluttered Malcolm.

"Home James," said Brett. "Think of your blood pressure."

"Are you going to let him get away with that? Strangers. That's what we are and that's what we'll always be," he said, with more than a hint of self pity. Brett clocked his partners look of weariness, and, in that instant, something snapped inside him.

Taking up a sort of Clint Eastwood stance he fixed his eyes on Snidey. Slowly he negotiated the spit and sawdust floor and began fingering the town councillor's felt collar.

A bead of sweat sprang through a pore on Snidey's upper lip. His mouth went dry, his Adam's apple bobbed alarmingly, and yet, when Brett ruffled his toupee, Snidey felt a not entirely unpleasant sensation deep within.

"Is that a gun in your pocket, or are you just pleased to see me?"

Snidey twitched. Silence.

Suddenly a piercing screech came from Iris Pillows who normally sat, expressionless, next to her husband Percy. "Thass just like...you know, that...whassername...you know...'er in the pictures ."

"Mae West," shouted Sammy from behind the bar.

"Thass 'er," squealed Iris.

Brett took out a handkerchief. "My, but it's hot in here," and he slowly wiped the perspiration off Snidey's forehead. The greengrocer's face now turned the colour of red cabbage. Tucking the hanky into Snidey's breast pocket, Brett said, "Keep it honey. That's a gift. From one cream puff to another."

Then he heard the sweet sound of applause. Walking back to Malky, in the middle of the floor, he suddenly stopped and turned.

Malcolm squirmed, but nothing would stop Brett now. "Of all the bars in all the world, you had to walk into mine!"

"Humphrey Bogart!" shouted Sammy.

"Thass him alright," said Percy. "Recognise that 'un too."

"Get out while you're ahead, dear," muttered Malky.

But Brett was on a roll. "You lousy stinkin' cops."

"James Cagney!" shouted Percy.

With consummate ease, Brett went on to perform his Marlene Dietrich, his Tony Curtis, John Wayne and a Judy Garland which left everyone in fits.

286

He was doing Cary Grant when his top set suddenly came loose. The vintage dentures slipped out, arched in the air and fell dangerously close to earth, but Brett's amazing overhead flip saw them safely returned to his gaping mouth. He returned triumphantly to Malky at the bar and downed a celebratory Guinness.

Applause eventually gave way to excited chatter about the films they used to see when the town had a cinema of its own.

Back in his corner, Snidey slurped his dregs and made for the door. He was about to exit when Percy Pillows suddenly found his voice. "You mind what you do say, Snidey. You 'ent so bleedin' shinin' white theeself."

"Now you said summat!" cried Sammy from behind the bar.

"There's a few here as remembers the bus shelter kerfuzzle o' farty seven! Where was you on the night, Snidey?"

Snidey froze. A rabbit in the headlights.

There were more than a few in that company who remembered the bus shelter scandal that rocked Crancombe during the hard winter of 1947. Snowed in and unable to leave the village, the behaviour among certain of the townsfolk had raised more than eyebrows.

It was the vicar, caught characteristically on his knees, who bore the brunt of the publicity. He was given a conditional discharge at the assizes and told to 'take himself in hand'. He and his mother left Crancombe immediately for an office job at Gloucester Cathedral.

Exhaustive investigations failed to discover the other malefactors. The village closed ranks, but there was no one who didn't know someone involved. The police told them quietly to pull themselves together and that was the end of the matter.

You don't see so much of the boys in Crancombe these days. A glimpse maybe of Malcolm's purple head amongst the incessant traffic. Sammy's nephew, Wayne, now runs The Jovial Forester. The regulars are nice folk, but too bogged down with mortgages and school fees to enjoy a proper good night out.

Except perhaps for the night of Malcolm's 70th birthday. As Malcolm and Brett entered a darkened snug, the lights suddenly went up on a room full of regulars.

"Happy birthday, you blummin' ol' cream puff!" shouted Winnie Sawyer.

They all raised their glasses. Malky couldn't believe his eyes. Every single head was purple rinsed, and, believe it or not, some swear to this day, they saw a hint of purple in Snidey Graves' toupee.

CHLOE TURNER

I Won't Tell You about all the Days I Spend Looking for Her

There are probably tanks rumbling along the overpass above us, but it's dark, and the carousel's speakers are blasting out Beyoncé, and we've got used to them now anyway.

Andriy and me are waiting in line for the Skydiver. The air's sticky with cherry jam from the pampushky fryer at the gate, and thick with generator diesel. I've been on this ride so many times, I could shut my eyes and feel it without even clipping into the harness. Every year, the same – they've not even painted out Michael Jackson on the archery stall backdrop beside us. It's him and a duck and this girl with weirdly shining cleavage, like that's just what would make you take up arms to win a light-up frisbee. Still, we keep dragging ourselves out here. Strapping ourselves in. What else are we to do?

Up ahead of us, there's a woman with a dog dressed up like a lion. Tiny little rat of a thing, with this big, curly mane at the collar of its coat, and she keeps pulling on its lead and making roaring sounds like it's going to copy her: it makes me think of that old toy of Petro's, the one he took everywhere, long after he should have done. But my older brother is somewhere in the north, and it's best not to think too much about that. In front of the lion-dog woman is the Carnival King, still in full costume with his floppy ears and lopsided, embroidered mask, like some mutant sock-puppet come to life. He's doing his strange jig while he waits for our turn to come around.

I don't spot the girl immediately, because she's behind us, and what with the dog and the King, there's a lot going on. When I look back, I see pink trainers and the string of little plastic sunflowers in her hair. Her friend's much taller, blonde as she is dark, and I know immediately where Andriy's eyes will go. I'm probably looking like a marten caught in headlights when Sunflower Girl smiles. I'm halfway through smiling back, but Andriy's yanking on my sleeve because the bell's gone and the gate's open and we need to get on. And then the lion-dog woman's squeezing back past us, red-faced, though we all know no dogs on the ride, and Carnival King is high-fiving us on the way to his chair. By then the safety bar's down, and no chance of reaching back to catch a glimpse of her.

We're off. The speakers are ruining *Born Slippy*, but it's loud and we're spinning out wide, and then I spot her right opposite. She's laughing and her hair's flying out blue and pink and green in the lights, and I've got that sucking feeling in my gut that might be centrifugal force, but if I'm honest, is more to do with just how pretty she looks.

I could ride the Skydiver all night, but Andriy always wants to go bigger and better so we make our way towards Doom Drop. He stops for a hot dog. We pass the dodgems and a fat man squeezed into the smallest car. Someone's screaming on the tea cups, and the gang of boys taking it in turns to pummel a boxing bag snort and jeer. They're big men tonight, in their vests and bomber jackets, with their older brothers on the trains following the tanks north towards the border. And while they punch and hoot, a little girl with ice-cream dripping down her t-shirt stands watching them.

The lights are out when we get to the Doom Drop kiosk, but there's a workman on his knees who says we won't need to wait long, we'll be first in the queue. And then the Sunflower Girl walks up right behind us. No sign of her friend, but Andriy gets chatting anyway. I'm rolling the coins in my pocket, half-wondering why I'm friends with this boy who can get anyone he wants, but then her blonde friend turns up with pastries in a bag and his gaze switches like a lighthouse beam.

The lights are just flickering back up when she tells me her name's Kalyna. We ride together, and then again, and the second time she grabs my arm when the cart drops like a stone. She wants a drink so I buy her a soda from the stand - the owner's face is old as the knot in a tree - and Andriy disappears for a while with the friend. Kalyna and me hook ducks and I win her a toy panda. We see the little girl again: she's finished her ice-cream and now she's shooting a cap gun out into the dark. Kalyna gives her the panda and she takes a minute to clip it to a hoop on her shorts.

When Andriy and his girl find us again, we're in the queue for the rollercoaster. We watch the Carnival King whip past on his final loop, his rag coat swollen with the breeze. The fat, spun yarn of his eyebrows has slipped on one side so he looks even more manic than before.

It's four to a cart, so we can ride together; ours has 'Miami' painted down its side. There's a strip of neon along the seam of Kalyna's jeans as her thigh presses against mine. I can smell the plastic toys in the rack at the archery stall, warming under the lights. Taylor Swift's *Ready for It* is pounding out of the speaker alongside us.

You know that lurch when the thing starts? Then we're inching higher until we can see that ribbon of dull orange along the northern horizon. Andriy's making the friend giggle on the far side of the cart. I want to take Kalyna's hand. Her nails are a painted rainbow and she fans them out on her thigh. I take that for a sign and lay my palm on the back of hers.

We're almost at the top when the lights fail. Someone further back in the train boos. The lights come back, then off again. Taylor Swift dies away just at the peak of the chorus. There's a horrible crunch of gears, and I remember the screech as we begin to roll backwards. Someone screaming: a girl, or maybe me. The smell of pancakes in hot fat and a siren on the overpass. The taut tendons on the back of Kalyna's hand and then nothing.

*

I won't tell you about all the days I spend looking for her. *No-one by that name was treated at this hospital* – I check as soon as I am patched up enough to ask. And she doesn't come to Andriy's funeral, though it is held in the mountains near his father's place, so she wasn't to know.

It's too late now, anyway. My letter comes this morning, as expected. My mother stands up from her breakfast and drums her

291

fists on the wall; my father has to hold them still before she breaks her fingers. I will report at 1800 to the station near my old school, joining a new signals' unit for training in the capital. It may be weeks, months, before I see the front, though in my brother's childish script he wrote to say that there's room in his barracks when I do.

I have a few hours spare so I take the old road out to the fairground field, even though I know the rides will be long gone. Sure enough, there's nothing there except a flock of pink-footed geese. But I stand there for a while, listening to them pecking at the muddied grass, before turning for home. Those geese have me thinking about her pink trainers as I pass the old farm cottage that's tucked under the concrete beams of the overpass. And then I see her. She's hunched on a bench in the garden, two bowls in her lap. When she glances up from her work, she jumps and we laugh and hug with sunflower husks spilt all around.

It's only a little time we have together. She will not be retreating west like many – her grandmother is too old to make the trip. She fills my pockets with seeds, though the army are always well fed. She shows me the apple tree she planted as a child and the new stick she has whittled for her grandmother. I don't have anything to give her, except my football key ring with its lion motif – she takes it anyway, says it reminds her of the little dog at the fair and therefore me.

She stands at the gate to watch me go. When I kiss her goodbye, she tastes of baked milk and raisins. There are no tanks on the overpass today; everything is in place now. Tomorrow I will eat sunflower hearts on the train, and try not to think about whether I will return.

JASON JACKSON

He Loves to Stand on Clifftops

He loves to stand on clifftops.

Or bridges.

Or beaches in winter where the sea meets the sand.

And there's always a moment — the wind behind him, a particular unsteadiness, an uncertain vertigo — where it would be easy, so easy...and wouldn't it just?

He lives for these moments.

Sips at them, fine wine.

And smiling, always smiling.

Once, a young woman came up behind him, gently put a hand on his arm. *Excuse me, but you're not going to...are you? Do you need to talk? We could grab a coffee?*

Her fingers were long, thin, the nails painted silver and green.

In the café, he asked her — as she wrapped those same fingers round her steaming mug — *have you ever had a someone...? Have you ever had a moment...?* And each time he tried, his words came out empty, his heart full to bursting.

Whatever it is, it's not worth it, she said.

And all he could do was turn to poetry, to Eliot, to Prufrock, and all he could say was, *that is not what I meant at all.*

*

January 1985, and two lads — two not-quite-men — take to spending their evenings together, outdoors. One is six months the younger, a significant stretch of time at that age, and the elder is tall, thin, with dark eyes, long lashes. His cheekbones catch streetlamp shadows, and his voice is low and soft, a velveteen whisper.

The younger is already in love, or something like it, although he doesn't know it, can't name it, won't admit it, tries to hide it or ignore it or forget it.

Anything to stop things spinning out of control.

And the elder knows. Teases. Touches. Smiles. An arm around a shoulder. A glance held at goodbye.

Theirs is a specific and sweet unhappiness, distinct from one to the other, yet held between them, precarious and fragile. It could easily die — and quickly — in these biting winter winds, but unhappiness of this sort — young love, uncertain perhaps, but true — can find a way to thrive in such conditions in northern towns, between those who love to talk about music and poetry and art and the colour of the night sky at the horizon, how it greys out, how traces of the day's light remain.

These two, they take to walking by the sea or by the river; something about the space above water, its emptiness, its potential to be filled, draws them in. They like the wet sand as it kicks up behind them, their boots making sucking sounds, leaving imprints which morph into hollows before completely disappearing. They like the cold, how it comes alive in the wind, becomes something sharp and dangerous. They like to throw stones. They like the waves. They like deep, black water and the way they can look over it, beyond it, to a bank on the other side, or right out into dark spaces where occasionally they'll see lights flickering, ships or stars or other unknowable things.

London, says the elder. They're standing on a bridge, looking out over the docks to the mouth of the river away in the gathering evening. Two hulking boats sit huge, grey-blue and silent. This is no longer a place where ships are built; occasional repairs and refits are all the docks are good for. Desolation and decay drip with the saltwater from the wet ropes which tie the vessels to the docks.

I'm going to London, he says again, like it's true.

When? What for? says the younger. What he wants to say is, *Don't.*

Soon. Next month. I can't stand it anymore.

Your dad, you mean?

294

All of it. This place.

I thought you liked it. The grit and the bleakness, you always say.

I like us, he says, the taller, elder, more beautiful not-quite-man. *The rest of it, not so much.*

What are you going to do?

Rent a place. Get a job. Drink. Take drugs. Fuck.

You're seventeen.

No, he says. *You're seventeen. I'm eighteen in exactly three weeks' time.*

I don't know what to say.

Come with me.

And just like that, life splits in two. To stay, to go. To be, or not. A moment. A someone, there on the bridge, and lips offered for the first time, a kiss in the lights of passing cars while the river rushes below and the ships ease against their moorings with quiet, animal groans.

That first kiss is not their last. They spend more hours on beaches, on bridges, the precarious edges of clifftops, looking for shadows to hide in, looking to hide from themselves. And in truth, sometimes there is more than just kissing. Eyes wide in the winter dark, they find themselves in fleeting, clumsy contortions.

But mostly, they talk. Not of London — not yet, not again — but of things they've always talked of: how Gilmour's guitar sound is a stretched scream, how even one line of Larkin can hold all the misery and mess of the world, how van Gogh's tree roots are the twisted limbs of a grasping past. These pretentions keep them happy, keep them safe. Only when their lips meet — hurriedly, on some dark coastal pathway, or in the absence cast by a brick-broken streetlight — do they recognise the dangerous pull of the future, the quiet threat of what-next.

The younger of the two cannot sleep at night, will not wake in the morning. Those three words — *come with me* — are a poem, a question, a command and a promise. He writes a song, his fingers stretching into unforeseen shapes on the fretboard, verse and chorus the same, the repetitions, the beat, those three monosyllables sung in a gradually disintegrating loop.

He wants it to end in a whisper.

He wants that final, empty silence to be part of the song.

London: an impossibility. He knows he can't go. Although he's young, he's read enough: love can't last, passions fade. But more than that — more than anything and everything — it's the darkness, the space-above-water, the stepping off, the stepping out, the wave-become-sand, the ground-become-air, the vertigo, the nausea, the desperate, churning anticipation, the terrible pull of it all.

He's not ready.

Not sure.

Not frightened, but cautious.

It's a mundane truth, but he's not yet the man he hopes he can be, one who might stand on a clifftop in darkness and jump, reaching for the mystery of distant lights, expecting to fly.

And in the end, these two don't even say farewell. A wet Sunday evening, a shadowed beach, the younger waits, the elder already gone.

A deception, a kindness, a trick.

And the rain getting harder until the drops make sad little hollows in the sand.

Three days. A postcard. Big Ben, and no forwarding address. Six words: *You know it's better this way.*

And it is, of course.

It is.

*

He still loves to stand on clifftops.

And bridges.

And beaches in winter where the sea meets the sand.

But in the café, he told the woman nothing of his reasons. Platitudes, that's all. The view. The bracing breeze, good for him, now he's in his fifties. And she was already looking at her watch, having to meet her husband, glad — at least — that he was not some pity-case, something she'd have to worry about, but just another story to tell.

I'm fine, he said. *Thank you.*

Well, if you're sure.

And he thought to himself, as he watched her leave, I'm happy. I have a life. A family, a home.

There are dark open spaces above stretches of water, and there is always, always a pull, but there are memories.

A kiss, that first time.

The lights of passing cars, and somewhere close, the slow shifting of tethered boats.

ANDREW STEVENSON

Relatively Dead

To the Editor
Practical Taxidermy

Dear Editor,
Last year, in a letter you chose not to publish, I wrote to you describing how I managed to squash a top hat and a rabbit in one swift movement. These squashings were inadvertent, caused by a violent sneeze at the high point of my conjuring act, as I bear no grudge against rabbits, or indeed, top hats.

To try to rectify matters, I employed a milliner to repair the hat and a taxidermist to repair the rabbit: the milliner being more successful than the taxidermist. Nevertheless, I was able to continue my act for some time, pulling the partially-repaired Snowy out of the fully-repaired top hat, until I was forced to discontinue the practice by popular demand.

Looking for a new interest after the demise of my conjuring career, and inspired by Snowy's courageous posthumous performances, I resolved to become Froghampton Magna's resident taxidermist - despite a complete lack of knowledge, qualifications and aptitude.

My initial attempts at the craft did not go well. However, memories of my work on Mrs Bright's Dachshund soon faded from the Froghampton collective memory, as the eminent psychiatrist, Carl Jung, would have put it.

As my skills approached a degree of near-competency, villagers began bringing their dead pets for me to mount. I should point out at this time that the phrase *to mount* is the professional term for preparing a dead body for display, and apologise for any regrettable images the ambiguity of the term brings to mind.

My taxidermy business took an unexpected turn when Mrs Wallace, horrified at the cost of her vet's bills, decided not to wait for the natural end of her dog's life, but to curtail it there and then, and have Napoleon stuffed and mounted.

The logic of Mrs Wallace's argument was unassailable. My fee would be easily offset by savings, not only in vet's bills, but also in dog food, dog toys and all other paraphernalia considered necessary to the life of the twenty-first century dog. Furthermore, Napoleon, in his mounted form, would be much less trouble than in his living one, no longer requiring exercise, love and companionship. And like film stars who die in their prime, the dead Napoleon would be preserved for ever, full of life.

I mounted him in his familiar pose with bared fangs as requested by a delighted Mrs Wallace, who proudly put the finished item on view in her living room window. Thus, news of her brainwave spread quickly through the village, to owners of dogs, cats, hamsters, gerbils, rabbits, tortoises, turtles, lizards, budgerigars, canaries, pigeons, goldfish and other more exotic creatures. People in their droves began bringing me their pets, prematurely deceased by a variety of innovative methods. Front windows throughout Froghampton Magna were soon adorned with dead animals in an assortment of captivating poses.

My career took another turn for the better when I discovered the circumstances surrounding the death of the philosopher, Jeremy Bentham. Still dressed in his clothes, Bentham's body was mummified and put on public show. The mummification of the head, however, went badly wrong, leaving it hideously disfigured. In its place, Bentham now has a wax head with glass eyes, which is so life-like that he looks exactly as he would have done had he been born with a wax head and glass eyes.

I thought that Bentham's idea would prove popular among the villagers, given their enlightened attitude towards the evisceration of loved ones. No longer would I limit myself to stuffing and mounting my customers' pets, but would now stuff and mount their relatives as well. With the high price of funerals these days, the practice would be a welcome cost-cutting method of disposing of cherished family members.

I put an advertisement in the newsagent's window detailing my scale of charges, choice of poses and disposal of innards. The next week, I received my first corpse. The late Mr Hodgson arrived in the passenger seat of his Fiat 500, from which his widow and I pulled him with negligible damage, and dragged him as sensitively as possible to my garden shed.

Mrs Hodgson chose a golfing pose for her husband, a number three iron in one hand and a large Scotch in the other. So pleased was she with the result, that the following week she took the stuffed Mr Hodgson to the Rotary Club dinner and dance. His presence was extremely well received, especially by Mr Gilfoyle who kept topping up his glass with Glenfiddich, while engaging him in a long conversation about maritime insurance.

On hearing the news of this social triumph, others followed Mrs Hodgson's lead, bringing me corpses of relatives, friends and even passing acquaintances. Nowadays in the village, displaying at least one dead body in one's home is more or less de rigueur. They are accomplished icebreakers at parties, livening up the proceedings of many an otherwise hopelessly dull evening. A stuffed grandfather standing in the hall, for example, will get any occasion off with a swing. He can also double up as a coat stand, and, if wearing wide-fitting wellington boots, an umbrella holder.

In light of this success, I recently began to offer, as an optional extra, battery-stimulated arms and legs, which can move in time to the beat of various musical rhythms: a useful social skill when the bodies are invited to join in the dancing. The three movements I offer at present are those of the waltz, rhumba and a random flailing of limbs that covers all contemporary styles apart from Hip-hop.

Stuffing dead bodies is not all fun and frolics though. An occupational hazard in common with dry cleaners, watch repairers and shoe menders, is that of the uncollected item. A typical example is one in which the relatives of recently deceased ninety year-old Aunt Elizabeth asked for her to be set in the pose of an Olympic high jumper in mid-leap. Unfortunately, just before the collection date, those same relatives discovered that the

300

considerable inheritance they were expecting had been left instead to a donkey sanctuary in Torquay.

As a result of this, and similar cases, my garden shed is full of abandoned corpses in an array of poses ranging from serene to sprightly, and I have been obliged to transfer the overspill to the house. Aunt Elizabeth, repositioned from her spirited stance as a champion high jumper, now sits in a reclining Parker Knoll chair in the living room with a firm grasp on the television remote control. Not only is her bill unpaid, but my wife and I can watch nothing but endless repeats of *Crossroads*.

Putting such drawbacks on one side, however, I shall leave you with the tale of a recent amusing incident. Only yesterday, Mrs Seale brought me her husband before the legal formalities regarding his death had been completed, or, indeed, started. She wanted to pre-empt rigor mortis by having Mr Seale preserved in the pose he had adopted when dying of laughter at a joke during a long night at the Froghampton Arms. It was quite a shock when, at my first scalpel incision, he let out a piercing scream.

Yours faithfully,

Herbert Pennywhistle
Cell 3
Froghampton Police Station

PS Please note change of address

301

AUTHOR BIOGRAPHIES

Nick Adams
Nick is a restless writer who has lived in various parts of Europe and now calls Stroud home. *Demolition,* the story in this volume was selected for *The Best of British Fantasy 2019,* and Nick's work has also been published in two *Storgy* collections, *The Shadow Booth* and elsewhere.
Twitter - @_nickadams

Peter Adams
Peter always wanted to make on impact on the world. He has tried many creative endeavours - art, pottery, stand-up comedy, poetry, short stories, long stories and non-fiction. Some of his non-fiction books - his writing on health and homeopathy - have been published by Penguin, Element Books and others. He has also been poet in residence at The Celebration of Life, a spiritual gathering in Stroud. His main endeavour is homeopathy and running Stroud Natural Health Clinic (www.snhc.co.uk). Peter lives in Edge.

Sallie Anderson
Sallie is a reader, writer and bookseller living in Cheltenham. Her stories have appeared in print and online, including *Stand Magazine* and *Visual Verse,* as well as on competition lists.
Twitter - @JustSalGal

Ali Bacon
Ali was brought up in Fife and studied Classics at St Andrews University. She now lives in Emersons Green in South Gloucestershire where she writes contemporary and historical fiction. Ali first appeared at Stroud Short Stories in 2015,

since when she has had five more stories selected and has acted as co-judge for several SSS events. At the time of writing, her latest novel, *The Prose and the Passion*, an exploration of the love life of R L Stevenson, is in the final stages of preparation.
Website - alibacon.com
Twitter - @AliBacon

Georgia Boon
The first time Georgia showed her writing to anyone was when she entered Stroud Short Stories. Since then she's read twice for SSS, been published in *Shooter* literary magazine and been shortlisted and commended in international competitions. She likes to write about gender and belief, and is working on two collections of stories and a novel. Georgia lives in Rodborough, Stroud.
Website - onlyticksinthemargin.wordpress.com
Twitter - @GeorgiaGabriell

Robin Booth
Robin moved to Stroud from London in 2014. He works for an independent publishing company specialising in theatre, and does some freelance editing. His story *Two Towns* won the Local Prize at the 2020 Bath Short Story Awards. He runs a Stroud-based writers group, Wild Writers, founded with other writers who have appeared at Stroud Short Stories events.
Twitter - @BoothRoom

Nimue Brown
Nimue Brown loiters about in damp corners of Stroud, writing blog posts, short stories, poetry, novels, graphic novels, non-fiction books, songs and shows. You can find her out and about performing with The Ominous Folk of Hopeless, Maine, or hunched possessively over a cup of coffee somewhere, looking like a scruffy goblin. *Hopeless, Maine* graphic novels are published by Sloth Comics in the UK and Outland Entertainment in the US, and her non-fiction is mostly published by Moon Books.

Website - druidlife.wordpress.com
Twitter - @Nimue_B

Cheryl Burman
Cheryl lives in Lydney in the Forest of Dean. She's the author of two novels for grown-ups and a trilogy and its prequel for youngsters. Some of the stories in *Dragon Gift,* her collection of flash fiction and short stories, have won awards. Cheryl is the chair of Dean Writers Circle and a founder of Dean Scribblers, which encourages creative writing among young people in her community.
Website - cherylburman.com
Twitter - @cr_burman

Joanna Campbell
Joanna lives in Bisley where she writes full-time. As well as her collection of prize-winning short stories, *When Planets Slip Their Tracks*, she has also had two novellas-in-flash published. The most recent is *Sybilla*, winner of National Flash Fiction Day's Novella-in-Flash Award. Her novel, *Instructions for the Working Day*, is published by Fairlight Books. It is about a man who buys a village and a woman who confronts a city.
Website - joanna-campbell.com
Twitter - @joannacampbell_

Stephen Connolly
Born in Canada, but raised in Scotland and South Africa, Stephen began publishing short stories before concentrating on scriptwriting. He graduated with an MA in scriptwriting from Bath Spa University in 2015. He was joint-winner of the BBC Solent Radio Playwright competition 2018, selected for Bristol Old Vic Open Session Writers and Dialect Resident Writer 2021. Inspirations include Umberto Eco, Terry Gilliam, Shaun Tan and Alan Bennett. He has recently completed a play about Scott of the Antarctic and the 2012 Olympic Games.
Website - stephenconnollywriter.com
Twitter - @SteveConnolly3

Philip Douch

Based in Stroud, Philip is a frequent contributor to Stroud Short Stories and to Story Fridays in Bath. He is a past winner of the Gloucestershire Writers Network short story competition and has read twice at Cheltenham Literature Festival. He knows that it is amusingly ambiguous to say that he closed the 2021 Nailsworth Festival with his own story show. Philip is also a playwright and a regular presence as both writer and performer at the Stroud Theatre Festival.

Website - www.philipdouch.org.uk

Louise Elliman

Louise lives near Cirencester and has more ideas for stories than she has the time or self-discipline to write. She manages to write short stories occasionally though, and some make it into competition short lists or anthologies, including this anthology and the 2019 *To Hull and Back* short story anthology. Louise is a member of Cheltenham's Wild Women Writers' Group who inspire her to keep writing.

Sophie Flynn

Sophie is based in Moreton-in-Marsh and is the author of the novels *All My Lies* (Simon & Schuster, 2021) and *Keep Them Close* (Hera, 2022). Sophie's short stories have been published by *Stylist*, *Writing Magazine* and of course Stroud Short Stories. When not writing, Sophie can be mostly found on muddy walks, or beside the sea in Cornwall.

Website - sophieflynn.com
Twitter - @sophielflynn

Hannah Glickstein

Hannah lives and works in Stroud. She used to be an English teacher and is now a counsellor for young people. Whilst teaching, she self-published graphic stories about a skeleton called Skinny Bill. Her writing has appeared in non-fiction publications including *Huffington Post*, *The Catholic Herald* and *Spectator Schools*. Her stories have been published by *Platform for Prose*, *Litro* and

Stroud Short Stories. She was once shortlisted for the Fish Poetry Prize. Her ambition is to write compelling novels.
Website - hannahglickstein.blog

David Goodland

David has transitioned from Drag Queen to Stroud Short Stories writer over eight decades. An actor and prolific performer on BBC Radio, his play writing includes *Making Up*, *Anzacs Over England* (Radio 4), *The Life and Death of a Buffalo Soldier* (Bristol Old Vic), *A Child in the Forest* (book by Winifred Foley; Everyman, Cheltenham), *Beyond Milk Wood* (Tobacco Factory, Bristol) and *The Pied Piper* (Arts Theatre, London). He lives in Nailsworth.
Twitter - @davidagoodland

Mhairi Gray

Mhairi lives in Woodmancote, near Cheltenham. She has written software for aircraft displays and indexes to science books. More recently Mhairi has started writing short fiction. *Forgetting to Heal*, her story in this anthology, is her first for Stroud Short Stories.

Claire Harrison

Claire is a freelance copywriter, author, part-time creative writing lecturer and joint managing editor of *The Phare* online literary magazine. Her plays have been performed at the Stroud Shakespeare Theatre Festival and *Script in Hand* at The Everyman Theatre. She has written three children's books, and her prose and poetry have appeared in anthologies and short story collections. She lives in Cheltenham, has an MA in Creative & Critical Writing and currently writes for Oxford University Press.
Website - claireharrison.blog
Twitter - @ClaireHWriter

Anthony Hentschel

Anthony was born in Israel and lived in Mexico, Finland and Jamaica before being despatched to a boarding school in England. He settled in Nailsworth thirty years ago. Though working primarily in Special Needs, he also taught Creative Writing at

Stroud College. Once crowned The Bard of Hawkwood, Anthony is now better known for his angry letters to the press. He has written three (currently unpublished) novels and, during lockdown, a work of non-fiction *Bottled Rage: The Diary of an Angry English Teacher.*

Sarah Hitchcock

Sarah lives in Stroud and works in Cirencester Library where she gets paid for indulging her passion for books. She has read for SSS three times, was included in the last anthology, and has also had her work published in *To Hull and Back* and *Beyond Realities Volume 2.* She has published her own anthology of short stories for adults entitled, imaginatively, *Anthology,* plus a middle-grade novel called *Stan and the Enchantress* and is currently working on a series of contemporary fantasy novels for young adults.

Diana Humphrey

Di, who moved to Stroud over twenty years ago from the New Forest, turns everything into a narrative. She thinks it may be something to do with years of obsessive people-watching. Di now has hundreds of stories crowding her brain and her shelves, and is delighted that you can read her second story for SSS, *That Old Tune,* in this anthology.

Michael Hurst

Michael's short stories have been published by *The Fiction Desk, Ellipsis Zine* and *Gemini.* As well as writing, he is interested in photography, playing the piano and walking in the Cotswold countryside. Michael lives in Cheltenham.
Twitter - @CotswoldArts

Jasmin Izagaren

As a naturopath and systemic therapy practitioner, Jasmin enjoys looking for the connection between things. An aspiring writer since she was a child, she has recently rediscovered her love of storytelling, especially the stories we tell ourselves and those we tell others. Jasmin lives in Chalford near Stroud.

Jason Jackson

Jason is a writer from the north east who has been living in the south west for over twenty years. His prize-winning fiction appears regularly in print and online. His stories have been nominated for the Pushcart Prize, as well as appearing regularly in the *BIFFY 50* and *Best Microfictions*. Jason is also a photographer and his prose/photography piece *The Unit* is published by A3 Press. Jason co-edits the online magazine *Janus Literary*.
Twitter - @jj_fiction

Claire Jaggard

Claire lives in Cromhall in South Gloucestershire. She has an Oxford University degree and a background in broadcasting and online journalism. Claire began writing creatively during the Covid lockdown and was delighted to read *The Wild Woman* at Stroud Short Stories within a year. BBC Radio Bristol has broadcast several of Claire's pieces, which are available to read on her website. She is a member of the Thornbury U3A writing group, and, inspired by a Changing Stories course, is now writing a murder mystery.
Website - clairejaggard.com
Twitter - @clairejaggard

Sally Jenkinson

Sally is a poet, community arts producer and care worker with an almost-completed Masters Degree in Creative and Critical Writing from the University of Gloucestershire. Her third poetry chapbook, *Pantomime Horse, Russian Doll, Egg* is a poem cycle exploring labour and birth, which will be published in September 2022 by Burning Eye Books. Her work has recently appeared in BBC Radio 4's *Power Lines, Lighthouse Literary Journal* and *Emerge Literary Journal*, NYC.
Twitter - @sallysomewhere

Kate Keogan

Kate is a poet and writer of short fiction. Her work can be found by the determined in various anthologies and she is currently seeking publication of a poetry pamphlet written during her mentorship with Pascale Petit. Kate lives in Gloucester.

Emma Kernahan

Emma lives in Stroud. At work she writes about the UK welfare system, and in her spare time she writes short fiction and satire which can be found in places such as *Ellipsis Zine*, *The Independent*, *Yorkshire Bylines*, *Writers' HQ*, *The F Word* and *McSweeney's*. She has won the Gloucestershire Writers Network Prose Prize, the *Funny Pearls* Short Story Prize and has been shortlisted for the Bath Flash Fiction Award.
Website - crappyliving.wordpress.com
Twitter @crappyliving

Laura Kinnear

Laura is originally from Cheltenham, although she has lived in Stroud since 2006. She's been published in *Pen Pusher*, *Aesthetica* and the first Stroud Short Stories Anthology, having read at our event three times. She has also been long listed for the Fish Short Story Prize. In 2021, Laura was selected for the Curtis Brown creative three-month novel course, which she spent developing her historical novel set in 18th century Poland and Scotland. Inspired by the past, Laura has worked in museums for over fifteen years and is currently Curator of the Holst Victorian House in Cheltenham. She also works as an English GCSE Language Mentor at Gloscol.
Twitter - @Laura Kinnear4

Rebecca Klassen

Rebecca is a freelance editor from Gloucester. She has a Masters Degree in Creative and Critical Writing. Her short stories have been published in *Graffiti* and *Write up Your Street* magazines, and anthologies for Worcestershire LitFest, University of Gloucestershire, Superlative, *Glittery Literary*, *The Phare* and Dean Writers Circle. She has performed her work at the Coleford Festival of Words, Cheltenham Literature Festival and Stroud

Book Festival. In 2021 Rebecca's flash fiction piece won the London Independent Story Prize.
Website - bex350.wixsite.com/rebecca-klassen
Facebook   -
www.facebook.com/profile.php?id=100070261364179

Pauline Masurel

Mazzy is a gardener who lives in South Gloucestershire. Her short and tiny fictions have been included in anthologies, published online, broadcast on radio and performed at events around Gloucestershire, Bristol and Bath. She won the Gloucestershire Writers Network prose prize in 2021 and read her winning story at Cheltenham Literature Festival.
Website - www.unfurling.net
Twitter - @unfurlingnet

Geoff Mead

Geoff lives in a house appropriately named Folly Cottage in Kingscote. The first thing he ever wanted to do as a child aged 8 was to write stories. However, it took him another 50 years to find his voice as a writer. In the past few years he has authored eight books of fiction, non-fiction, poetry and memoir. He is currently writing his second novel and looking for a publisher for his first.
Geoff's website www.cominghometostory.com includes a regular blog.
Twitter - @NarrativeLeader

Gillian Metheringham

Gillian is a relative newcomer to Stroud who loves to write short stories. *Release* is her first story for SSS. She was born in England and brought up in California. At the age of 13 she started a diary, which she has continued up to the present day. She began her adult life in Seattle and later moved to West Sussex, working in the IT industry in many different roles. Since 1986 she has been a Quaker.

Nastasya Parker

Nastasya lives in Dursley and works in the secondary school there. She has read three times at Stroud Short Stories, and her contemporary literary fiction has appeared in two Bristol Short Story Prize anthologies, a Retreat West anthology, *Perhappened* magazine and *The Phare*. In 2017, she won the Gloucestershire Writers' Network Prose Prize. She is currently editing her irreverent novel giving Eve's perspective on the creation myth, and blogging about the random stories we find in daily life on nastasyaparker.com, her website.

Simon Piney

Simon has been writing stories, articles and poetry for some seventy years. He was twelve when his first letter was published in *The Evening Standard*. His poetry has appeared in a number of now-defunct magazines. He has read a few of his short stories at Stroud Short Stories events and been published in both previous SSS anthologies. As well as fiction, Simon continues to write on academic subjects and is a member of a local writing group. Having lived in Stroud for nearly thirty years, he has now moved to the nearby village of Eastcombe.

Ken Popple

Ken has now moved from Stroud and returned to his home county of Lincolnshire where he lives in the small Georgian town of Horncastle. For many years a secondary English teacher, he is still working in education but in a more pastoral role. Ken sings his wry, melodic songs and reads his poems anywhere and everywhere around the flatlands of Lincolnshire. Please view his work on YouTube through *Ken Popple*, like it and subscribe.

Sean W. Quigley

A graduate of Rose Bruford College, Sean has co-written comedy sketches for the BBC. These days he lives in Longlevens, Gloucester and has two stories in this anthology, having read for Stroud Short Stories in May 2021 and May 2022. Sean writes for the glamour, adulation and cash - and hopes that, by the time of

311

this anthology's publication, his novella *The Pylon Man* will have been optioned by *Disney+*. Or *Dave*. He's not fussy - just give him the cheese.
Twitter - @seanquigley101

Mark Rutterford

Mark is a writer-performer who works in South Gloucestershire. His stories are humorous and emotionally engaging, told in the first person, sometimes in character and often with props. With over ten years of performing stories at live lit events across the south west from inner-city Bristol to the Women's Institute, Mark is currently writing about his two favourite things in a project he calls 'Love.Stories'.
Website - www.markrutterford.com
Twitter - @writingsett

Clive Singleton

Clive lives in Nailsworth and is an occasional writer. Now retired, he hopes to be able to write more in the future, but gardening and DIY seem to be filling his weeks. He has a long-term ambition to write and illustrate a comic strip, harking back to his childhood reading habits.

Amanda Staples

Amanda is from Staple Hill in South Gloucestershire. She says she has sent a lot of stories to a lot of places. Some made it into magazines and anthologies. Some didn't. She has finished a novel; hated it, and started another. Amanda has also written a recipe book about eating for energy. Her plays have been staged in Bristol and Croydon. Amanda has performed her stories at events in Bristol and Bath, as well as Stroud.
Website - scribestaples.wixsite.com/mysite
Twitter - @scribestaples1

Andrew Stevenson

Andrew Stevenson was a television producer/director until he moved from London to Nailsworth to write in peace. Here, he graduated from writing films scripts to writing short stories on subjects as diverse as invisibility achieved by the power of concentration, amateur taxidermy and the difficulty of determining the precise moment at which bread becomes toast. He has read many of these on radio and at public events, including the Cheltenham Literature Festival. He has now finished writing his first novel.

Chloe Turner

Chloe's short fiction has appeared in many journals and anthologies, including *Best British Short Stories 2018*. She has won the Fresher Prize for short story, twice been shortlisted and won the Local Prize in the Bath Short Story Award, and her first collection, *Witches Sail in Eggshells* (pub. Reflex Press) was awarded the 2020 Saboteur Award for Best Short Story Collection. Chloe lives in Minchinhampton.

Website - www.turnerpen2paper.com

Twitter - @turnerpen2paper

Rick Vick (1948-2019)

Rick was a mainstay of Stroud Short Stories, having read at SSS a record seven times, including at the very first event in 2011. He moved to Stroud in 1997 and became a creative writing tutor as well as working as a teacher with charities like the Nelson Trust. Rick wrote both poetry and prose, some of which were collected in three publications: *Indian Eye*; *Ask the Ferryman - He Passes all the Time* and *A Coat of No Particular Colour*. His story in this anthology, *Mazurka*, was read by his son William at our November 2019 event. A personal friend of Leonard Cohen and documentary maker, Nick Broomfield, Rick was the subject of a *Guardian* obituary in December 2019. A retrospective collection of Rick's work, *Ways of Seeing,* was published by Chapeltown Books in 2021. His motto was 'Let the pen do the writing'.

Sharon Webster

Sharon lives in Cheltenham. A doctor by trade, in recent years she has had more time to write, inspired both by the strength and complexity of the human condition and the beauty of a county which she now considers home. She volunteers for Gloucestershire Writers' Network and has had some of her poems featured in *Wildfire-Words*.

Steve Wheeler

Five times Stroud Short Stories reader, Steve Wheeler's short fiction has appeared in numerous online magazines and printed anthologies, usually under his nom de plume, Steven John. He is Joint Managing Editor of the online literary magazine *The Phare* and an occasional Creative Writing Lecturer at the University of Gloucestershire. Steve lives perilously close to a river in Tewkesbury, in a house someone described as 'a bit *Wind in the Willows*'.

Website - www.stevenjohnwriter.com

Twitter - @StevenJohnWrite

Melanie White

Melanie is editor and publisher of *Shooter Literary Magazine*. She has worked as an arts editor at a newspaper in the Rockies, a freelance journalist in New York and a book reviewer in London. Her fiction has been published or performed by *Liars' League*, *Londonist*, *The Curlew*, *Cent Magazine*, *Lunate* and others. *City Girl* is her first piece to appear at a Stroud Short Stories event. Melanie lives in Cheltenham.

Website - shooterlitmag.com

Twitter - @melaniecwhite

Alwin Wiederhold

Alwin lives in Hucclecote, Gloucester. He was born in the Netherlands and grew up in South Africa. His writing is influenced by his experiences when living in South Africa. His novel *Getting Hold of a Gun is Easy* is set there at the end of apartheid. Alwin is a physicist who started writing in 2019. He has had a love for literature since he was at school and enjoys learning languages and travel.

Naomi Wilkinson

Naomi is a gardener, Systemic Constellations practitioner and multi-disciplinary artist living in Stroud, and is part of the Silver Spoons Collective. Writing is Naomi's passion. Mostly she writes on nature, wild swimming and womanhood, so she was surprised, as she finished the free-writing session at her village writing group, to discover she had written the dystopian short story which appears in this anthology. She describes her story *Animate!* as a peculiar little fruit.

Katie Witcombe

After graduating with a BA and an MA in English Literature from Newcastle, Katie has spent her twenties and early thirties working in higher education. She's currently living in Bristol and working as a social media manager. As an avid reader and lover of all things gothic, Katie is continuing to write short stories - inspired by the large Victorian cemetery she lives next to.